Sorrow Wood

a novel by Raymond L. Atkins

Medallion Press, Inc.
Printed in USA

Previous accolades from Raymond L. Atkins' novel,
The Front Porch Prophet:

"*The Front Porch Prophet* is a fine piece of Southern fiction—by turns poignant and hilarious. Atkins knows his front porches; the rustics who inhabit his novel are real people who walk right off the page, but he's also had some book learning . . . in the rich, lucid prose, one finds moments of breathtaking elegance.
With a knack for storytelling, a sly sense of humor, and a Faulkneresque sensibility, Ray Atkins enters the literary scene with aplomb, and he plans to stay."
    —Melanie Sumner, author of *The School Of Beauty And Charm* & *Polite Society*

"Raymond Atkins tells a story at once comic and deeply tender, a story of friendship, love, unexpected brotherhood, and redemption. The world he paints is so full of wonderful eccentrics you'll wish you could stop off for a cup of bad coffee at The Wages of Sin Are Fried Chicken Diner. I don't have to be a prophet to predict you'll adore this book."
            —Man Martin, author of *Days Of The Endless Corvette*

"Atkins is the new Twain . . . This is what you get when you blend the best sense of humor in the world and the biggest heart: *The Front Porch Prophet*."
            —Ken Anderson, author of *Someone Bought The House*
                On The Island and *The Statue Of Pan*

"In *The Front Porch Prophet*, Raymond L. Atkins whisks the reader into a world of Southern quirkiness, a world that is well-populated by many novelists and story-tellers from the Deep South. The novel is reminiscent of the longtime favorites coming from such Georgia penners as Erskine Caldwell and Flannery O'Connor but with Atkins' unique voice leading the way into and through the tradition of quirky characters doing quirky things in quirky ways."
    —Kenneth Robbins, author of *The City Of Churches* and *Buttermilk Bottoms*

"It's creative and clever beyond comment. I'm simply blown away. I laughed out loud, chuckled, grinned, felt sad, found hope, and burst into tears. That's pretty powerful writing to my way of thinking."
            —Terre Gorham, Editor, *Memphis Downtowner Magazine*

"*The Front Porch Prophet* is a deep, poignant look at friendship in a small Georgia town . . . Fans will appreciate this insightful glimpse at life in the South, where sipping Georgia ice tea on a cabin's porch might be dangerous, as anything can fall from the sky. . . ."
            —Harriet Klausner, Gotta Write Network

"*The Front Porch Prophet* is an intriguing and clever tale, highly recommended for community library fiction collections."
                    —*Midwest Book Review*

"Atkins' writing is impeccable, and he is clearly in his element with this wonderful piece of Southern fiction."

—Literarily

"I really enjoyed this book, and I hated to reach the last page."

—Ferris Yawn, *North Georgia Living Magazine*

"There is much to enjoy in this wonderful book . . . The characters are fascinating, quirky, and they come in and out of the story with ease. The dialogue is some of the best ever written. It is natural, true to character, and so funny in places readers will be hard pressed to stifle their laughter when finishing the book at work because they couldn't bear to leave the story at home."

—Maryann Miller, Blogger News Network

"This is an absolutely wonderful novel . . . It is so wildly humorous, so unrealistic, and so down-to-earth at the same time, so gosh darn in-your-face enjoyable."

—Brad Canfield, B&B Ex Libris

". . . the funniest book centering on the inevitable death of one of the central characters you will read in a long time. Yes, it's a book about death, but it's also about life."

—Michael Scott Cain, Rambles.net

"This may very well be my favorite novel of 2008. I can't recommend it enough."

—*The Literate Housewife Review* (December 2008)

". . . no one should miss out on this touching tale of friendship, family, and Southern culture."

—Brooke Carleton, *Apex Reviews*

"Atkins writes with a sly wink . . . a wonderful story of friendship, personal growth, sacrifice, and love . . . made me both laugh and cry . . ."

—Dawn Rennert, *She Is Too Fond of Books* (November 2008)

"Once I was drawn in I had trouble putting **The Front Porch Prophet** down. I loved the characters; I loved the town . . . I was sad that it was over."

—Cam Robbins, *NovelSpot*

DEDICATION:

To my beloved wife, Marsha, and our children: Natalie,
Daniel, Caroline, and Tyslon.

Published 2009 by Medallion Press, Inc.

The MEDALLION PRESS LOGO
is a registered trademark of Medallion Press, Inc.

Printed in the United States of America
Typeset in Adobe Garamond Pro

Library of Congress Cataloging-in-Publication Data

Atkins, Raymond L.
  Sorrow Wood / Raymond L. Atkins.
    p. cm.
  ISBN 978-1-934755-63-1
  1. Police--Fiction. 2. Women judges--Fiction. 3. Witches--Crimes
against--Fiction. 4. Married people--Fiction. 5. Religious
life--Fiction. 6. Alabama--Fiction. 7. Domestic fiction. I. Title.
  PS3602.T4887S67 2009
  813'.6--dc22
                                    2009013544

10 9 8 7 6 5 4 3 2 1
First Edition

ACKNOWLEDGMENTS:

Thanks to my most enthusiastic supporters: Charise McNeely, Tammy Dempsey, Dawn Hefner, Kelly Wilson, and Marcey Yancey.

Thanks to Ken Anderson, Anna Nichols, Melanie Sumner, and Jeanie Cassity for reading and critiquing along the way.

Chapter One: 1985

Wendell Blackmon considered the dead dog lying before him and wiped his sweating brow with a white handkerchief pulled from his back pocket. He looked a bit incongruous producing the starched hanky, like a teamster holding up a pinky as he slurped coffee at the truck stop. He was a tall, broad-shouldered man with thinning brown hair and a full beard gone mostly white. He sported a nose that had profiled better before it was broken those three times. His creased forehead was high and getting higher as his hairline receded, and there were laugh lines at the corners of his blue eyes. The passage of the years had added a few extra pounds to his frame, and these had the effect of enhancing the sense of largeness that he projected.

The August afternoon was as humid as a rain forest and hotter than the sixth circle of hell. The weather report that morning had called for a near 100 percent chance of rain, locally heavy at times. Miniature dark clouds with petite lightning bolts had been superimposed on the weather map, and the meteorologist had gravely advised her viewers to pack an umbrella in anticipation of the inevitability of precipitation. Wendell looked up at the cloudless blue sky and mentally declared another triumph for modern meteorology. He noted a mountain hawk hanging on the wind, floating effortlessly over the landscape. Its mournful *kee kee* came to his ears from what seemed a thousand miles away.

The weather woman had annoyed Wendell. In his opinion, his own mother, Eunice, had a better track record than any of the professional prognosticators, and her predictions did not rely on satellites, radar, or computers—a fact he believed may have enhanced her success rate. Her method was simple, a venerable system of forecasting that had been refined for millennia by the arthritic masses. If her elbow hurt, it was going to rain. If her knee hurt, too, it was going to rain a lot. If her elbow, knee, and hip—all three—hurt, then it was time to make peace with God because the end was near. That was her system, and she was reliable 80 percent of the time, provided she stayed away from the aspirin bottle. Still, Heather McDowell of Channel Five Weather Alive did have nicer legs than Eunice's, and maybe the poor girl would be fortunate enough to develop a good case of rheumatism over time.

"If you've got straight teeth and can point, you are qualified," Wendell had noted to his wife, Reva, over breakfast eggs and bacon. He was watching the weather report while she read the paper and paid scant attention to his monologue. His comment was an unfair generalization, anyway, since many of the practitioners of the trade also gestured with the backs of their hands, and a couple of the real old-timers used little batons, as if they were conducting an orchestra of meteorological events, a symphony of storm. "You can be wrong every time, and you still get paid," he continued as he pointed his fork at the television on the kitchen counter. "You're protected by the Act of God exemption. You can't lose." Reva poured herself a little more coffee and turned the page. They had been married for over forty years, and she had pretty much heard it all before. Her husband's gentle tirades against the real and imagined insults of the world were the background noise of her existence, always humming just outside the borders of her perception.

Weather people were not even really the problem, although in his later years, Wendell had come to view himself as a trace underemployed, a smidge below maximum potential, and he tended to grow touchy when mulling trades he felt to be better, or at least easier, than his own. As a humble policeman in Sand Valley, Alabama, he felt that category included many occupations. Maybe not coal mining or steel working, but certainly a large group of others. The real issue with Wendell was a general, vague dissatisfaction with almost everything, a mildly negative outlook on the world that was coupled with a quiet, nagging yearning for something he could not identify. This phenomenon had descended upon him later in life, and he often wondered if he was alone in this unidentified feeling of emptiness and loss. Certainly his wife, Reva, seemed immune and took each day as it came, happy as a sailor in a liberty port to be drawing breath and seeing another sunrise. The last time they had discussed their different points of view was on the occasion of Wendell's fiftieth birthday, a day that dawned dark and rainy and matched his mood to a tee.

"Being fifty really sucks," he had noted. It was going on noon, he had been up for several hours, and these were his first words of the day. He had contemplated the phrase since early morning, had crafted and honed it in his mind, and it said exactly what he wanted to say.

"Why can't you be happy?" Reva had asked. "You used to be." They sat on the front porch and watched rain drip from the leaves on the sickly magnolia tree in the yard.

Wendell and the tree were not friends. He claimed it was the only tree in the world that shed something each and every day of the year. Even on the only day in living memory that nothing had fallen off the tree, a bird had dropped dead from a branch, thus continuing the unbroken record. The magnolia had been planted by their neighbor, Miss Rose Lowery, when she was seven, and now she and her tree were both over ninety. The tree was drooping and had been losing branches with increasing regularity, and its occasional few blooms were more mottled brown than white. Miss Rose, on the other hand, was still as spry as a girl of seventy, and nothing major had fallen off of her in a long time, so it looked like she might outlast her tree. If the current drought extended another year, it was almost a certainty.

"I really don't know," Wendell had replied with a sigh to his wife. He was a man who began each day with the intention of being carefree and gay, but the harder he tried, the less it rang true. "I want to be as happy as a fat pig in deep mud, but it just isn't there. I'm not unhappy. I'm just not happy. There is always a feeling in the back of my head that I'm missing something, that the party has started and my invitation got lost in the mail." In Wendell's view, given the state of the postal service in recent years, this was entirely possible. "Maybe it's the job, or maybe it's Sand Valley, or maybe it's just me. I remember being content when we lived in Seattle."

"There is no party, and this is not a dress rehearsal," Reva pointed out. She took his hand. "It doesn't matter where we live, as long as we are there together. And a job is a job. This is the real thing. We are both on the wrong side of fifty now, and time is not going to stand still. Eventually, it will all be over for us. First one of us and then the other will pass on from this world. My mama died young, so it will probably be me that goes first. But you know what I believe, and I'll say it again. I am sure that I have loved you over many lifetimes, but I think that this will be my last time through this world. I hope that we are going to be together for whatever is next, but if you don't quit dragging around this baggage, I don't honestly believe it's going to happen. If you don't find some peace in this life, you will have to come back and look for it again in the next. And I don't want to go on without you."

Reva's vivid dreams of what she believed to be her past lives with Wendell were at the core of her belief system. She had experienced them for as long as she could remember, but she had never understood what they signified until she'd met her husband. She did not know why, but she always seemed to dream of just the endings of those lives, as if the imprint of the conclusion of one existence could carry over to the next and somehow burn itself onto that new consciousness.

In one dream, she and her fellow villagers were corralled by Roman soldiers at the edge of a cliff by the sea, and there was no escape. When awake, she believed the setting to be a rocky coast on the Irish Sea, but in her dreams she was not sure. The women fought savagely and well beside the men, with faces painted in blues and grays, but the Romans were too numerous and well equipped. As the end neared, the man who had battled the entire time by her side threw his axe at a Roman, cleaving the soldier's shield and the arm that held it. Then he turned his back to their enemies and placed himself between her and their foes to protect her as long as he could. He spoke to her in a language that her modern mind did not understand, although in her dream she knew what the words meant. Then, together, they stepped off the precipice. Reva knew beyond a shadow of a doubt that those two ill-fated lovers were previous incarnations of Wendell and herself. She had experienced the dream dozens of times, and each time she re-played the episode, a new fact or image was revealed. The first time

she had viewed the scene was when she was six, long before she knew
what a Roman was, or where the Irish Sea was located. Every time she
had the dream, she awoke feeling sad on one hand and deeply peaceful
on the other.

There were many other dreams as well. Some were frequent, some
were occasional, and some were one of a kind. But they all had as their
subject matter the ending of a relationship between the same two people. The appearance of the characters differed from one recollection to
the next, but she was always certain that it was the life forces of Wendell and Reva Blackmon that were bidding farewell to one another.
The *adieu* was the constant. Sometimes both were passing away, while
other times it was one or the other. In one of her saddest and most
vivid dreams, she was riding in a freight car. She knew it was a prison
train of some type, and in her waking hours she always assumed that
her dream persona was on the way to a penal camp in the vastness of
Siberia. It was bitter cold, and she did not have sufficient clothing, so
she was suffering from pneumonia while slowly freezing to death. The
odor in the car was a mixture of rotted hay and hopeless humanity.
She was an old woman who had been alone all her life, and she wanted
to die and be out of her misery, but she could not. Her heart would
not stop beating, and her life force simply would not let go. Then the
train stopped, and more prisoners were punched and kicked into the
car, herded by roughly dressed men with sticks and clubs. Included in
this influx was an old man who appeared to be a farmer. He sat next to
her just as she began to have a coughing fit. Without a word, he stood,
removed his greatcoat, and wrapped her in it. Then he sat back down,
encircled her frail form with his large arms, and tried to warm her as
best he could. As the *thump-thump* of the rails passed beneath them, he
held her, quietly singing an unfamiliar tune while gently rocking her.

He continued this comfort until she died. The dream always made her sad, because she knew that in that particular life, they had almost not found each other and had missed much happiness in their individual isolations. But the dream also encouraged her because they had, in fact, discovered each other before the end.

"Thanks for cheering me up," Wendell had said, back on the occasion of his fiftieth birthday. Reva had just informed him that from a cosmic standpoint, his prospects were limited. "You always know just what to say to make me feel better. You're going to die young, and I am going to come back as a barnacle. It doesn't get much better than that. Excuse me while I go sit in the highway. Maybe a chicken truck will come along and put me out of my misery."

"I am serious," she replied.

"I know you're serious, babe," he offered. "Maybe I'm in better shape than you think, and I could be your dog."

"This isn't funny," she had told him. It was Reva's belief that the soul went through many incarnations before purifying itself enough to pass to a higher state of existence. The concepts were called the *samsara,* the continuing cycle of birth, life, death, and rebirth, which formed the core of many Hindu beliefs, and the *moksha,* the release from the earthly plane for those souls ready for oneness with the universe. Reva had believed in these concepts long before she'd known their names or realized their Hindu origins. Hers was admittedly an unusual belief system to be held by a good, solid Methodist who sang in the choir on Wednesdays and Sundays, but she did not consider the two views to be mutually exclusive. The Methodist pastor, Dr. Stephen Rideout, was not as liberal as his parishioner, however, as was indicated by the "Hinduism or Heaven?" sermon that he dusted off from time to time, whenever Reva became too vocal with her arcane philosophies.

But Dr. Rideout's narrow-mindedness did not bother her in the least. She knew what she knew, and she believed what she believed. It was a certainty in her heart that this current life with Wendell represented her final trip through the earthly plane, and her great apprehension was that her husband was not yet ready for bigger and better things, cosmologically speaking. As with a child who could not learn his sums, her husband would flunk the great cosmic test and be held back at promotion time. Wendell was aware of his wife's views on the state of his inner light, and he really could not mount an argument. She was happy, he wasn't, and her explanation was at least as good as any of the others he had heard. It made as much sense as the fire and brimstone Christianity that he had been raised upon, and it was a more hopeful and forgiving system, given the fallible tendencies of the human race. While Wendell didn't buy into Reva's convictions, he believed that she believed every word. And he wished that he did, too, because then he would believe in something definite, and more importantly, he would believe in something that he wanted with all of his heart to be true.

As for Wendell's discontent, which Reva took as the major sign that his spirit needed seasoning, the matter had grown acute as he entered his fifties, as if he could hear the individual sands trickling through the hourglass, each one booming like cannon fire as it landed in the pile of time past. By the time he eclipsed fifty-five, he found himself in the doldrums more often than not. He felt he was squandering his allotment of eternity, was spending his days on substandard merchandise. But he could see no cure for the dilemma. He had long ago learned to spot a lie, but he did not know how to discern the truth. He had spent his entire life attempting to decipher what he desired to be and do, but the only progress he had managed so far was to develop an ever-expanding list of what he did not want.

At the present moment, Wendell knew with certainty that he did not want to be the individual who had to ferret out the facts surrounding the apparently radical departure of the cur on the ground at his feet. The deceased canine was in shabby condition, but that was not entirely his fault. He was a German Shepherd, and he had come up on the short end of a dog fight, a sporting contest much like the proverbial cock fight, with the primary difference being that the loser wasn't quite as tasty when served up with dumplings. Wendell looked at the dog's owner, Deadhand Riley. He leaned up against his patrol car and watched as Deadhand fidgeted and scratched at his grizzled chest hair. It was coarse, tangled, and matted, like white steel wool. One of his overall straps came undone, and his nimble fingers re-buttoned it without any conscious assistance from their owner, who was busy at that moment attempting to look innocent.

"I'm getting too old for this kind of shit," Wendell noted to Deadhand. He spoke in a conversational tone. Wendell would be sixty in the fall, had been a policeman since he and Reva had relocated from Seattle to Sand Valley during the first year of John Kennedy's reign, and was indeed getting too old for that kind of shit. Deadhand was caught short and didn't quite know what to say, so he compromised by nodding in agreement.

Opposite Deadhand stood Otter Price, the owner of the winner of the recent festivities. Otter looked as nervous as an apprentice firewalker and appeared to be contemplating the wisdom of becoming sullen,

an avenue that represented one of his two favorite responses to authority. Historically, it had not been a particularly effective reaction, but it
beat high-speed flight in his old Chevrolet, which was the other trick
in his bag. He noticed the shadowy look on Wendell's face and decided
against trying either. Wendell usually sailed on a fairly even keel, but
today he looked testy, and the Chevy needed a tune-up and two front
tires before any swift roadwork could be seriously considered.

Wendell slapped a mosquito. They were bad this year, bantam
striped demons that he called tiger mosquitoes. There were few things
in the world that he hated more, but the species as a whole did not take
his dislike personally and attempted to drain him at every opportunity. He did not know what it was about his personal chemistry that
drew them in, but he was like a living, breathing mosquito magnet
and had been ever since before he could remember. Indeed, his mother had once told him that he was bitten when he was three hours old.
Another time, he had been nailed while on a destroyer in the middle of
the Pacific Ocean, a thousand miles in every direction from anything
even resembling dry land. It was a curse, but Wendell had grown accustomed to it, and he supposed it could have been worse. What if he
had attracted cottonmouths all of his life, or vampire bats? At least he
could swat mosquitoes with the newspaper.

Wendell wasn't surprised that he had encountered mischief at the
Riley homestead. He had actually come looking for it, and Deadhand
was not one to disappoint. Wendell was a good policeman and had
the knack of knowing where to direct his gaze. Deadhand Riley was
one of his best customers, a frequent flyer in a manner of speaking,
and he had been too long quiet. Thus, Wendell had decided early that
morning that an unscheduled visit was in order. This tactic resembled
gunboat diplomacy in the old style, just a trip through the neighbor-

hood to fly the colors and see what trouble popped up. The silent mutt before him indicated that his intuition had been correct. The dog's paw was flopped up over a lifeless left eye, a salute in tribute to Wendell's hunch.

"Deadhand," Wendell said, "tell me about the dog." He knew it would take a minute for Deadhand to get started, that he would need time to hone his story to its sharpest edge before presentation, so he let his mind momentarily wander. He wished he had a cold drink, an ice cold Coke served up sixties-style in a nickel-deposit green glass bottle, slushy and crisp with a handful of peanuts dropped in so that every mouthful was cold, crunchy, salty, and sweet, all at the same time. Then he wished that he did not have a dog evisceration to examine, a reasonable enough desire even when the heat index wasn't over one hundred degrees. Finally, he wished both Otter and Deadhand had been sold to Yankees at birth on a buy one, get one free arrangement, thus providing better value for the shopping dollar. Then it would be some poor unsuspecting Northern lawman and not Wendell who would have to deal with the pair.

"Rusty," Deadhand finally said. "His name was Rusty." Deadhand smelled like a distillery fire and looked about as bad, sort of burned out and fallen in on himself. Wendell couldn't believe that he had been there ten minutes and all he had was the dog's name, and he didn't even need the dog's name.

"I don't care what you called him," he said. "What happened to him? Why is he dead? Why did Otter's dog kill him?" Deadhand shrugged, as if to say that it beat the living hell out of him.

"Harley," Otter Price interjected in the name of clarity. "My dog's name is Harley. Like the motorcycle." The hound looked like he might have mostly bulldog ancestry, with a little of one breed and another thrown in for variety.

Otter could be a cooperative man when the drop was on him. Arthur was his given name, and most people believed that his nickname resulted from his uncanny resemblance to the sleek mammal of the same name. Actually, his mama was afflicted with a lifelong speech impediment but had, in spite of this malady, named her bonny baby boy with a combination of syllables that she could not quite get her lips around. *Otter* had been the result.

"Harley," Wendell said. "Like the motorcycle." Now he had two dog names that he did not need, and the sad part was, he felt like he was making progress. He continued. "So Harley jumped on Rusty for no apparent reason and did that to him? That's the story?" He pointed at the remains, silent testimony to Harley's mean streak and Rusty's bad day.

"That's what happened," Deadhand said, nodding. He was honesty personified, a choirboy in the rough. The sincerity in his voice was as absolute as the atomic weight of lead.

"Swear to God," Otter added, placing his right hand over his heart while holding his left hand in the air. He looked like a poorly dressed Boy Scout with a hangover who was in bad need of a shave, a haircut, and several thousand dollar's worth of dental work. Wendell wasn't impressed, solemn vow notwithstanding.

He scanned the area of the lawbreaking. Deadhand's trailer was in the background, a structure long past its prime that would never achieve the status of mobile home. It was twenty feet in length and had two fins on one end—presumably the back, since there were tail lights below them—and between the fins was attached the insignia *Fleetwood*, a name long associated with style and grace, even if it was hanging down at a forty-five degree angle. The moveable structure was propped on a variety of objects, ranging from standard fare such as bricks and concrete blocks to the less-traditional Pontiac engine that supported the southwest corner. Pieces of the aluminum siding were missing along the sides of Deadhand's home and had been replaced by irregularly shaped squares of plywood and tin, nailed in haphazard fashion. One of the patches was a license plate, another a stop sign. One window was completely gone, and a sheet of opaque plastic was permanently duct-taped over the hole. There was no air conditioning, and the door hung open like a slack jaw. Wendell shuddered when he thought of how hot it must be inside, like an oven that was equipped with Naugahyde furniture and shag carpeting, and he figured Deadhand was probably the way he was at least partially because his brain had been baked.

The dirt yard was littered with an impressive assortment of beer cans and liquor bottles, thousands of cigarette butts, four defunct vehicles in various stages of decomposition, a dog pen, and an old John boat with a hole in the bottom, courtesy of a shotgun blast. Plus Rusty, of course, now gone to that great fire plug in the sky, just another chewed-up dog in search of a better deal who had almost certainly found one. Wendell wondered what assumptions some future archaeologist would make about the culture of twentieth-century America if he happened to dig up Deadhand's yard.

"Harley is kind of skittish, isn't he?" he asked of no one in particular as he nudged Rusty with his toe. In his line of work, he heard the occasional broad story, and he was a little disappointed that the boys hadn't come up with something more creative. Given their past history as tellers of epic tales, and considering the sheer amount of practice that both of them had acquired at adjusting reality in their favor, he had expected a better effort from the pair.

As an example, Wendell had once found both of the men standing naked, at four o'clock in the morning, next to a burning GMC pickup truck parked in the middle of U.S. Highway 11, just down the road from Whitehead Baptist Church. The truck had been reported missing the previous day by Deadhand's brother-in-law, Larry Franklin, or as Deadhand liked to call him, "That-no-good-son-of-a bitch-who-stole-my-baby-sister-right-off-of-Mama's-tit." This moniker was admittedly long for a nickname, but Deadhand liked the way it scooted across his palate and declined to discontinue its use. It was about twenty degrees that night, and the clouds were spitting the occasional flake but looked as if they might decide to find some gumption and produce a real storm at any moment. Under questioning in the eerie light of the pickup truck bonfire, both Otter and Deadhand swore on their mama's heads to have been abducted by "little green midget-looking fuckers" who had taken them up in a spaceship for observation before releasing them on the highway. Wendell thought the cold west wind had likely frozen the men's synapses, thus causing stupidity to tumble from their mouths, so he wrapped them both in blankets and placed them in the back of the police cruiser with the heater turned on high. From the odor that soon permeated the close confines of the car's interior, it became apparent that the green midgets had forced Deadhand and Otter to drink large quantities of bourbon while stealing their pants and burning the truck.

"Tell me more about your abductors," Wendell began.

"Who?" Deadhand asked.

"The little green midget-looking fuckers," Wendell replied.

"Well, they were these little green fuckers," Otter offered.

"Like midgets," Deadhand added.

"Thanks," Wendell said. "Why did they take your pants?"

"Oh, shit, our pants are gone!" they both cried when they looked down.

"Why did they burn that truck?" Wendell probed.

"Oh, shit, they burned Larry's truck!" Otter wailed while Dead-hand sat silently, looking distraught, as if he might be in the early stages of post-abduction stress syndrome, or a hangover of mammoth proportions. Since neither of the abductees could produce an abductor to corroborate the story, Wendell was forced to look for earthly solutions to the mystery, although he was more than fair with Deadhand and Otter during the evidence- gathering phase of the investigation.

"It's not that I don't want to believe you, but I need to see an alien," he explained. "Any size, any color. Otherwise, I'm going to charge you with public drunkenness, public indecency, and someone has to pay for Larry's truck." Larry Franklin had decided to forego pressing charges after Bonnie, his wife and Deadhand's baby sister, explained to him how difficult it would be for her to keep her mind on sex for the next five-to-ten years if her big brother ended up serving a prison sentence for truck theft. The pantless truck burners were fined two hundred dollars apiece and had to split the cost of the vehicle, but it had been a world class lie worthy of fond remembrance, not the uninspired little fib that Wendell was currently being handed. He shook his head and yearned for the old times. They just didn't make scoundrels like they used to.

"Well, I guess it makes sense," he said, referring to Harley killing Rusty for no particular reason, and not to the little green midget-looking fuckers flying in for a truck burning. Deadhand and Otter relaxed. The relief was visible on their faces. The matter was cleared up, and their good names were restored. Deadhand felt that the occasion called for a drink, so he took a generous sip from the pint bottle he had sequestered in the bib pocket of his overalls, tucked in next to a can of snuff and a thirteen-year-old condom. He was an optimistic man.

"Except for one thing," Wendell continued, and the boys tensed right back up. "Why were you here with Harley in the first place?" He directed this inquiry to Otter. It was sort of the inevitable question, the keystone that held the entire lie structure aloft, but for some reason, it threw Otter. Perhaps he had thought it wouldn't occur to Wendell to ask.

"Uh," Otter said, and Wendell could almost hear the gears grinding as they attempted to mesh. "Uh," he repeated. Then his clutch engaged, and he was able to move forward. "I brought him over here to *play* with Rusty," he blurted. Both he and Deadhand nodded earnestly. Harley growled from his cage on the back of Otter's truck and lunged playfully at Wendell, as if he were agreeing with the story. The cage scooted a few inches when the dog hit the chain link. He cast a baleful eye in Wendell's direction.

"I think he wants to play some more," Wendell noted. "How much gunpowder have you been feeding him?" he asked, referring to the practice of serving gunpowder to a dog to drive it insane and make it savage.

"I don't feed him gunpowder." Otter said defensively. He was sliced to the quick at the implication that he was capable of cruelty of that magnitude. Besides, he had used turpentine. It was cheaper, easier to get, and the dog was much less likely to explode if someone smoked in his vicinity. Wendell needed a break from dealing with Otter, so he turned his glance upon Deadhand, sportsman extraordinaire and bereaved dog owner, who seemed to be bearing up well after his recent loss.

Deadhand Riley appeared to be a well-preserved seventy, which was a problem for him, since he was forty. But they had been forty hard years, dog years, as it were, and the toll had been taken. His downward slide had begun early, due to poor judgment regarding his first choice of professions, which had been opening up the barrels of Agent Orange before that substance was sprayed over a variety of Asian people who were trying for the most part to mind their own business and stay out of the way. Admittedly, he had not had an entirely free hand in his selection of occupation, but fate has always been more oriented toward outcome than process.

Deadhand's given name was Huford Riley, but he became Deadhand due to another questionable decision concerning employment. After being the Agent Orange man for eleven months, three weeks, and four days, Huford came home to Sand Valley, Alabama, with a chronic cough and an understandable dislike for fifty-five-gallon drums. He got a job in the joist factory, and over the next few years, he worked hard at his trade and smoked a lot of dope on the side. He was attempting to forget, and while his selected method was not as traditional as joining the Foreign Legion, it at least had the advantage of not involving firearms, French people with curtains on the backs of their hats, or stone forts in sandy locales.

He worked diligently, and he eventually rose to the coveted machine-shop foreman's position, which was the top of the pile in his selected venue. His job was to machine the steel to a precision fit, and it was while checking a lathe bit for sharpness one day that he began the journey from Huford to Deadhand. The testing of a bit for a honed edge was a routine task and should not have produced mishap, but performing this function while the lathe was still turning at eight hundred rpm's added an element of risk that Huford had not foreseen, due to the large quantity of high-quality cannabis he had smoked throughout the day. His right hand was mangled almost beyond recognition, and he was still looking with interest at the affected paw when his coworkers dragged him to safety while gagging at the gore.

During the hand-rebuilding process, several grafts from his back and buttocks were taken, but the process went awry, and the resulting extremity had no feeling in it whatsoever. It also exhibited a pronounced mound of flesh on the back of the hand that resembled a mallet. These new features proved to be advantageous to Deadhand during fistfights, toward which he was prone, and it was widely held by his many opponents that his right fist had an impact velocity similar to that of a runaway Mack truck. One of them, Art Duarte, had actually been *hit* by a runaway Mack truck, so he was in a position to know. But all of that was long ago and far away, and none of it would bring back poor Rusty.

"Let me tell you what I think," Wendell said, looking at Otter and Deadhand in turn. "I think you had a dog fight here." The miscreants made as if to protest, but Wendell held up his hand. "I've told you before that I don't like this kind of business. It makes me think that you are not classy people. It makes me want to forget that I am a nice guy. It makes me want to send you away until your dicks dry up and fall off." Penile desiccation had probably already occurred in Deadhand's case, but Otter considered himself to be a swordsman, and the threat seemed to impress him a great deal. He winced, and his left hand drifted of its own accord down to his genital area to make a quick check for missing or dried-up pieces.

"Wendell," Deadhand protested, "you have never said a damn word about dog fighting." He had Wendell on a technicality on this matter, but the lawman was not fazed. It was not the first time that a rogue had tried to argue the finer points of the law.

"No," Wendell agreed, "we didn't talk about dogs. We talked about roosters." Otter and Deadhand nodded, vindicated, and Wendell continued. "As I recall, Deadhand brought his rooster over to your house to play with your rooster, Otter, and your bird ended up like this dog." Otter looked morose, as if the memory brought him great sadness. Satan—Otter's rooster, not the cloven-hoofed evil Prince of Darkness—had been a fine yard bird, a chicken among chickens, and he was missed by all who had known him. Harley whined in his cage out of sympathy for a fallen comrade, or maybe because he had wanted to eat the deceased. Deadhand shooed some blue flies from Rusty and said nothing. He seemed to sense that it was his best course.

"I like you boys, so I'm going to cover this one last time," Wendell said. He actually didn't like the boys that much, but he had always believed that it was a good idea to give something before taking something away. "And you both need to listen because it is important. I don't like dog fighting, cock fighting, or rat fighting. I don't like cat fighting, coon fighting, or snake fighting. If you two ever decide to get married, I don't like wife fighting." Wendell tried to imagine a tussle between two women who would actually marry Deadhand and Otter, and he had to concede that it would probably be a fairly interesting contest, at that. Deadhand did not currently have a romantic attachment, but Otter's girlfriend, Rita Hearst, was a woman who looked like she might kill someone for their shoes. "Basically, if it involves two living things fighting and a bet from either one of you on the outcome, then you are not allowed to do it. The next time I catch you, I'm throwing both of you *under* the rock castle."

The rock castle was Sand Valley's jail. Deadhand and Otter had sampled its hospitality on many previous occasions, and they did not wish to partake of it again. It was a solid edifice constructed of mountain rock, the Alcatraz of rural Alabama, complete with two turrets and a moat. It had been built during the thirties by a group of unemployed mill workers from Dogtown who had nothing to fear but hunger, itself. They were willing to do nearly anything for some pinto beans, cornbread, and a little fat meat, and their government in its wisdom had put them to work building a jail. Admittedly, it was a humble project when compared to the great public works of the time, such as Hoover Dam, but it was impressive by local standards and had the added advantage of not containing the entombed remains of any of its builders. Franklin D. Roosevelt himself had viewed the completed project while on a long weekend furlough from Warm Springs and had dubbed it "the rock castle" on the spot. He had commended the workers and ordered extra cornbread and fat meat plus a day off for each of them.

Deadhand and Otter hung their heads, overcome with humiliation. Even Harley looked a bit shamefaced, as if he wished the killing of his opponent had not been a necessity.

"Speaking of bets," Wendell asked, "how much was riding on this fight?" There was no sound, and neither of the men met his eye. They had the Constitutional right to remain silent and were doing just that. Wendell continued. "It looks like a one hundred-dollar fight to me, so I'm going to make your fines one hundred dollars apiece." Technically, Wendell did not have the authority to levy fines or mete out justice, but he and the judge were of like mind most times and made an effective team when it came to crime and punishment. He knew that she would back him up.

Wendell had decided that a deterrent was in order, a penalty with some bite so they would remember to behave next time. He settled on a fine because if he ran them in, he would be stuck with them for the duration of their sentences. No one was likely to bail either man out of trouble, and Wendell didn't want to have to feed, clothe, and talk to them for thirty days. It would be a poor fiscal move for the town and hard on his nerves as well. Plus, he lived upstairs at the rock castle with Reva, and he really didn't want Deadhand and Otter in his house. It was bad enough to have them in his community.

"A hundred dollars?" Otter asked. "Where the hell am I going to get that?" Otter's portfolio was not particularly liquid since having to pay for half of Larry Franklin's truck when the aliens burned it. Deadhand could find no voice at all to express his dismay. His mouth moved, but no words escaped. He reminded Wendell of a ventriloquist's dummy whose owner had a touch of laryngitis.

"Why don't you sell Harley to Deadhand?" Wendell suggested. "It looks like he needs a dog to me. If you throw in the truck and the cage, the package should be worth close to one hundred dollars." Harley growled low, as if he objected to the idea of being Deadhand's dog. Wendell could understand his point.

"This ain't fair!" Otter said. Deadhand nodded.

"I'll tell you what's not fair," Wendell replied, pointing to the defunct hound. "That's not fair. But if you think I have been too harsh, you can always throw yourself on the judge's mercy." He knew what was coming next, and he loved it every time. It was often the high point of his day.

"But your *wife's* the judge!" Deadhand said, finding speech at last. "She'll put us on the chain gang!" Considering Deadhand's and Otter's checkered pasts and Judge Reva's legendary dislike for anything even resembling cruelty to animals, it was a definite possibility.

Reva had been the temporary probate judge for close to ten years, ever since Miss Effie Beecham had gone to that big courtroom in the sky. She had been handed the job the day after Miss Effie's funeral, just until a more permanent arrangement could be made, and she had been trying to hand it back ever since. The townsfolk were happy with her work, however, and would not let her quit. Even her regular clientele, such as Otter and Deadhand, had to admit that she was better than Miss Effie, who was the only probate judge in Alabama history to ever attempt to impose the death penalty. So Reva was reelected every two years by write-in vote, even though her name was never officially on the ballot.

"I don't care if they do elect me again," she had said the last time the polling place had been open. "I'm not going to do it!" The exit polls were looking ominous, however. Nearly every voter who stepped out from behind the curtain smiled and waved at the unwilling incumbent. Some winked at her and flashed the V for victory, while others gave her thumbs up or clasped their hands and shook them over each shoulder, like boxers on the way to the ring.

"I've gotten kind of used to sleeping with the judge," Wendell observed conversationally. "I would hate to have to start bunking in with Ralph."

Wendell was a creature of habit, and there could be trouble if Reva declined to serve and the town's only official candidate, Ralph Harp, was elected by default. Ralph was not a regular bather, which is a bigger issue for chicken farmers than it is for the practitioners of a large number of other trades. Thus, Ralph was not a popular man, but he was a tenacious one. He had run unopposed for the probate judge's position once every two years for the last ten, and in that time, he had received a total of five votes. His own mother did not even vote for him, although she told him routinely that he needed a shower, and her voting record and bathing advice were a constant source of trouble between them. Reva was reelected by a vote of three hundred six to one, and as usual, she agreed to take the job.

"I guess it beats working at the sock mill," she said in her informal remarks in front of the rock castle. The people cheered. Reva's way with an acceptance speech was always a crowd pleaser.

"And you get to meet such interesting people," Wendell noted helpfully.

"Boy, howdy," Reva replied as she once more strapped on the yoke of responsibility thrust upon her by the townsfolk. At the back of the small crowd, she could see Ralph Harp shaking hands and giving out cards in preparation for the upcoming election, two years hence.

The reason that Reva was so popular was a simple matter of comparison with her predecessor's legal decisions and her opposing candidate's odor. Miss Effie had become a little touched in her waning years, and many of her legal renderings were subject to question. The probate judge was supposed to levy and collect fines on small legal missteps, process the paperwork on civil claims, and bind all serious cases over to the county court. Over time, however, Miss Effie began to exceed this mandate. As a result, Wendell spent a good deal of his time cleaning up behind her. The problem came to a head when she sentenced a speeder from New Jersey to thirty years and a day at hard labor because he had given her sass. The perpetrator was remanded into Wendell's custody for immediate execution of sentence. He aimed the scofflaw, who was a bit sassy, in a generally northeasterly direction and quietly advised him to stay out of town for a few years. The town council met that very night to decide how to get rid of Judge Beecham without hurting her feelings, but the poor dear beat them to the punch by having the good grace to suffer a fatal stroke in her sleep. She quietly weighed anchor and set sail for heaven's shore, where hopefully she was not given gate duty.

"If I were you," Wendell said to Deadhand, back out at the dog-fight, "I wouldn't give Reva any lip while I was paying my fine. She won't put up with it." Deadhand nodded, subdued. "You, either," he continued to Otter. Like Miss Effie, Reva did not care for sass. If they weren't careful, she would land on them with both feet, in a legal manner of speaking. He gave the rowdies one last stern look to dem-onstrate that he meant business before climbing into his cruiser. Rusty was tenderizing, and the flies were beginning to gather in earnest. It was time to vacate. Wendell rolled down the window and leaned out for one final word.

"You had better get that dog under some dirt before he becomes a health hazard. That would cost you another fifty dollars. Bury him deep and pile some rocks on him. I don't want a coyote digging him up and dragging him out into the highway." Deadhand nodded. Otter scowled, but he knew good advice when he heard it. Wendell backed out of the yard, shifted the cruiser into drive, and headed to-ward town. "Way, way too old for this kind of shit," he muttered.

The riverbanks were steep and barren, a red clay canyon carved by a slow-moving green current. Above the clay banks on both sides of the water course stood tall, old-growth trees: chestnuts, long-leaf pine, hickory, elm, and river oak. Wisteria hung in curtains from the canopy of branches, a fragrant lavender barrier between wood and water, the vines as thick as a grown man's arm. Here and there, a fallen tree met the river and provided a handy avenue for river turtles to take the sun, and they were stacked on these makeshift platforms like flat rocks on a beach. A brace of geese dropped in low and skimmed the river's surface. The splash of a

catfish quickly diving sent ripples out to greet them. A muskrat made his slow way against the current toward his den in the far bank. It was late afternoon. The sky was a cloudless cerulean canopy.

The canoe glided silently into this idyllic scene. Its construction of skins stretched and dried over a supple ash frame lent lightness and buoyancy, although the two occupants were not much of a burden for the craft to bear. The woman rowed, and the man lay still. They were of a brown-skinned race with long black hair, members of the Ani-Yun-wiya. They were not children as their people reckoned age, but they still had the bloom of youth about them. They were man and wife, and they were on the river that day trying to outrun the sickness that had come with the Spaniards, the disease that had obliterated most of the rest of their village. The woman was covered with pustules. Her fever was high, and a deep weariness had settled over her. Her joints had ached until they were numb. Her companion had been ill for a longer time, and all of his lesions had joined to form a single scale, like a turtle's shell. He had lost consciousness soon after they had climbed into the vessel. His fever raged, yet he shivered. His breathing was raspy and uneven.

She rowed to the bank and tucked in behind a snag. They needed water and rest before their journey could continue. She dipped her hand into the cool stream and drizzled water onto her husband's parched lips. He moaned but did not awaken. She knew that without intervention from the Red Woman, his time was near. She prayed to this deity until her head fell forward with fatigue. Then she took a drink herself before collapsing from exhaustion.

The rain arrived in the darkness of the night. It began as a light sprinkle, but it gained momentum as the stars retired. The dawn was cloud-covered. A heavy drizzle outflanked the sun and continued until midday. As the river rose, it turned from green to brown, and the small *canoe floated free from its snag and made its way out into the current. The pair lay, heads touching, with her feet pointing to where they had been and his pointing toward their destination. They were still, and her hand rested on his cheek. Their pain was gone, their fevers abated. They, too, had floated free, and now they drifted down the river toward the wide, cool sea.*

Chapter Two: 1942

Years uncounted have meandered through the corridors of the ages to become dog-eared pages in dusty history books, and 1942 was no exception. But to those who lived the time, it was a great and terrible season. Enrico Fermi split an atom he could not see and became the father of the Apocalypse. Adolph Hitler warmed the gas chambers in Buchenwald and began the attempted extermination of a race of people. Jimmie Doolittle flew a desperate mission into the rising sun in defiance of the Asiatic hordes. And late in 1942, when Wendell Blackmon was sixteen, he hitchhiked to Chattanooga, Tennessee, and joined the Navy. It was his intention to see the world, fight for his country, and place at least one ocean between himself and Sand Valley, Alabama, where he was born and raised.

Wendell was a tall, slim boy with thick brown hair who wasn't as patriotic as his actions seemed to indicate. He had trouble at home on two fronts, and those were two more fronts than he cared for and one more than he could manage. His biggest problem was Glennice Olive Cole, an older woman of twenty-five from down the valley. She was not a beauty in the classic sense. She had bad teeth due to her unladylike habit of dipping snuff, and her right eye always seemed to be looking elsewhere. She was thick across the middle courtesy of her Slavic ancestry and wide across the hips thanks to birthing too many babies, too soon, but beauty always resides in the eyes of the beholder, and her attractiveness to Wendell was in direct proportion to her accessibility.

Glennice had recently informed Wendell that she was with child, and that the child she was with belonged to him. When delivered, the baby would bring to five the members of her brood, so Wendell was faced with the prospect of a wife and a ready-made family. He had been raised as one of eleven children, the oldest child of a loving mother and a vicious, spiteful father, so the concept of a large family did not daunt him. The idea of setting up housekeeping with Glennice did not faze him much, either. He was a young man just looking for another excuse to leave home. He had already run away five times by his sixteenth birthday, and five times his father, Happy Blackmon, had tracked him down and dragged him home. The last time, Happy had tied Wendell to a tree in the dooryard and had beaten him unconscious in front of his mother and ten sisters with a length of knotted rope, so that none of them would get any foolish ideas about running off like the prodigal son. Wendell's sisters screamed and cried, his mother got a dose of the knotted rope herself when she tried to stop the whipping, and Wendell called Happy seven different kinds of low down son of a bitch right up until he lost consciousness. It was a horrid interlude even by the liberal standard in force at the Blackmon farmhold, and none who witnessed it were ever quite able to retire the scene from their mind's eye.

Wendell was planning on doing right by Glennice and marrying her, when he was informed by his good friend, John Frank Henson, that Glennice had told *him* the same story, and two other boys had also been nominated as patriarchs of the burgeoning Cole clan. In her defense, she wasn't quite sure *who* the father was, but she had told Wendell before all of the others because in her heart of hearts she wished that the baby she was carrying was his, or that he would marry her anyway, even if it wasn't. She liked that he brought her little gifts, and she liked his blue eyes and his big hands that looked like they should be clumsy, but weren't, and she liked the way he talked to her when they made love. Glennice was a bit on the dull side, but she was not working her wiles out of spite. She merely wanted a husband, and she was using the only tools in her kit to try to obtain one. She hoped it was Wendell, because he was nice to her, and in her experience with the male gender, men who were nice were a rarity.

"She's not like that," Wendell had said to John Frank, defending the honor of the woman he felt duty-bound to marry. He wasn't sure that he loved her, but he was very fond of several *parts* of her, and he was willing to take the rest of her on faith.

"Damn, Wendell," John Frank said, but not unkindly. He was eighteen and had been around the track a few more times than his younger friend. "She has screwed damn near everyone in the county. Did you think you were the only one?" Actually, Wendell hadn't given it much thought, but now that he did, he supposed that the four children she already had plus the one on the way did imply a history of sexual intercourse. Wendell had a heightened sense of propriety, however, due to having been raised in a household where nearly every human interaction had been performed incorrectly, and he thought it disrespectful of John Frank to be discussing Glennice's personal life in broad daylight, in front of God and everybody else, even if he might have a point.

"Just don't talk about it anymore," he said to John Frank. His friend shrugged, and then he proceeded to tell Wendell that Glennice's daddy, A.B., was looking for all four of his potential sons-in-law, and Lord help the one he found first.

"He'll either kill you or make you marry Glennice," John Frank told Wendell. "I don't know which would be worse." Then, since he could not swim, John Frank went to join the Army. "If she don't find a husband soon," he said to Wendell before heading for a foxhole, "the whole state will be in service." John Frank knew A.B. Cole to be a crack shot; thus, he was willing to take his chances with a collection of faceless Germans instead, some of whom were bound to be city boys and, therefore, fairly useless with a rifle. Wendell was left impaled on the horns of a dilemma. He had been prepared to step up to the plate and marry Glennice, but the new information provided by John Frank had weakened his resolve. Too many cooks spoil the stew—or at least they get one of the cooks to thinking with his brain instead of his penis.

So Wendell was already mulling his duty to God and country as the likeliest escape route from either matrimony or shotgun wounds, when the well went dry at the family farm. This was his other problem, and although it was not quite as severe as having A.B. Cole wanting his hide mounted on the side of the barn, it was sort of the straw that broke the camel's back. Wendell was the oldest of the Blackmon children and the only boy in the batch, so it fell to him and his father, Happy, to dig a new well. His mama, Eunice, and his ten sisters could haul water from the spring for a short while, but it was a mile there and back straight across a series of fences and furrowed fields, and this was a short-term solution at best, especially considering that three of the girls were too young to be of much use in the bucket line and a fourth suffered from infantile paralysis and could not even walk, never mind haul.

Happy Blackmon's name implied that he might be a carefree fellow, but alas, that was not the case. He had been born crying in a fit of rage, and his disposition had not improved much in the ensuing years. His father was an alcoholic schizophrenic who blew out his own brains just two weeks before Happy was born, much to the delight and gratitude of all the poor souls who knew him. His mother, Rhoda, named her new fatherless baby *Happy* in a moment of wishful thinking, but her optimism had been misplaced. Happy took after the father he never knew and remained unhappy for the entire span of his existence, and he behaved as if it were his mission in life to make those around him as miserable as he was. So he abused his wife and daughters constantly, and they all learned to fear the keen edge of his tongue and the sharp sting of his open palm when he was in one of his midnight moods. As for Wendell, Happy first beat him three days after the boy's third birthday, for the offense of crying. It was his theory that a lad must be toughened into manhood, and it was his intention that Wendell become a hell of a man, just like his old dad. After that first thrashing, Happy beat the boy like a dirty rug, regularly and for not much reason, and Wendell learned to hate him, but not to fear him.

Happy was a lazy man, and the fact that he had only managed to father one son was a source of bitter disappointment. The family farm was ninety-three acres of toil, and he labored year after year to produce additional sons to help work the land, much to the unending chagrin of his long-suffering wife, Eunice, who seemed to have a knack for bearing little girls. The girls worked too, of course, but Happy was convinced that more boys were needed, especially when a large task, such as digging a new well, arose. Eunice had married Happy when she was seventeen, and by the time she turned eighteen, she realized what a horrible mistake she had made. The handsome young scamp

she had wed possessed no conscience or any capacity for feeling. She
had tried to leave only once, while she was pregnant with Wendell.
Happy had thrown her to the floor and kicked her first into submis-
sion, and then into labor. She gave birth to her first child while her
husband whispered into her ear.

"If you ever try to go again," he hissed, "I will kill you and every
child we have." Eunice knew without a doubt that he was telling the
truth, and she never again attempted to flee. There was really no place
for her to go, anyway. Her parents were dead, and her sisters had trou-
bles of their own. But that night, as she held the newborn Wendell
to her breast, she quietly swore to someday escape the man who had
threatened her child.

Happy was not pleased when the well went dry. He hired Dock
Farris to come out with his divining rod to find water, and for one
crumpled dollar, that old man stayed half the afternoon, praying and
mumbling as he shook his forked stick. Dock was a local institution,
and fully half of the wells in the area had been located with his assistance. But he also had a roving eye, as if he were a human divining rod
capable of discovering women who were not too particular. He had
fathered several children around the county, including the oldest of
Glennice Cole's progeny, but that foible was not common knowledge,
and Dock was too old to join the service, in any event.

"Blessed God," he prayed, "bring forth the eternal breast and
suckle thy children." He was shaking his branch and beseeching the
Almighty, but his gaze was on the firm young bosom of Louella Blackmon, Wendell's fifteen-year-old sister, as if there might have been some
confusion in his mind about the location of the proposed suckling. He
continued the hunt for water until he began to talk in tongues, and
when he fell out, the spot where he landed was chosen as the new well

site. "Just scratch the dirt," he said, as he rubbed the back of his neck, "and she'll come bubbling up."

Dock had no particular talent for finding water, but Sand Valley and the surrounding area sat mostly on top of a huge underground lake, so discovering a good well site was not difficult. A blind pig could do it. It was only around the western edge of the valley, where the farms butted up to the foot of Sand Mountain, that the lake petered out and finding water became hit or miss. Dock knew that the Blackmon farm was in the danger zone, but he figured that he had a fifty-fifty chance, and dollars were hard to get. Still, he wanted to be long gone before the digging began. He knew how moody Happy could become, with not much provocation.

After Dock Farris pocketed his greenback and left the premises, Happy made an X to mark the spot, rolled up both sleeves, spit on the palms of his hands, and handed the pick to Wendell. The reason that he had sired children in the first place was to have spare hands around when chores such as well digging came up, and now was the time for the payoff. He just wished there were a few more peckers in the crowd. It was just bad damn luck. He had gotten off to a good start by producing a son on his first try, but then his fortunes had reversed, and the next ten children were girls. It was almost as if that bitch he was married to was doing it to him on purpose. She would lay there with her eyes closed and her fists balled, and if he ever let go of her arms, she would try to hit him or scratch him. Then, nine months later, there would be another damn girl.

"Get to it," he said to his son. "We can't drink dirt." He was not a verbose man, and Wendell knew that no other instructions were forthcoming. He set to with pick and shovel, and once the hole got deep enough, his three oldest sisters—Louella, Lucille, and Mary Alice—

assisted as much as they were able by pulling up the washtubs full of dirt that he dislodged. Happy took the occasional turn in the well at first, but his times on the pick were short and infrequent, and by the end of the third day, he no longer even pretended to help, preferring instead to sit underneath a shade tree about fifteen feet away from the actual work, supervising the job while he sipped on white whiskey.

"Damn it, Louella, *pull,*" he instructed, as his daughter strained on the rope. "I reckon I'm going to have to do it my damn self!" The girl knew that this was an idle threat, although she was not foolish enough to say so out loud. Wendell wasn't the only Blackmon to have experienced the loving caresses of Happy's fists. The well was now over twenty feet deep, and each shovelful of dirt was drier than the last.

Happy was disgruntled. He had two dry wells, an old one and a new one, and that was a sorry state for a farmer to be in. He had ten daughters on his hands—one of them a cripple—and he knew that they would soon begin to marry and move off, thus depriving him of what little help they provided. Indeed, he had twice had to shoo Dock Farris away from his oldest girl when the old man had been out to find the well, and maybe if Dock had spent a little less time looking at Louella's bosom and a little more time shaking his stick, they would be having better luck finding water. Now, on top of it all, it seemed that Happy was out a dollar—and money, like sons, did not grow on trees. He didn't know how his luck could get any worse. But then, he was an unimaginative man.

As the well deepened, Wendell grew as despondent as Happy, but his low mood had nothing to do with his large number of sisters. Foremost on his mind was his father's legendary frugality, and he was certain that the cheap old bastard would make him dig all the way to China before he gave up on that dollar. Additionally, Wendell had

discovered that he was claustrophobic, and the condition was aggravated by standing in a hole twenty feet deep and five feet across, with
loose dirt raining down while the dank smell of raw earth filled his
nose. It was like being in a deep, round grave, and he was sure he was
going to be buried alive long before he hit water, or he would drown if
he managed to live long enough to pierce the aquifer. And even if he
did survive the well, Glennice's daddy was still looking for him up in
the world of sunlight, and A.B. Cole did not miss what he shot at. It
was a no-win situation, and all Wendell knew for certain was that he
had to get out of that hole. So he peed on his own boots and called to
be pulled up.

"I hit water," he said, when he clamored out of the well on all
fours. He pointed to his wet footwear, his bonafides. He had hastily devised a plan as he scrambled toward the sun that relied heavily
on Happy's naturally suspicious nature, and he prayed silently to the
gods of agriculture that his father would want to go down for a look.
Otherwise, Wendell was going to be forced to brain him with the wash
tub before throwing him down the well and running like hell. But
whatever happened, whichever way it went, Wendell was not climbing
back down that rope. If he had to kill Happy, that was fine by him. If
he had to marry Glennice Olive Cole on the spot, so be it. If he had to
sell his mama and his three oldest sisters into the skin trade in Memphis, well, Mama had always wanted to travel.

"By God," said Happy as he touched the damp leather of Wendell's boots. "Dock did it again!" He put his fingertips to his tongue
and looked over at his son. "It sure tastes sweet." Wendell nodded
earnestly. Happy picked up one end of the rope. "Lower me down,"
he said. "I want to see it." A relieved Wendell grabbed the rope and
began to play it out, and his father disappeared from sight. Presently,

the rope went slack. Wendell knew that Happy was at that very moment inspecting the damp spot at the bottom of the well.

"Damn it!" came the disembodied voice from the depths. Wendell flinched as the rope went taut. Happy was on the way back up, and he did not sound like he was in a good mood. Wendell released his end of the rope, and the thud from the hole indicated that his father had once again arrived at the bottom. Wendell looked over at Louella, who had witnessed the entire event. He gave her a rueful grin and shrugged. Her eyes were as round as two dinner plates in her pretty, young face.

"Daddy's gonna kill you when he gets out of that hole," she whispered. Wendell considered her appraisal and concluded that she was correct. Happy had a long history of violence and would beat him like a rented mule for the smallest infraction, but this time Happy would likely bludgeon him to death. Wendell knew it in his heart. Luckily, Happy could not fly, and it would be difficult for him to climb out of the hole while the rope was in there with him, so Wendell figured that he should have a fair head start. He knew he needed to go right away, but he hesitated as he looked slowly around the rundown dooryard of the squalid farm that had been his home for sixteen years. There was the weeping willow by the front doorstep, an apt door warden for a sad home. To the right of it was his mama's flower garden, her pride and joy, filled with wild flowers that she had transplanted with love and care from all over the valley. There were purple and pink blazing stars that stood like spears, delicate blue asters, white and orange lilies that fluttered like triumphant flags in the breeze, red bee balm and fire pink, blue salvia and phlox, knee-high brown-eyed Susan's, and sunflowers as tall as Wendell. There were rhododendrons that bloomed white and azaleas that sprouted gentle pink to velvet rose. Around the remainder of the dooryard stood white cedar trees intermixed with sourwoods. Along the path to the barn and on out to the road stood a long line of gnarled hackberry trees.

Wendell would miss seeing his mama in her bonnet working her garden, snipping and fussing as she attempted to coax some beauty into their bleak lives. He would miss his sisters, and he would miss Glennice Olive Cole's sweet attentions. But he would not miss this *place,* he decided, and he would not miss the coiled viper in the well.

"He'll have to find me first," Wendell replied over his shoulder as he ran into the house through the open front door. Again, he stopped a moment and looked, although he did not have the time to spare. The house was sad and threadbare, and his mama's attempts to make it less so by hanging pictures from *Collier's* and *The Farm Bureau Gazette* on the rough pine boards that formed the wall served to amplify the shabbiness rather than ameliorate it. The theme of the gallery had always fascinated Wendell, as it seemed to be a pictorial collection of places his mama wanted to go combined with people she would rather be. He really could not begrudge her fantasies. The nicely dressed, beautiful people in the pictures lounging against fine automobiles or dining in palatial settings contrasted starkly with the squalor of the Blackmon existence, even to a sixteen-year-old plowboy like Wendell, who had not been to town that often. He shook his head. It was time to leave Sand Valley behind. He poked all of his worldly possessions into an empty flour sack, along with four cold biscuits from the table and the family tree from the front of Eunice's Bible, which he had heard the Navy would take in place of a birth certificate. Then he headed back to Louella at the well. As he neared the scene, he could hear the voice drift from below. It sounded a bit closer than it had before, as if Happy were trying to shinny up the side.

"Wendell, I'll nail your ass to a tree when I get out of here!" This promise had a vaguely biblical sound to it and was followed by a *thud* and an "oof." Wendell stepped over to his sister. He looked at her a minute, at her blue eyes and short brown hair, at the freckles that peppered her nose, at the telltale dips and curves that marked her transformation from his skinny little sister into a young woman. Then he gave her a hug and patted her back.

"I've got to go," he said to her. She nodded at the inevitability of the action. "If Happy ever gets out of there, tell him you tried to stop me, but I pushed you down. Tell Mama I love her. I love all of you girls, too." She nodded again. "Don't let Dock Farris get near you if no one else is around. He's a dirty old man, and you can't trust him. Wells aren't the only thing he likes to shake his stick at. Now, go find Mama and tell her I've gone. Tell her I don't know when she'll see me again, but I'll send her some money every month." Louella began to cry as she ran toward the spring. Wendell started to go but then felt compelled to say something, anything, to his father. Without even being aware of the concept, he needed closure, a definite end point to his sixteen-year relationship with the man down in the hole.

"Happy," Wendell hollered down at his father, "I'm leaving now. Don't come after me, because you won't find me." This was not what he had intended to say, but it was what had come out.

"I'll kill you when I get out of this hole!" came the reply. "You can't run far enough to get away from me!" Hatred flowed from Happy like cool air from a smoke house. Wendell mulled his father's response and had to disagree. He knew good and well that he could run far enough. Then, without conscious thought, Wendell unbuttoned his fly and relieved himself a second time into the well. It had not been long since he had peed on his boots, and his bladder was mostly empty, but he managed to produce enough to get his point across.

"Piss on you, Happy," he said as he finished. He shook off the drops in aggravated fashion as Happy screamed, speechless with rage. Wendell supposed that, after all, he really had nothing else to say. He shouldered his sack and began his long walk toward the relative safety of a world war.

He met scant resistance at the recruiting office because the war was ratcheting up by that time, and the Navy was in need of all the deckhand candidates they could find. The recruiter, an old chief petty officer with a plate in his head, took Wendell's word that he was eighteen and did not even glance at the forged family tree from the Bible. If the boy wanted to be a sailor man, it was okay by Boats Chadwick. He had lied his own way into the previous war, the war to end them all, at the tender age of fifteen, and the Navy had given him a home and a good life, that steel plate notwithstanding. Besides, Boats knew that if he didn't take Wendell, the Army would because these days they were signing up anyone who could fog up a mirror. So Wendell was sworn in and shipped to Nashville for sorting, and by the following Friday, he was on a bus headed for San Diego, California.

Wendell made two friends during the three days he was in transit from Nashville to the San Diego Naval Air Station. The first was a buck-toothed, white-skinned, and red-headed young man from Gatlinburg, Tennessee, who had joined up because he wanted to be a submariner. His name was Walter Smith, and he was easily the homeliest person that Wendell had ever met, including Dock Farris, Boats Chadwick, and Glennice Cole's daddy, who was no looker for sure, although he did wield an impressive shotgun.

"Call me Smitty," Walter Smith said. He and Wendell shook hands as the Greyhound made its way toward Memphis, birthplace of the blues and future home of Elvis. There was an abundance of

Smittys in the military during the war years—the only moniker more common was *Jonesey*—but Walter was Wendell's first and remained his favorite. Smitty was a luckless soul, however, and his fortunes did not improve when he enlisted. There was a chronic shortage of submarine sailors in those days, for the obvious reason that most of them were drowned fairly quickly, so Smitty was given his wish and allowed to train to be a submariner. He was lost at sea during his first voyage when the skipper was forced to dive the boat due to unidentified aircraft on the horizon, while Smitty was on deck dumping the slop bucket from the galley. When the submarine returned to port, Walter Smith was officially listed as being still on patrol, a designation that he and his slop bucket will retain until the seas give up their dead.

Wendell's other new acquaintance was Raymond Brown, and he boarded the bus in St. Louis. He was a short, oily-looking boy who chain smoked Luckies. He had a wild look in his eye, and he wanted to be a sailor like his father before him, hopefully with a better outcome. Raymond's sire, Alonzo Brown, had been a seaman in the Merchant Marine, until a Nazi U-boat commander had taken a dislike to his ship and sent it and him to a watery, unmarked grave in the wintry North Atlantic.

"I am going to kill some Krauts," Raymond said to Wendell by way of an icebreaker. The young men shook hands. "Those German sons of bitches will regret the day they decided to cross the Browns." Raymond was eighteen and knew just what he wanted to do, which was an unusual trait in one so young.

"This bus is headed west," Wendell felt compelled to say. He hated to point out the flaw in the plan, but the points of the compass were not subject to interpretation, and maybe Raymond was on the wrong bus. "I think you have to go east to get to the Krauts." He did not know this for sure, but it seemed to be a pretty good assumption.

"Are you sure about that?" Raymond asked.

"Pretty sure."

"I guess it will have to be Japs, then," Raymond replied after a pause. As long as he had someone to kill, he was apparently pretty flexible.

Wendell liked the Navy or, at least, he preferred it to digging wells, dodging matrimony, and being beaten by his father. In fact, compared to his Spartan existence down on the farm, boot camp had an aura of surreal luxury about it, like a trip to a fine hotel where the concierge yelled a great deal while making the guests do push-ups. There was electricity, a scientific marvel that he had only experienced from time to time back in Alabama. He received three square meals a day, and he didn't have to stare at the business end of a mule from sunup to sundown. He took hot showers, and he sat on indoor plumbing, and he didn't have to sleep with three small sisters, one of whom had the habit of soaking the corn shuck mattress in her sleep. He wore clothing that no one else had ever worn—crisp, unpatched garments that were his and his alone. And on top of it all, they paid him to be there. Half of his salary was sent to his mother every payday, so the girls would not starve in case Happy was still in the well. Part of the remainder went to Glennice Olive Cole each month, just in case, and the rest trickled down to Wendell Blackmon's pocket. He'd never had it so good.

The makeshift surgery was set up in a red brick barn on the outskirts of Fredricksburg, Virginia. In the distance the battle raged as Ambrose Burnside attempted to advance his army against the strident objections of

*Robert E. Lee. It was December of 1862. The operating theater was an
oak door laid across sawhorses, lit by two sputtering lanterns. The wounded came in the front door of the round barn, and the patients who survived
treatment exited by the same route. The dead and a collection of ownerless
limbs were taken out the back and stacked for burial.*

*The surgeon had been working nonstop for eighteen hours, and Mary
McCray had been with him the entire time. She was a local woman who
had volunteered to help. Her husband, son, and son-in-law were all out
there somewhere, fighting for the Confederacy. Mary and the doctor were
averaging better than one patient per hour, some blue and most grey, and
of the twenty-one poor souls they had treated, seven were dead and three
more were likely to join them before another day passed. The doctor's tools
were getting dull. They were out of laudanum, whiskey, and bandages.
Their clothing was drenched in blood.*

*On the table, the doctor pulled a blanket over the head of a corporal
from the Stonewall Brigade who was missing both legs and his right arm.
He had never had a chance and had lived just long enough to doom another man by taking his spot. The doctor sighed.*

*"It would have been a mercy to this man if someone had put a bullet
in his head." Mary agreed but said nothing. It was an irony to her that
it was somehow unthinkable to ease the suffering of a poor soul who could
not possibly survive. The orderlies transported the corporal's remains out
the back door. The doctor washed down his makeshift table with a bucket
of water. Mary threw a shovelful of sand for traction onto the floor under
the sawhorses. Then she ripped a few more strips of cloth from her petti-
coat to use for bandages.*

*"Next!" the doctor yelled. The orderlies brought the next man in. He
was under a blanket, but it was elevated in the middle, as if he were lying
under a small tent. His face was black, but whether this was from soot or*

the result of a burn, Mary could not tell. There was a bandage covering both of his eyes. He groaned in pain, panting. The doctor removed the blanket and looked upon his latest patient.

"Damn," he said quietly. The soldier had been shot from behind, obviously by an enemy who had panicked and had forgotten to remove his ramrod from his musket before firing. The wooden ramrod had entered the back of the unfortunate soul and had nearly passed through him before breaking in half, causing two exit wounds, twin Yankee arrows protruding from the front of a dying Confederate torso. The doctor attempted to ease the patient up on his side so he could determine the path that the ramrod had traveled and was rewarded with a scream so full of pain and bereft of hope that it did not sound human. Mary bathed the unfortunate's brow and cheeks with cool water as she whispered, "Ssshhh, ssshhh." Then she stopped before staggering back with a look of horror on her face.

"It's hopeless," the doctor said, misunderstanding her reaction. He, too, wished to turn away.

"It's my husband," she whispered.

"What?"

"It's him," she repeated. "We have to help him."

"Mary, I can't fix this. There is a ramrod shattered inside of him. I don't know why he is still alive." The soldier groaned again. His panting continued.

"We have to put him out of his pain, then," she said. "Can you get some laudanum anywhere? Or some chloroform? He is a strong man, and he won't give up. His father lived for two days after a wagon ran over him. We can't let him suffer for two days!"

"They may have some chloroform at the officer's hospital. I'll have to go myself. They won't let any of the men have it. I can be back in twenty minutes." The doctor rushed out, leaving Mary with her dying, suffering

husband.

"*John, can you hear me?*" *she asked, taking his hand. She was sure he could not speak, but she felt a slight squeeze from his hand. "This is Mary." She felt another squeeze. "John, you are hurt too badly. We can't help. All I can do is make the pain end. Is that what you want?" She felt nothing for a moment. Then a squeeze. Near the table was a pile of gear stripped from patients as they were brought in. Boots, knives, sabers, belts, pouches, and pistols. Mary picked up a pistol and checked the prime. Then she cocked it and aimed at her husband's head. "John, you won the battle. The war is over, and the boys are safe. So it was worth it. You saved them." She was quiet a moment. Then she spoke again. "I will always love you." He squeezed her hand, and she squeezed the trigger. Her aim was true, and another shot was not necessary.*

Chapter Three: 1933-1942

Reva Blackmon was born Reva Anne Martin, and in 1933, when she was ten, she and her kin moved west from Arkansas after the family farm dried up and blew away to Texas. The topsoil on the Martin's forty acres had been thin and weak to begin with, like a malnourished child, and nine straight years of drought had finished off what King Cotton and poor farming skills had begun.

"If we stay here, we'll starve," Reva's father, Harry Lee, said to his wife, Avonnel. "I reckon we better head on to California." They had been discussing the possibility of westward flight since May, but they were loath to leave their home. It wasn't much, but it was all they knew.

"We're nearly starved now," Avonnel agreed, relieved that her husband had finally arrived at the inevitable decision. "We had best go." She looked at him with pity. He was tracing zeroes in the dusty dooryard with the toe of his decrepit boot. His failure was as heavy as a timber upon his broad shoulders, and he looked as if he had aged twenty years during the last five. The farm had been his father's, and his father's before that, and had passed from father to son for well over one hundred years. But it was about to be owned by the Farmer's and Merchant's Bank of Arkadelphia, Arkansas, even though the bank did not want the parcel and made no secret of the fact. That institution had been swamped with foreclosures and was land-poor already, but business was business, and Harry Lee Martin had been informed that he could not stay if he could not pay.

The original Arkansas Martin, Roger by name, had claimed the homestead back in the latter part of the eighteenth century. He was a Scots-Irishman from near Ulster who had decided to emigrate soon after he was forced to throw the Catholic rent collector out of the closed window of his small cottage, after that unpleasant fellow had called Roger a lying, cheating, Presbyterian pig. Roger was a Presbyterian, had indeed been lying at the time, and had cheated on his rents on many occasions, but he felt that none of these facts entitled the bald retainer with the weasel eyes to call him a pig. Unfortunately for Roger, the landlord sided with his hired man and evicted the Martin family. They took ship for want of a better option, and they came to the port of Charleston in January of 1789. One year later, they arrived at the Quachita Mountains in the Arkansas Territory. They settled in a small valley at the south of that range and began to farm the tract that was to support the Martin family for the next one hundred and forty years. But all things of this world, good and bad, come to an end, and in the fall of 1933, Harry Lee Martin was about to lose the title to the family home.

"Harry Lee, you owe us four hundred sixty-seven dollars and thirty-three cents," said Aldred Sexton of the Farmer's and Merchant's Bank, when he and Harry Lee met to discuss the Martin financial embarrassment. "And you haven't paid us so much as a buffalo nickel in three years. If you can't pay me something, I am going to have to take your farm." The last thing Aldred Sexton needed was another ramshackle house adjacent to a forty-acre dust field, and he hoped he wouldn't have to repossess. Perhaps Harry Lee could come up with fifty dollars, or maybe even twenty-five.

"I can give you the LaSalle," Harry Lee offered, knowing as he made the gesture that the old rust bucket was not worth anywhere near four hundred sixty-seven dollars and thirty-three cents. He had only given forty dollars for the heap to begin with, and it had gone down considerably since then. When the silence grew long, he spoke again. "I was going to throw in the mule, too, but he died." Actually, old Rex had been shot and eaten, and he hadn't gone down too bad, at that, considering the lack of condiments available. Avonnel was a marvel with a skillet, as Harry Lee had observed on many occasions.

"I got a look at your mule, once," Aldred replied. "He has to be worth more dead than alive. And the LaSalle is worth less than the mule." The banker shook his head. The sins of the monetary world were weighty on his soul, and because he had no choice in the matter, he was about to put yet another family out of their home. He felt sure there was a place in hell waiting for him as a result of the unhappiness he had spread, but if he didn't evict the folks who couldn't pay, the bank would find someone who would, and his own family had to eat. So he would just have to let the afterlife take care of itself. "I'll give you a month to sell out and go," he said. "I'm sorry." Harry Lee merely nodded. He was ruined, and all he could do was stand like a captain in the wheelhouse, watching as the ship sank beneath the waves.

"I don't want to move away, Mama," Reva said when she was told the news. "I like it here." She was sad but did not cry. She was a quiet child, no trouble at all to raise, according to her mama. She had known hard times her entire young life, so she was accustomed to them and didn't recognize them for what they were, but she did not realize that the transition to even harder times was upon her family.

"I like it here, too," Avonnel said as she took her daughter onto her lap and smoothed her curly hair. "I like it here, too." She hugged Reva for a long while as they sat in shared silence at the rough-hewn kitchen table. It was covered in a light layer of dust, fine as talcum powder, that had sifted in around the windows and under the door.

So the Martins cashed in what little of value they could spare. The plow and the stove were sold for scrap, and most of the furniture was burned along with the house, because Avonnel could not stand the thought of strangers living in her home. They loaded what was left into a car that should have gone with the stove and the plow, and found their way to Oklahoma City, where they picked up the great westward road, the Mother Road, Route 66. They began their journey toward the setting sun in a 1927 LaSalle that belonged in a junkyard, and over the course of the coming weeks, they traveled to what they hoped would be the Promised Land.

In later years, Reva came to remember the diaspora as a series of photographic stills of an heroic journey, as if the trip to the Pacific had transpired in pieces rather than as a process. She remembered a rusted truck by the roadbed somewhere in Texas, an old hulk made oddly beautiful by the wildflowers growing around it as the sun settled down for the night in the background. She recalled the profile of her father as he laid his trusty shotgun across the top rail of a fence and took aim at a wild pig, and it was only after she reached adulthood that she realized that wild pigs do not live inside fences, and that Harry Lee had actually been practicing a rude form of communism by redistributing the wealth, or at least the pork, from those who had it to those who needed it. She could see her mother bent down, cooking over a campfire, humming "Amazing Grace" as she fried the potatoes. She recollected waking up in the gray canvas tent and looking with wonder out across a dry, grassy plain to see the sun shining brightly down on the left side of the tract while the rain fell hard and cold on the right. It was a weather war, with the front line directly before her, two elemental forces fighting for control of an abandoned prairie.

They traveled at the pace they could manage, sometimes alone, sometimes in spontaneous caravans, and they camped each night in the best spots they could find. Sometimes they overnighted with other travelers in makeshift campsites, small temporary towns peopled by homeless optimists, all engaged in the pursuit of survival and perhaps some happiness. Other nights, they slept with the stars. There came days when they stayed put because they were just too tired to go on, or because the LaSalle would not budge, but most days they were on the highway that led from shattered dreams toward unfounded hopes. They gravitated to the uncertainty of the new existence because they were afraid to go back to the cruelty of the old. They lived on a diet of cornbread, fried dough, and faith. And as each day passed, they had less of each to quell their hungers.

Harry Lee, Avonnel, and Reva reached California early in October, but countless other unfortunates had arrived ahead of them and had already sopped up the legendary river of gravy that welled up from the San Andreas and flowed to the sea. California had failed the Martins in its covenant of milk and honey and could not accommodate even three more hopefuls in an old LaSalle, so they drifted north and finally settled in the small town of Timberline, Oregon. There Harry Lee got a job logging for the sawmill. They lived in the LaSalle until he pocketed a couple of pay envelopes. Then they rented a small house on an acre of land and bought a pair of pigs and an armload of chickens. It looked as if their search for a new home might be over. But their newfound security was a phantom in the cool Oregon mist, and when the family fortunes began to fall once again, they plummeted like a dropped stone on a windless day.

Reva became the barometer of the family woes lurking just over the horizon when, at thirteen, her right leg was severed just below the knee by a gin-swilling engineer on the Southern Pacific. His name was Banks Clifford, and he never even saw the schoolgirl who had tripped and fallen on the tracks, but that oversight saved neither of them from the rupture in the Martin karma. Reva lost her leg, and Banks lost his job and pension, but not his taste for rotgut liquor. It took another year after the accident, but he finally managed to drink up enough courage to kill himself, and as he lay on the tracks right before the train arrived, he wondered if it was going to hurt. There was a note in his pocket when they found him that said, "Tell the little girl I'm sorry."

Reva survived her ordeal and healed, and by the time she turned sixteen, she had learned to walk again with the aid of a used wooden leg that the local doctor had secured from the county morgue. The secondhand appendage had previously belonged to Ronald Applewhite, who was the only one-legged gay Seminole to ever reside in Timberline. Unfortunately, he had fallen fatally afoul of a lumberjack with a twitch who went by the name of Buck Neveau. Buck and his chronic eye spasm ran into poor Ronald one night at the Main Street Tavern, and the Seminole had the misfortune to mistake the logger's tiny ocular convulsion for a wink. One blunder led to another, and before Ronald could explain his error, he had been beaten to death with his own leg. Luckily, Reva knew none of this, and the leg fit well enough, provided she kept the strap tight. She was big for her age, and Ronald had been a very small Seminole. So for her, life seemed as if it might be inclined to return to normal. Then one day her father met her at the gate when she came home from school. It was March of 1941, and she was eighteen. It was her last year of school, and she hoped to win a scholarship and go on to teacher's college. She had grown into a beauty, with jet-black hair and eyes like midnight velvet.

"Your mama's real sick," Harry Lee said. He had not shaved that day and looked scruffy. "I don't believe she's going to pull through." Harry Lee was not a medical man, but his diagnosis in this case was correct. His wife had suffered a heart attack. Fifty years of fried pork and buttermilk biscuits had rendered her coronary arteries insoluble, and a lifetime of wondering how she and her husband—and later, her daughter—were going to make their next meal had added stress to the mix. It had been a significant infarction, long overdue, and surviving it was going to be out of the question. Reva started for the house, but in her concern for her mother she forgot her own physical limitations, and as was always the case when she tried to run, her prosthesis slipped and down she went.

"Damn the Southern Pacific!" she cried, ironically mimicking the last words of the drunken Banks Clifford as he had caught that train to glory. It was her first use of profanity, and she wouldn't have done it then if she had not been so upset. Still, it was strangely cathartic and satisfying. She sat and rearranged her leg before proceeding at a slower pace, arriving just in time to hear her mother's last words, which had nothing to do with trains, fried pork, or swearing.

"Aunt Velma," she said, "take me home to Jesus." Aunt Velma had been dead for better than thirty years, but that didn't seem to bother Avonnel in the least, and off she went.

"Goodbye, Avonnel," Harry Lee said as he began to cry. The woman he had lived with since he was little more than a boy had just left him and gone way over yonder. He did not know what to do.

"Goodbye, Mama," Reva said as she held the lifeless hand. She was too sad to cry, so she sat there in the slowly darkening room and stroked her father's hair while he sobbed for the both of them. Around sundown, a cold rain began to fall, and the mist embraced the ground. It was the bleakest day that Reva had ever known, and she had encountered some bad ones in her time.

Reva had lost her childhood home, her leg, and her mother, and she hoped that fate might now spare her and Harry Lee further trouble, but that was not to be the case. The week after her mother was buried in a pretty spot overlooking the Columbia River, her father was killed at the mill when an arbor shaft broke, and a rogue saw chased him halfway across the log yard before splitting him right down the middle. It was a bad way to go, and even the veteran lumberjacks and sawmill hands were shaken by the incident. Both pieces of Harry Lee were tucked in beside his wife, and Reva planted some azaleas on top of her parents. Her mother had always loved them. Reva somehow felt better that their remains were together, and perhaps Aunt Velma would take it as her eternal duty to lead them both to a better place. Or at least to a better place than Oregon, which had had its drawbacks for the Martins. Reva returned home to the rented acre and went about the business of being an orphan, and over the ensuing days, an odd normalcy descended. She had become the last living member of the newly established Oregon branch of the Martin family, and her plans did not reach out much past the next hour of any given day.

She was at a loss. She had lost her Arkansas home at ten due to decades of unsound farming practices coupled with a dry, hot wind that would not cease, and she had lost her leg at thirteen thanks to Southern Pacific's questionable policy of hiring a drunk. She had been orphaned in stages at eighteen due to pork on the one hand and metal fatigue on the other. None of it was her fault, but all of it was her problem. It was as if the fabric of her life were a shroud. She did not know what to do, but she had to do something. She had no job, and she had no leg, and the rent was only paid through the end of the month. For the first time in her life, she was utterly alone.

The gene pool was shallow around Timberline, just ankle-deep in most spots, and unrelated and available females of marrying age were rare. So scarce, in fact, that the number of limbs possessed by any given candidate was not the issue that it might have been in the city. Thus it was that only three weeks after she had buried her parents, Reva received a proposal of marriage from Theodore Nichols. He was a nice boy who had known Reva since the Martins had moved to town, and he had grown to love her from afar. Now he had worked up his courage, and he wished to conduct his love affair from a closer proximity.

"Reva, I love you and I want to marry you," were the words he spoke on her front porch. She was sitting in the porch swing, and he was down on both knees with his hands clasped, as if he were praying. His hair was slicked back, his shoes were shined, and he wore a tie. He was trying his best to do it up right. Reva had always liked Ted, and she still did. But she did not love him.

"Ted, you are sweet," she said as she leaned forward and straightened his tie. "But I'm not sure that I love you." In truth, she was quite sure that she didn't, but the look of hope and yearning on his face had caused her to soften the blow.

"Well, do you like me?" he asked, grasping at straws.

"Yes, I like you, Ted," she replied. He looked down a moment, then raised his head and met her gaze. There was a look of desperation in his eyes when he spoke.

"That would do for starters," he said. "How about it?"

While searching for the nicest possible way to turn Ted down, Reva gave his question some consideration. She was a practical girl, and she knew that she would soon be out on the streets. Her sex, her education level, and the number of legs she possessed all guaranteed that finding employment would be no easy task. She did like Ted, and after some thought she determined that she could grow to love him later, and even if true love did not find its way to her heart, she could and would still be a good wife to him. So she said yes and became Reva Nichols, and she cleaved to her young husband till death did them part.

Unfortunately for Ted, he had placed himself squarely in the path of a woman whose run of bad luck was winding down but was not quite yet over. Six months after they married, he was drafted into the Army. Three months later, she gave birth to Charles Parton Nichols, a nine-pound baby boy. Six months after that, Ted was run down by one of Irwin Rommel's panzers in French North Africa. Mercifully, he was asleep in his pup tent at the time and never saw it coming. Ironically, the German tanker and his two-man crew had deserted the Third Reich for greener pastures earlier in the day, and they were driving around in the Saharan night looking for someone to surrender to. After they flattened Ted, however, the opportunity to apologize was not afforded, and they were shot one by one as they came out of the tank.

"Nein! Nein!" Corporal Willie Gruber screamed as he clamored out of the hatch. He was the last man onto the turret and felt cold terror descend as he saw his two deceased crew- mates. His hands waved frantically in the air, as if he were trying to take flight from the horror of the moment.

"Ninety-nine, my ass," Sergeant Riley Goodman muttered as he pulled the trigger of his carbine for the third time, sending Corporal Gruber to another, hopefully less martial, plane of existence.

When Reva received the telegram regretting to inform her of the loss of her husband, she was sad but somehow not particularly surprised. It was a Friday, near sundown, and she heard a vehicle bumping up the road to the house. She expected it was her neighbor, Flora Hutton, arriving in her timeworn truck for her weekly visit. Flora was an older woman from across the ridge whose own grown children had moved off, and who had no grandchildren to hold. She was about the same age that Reva's mother would have been if she had lived. Flora had taken to bringing over supper on Friday nights while her husband, Luke, was out drinking with the other timbermen. But when Reva stepped out onto the front porch, she was greeted by the sight of the county sheriff's Dodge. Fear cinched her throat like a noose. The tall deputy stepped out of the sedan and removed his hat. He cleared his throat and cast his eyes at the ground. The universe held its breath, and no sounds could be heard, but it was a false calm, a short remission, a deep breath before the plunge.

"M'am," he said, "I have bad news." Reva nodded, turned, and walked back into the house. She had seen the yellow telegram in his hand and knew why he was there. There was nothing to say. She had known, somehow, that it was just a matter of time. The baby began to cry from his cradle, and she snatched him up like a wolf was nibbling at his toes and held him tight as she gently rocked him back to his infant dreams. A tear fell from her cheek and landed on his forehead. He frowned and rubbed the wet spot with his tiny fist. Reva cast her eyes to the ceiling.

"I don't know what I've done," she said in a clear voice as calm as a summer lake, "and I don't know when you will be satisfied." She paused, looking for the right words, the phrases that would redirect the gaze of the Almighty. "If you need more, take me. You already have my leg anyway. But not him. Please leave him be." She took a shaky breath and held the baby tighter still. "Please leave him be."

She was old, and she was dying. She could feel the magic gift of life ebb from her, like water draining from a tidal pool as it found its inevitable path back to the sea. Leaving this world was painfully slow work, but it would not be long now, not nearly so long as it had been, and she was ready. Her long life had been her punishment, crueler by far than fire raining down from above or transformation into a statue of salt. Her sin had been fear, and endless days of regret had been the price that had been exacted for her transgression.

She sat alone in her parlor, surrounded by silver and gold trinkets that performed no function, mother-of-pearl frames embracing pictures of strangers, lace pillows and throws that did not ease or warm, empty cut-glassware, and hand-painted vases that had never known the intimacy of a flower. They were mute companions that gave no comfort. The love of her life had been gone for better than sixty years now, gone by her actions and by her hand, and she wanted nothing more here at the end of her time than to talk to him once again, to explain to him why she had acted as she had, and to beg him for his absolution before she made her final journey.

They had been in love, and they had been lovers, and for a time that had been enough. By day she was a lady, a woman of property and position, and he was a tanner, a man with calloused hands who had known the rigors of a hard existence. But at night they lay in each other's arms and whispered their dreams of freedom. They would run to where no one knew them, and they would live as man and wife, and they would build their lives around their love for each other.

But in the end, it was just talk. She loved him, but she loved her comfort more. She was afraid of being poor. So she sent him away and married a boy from the local gentry, and lived a loveless, barren marriage. But now her time was done. As she slipped away, she remembered one last time his broad shoulders and his gentle hands. A single tear traced her cheek as she weighed what she had gained against what she had lost. Her final thought was that she wished she could see him just one more time. And then she was gone.

Chapter Four: 1985

Sand Valley was a compact community, a molecule on the Alabama map, equidistant from Pisgah and Ft. Payne. That small dot contained one bank, seven churches, two gas stations, and a feed-and-seed. It boasted a general store, a school, two restaurants, and a truck stop. It sported a rock castle, four red lights, twenty parking meters, and a garage. In short, the town of Sand Valley represented the lives and hopes of the souls, good and bad, who called it home. It was a small island of ungarnished Southern humanity lapped by the turgid seas of the wide, cold world.

Sand Valley the town was small, but Sand Valley the *township* was a different matter. It was huge and contained mostly pigs, chickens, cows, and the relatively few humans who tended them. The town lines had marched outward in June of 1975 at the insistence of most of the then-incumbent town council, a farsighted group who had wanted to position Sand Valley for the future.

"Why does Sand Valley need to be one hundred square miles big?" Wendell Blackmon had asked at the council meeting. He was a member because he was the chief of police of the town force of one, and on this occasion he seemed to be missing the bigger picture. Because it seemed to him that there was quite a bit of empty space between the people in Sand Valley already. His was the lone voice of dissent.

"To attract industry and commerce!" was Gilla Newman's reply. "We have to think big!" He spoke of the concepts as if they were already loaded on trucks, twin eighteen-wheelers loaded with, respectively, industry and commerce. Wendell could just see them pulled off the side of the road about ten miles out in the country, a big Kenworth and a Peterbilt, the drivers leaning up on the fenders, smoking cigarettes and enjoying a cold drink while they worked on their log books.

"I hope they get the town line out here soon," one of the drivers would say.

"Maybe they'll think big," would be the other's reply.

Gilla Newman was the mayor during Sand Valley's Big Bang. It was an extremely part-time job that required about four hours per month of his time, and he was a slow worker. His full-time occupation was that of ne'er-do-well son of the richest man in the county, which some would say is good work if it can be found. Unfortunately, none of the local folks were much inclined to explain to him the full extent of his inferiority. The exception to this rule was Wendell, who never missed an opportunity to inform Gilla of his general stupidity, but young Newman just would not listen. As a result of this lack of civic responsibility by most of his peers, Gilla was under the mistaken impression that he was important, that he had a point of view worth sharing. His given name was Stanley. Gilla was short for Magilla, after the cartoon gorilla of the same name. Gilla was living proof that, Godless heathen though he was, Charles Darwin may have been correct.

"I haven't seen all that much industry and commerce circling for a landing," Wendell noted, but he had not been looking up much, so he might have missed it. He had scant use for those of his fellow citizens who had pretensions of urbanizing his home. If they wanted to live in a city, then they should move to a city. There were several to choose from. And it wasn't as if Sand Valley was going to become the commercial hub of the New South, no matter how far out the town lines were moved. The only new business that had opened in a long time was Jimbo Cox's Snowball Stand, and poor Jimbo was currently down on short- time, due to a fluctuation in the flavored-ice industry. The jury was still out concerning whether or not he could weather the storm.

The rest of the council looked at Wendell like he was a leper, unclean and untouchable. They were fully behind Gilla because his father, Mr. Frank Newman, had suggested to each of them individually that it would be a good idea to back the lad. Mr. Frank understood that the main component of power is fear, and he liked a great deal the fact that most of the people on the council and in the town were afraid of him. It gave him a warm feeling inside. He was a visionary who could see so far because he was standing on the uncounted bodies of the hapless souls who had gotten in his way.

Mr. Frank had not bothered to have one of these chats with Wendell for two reasons. The first was that in the Newman grand scheme, Wendell was of no consequence. He had no money. Thus, he was beneath notice, a speck on a flea's back, a bump on a log in a hole in the bottom of the sea. The second reason was that Wendell, inconsequential though he was, could not be bought. Mr. Frank had once made the error of trying—over speeding, of all things—and had found himself paying a five hundred dollar fine to Judge Reva as a result. The charge was for disturbing the peace.

"Whose peace am I disturbing?" Mr. Frank had demanded. He had a solid white unibrow that looked like a V when he frowned, as he was doing presently. He was not happy over the turn of events. It had been a long while since anyone had confronted him, and he had forgotten how much he disliked the feeling.

"Mine," Wendell said. He had stopped Mr. Frank for vaulting a speed bump in front of the school, and it had been his original intention to let the old man off with a warning about driving too fast around the children. But when he stepped up to the driver's side window, Mr. Frank had casually handed out his registration wrapped in a fifty-dollar bill. It was a draw as to which facet of this gesture made Wendell angrier: the fact that Mr. Frank had assumed his integrity was for sale, or the discount price he had tried to place upon it. It was a double insult, and Wendell decided that more than just a slapped hand was in order, after all.

"Why in the hell are you arresting me?" the elder Newman had challenged, not quite able to fathom the effrontery. Wendell had him out of the red Lincoln, legs spread and hands on the roof as he frisked him.

"Mostly because I can," Wendell admitted as he slapped on the cuffs. He couldn't remember the last time he had enjoyed an arrest so much.

"I'll have your job!" Mr. Frank shouted. A vein pulsed on his temple.

"Put me out of my pain," Wendell stated, as he helped his prisoner into the back seat of the cruiser. "Watch your head." Mr. Frank had used his one phone call to summon his attorney, Charnell Jackson, to come help straighten out the misunderstanding. Charnell had been playing golf when he was tracked down by the golf pro on the fifteenth fairway, but he was three strokes under his handicap coming off of the fourteenth green, and he was currently lying a two just seventy yards from the pin on a par five, so Mr. Frank had to wait an extra hour while Charnell finished the round. When he finally arrived, he was still in golfing attire, a Southern study in what not to do with pastels.

"Sorry I took so long, but I was in court," Charnell said as he entered the rock castle. "What is all of this about?"

"What color are those pants?" Wendell asked. They shimmered, looking almost alive. They made Charnell look like a tall, balding frog with a pot belly.

"Forget the damn pants!" Mr. Frank yelled from the cell in the back. "I am in jail! Get me the hell out of here!" The rock castle only had one cell, and Mr. Frank was sharing it with Deadhand Riley, who had engaged in a slight difference of opinion over the weekend with five construction workers from Montgomery, and who was now serving three days as a result of those discussions.

"They are green," Charnell responded to Wendell. "Why is Frank in the cell?"

"Frank is in the cell for disturbing the peace, because he offered me a fifty-dollar bribe to not write him a ticket that I wasn't going to write him anyway. I did him a favor and didn't arrest him for attempted bribery, which is a felony. I won't ever do him that favor again." He was still looking at the pants. He was about half color blind, but even so, that didn't look like any healthy shade of green he had ever seen. Charnell stepped back to the cell and conferred with his client a moment. Then he came back to talk to Wendell.

"If Frank pays his fine, will Reva let him go?" Charnell asked.

"Reva has gone out to visit my mama, but she left word that Frank can go when he pays his fine. You, however, may have to do a little stretch for wearing those pants." So Mr. Frank paid his fine, and Wendell let Charnell off with a stiff warning on the pants.

"You may have to hit the streets if I get fired for arresting Frank

Newman," Wendell said to Reva that night. "I'll get some sharp clothes and a hat with a broad brim and become your pimp. I already know where I can get a cool pair of pants. Maybe I can even find one of those long watch chains to wear. It will be great. We'll still be working together."

"It'll never work," had been her reply. "Mr. Frank will end up wanting to buy me something nice." He had been a widower for many years. His wife, Jeannette, had seemingly lost the will to live shortly after giving birth to Gilla and had journeyed to the far shore. "Then there will be trouble between you two, and I will have to fine you heavily. Besides, the police cruiser doesn't have whitewalls." Wendell had to concede the validity of these points. As it turned out, he did not lose his job over arresting Mr. Frank, but he had made a nasty adversary, an enemy with a long memory and deep pockets who still held the grudge when the big town-line vote came up a couple of years later, and who had the capacity for holding that same resentment until the Second Coming. In Mr. Frank's world, the worm always eventually turned.

"We've got to think big!" Gilla reminded the group, waxing enthusiastic on the subject of Sand Valley, the new megalopolis of rural Alabama. "Think of the tax base!" he continued. He had Wendell on that one. Wendell hadn't been considering the tax base at all. He rubbed the bridge of his nose while wishing that Gilla had not taken that correspondence course in real estate development. The juggernaut rolled on, and the final vote was four to one in favor of annexing what seemed like half of the county. The opposing vote just shook his head and wondered how he was going to police all of that area. Poorly, he supposed.

"How did the meeting go?" Reva asked when Wendell arrived

home. It had been conducted downstairs at the rock castle, and home was upstairs at the same address, so it had been a short trip.

"You can go anywhere you want to in north Alabama and not leave town," he replied.

"Well, I guess that could be handy," she said dubiously.

"If they decide to move New York City down here, we'll have room for it," he said. "But they are going to give me a deputy. That's something, I guess." Wendell had managed to win this sole concession from his fellow council members by reminding them of the need for deliberation on the grand scale. Wendell hired his only applicant, T.F. Morgan, to help him watch the sprawl that Sand Valley had become. T.F. was a profane but friendly man who weighed in at about three-twenty in his boxer shorts. He had always wanted to be a police officer, and he offered to supply his own car if Wendell would take care of tires, gas, and the installation of a blue light up on top. His mama had named him Clarence, but everyone else called him T.F. This was short for tractor fuck, an expression he had once employed when referring to a situation grown unwieldy.

He had coined the phrase late one summer evening in the dim and unforgiving past. He and several other then-teenaged boys were drinking beer in downtown Sand Valley while taking turns using a homemade slingshot to shoot M-80 firecrackers at the abandoned railroad depot. The building was decrepit and contained only some rusted farm implements, two old tractors, and several bales of hay. It was a dry summer that year. That fact plus the presence of the hay should have been a clue that the depot might be combustible. But the boys' thinking was muddy that night, a phenomenon often associated with collective mentalities when the group's average age is seventeen and its average Schlitz Tall Boy consumption is three, and they were actually somewhat surprised when the train station whooshed itself into the middle stages of nonexistence. The amateur arsonists beat a hasty retreat as the flames reached out and fondled the summer sky.

"This," Clarence observed as he roared out of town with the other perpetrators, "is a real tractor fuck." The depot was history within the hour, but the phrase stuck to the young vandal like pine resin to an axe head. More importantly, T.F. had discovered his talent for incongruous adjectives, and from that point on, his descriptive parlance approached art. The old standards such as jug fuck and cluster fuck simply would no longer do. A football game gone awry in the rain became a mud fuck; a traffic accident blocking both lanes of the thoroughfare evolved into a fender fuck. A busted royal flush was a club fuck, and a fish that slipped the hook was a trout fuck. T.F. even referred to his ex-wife as the shrew fuck, although he was under court injunction to no longer do so in public.

So T.F. became Wendell's deputy, the city limit signs were moved way on down the highways, the tax base was enhanced, and everyone took a deep breath and hunkered down to await the frenzied influx of industry and commerce. Ten years later, the big time had yet to arrive.

After he left Deadhand's trailer, Wendell settled in for the long drive back to town. Deadhand lived at the end of Shake Rag Road, which marked the western border of Wendell's territory. It was nine miles to civilization along a narrow strip of blacktop not suited to either industry or commerce. At the approximate midpoint of his journey, he made a left turn on impulse and headed up a dirt road toward a mountain that formed the horizon. He hadn't seen his mother in three days, which was a long time for him to go without a visit, and he decided to take the opportunity while he was in the area. Two miles up the dirt road, he came to a clearing containing the small farmhouse that had been his boyhood home.

The house was laid out in the shotgun style, with the front porch facing west to avoid the early morning sun and to catch the prevailing breezes in the valley. The house had no hallways, and each room led into the next through a series of in-line doors. The shotgun style of home had reputedly acquired its unusual name because it was said that a person could stand on the front porch, shoot a shotgun straight through the house, and kill a chicken standing on the back stoop. They were cheap, easy to build, and had no wasted floor space. At Wendell's family home, the front porch opened into the living room, which in turn led into two back-to-back bedrooms. The back bedroom accessed the kitchen, and the kitchen was the portal to the back porch. When Wendell was a boy, the front bedroom was occupied by Happy, Eunice, and one or two of the youngest children. Everyone else slept in the second bedroom. There was no bathroom until 1963, when Wendell installed one in the second bedroom. The house was shingled top and sides with asphalt shingles and was resting on piers made of mountain rock. There was no underpinning. It didn't look like much and never had, but it was Eunice's home, and it was where she intended to live until she was summoned across the river.

Wendell rolled to a stop under the massive oak that stood at the far end of the dooryard. He killed the motor, exited his vehicle, and leaned against the trunk of the tree. Closing his eyes, he listened. At first he heard only silence, but as his ears adjusted themselves to another time and place, he began to pick out the quiet sounds of the country life of his youth. It was no longer odd to Wendell that he almost never recalled the bad memories of his childhood. Certainly there was an almost inexhaustible supply of these, but he chose rather to concentrate on the small handful of fine moments that had managed to squeeze themselves in around life with Happy.

He remembered a hot summer evening when he and three of his sisters caught fireflies in the dooryard, while Eunice rocked two additional sisters on the porch. The sky had been so clear and the constellations so bright that it had been difficult for his young eyes to tell the flash of the fireflies from the twinkle of the stars. He recalled his mother's delight at her children's laughter, and he could still hear the tree frogs and the crickets as they serenaded the moment. In his mind's eye he could see the barefoot, ragged children as they danced with the moon and the constellations.

He recalled another memory, a winter scene this time, when he and seven sisters sat with his mother at the kitchen table and sang along in the lamplight with the battery-powered radio. It was bitter cold that Saturday night, but the fire in the stove was stoked high, and the family, minus Happy, listened to The Grand Ole Opry broadcast as it sailed in over the airwaves from WSM in Nashville, Tennessee. Wendell believed that it must have been in 1939, because that was the year that Happy had worked at the foundry in Chattanooga and only came home once per month. He could still hear Bill Monroe and the Bluegrass Boys, and Roy Acuff as he sang "Wabash Cannonball." He remembered Eunice handing the baby to Louella before jumping up to dance a jig as DeFord Bailey played his harmonica hundreds of miles away. She had seemed like a young girl to him at that moment, carefree and alive. And he could still make out the finger-picking banjo of Uncle Dave Macon as he played *Hold That Woodpile Down*. Eunice had made sweet biscuits for her children, a rare treat, and coffee loaded with cream and sugar. It had been a fine night.

Wendell's reminiscences flicked on like lightbulbs in a cavern, burning dimly at first, then brightening as the details of each moment etched themselves into full remembrance. Above him, the slightest of breezes rustled the leaves of the leviathan oak, producing what sounded to Wendell like a sigh of relief. He heard the creak and slam of the screen door, the tone and decibel matching exactly the pattern of *scree, bam* that he had heard so many times. An unknown dog barked as he chased a rabbit across the back twenty. From the far side of the valley drifted *whip-poor-Will, whip-poor-Will,* as if poor Will had fallen afoul of his own version of Happy Blackmon and was reaping his just reward. Barely audible at this distance was the sound of a diesel truck straining up the mountainside behind the farm. The audible sequence of *roar, silence, roar, silence* as the driver searched for the gears was so familiar that it seemed as if that same truck had been climbing that pass for all the days of Wendell's life.

The smells, too, drifted slowly into his consciousness. From the direction of the barn wafted the slight odor of manure and hay. The fragrance was strangely sweet, and Wendell was almost convinced that a single "Yip-ha" would bring his old mule, Jerry—dead forty years now—trotting up for a piece of turnip or a sugar cube. Wendell detected the unmistakable aroma of biscuits browning in the oven in the kitchen, a complex mixture of flour, grease, and buttermilk that never varied from the first time he remembered smelling it, one hot Saturday morning somewhere down the long corridor of his personal time. He smelled his mother's flowers, and in his mind he could see her on endless summer mornings, wearing her gardening bonnet as she quietly snipped one here, one there, before placing the flowers into her basket with a care that bordered on reverence.

Wendell's eyes opened, and he was back in the present. The poignancy of the moment robbed his breath. It was always this way. His boyhood recollections were beautiful to him in a way he could not voice. Perhaps his memories of the good times from the past were so precious because of their rarity, like gems without flaws. They were threads in the tapestry that was Wendell Blackmon, good husband and father, passing fair policeman, and failed modern man.

Wendell walked to the back door, climbed the stoop, and entered the kitchen. His mother sat quietly at the table, cutting up the okra she had harvested that morning from her garden. Her back was to him, so he walked around the table into her line of sight and pulled up a chair. She had become hard of hearing with the passage of the years, and he did not want to startle her. She looked up from her work, saw her son, and smiled.

"Wendell!" she said. "I'm glad you stopped by. I was just thinking about you."

"Hey, Mama," he said. He reached and took both of her hands in his. They trembled with a quiet insistence. "You're going to cut off your fingers messing with that okra." Her Parkinson's was getting worse. Doctor Mize said that the condition would eventually debilitate her completely. In layman's terms, Eunice was shaking herself to death. Wendell put the unpleasant thought from him. It was a talent of his. There was no use dwelling on what he could not change. It was an exercise in futility, like trying to walk on air. He took her knife and began to cut the okra. He noted that each pod was about as long as his index finger. His mama did not let her okra grow too big, lest it become tough and stringy.

"I can't cook like I could when I was a girl," Eunice admitted. "But Jacob likes his okra. I thought I'd fry some for his dinner. Maybe I'll make him some steak and gravy. The bread is already in the oven. I wanted to get it brown before the heat of the day." She took the cotton dishcloth from her apron pocket and dabbed at the moisture on her forehead and cheeks. The oven was making the kitchen unbearably hot. The lone window fan whirred away as it pumped still more stifling air into the room.

"Too late," Wendell observed, sweat trickling down the small of his back. He didn't even mention the window air conditioner propped, forlorn and forgotten, in the window over the sink. He had bought it for Eunice and Jacob a few years back, and to his knowledge, it had never been turned on. Wendell's mother and her second husband, Jacob Gribble, were card-carrying members of a generation that did not hold with comfort. If the good Lord had wanted them to be cool, He wouldn't have put them in Alabama.

Wendell had acquired his stepfather after the original article met a bad end at the bottom of a deep hole. The well that Wendell had begun never did produce water, but Happy was unwilling to forego value for his dollar, and since Dock Farris had a no-refund policy, Happy built a makeshift bench over the hole and a ramshackle shed over that, and turned it into the deepest outhouse east of the mountains and north of the sea. One day early in 1952, after a full morning of harassing his family, he stepped into the outhouse to make water. As he stood there, ironically in the identical stance taken by his son ten years previously, he suffered a heart attack and collapsed onto the bench, which then splintered, sending him down into the hole. Eunice was outside the outhouse and heard the noise and the splash. She stepped in and looked down. She could hear Happy floundering, so the heart attack had not been fatal.

"Help me, damn it," he croaked as he tried to remain afloat. Eunice considered her options. She could attempt to rescue her husband and condemn herself to more long years of cruel abuse, or she could go work in her garden for a while. She had always believed that the good Lord helped those who helped themselves, and it was that certainty, along with her firm faith in divine providence, that guided her to her decision of how best to proceed. She hiked up her skirt, propped her left leg up on the back wall of the shed, and made a little water of her own. When she finished, she stood a moment and looked down the dark hole. She could not see the bottom.

"Piss on you, Happy," she said. Then she stepped out of the door. It slammed behind her with a resounding bang. She had lived in fear for her children's lives, and to a lesser extent her own, for many years, but it was time to break a bad habit. She had wished her husband dead many times, although not necessarily from drowning in a dry well halfway full of excrement. But if this was not a sign from above, then her name was not Widow Blackmon. So she made the children all use the barn for their evening business, and next morning, *late* in the morning just to be on the safe side, she called for the sheriff and had Happy hauled out. It was a rather lengthy process, because the grappling hook kept pulling free, but they finally got him up, a little worse for wear, on the third attempt. The coroner concluded that no autopsy would be necessary, and had, in fact, pronounced the cause of death from the cab of his truck.

"Looks like a heart attack to me!" he yelled from about thirty yards away. Eunice felt that for the sake of decorum, he should have at least turned off the motor.

"My condolences, Miz Blackmon," the sheriff said, hat in hand. They dragged Happy straight across the near field and right into his hastily dug grave.

"Life must go on," Eunice replied. She was glad that Happy had moved on down the line. She was not a mean-spirited woman, although she had a right to be after close to three decades with Happy, and it would have suited her just as well if he had simply died in his sleep or wandered in front of a speeding automobile. It was just like him to make a big production out of his demise, but she was not one to look a gift horse in the mouth, so she dwelled on it no longer.

Wendell was stationed on a destroyer off the coast of Korea when he received the news that his father had met his maker. The telegram from Eunice was short and to the point. *Happy dead. Stop. Mama.* Wendell's response was equally efficient. *Happy Happy dead. Stop. Wendell.* As the fifties passed, more and more of Wendell's siblings moved as far away from Sand Valley as they could manage before their money ran out, so that by early in the new decade of the sixties, Eunice found herself in failing health and the sole occupant of the Blackmon family farm. As a matter of fact, she had received a diagnosis of terminal cirrhosis of the liver, even though not a single drop of alcohol had ever passed her lips. Wendell and Reva lived in Bremerton, Washington, a town near Seattle, and they tried without success to convince Eunice to sell out and move in with them. But she wouldn't do it. Her roots were too deep, and she wanted to die where she had lived. So, even though they and their children were happy by the Puget Sound, Reva and Wendell moved back to Sand Valley, so that someone would be there for Eunice.

Eunice met her second husband, Jacob Gribble, at the cattle barn in Ft. Payne about a month after Happy went on to his reward in the outhouse. It turned out that Happy had left a $250.00 life insurance policy, and Eunice decided that the best course of action for her was to spend it on some cattle and become a cattle farmer. She and Jacob hit it right off, and after a decent and proper engagement period of around fifteen years—she was taking no chances this time—Jacob Gribble and Eunice Blackmon were married late in the autumn of 1967. By that time, it had become fairly apparent that Eunice knew something the medical community did not and that if she were at death's door, then the porch was awfully large. Her continued survival was hailed as a miracle by the residents of Sand Valley, but Wendell had a different theory.

"God figured He owed her one, after Happy," had been his explanation for his mother's recovery.

"This heat reminds me of the summer your sister Louella was born," Eunice said, back in the kitchen with her son. Wendell knew the signs. His mother was about to reminisce. She loved the art of discourse and could talk for hours at a stretch. All she needed was an audience. Her running commentary on the defining events of mankind's excursion on the planet would soon be entering its eighth decade. Facts were not an issue for her. If she had them, she would use them, provided she liked the way they fit into the story. And if she was short on details, she just made some up. She told life from the omniscient viewpoint, and Wendell had heard many a tale concerning total strangers that included how they felt, what they said behind closed doors, and what their most secret thoughts were. One of Wendell's earliest memories was of an excerpt of a conversation, as told by Eunice, between the biblical Noah and his son Shem.

Shem: Daddy, one of the camels is looking bad.

Noah: He's probably just seasick. Give him some water, and pat his head. Don't you get behind him, though, or he'll kick.

Shem: Yes, sir.

Noah: And go ask your mama what's for supper.

Biblically speaking, the little slice of life on the ark could be neither proven nor disproven, but Wendell always liked to think that his mama was privy to some inside information.

"Where was I?" Eunice asked, back in the hot kitchen.

"You were talking about how hot it was when Louella was born," Wendell replied as he mixed cornmeal, flour, salt, and pepper in a bowl. It was time to dredge the okra. A thought occurred to him. "Where's Jacob?" he asked.

"He went out a while ago with his tool box," Eunice replied. "He said he needed to fix the roof on the outhouse." Wendell met his mother's eye but offered no comment. The outhouse had been burned, and the well beneath it had been covered with great ceremony, some two decades ago, right after indoor plumbing had been installed in the house. The privy had been packed with old cardboard and hay before being put to the torch, so that it would burn hot and bright. Wendell remembered it well because he had been given the honor of lighting it up.

"I hope he didn't take the ladder," Wendell said. That could be a problem.

"No, the ladder is put up," she said. "He's been hammering on something out there, but at least he's on the ground." Jacob was suffering from Alzheimer's disease, the old timer's disease, as Eunice called it, and slowly but steadily, fragments of his memory were flaking off and drifting away with the breeze. He was fading into oblivion one recollection at a time, losing the good along with the indifferent and the bad. It was a sluggish, merciless way to go, as bad as Eunice's Parkinson's in its own way, and no less final. Eventually he would forget how to eat, how to breathe, and how to live.

Jacob had never been much of a talker, even before the old timer's disease had sunk its talons into him, and his commentary on life in general was short and to the point. He had spent thirty years in the military before retiring, and as an example of his brevity, his description of World War Two took thirty-one syllables. "A lot of them boys tried to kill me, but I reckon I was luckier than they were, and I killed them first. Anyway, we won." Eunice had married a talker the first time around, actually a shouter and a hitter, but on her second outing, she cleaved to a man who could present the résumé of the greatest conflagration in the history of the world in two sentences while keeping his hands in his pockets. Jacob was not a man to fritter money, daylight, or words.

"It was hot the day that Louella was born," said Eunice Gribble, off of the side track and once again chugging down the main line, "and I was having back labor something fierce." Wendell put the big iron skillet on the stove and began to heat the grease for the okra. Eunice proceeded. "It was hot, and there was hammering going on in the yard, just like you hear now." Her voice took on a cadence, as if she presented a recitation. She and the material were old friends, and her rendition was flawless. "It was your Uncle John making all that noise. He was a cantankerous old so-and-so, as I've said on more than one occasion, and when he took it in his head to do something, then that's what he did. I don't know why he decided to fix the barn on the hottest day of the year, with me in labor in the front bedroom, particularly since that old roof had been leaking for longer than I could remember anyway, and the cows didn't seem to mind, and John wasn't much of a carpenter. But that was your Uncle John. Sometimes he could be as mean as two striped snakes, and he was always as stubborn as a blind and deaf mule." Uncle John was Happy's mother's brother, and he had come to live with the Blackmons after the black-hearted scoundrels at the bank took his farm.

Wendell occupied himself with the preparation of the okra while his mama's voice droned in the background. He dropped a pinch of flour in the grease to see if it would sizzle. It did, signifying that the pan was hot enough. He wasn't being rude to Eunice. It wasn't necessary for her audience to be responsive, just present. Indeed, an attentive listener sometimes gave Eunice pause. If a question was raised or a comment offered, she tended to lose the thread of the story line, which was often layered and complex, and the resulting impact on her rhythm was extreme. The occasional nod or "uh huh" was all the feedback she needed or wanted, and she could get by without even that. Wendell was reminded of his Aunt Muriel, who had spent her final twenty-four hours in a coma. Eunice had not left her bedside, and to Wendell's knowledge, she never once lapsed into silence as she strove to make her sister's last day pass a little easier. He dropped a handful of okra into the hot grease as his mama's anecdote unfolded. He knew it by heart anyway. He knew about the hard birth of his sister, Louella, in the front bedroom, attended by Merle Evans, the black midwife, who said afterward that she never saw so much blood in all her born days. He knew about the untimely death of his Uncle John when two opposing forces of nature—gravity and Uncle John's bullheadedness about climbing up on the barn roof—collided, and gravity won hands down. He knew about Happy coming in off of the county road crew that Saturday to a dead uncle, a half-dead wife, two squalling children, and poor Merle Evans, who had not signed on as nurse and undertaker in addition to midwife, but who was decent enough to stay until Happy rolled home for the weekend. Wendell knew the saga so well he could have told it himself, as was the case with most of her renderings.

"The fall came," Eunice continued with her eyes closed, as if she were reciting her lessons, "and then the winter. It was cold that year. Happy's mama, Rhoda, came to live with us and help out, and she brought her second husband, Edgar Brown, a bald-headed man with cross eyes. Everyone around here just called him Fish. Anyway, Rhoda took a choking fit one night on account of a chicken bone, and died right here in this kitchen. Your daddy was off working on the road crew again and wouldn't be back for a week. I swear I don't know what it was about his folks that made them want to pass on while he was gone, but it seemed to be a bad habit that a lot of them had."

"They probably all just died so they wouldn't have to see him again," Wendell noted. Due to being nearly as deaf as a post, Eunice did not exactly understand what her son had said, but she smiled and nodded politely anyway.

"The dirt was too frozen to dig," she continued, "so me and Fish toted her to the barn and dragged her up in the loft, and even though she was as limber as a wet dishrag, we only dropped her twice trying to get her up the ladder. We wrapped her in a sheet with the intentions of putting her in the ground come the spring, or at least after Happy got home on Saturday. I know this sounds curious, but in those days that was how it was done, and during a hard winter the departed would stack up like cordwood, and come warmer weather, the gravestones would spring up like daisies. So my mother-in-law went on to her reward and left me and you and your sister alone with Fish Brown."

"Even though I was a wife with two children to show for my trouble, I was still just a young girl, not worldly at all and too trustful to boot. So I was not on my guard two nights later when I was approached by Fish, who happened to be naked as a jaybird and drunker than a boiled owl at the time. I was in my room reading by the light of the lamp with you and Louella asleep beside me on pallets, when I looked up and there stood Fish Brown."

"That old man was on me before I knew it, pawing at my gown

and trying to put his hands where they ought not be, and he was a large man and I was no bigger than a gnat's ear. I have always had high, firm bosoms, and when I was nursing the first few of you they were sure enough ample, and I believe that this was the cause of the problem with Mr. Brown, or at least a part of it. I have lived a long time, and if I know anything at all, then I know that men are fools when it comes to a woman's bosoms and that liquor is the devil's tool." Every time he heard the story, Wendell wondered if all the other men got the chance to talk with their mamas about high, firm bosoms. He stirred the okra.

"Don't get me wrong," Eunice plowed on. "I have always believed in taking care of the men folk, because most of them I've known couldn't take care of themselves and would have starved to death as children if some woman wasn't putting food in their mouths, and I had already determined to take over Rhoda's duties after she went to the loft, and I had already told Fish that I would do this. But what I had in mind was the cooking and the cleaning, although he seemed to have other ideas on that subject. So there I was, struggling mightily to protect my virtue with my step-father-in-law all over me like a chicken on a June bug, and I would have been shamed for sure, but the good Lord sent me a sign in the form of a hot brick."

"It was as cold as a well digger's toes, and the only heat in this old house at that time was from the stove in the kitchen, so I had the habit of tucking a heated brick in beside you children to keep you warm. It was laying on the floor cooling off some because I had let it get too hot, when Fish came to my room and made his desires known to me. During the struggle, my hand struck the brick, and without thinking, I picked it up and whacked him a good one right on top of the head. This seemed to douse his flame, so I smacked him once more to be sure. He quit cutting up and dropped like a stone. It took me a while to get out from under him, because he was heavy as a sack of wet lead and not moving at all, but finally I managed. Louella had commenced to cry during the ordeal, and I calmed her by giving her the breast, which *she* was welcome to, while I looked at Fish and hoped that he wasn't dead. I was in a fix, and that is a fact, and I sat through the long, cold night and considered on what I was to do. Finally, the sun rose. I was sitting in here rocking you and your sister when I looked over at the doorway, and there he stood again. He still didn't have any britches on, and there was blood running down the side of his head from where I had whacked him, and I figured I was in for another round right then, and the brick was back in the bedroom."

Wendell spooned the okra from the skillet onto a doubled paper towel to drain. He turned off the gas ring and placed the pan to the side to cool. Then he looked at his mother and smiled. He had sailed around the world and had talked to people from twenty-six countries, and his was still the strangest family he had ever heard of.

"Then Fish Brown asked me where he was, and who he was, and who I was. I had knocked him silly with that brick, and he no longer had his memory. Or his desires, thank the good Lord. I got him dressed and fed him, and cleaned up his head, and you won't believe it, but from that day until he passed along two years later, he was the nicest man you could ever want to meet. It was like I had knocked the meanness right out of him, and if I had been sure it would have worked twice in the same household, your daddy would've been next. As for Happy, he had never took much to Fish anyway, and I don't reckon he had ever said a single word to him, so he never seemed to notice that Fish was a changed man. But I knew, and believe me when I say that it was a change for the better."

Had it not been for the sheer genius of Alexander Graham Bell, Wendell might have been in for a long afternoon of storytelling. But the telephone rang. He gestured to Eunice that he would get it. Then he wiped his hands on the dishcloth and answered.

"Hello," he said to the receiver.

"I thought you might be there," came Reva's voice all the way from the rock castle. "Is the story any good today?"

"She's got me on the edge of my seat," Wendell said. His mama made her slow, shaky way to the oven to check on the biscuits. He knew she couldn't hear him across the room.

"What is today's topic?" Reva had a fascination with Eunice's allegories and was attempting to commit many of her favorites to paper. She thought they would make a fine novel someday. Wendell agreed, although he needed to check on the statutes of limitations for the worst of them.

"Fish Brown just got whomped twice in the head with a hot brick."

"Fish Brown needed to be whomped with a hot brick. Did your sister have to be comforted with a high, firm bosom?"

"An *ample* high, firm bosom," he replied. He could hear his wife's chuckle.

"Anyway," she said, "the reason I called is T.F. He radioed in just now from out at Sorrow Wood. He said to tell you that he had a real sorrow fuck on his hands."

"He didn't say what the trouble was?" It was a long drive down a rough road to Sorrow Wood.

"He just said to tell you to get out there."

"Well," said Wendell, "I guess I better drive out and see what he wants. Probably a dead dog in the road. That reminds me. Deadhand and Otter will be coming in to see you. I told them that you were fining them one hundred dollars apiece for dog fighting."

"Those two are on my last nerve." She had warned them both the last time they'd seen her professionally that a long absence on their part would make her heart grow fonder.

"A couple of fine boys like Otter and Deadhand? They make their mothers proud."

"I'll go along with your fine this time. But there had better not be a next time." Her voice was ominous. Wendell was glad he wasn't Deadhand or Otter right then. Come to think of it, he was always glad he wasn't Deadhand or Otter. "Put your mama on the phone, and I'll listen to her for a while. Turn your radio on, in case T.F. needs to call you." They said their goodbyes. Then Wendell waved Eunice over.

"It's for you," he said as he kissed her cheek. "I've got to go." He handed her the phone before walking out the door. He had a sorrow fuck to investigate.

The storm had raged with fury for three days. None of the sailors aboard the Maria had ever seen the like, and most of them had been seafaring men their entire lives. All of the sails but one had been trimmed, and still they ran before a southeast wind like they were running from the demons of hell. The crew was white with fear, and many of them were praying openly on the decks and below, praying for a break in the weather, or for salvation, or for a quick and painless death when the ship foundered at last. Three seamen had already been taken over the bow, taken as if the very hand of the sea had snatched them one after another to their dooms in the frigid depths. The schooner had been two days out of Norfolk with a cargo of indigo and cotton when the storm attacked. But Captain Ramey

had not been able to take a sighting in three days or nights, and he had no idea where they were now. If the storm did not break soon, he feared the ship might be forfeit.

In the captain's cabin, his wife had tied herself to a chair and was attempting to read. Her name was Maria Ramey, and her husband had named his small merchant ship after her. The rolling of the ship combined with the swaying of the lantern was making her a bit seasick. She smiled grimly at that. She had been going to sea with her husband for twenty years and was hardier than many an old tar, but here she was with a touch of queasiness because of a few waves. It would not do for the men to get wind of that. Some of the older hands did not hold with women aboard ship. They thought it was bad luck to sail with a female. As she turned her attention back to her book, there was a knock at the cabin door. The first mate entered and doffed his hat.

"M'am, the captain wishes me to report that we have sighted a light off the starboard bow. He thinks it may be Cape Henry. He says to tell you that he'll steer north of it and we'll be in the Chesapeake soon."

It was a good plan, and if it had been the watch fire at Cape Henry they had spied, they would have made safe harbor. But the ship was over one hundred miles south of Cape Henry, and the fire spotted by the lookouts was at Bodie Island, on the North Carolina coast. Sailing north of it put the Maria onto the rocks in rough, cold seas. She broke up five hundred yards from the beach. As the ship foundered and began to come apart, Maria made her way to the deck. She was enough of a seafarer to realize that the situation was hopeless, but her one thought was to locate her husband, William. As another wave crashed over the bow, she saw him sitting beside the ship's wheel. There was a gash on his head, and his leg was at an impossible angle. She grabbed the lifeline and made her slow way.

"I'm here, my love," she said as she settled in beside him. There was a crash as the mainmast split and fell into the sea.

"We must get the men to the boats!" William said.

"We'll go in just a bit," she said quietly. "We'll go in just a bit."

Chapter Five: 1943-1944

R eva Anne Martin Nichols was a young woman who had seen more than her share of challenges during nineteen years of existence, and it appeared that the trend was going to continue into her twenties. After her husband met his early demise under the tracks of a wayward German tank, she discovered that she was entitled to a death benefit as a result of his ultimate sacrifice, but that this amount would be paid out monthly over twenty years rather than in one lump sum. These incremental payments didn't seem quite fair to Reva since Ted had died all at once and not over a period of twenty years to qualify for the stipend, but the ways of the government are complex and strange and not be understood by mere mortals.

The problem with this deferred settlement was that the resulting monthly allotment was not enough to allow Reva to continue to live in the house that she had occupied since coming to Timberline. At least, she could not maintain her residency if she wanted to feed and clothe her child while she stayed there, and God forbid that she or the baby got sick, because a trip to the doctor or the drug store would definitely be out of the question. Her only alternative was to obtain employment. She looked diligently around Timberline for a job, but there were simply none to be had. The only solution she could formulate was to move to the city, to Portland or maybe Seattle, where the job market would be more robust.

"Why don't you and the baby just move in with me and Luke?" asked her neighbor and friend, Flora Hutton. "We have plenty of room since the children grew up and moved on. Luke won't care. He's never there much anyhow. And I will surely miss you and little Charlie if you move to the city." This was a tempting offer, and Reva almost took her up on it. But she hadn't reached the ripe old age of just-shy-of-twenty short only one leg, two parents, a husband, and the family farm, by not listening to that little voice inside. And that voice told her that Luke was guaranteed to become a problem. It was as inevitable as the path of a dropped stone. He had the habit of coming home drunk, and when Reva was visiting, he would stare hungrily at her, like a starving man viewing a pork chop. Luckily, Flora had apparently never noticed this, but Reva had, so she thanked her friend and declined. She loved Flora like a sister, but Luke was not her problem, and she wanted to keep it that way. She began to make plans to move. Flora was disappointed that Reva was going to leave, but she agreed to help with the relocation.

Reva's plan was a simple one, and once she had sketched out the larger parameters, she consciously did not dwell on the smaller details, lest she should despair from the sheer audacity of it. Specifically, she decided that she would go to Seattle and become a welder in the Puget Sound Naval Shipyard, which in those days was called Navy Yard Puget Sound. This facility was quickly becoming the major repair facility for damaged ships in the Pacific theater of war. Reva had heard down at the diner that the shipyard was hiring anyone who could weld. She did not let the facts that she had no transportation to Seattle, no welding skill, no penis, and no leg distract her from her plan. She figured that she could resolve the first two of these issues, and that if she kept her pants on and her leg strapped tight, no one need ever know about the fourth. The third issue could admittedly be a tough one to resolve, although as the available supply of men continued marching off to war and not marching back, more and more women were finding employment in the industrial setting.

She set about the task of learning to weld with the help of Flora Hutton's brother, Peacock Calhoun. Peacock was an exceptional welder when he was sober, but he was not in that condition much of the time, and this handicap kept him from steady work in the field. Still, he was a better welder while inebriated than most other journeymen were in any shape, and he was a willing teacher, so welding school was conducted daily in the little shop behind his house. Classes commenced after breakfast, around nine o'clock, and continued until Peacock passed out, usually around two or three o'clock in the afternoon. Flora kept the baby during these hours, so that Reva would not be distracted from her studies. Peacock was a good teacher in his rough-hewn way.

"Damn it, Reva. That weld looks like a chicken took a shit on a piece of steel. Turn the welder up and slow down. *Push* your bead. You weld up a ship like that, and you're going to drown some sailors." Then he would take a nip and light a smoke, while Reva adjusted her welder and tried again. She had a steady hand and a good eye, and gradually she improved her skills, until finally the day arrived when Peacock pronounced her to be competent.

"I've seen plenty worse," he said with approval as he inspected her work. He took a grinder and cut into a weld to check her penetration. He nodded and mumbled to himself. Then he reached into his coverall pocket for a crumpled envelope, which he handed to Reva like a diploma. "When you get up to the shipyard, find a man named Mickey Porch and give him this. He was a foreman on Dry Dock 4 when I worked there. Tell him that Peacock sent you." He took a long pull from the ubiquitous bottle, sucked the air in through his teeth, and then belched. Reva ignored the breach of etiquette. She believed that every person had strengths and weaknesses, and she supposed that Emily Post probably could not put down a weld that would hold.

"I don't know how to thank you," Reva said. She gave Peacock a hug. She had grown attached to him over the course of her instruction and would miss him. The baby would miss him, too, but it would be difficult to say if that was due to Peacock's fatherly demeanor or his habit of slipping Charlie a sugar cube every time he saw him.

"Tell Mickey he's a sorry bastard, and see to it that your welds don't break or leak, and that will be thanks enough," Peacock said. He wasn't much on the small talk, and her gratitude embarrassed him. "Take care of that boy, and stay away from sailors." This last bit of advice was the extent of the goodbye that Reva could expect from Peacock, so she headed out into the great, wide world, and he turned and went back into his own small, safe portion of it.

Now that she had some welding skill to market and what she hoped was a letter of introduction, Reva needed a ride to Seattle. Luckily, Flora had both a pickup truck and an inclination to drive it. A window of opportunity was fast approaching in the form of Flora's husband's annual fishing trip with the boys. During that yearly outing, Luke and several of his logging buddies would head up the Columbia River as far as Bonneville Dam, where they would put their rowboats in and float fish for salmon all the way back down to Portland. Flora dreaded the annual fishing trip, not because she disliked salmon or because she was terribly lonesome without Luke, but because she objected to the method of fishing that the men chose. Rather than seining or spearing, which had been the preferred methods of harvesting salmon in the Columbia since the first Native Americans walked down from Siberia and decided that some fish would be nice for lunch, Flora's husband and his cronies chose instead the little known and much maligned art of dynamite fishing. As the name suggested, the methodology employed was to light up a stick of dynamite, pitch it far ahead of the boat, duck, and then float by and pick up the larger pieces of salmon. It was illegal and dangerous, but neither of these drawbacks gave much pause to the several rowboats full of rowdy, drunken timbermen, whose main occupation was to hike into primordial forests with sharp axes and wicked saws and fell huge trees without having them land on anyone they knew. Flora and Reva decided that the perfect time to make the trip to Seattle would be during the fishing trip. That way, Flora would not have to explain her absence, and having something new and different to do would keep her mind off of the possibility of sudden widowhood due to Luke drowning, exploding, or being shot by a game warden.

The women left early one morning at about the same time that Luke and his fellow fishermen were blowing up their first boatload of fish, and they made the trip without incident, which was a minor miracle, considering the condition of Flora's truck. By nightfall, they were cruising the streets of Seattle, looking for somewhere clean to spend the evening. They took rooms for the night at the YWCA, and after a supper of hoop cheese, bologna, and crackers, they slept the dreamless sleep of the exhausted stranger in a strange land. The next morning, Flora made her goodbyes. She had to get back before Luke did, or he would get fussy.

"Don't forget you've got a home in Timberline anytime you need one," she told Reva. She hugged her and the baby before climbing into the truck. She felt just like she had when her own children had left to make their ways in the world. "And don't forget to write."

"I won't forget," Reva said. She was exquisitely sad. Charlie was crying, and she felt like joining him. It seemed at that moment as if she had spent her entire life saying goodbye to people that she loved, liked, or would otherwise miss. She blinked back the tears and waved as Flora motored out of sight and out of her life forever.

On the way back to Timberline, about twenty miles from the relative safety of home, Flora had the misfortune to meet a log truck with no brakes. The driver of the rig had lost his ability to stop at the top of the pass, and he had been praying for a miracle to help him lose speed. When he rounded the blind curve, he was in the wrong lane with more tires up in the air than down on the road, and he met his miracle head on. The truck slowed down abruptly upon impact, and the driver was able to regain enough control to allow him to lay his rig up against an embankment. He survived, so his prayers were answered.

But they were answered at the expense of Flora Hutton. Her light winked out, and she went to join the ranks of the departed, including Ted Nichols, Aunt Velma, Harry Lee and Avonnel Martin, and Smitty Smith and his slop bucket. She also rejoined her husband, Luke, who had ceased breathing about six hours ahead of his wife. He had been very drunk on the final day of fishing. So drunk, in fact, that he had made the serious error of throwing his cigar at the salmon while clamping the lit stick of dynamite back into his jaw. It could have happened to anyone, but the boatload of fishing buddies that Luke brought with him to the afterlife didn't see it that way. Luckily, they had an eternity in which to get over it, and plenty of fish to eat as well.

The next few weeks were bleak ones for Reva. She learned that Flora was dead when she received a letter from Peacock about a week after the tragedy occurred. The envelope contained seven one-dollar bills and some very bad news.

Dear Reva,

I hate to have to be the one to tell you this, but Flora got herself run over by a log truck on the way home from Seattle and now she is dead. She was a good woman, and I ain't just saying that because she was my baby sister. I will miss her. Luke is dead too, but that don't bother me much, and I expect you ain't too tore up over that news, either. I wish he hadn't blown up my boat though. It was a good boat. Anyway, I thought you needed to know. She loved you like you were one of hers. Give that boy a hug and a sugar cube for me. Keep your mind on your business out at the shipyard, or you will end up with Flora.

Pea

After she read that letter, she cried for three days. It seemed to her that every time her life began to gel into some semblance of normalcy, someone else close to her would die. Although she knew, objectively, that it had to be just a long series of bad coincidences, the fact remained that the list of people she had loved who were now dead was growing longer, and each new name on the list, except maybe Luke's, added to her ever-growing sense of sadness. Even though she did not know how she could have prevented a single death in her personal arena of sorrow, she nonetheless felt responsible for them all. But sad or not, responsible or not, she had a baby to raise, so she had to swallow her grief and get on with the business of trying to build a life in Seattle.

She found lodging for herself and Charlie at a combination group home and boarding house down near the mission district that catered mostly to working women whose husbands were off in the service. Technically speaking, Reva did not actually fit this profile, because her husband was no longer actively engaged in fighting the enemy, and she didn't have a job. But she was a war widow who had the first month's rent in advance, and she intended to secure employment if she was able, so as far as the landlady was concerned, her credentials were impeccable. Two of the other tenants also had children, so they and Reva worked out childcare arrangements that were sufficient to everyone's needs.

She had completed an application at the Navy Yard, which was across the harbor at Bremerton, but she had not heard back, and she was starting to believe that she was getting the runaround. She thought that she might make better progress if she could take Peacock's advice and talk directly to Mickey Porch, but with the war on, security was tight at the shipyard, and she could not gain access to him there. She was in a pickle, and her small reserve of money was growing smaller by the day.

"I don't know what I am going to do," Reva said to her new friend, Hallie Lou Albert. Hallie had a small daughter in her arms, and the remains of a husband on Guadalcanal, but she was not yet aware of the second of these two facts. She was a riveter on the B-17 line out at the Boeing plant. Like Reva, she had just turned twenty.

"Find out where he drinks, and ambush him there," Hallie proposed. It seemed to be an obvious solution to her, and Reva liked the idea as well. So, through the husband of a friend of a brother of an aunt, it was discovered that Mickey liked to enjoy a cold Olympia beer at an establishment named Roscoe's while he read his evening newspaper. He stopped at Roscoe's each day on the way home from the shipyard. It was a waterfront bar close to the docks where the Black Ball Line ferryboats came in from Bremerton, and it was a popular watering hole for many of the workers at the shipyard. It was, in fact, a ship fitter's bar, and very few practitioners of other occupations ever darkened the swinging door. The walls were filled with photos of ships built or repaired at the Navy Yard, as well as with a grainy photographic record of many of the ship fitters who had worked at the yards since the turn of the century.

The following evening, Reva was sitting at the bar nursing an Olympia beer when the ferry from Bremerton, the *Kalakala,* docked and discharged its passengers. She didn't really like beer, but she was trying her best to blend. By wearing dungarees and a flannel shirt, she hoped she cast the general impression of someone who could fix a ship. As the yard workers filed in, the bartender nudged Reva and pointed to a balding, sixty-ish man in blue coveralls. He had a slight limp as he walked to a table in the corner. He sat and pulled the folded paper from his back pocket. Then he reached into his shirt pocket for a pair of reading spectacles. He held up one finger, signaling his desire for a mug of something frothy.

"That's him," said the barkeep. He pocketed the dollar that Reva slid him and placed two full mugs on the bar. Reva picked them up and went to sit with the man that she hoped would soon be her boss. Mickey looked up from his paper at the attractive young woman across the table. Reva slid him a schooner of Olympia.

"You look thirsty," she noted. "Why don't you have a beer?" She had decided that boldness was her best avenue. She also pushed a bowl of pretzels his way. There were bowls of peanuts, pickled eggs, and pretzels staged at strategic locations throughout the establishment. Roscoe was a tavern owner who believed in the revenue-enhancing properties of salt.

"I'm married, and I'm tired," Mickey said, misinterpreting Reva's intent. But he was also thirsty, so he accepted the beer before turning back to the war news.

"According to Peacock Calhoun, you are also a sorry bastard," came her reply. He looked back up from his daily. That was not the answer he was expecting, and she now had his full attention. She took the crumpled envelope from her pocket and handed it to Mickey. "And he said to give you this." Reva knew that this was the big gamble, the roll of the dice. Her future was in the hands of a man she did not know, and although he looked decent enough, how great could he be if he owed Peacock Calhoun a favor? With huge lined and calloused hands, Mickey slowly opened the envelope, pulled out the sheet it contained, and unfolded it. He smoothed it on the table top. His lips moved slightly as he read the note from Peacock Calhoun.

> Mickey,
> The girl can weld and she needs a job. Her old man got his killing in North Africa and she has a kid to feed. I know you need welders because half the damn fleet is blown all to hell. I have never once said that you did, but you always said that you owed me. If you still believe that, hire her and we will be even. Thanks, you sorry bastard.
> Say hello to Shirl for me.
> Pea

Mickey looked over the top of his glasses at Reva. Then he spoke.

"Did Peacock teach you how to weld?"

"Yes, he did." Reva replied. Her heart was pounding, and she knew she was at a crossroads. If he hired her, she had a future. She could pay the bills and feed her baby. If he didn't, she really did not know what she would do. She had heard that a one-legged girl could command top dollar in a seaport, but she didn't really think she was cut out for that kind of work. She supposed she could go back to Timberline, but with Flora gone, there was really no reason, unless she wanted to lie up all day and drink bourbon with Peacock Calhoun. Which was a tempting idea, if she didn't get this job. Mickey held her in his gaze for a long time before speaking.

"Do you think you can pull a ten-hour shift with that leg?" he asked. This question caught Reva by surprise. She had not mentioned her handicap, and she had assumed that the pants she was wearing had kept her secret just that.

"How did you . . ." she began.

"I spotted it right off when you walked over here. Got one myself." He tapped his faux appendage with his empty mug for effect. It made a hollow thumping sound. "I got this on December 6, 1917. It was my birthday, believe it or not. I guess you could say this was my birthday present from the kaiser." He waved for another beer. Reva slid her untouched mug across the table to hold him in the meantime. "We were on picket duty ahead of a convoy on the destroyer *Jacob Jones*—the original one, not the one in the fleet now—about twenty miles off of the English coast, when a U-boat put two torpedoes into us. Ship broke right in half and went down in about thirty minutes. Most of the crew got killed, I lost my leg, and Peacock Calhoun kept me afloat and alive for three hours until an English fishing boat picked us up. We probably would have both died that night, but the commander who sunk us made a radio call to the British to tell them that there were survivors in the water. He wasn't a bad guy, for a Hun."

The replacement mug arrived, and Mickey took a long and appreciative dram. "So anyway, if Pea says you can weld, you can weld. Meet me at the ferry at five in the morning. We just got a cruiser in that's more sunk than not and a minesweeper that by rights ought to be on the bottom, so there's plenty to do." That had been the extent of the employment interview. When Reva attempted to express her thanks, Mickey just held up his hand and went back to his paper and his beer. As with Peacock, gratitude embarrassed him.

Mickey did not become any more talkative the following day, or in the days after that, although Reva met and began to make friends with several women on the ferry who were also welders at the yard, and by the end of her second week of employment, she had settled into a routine. She arose at four every morning to be at the ferry at five for the hour-long boat ride to Bremerton. Her shift began at seven and ended at five thirty. With good luck, no extra overtime, and not much fog or chop in the Puget Sound, she was usually back home at seven in the evening. Then she and the other women at the boarding house tended to the children and the chores until they fell into bed, exhausted, by nine thirty or ten. Her schedule made for a long day, but she was grateful to have the job and voiced no complaint.

Thus the remaining days of 1943 elapsed, and 1944 eased in like a crippled warship to dry dock. Reva continued to ply her trade on vessels both grand and humble. Famous ships such as the *Tennessee,* the *New Orleans,* and the *Saratoga,* as well as unsung workhorses such as the *Halford,* the *Leutze,* and the *Killen.* The slow and terrible march of the war in the Pacific assured Reva and her thirty thousand colleagues at the shipyard a seemingly unending supply of work. The Marines, the Army, and the Navy advanced westward from island to island, from Guadalcanal, to the Solomons, to the Gilberts, to the Carolines, and each victory came at a great cost in ships, planes, and men.

The war in the European theatre was also in full force, and the tide seemed to have turned in favor of the Allies. The D-Day invasion of Normandy exploded upon the occupied shores of France, signaling the beginning of the long, agonizing German retreat to Berlin. On the Eastern Front, the Soviet Army pushed the last remnants of the Nazis out of the Motherland and began to exact retributions for twenty million lost countrymen. In Italy, the Axis forces were driven from Rome. The endgame had begun, and even though the final outcome was inevitable, the deadly dance still continued. As was the case in the Pacific, the enemies of the Allies were determined to fight to the last man. They would give no quarter and expected none, as they staggered down the bloody road to defeat.

On the home front, little Charlie was growing like a victory garden and thriving under the attentions of a houseful of surrogate mothers. Poor Hallie Lou Albert had taken her daughter and gone home to Kansas upon learning of her husband's sacrifice, but there were plenty of other young wives and mothers at the boarding house to help with childcare. When she considered the overall picture, Reva felt that her situation could have been much worse. She had overcome a great deal of adversity and was living her life to the best of her ability. It was not the life that she had envisioned, and it was not the one she would have chosen had she been allowed to choose, but it was the existence she had drawn, and it was her intention to make the most of it. Consequently, she was living it to the fullest at the end of August 1944, when Wendell Blackmon wandered into it.

To be fair, Wendell was looking for a cold beer on dry land and not the company of a woman, or the exhilaration of a fight, when he sauntered into Roscoe's on that fateful Friday night. Even though she had not been into the bar since the day that Mickey had hired her, Reva had accepted an invitation from three of her girlfriends and had stopped at the watering hole after work. Later in her life, after time had begun to edit her memories into an acceptable order and meaning, Reva would say that it was fate that had brought her to Roscoe's. But at the time, the factors in play were simply that it had been a long week, she was thirsty, and she wanted to have a little fun before she went home to her normal Friday routine. She was sitting at a table, chatting pleasantly, when Birmah Mae Peppers elbowed her in the ribs and cocked her head at the door.

"Don't look now," Birmah Mae said, "but we are about to see a squid get his ass handed to him." Reva and the other two women looked toward the door in time to see a lone sailor walk in. It was Wendell Blackmon, fresh in from Guam aboard a crippled destroyer that was scheduled for repair at the Navy Yard. He sat at the end of the bar, close to the door, and motioned to the bartender. He was tall and slim, with broad shoulders. His short brown hair was sun-bleached almost white, and he wore his cap on top of his head, rather than cocked at one of the gravity-defying angles that some of his shipmates preferred. His dark tan spoke of a long tour in the Pacific. Somehow, he seemed familiar to Reva. It wasn't his appearance—she knew they had not met. But there was something about him that struck a chord in her. It was as if she were again seeing a character from a scene in a movie she had watched long ago. Traces of memories danced through her consciousness.

"Maybe we should warn him," Reva said. Some of the fitters and riggers at Roscoe's were not always appreciative of sailors, particularly while they were drinking after a long week of difficult, hot, and dangerous ship repair. It was not a rational dislike, since the sailors were not intentionally getting the ships blown up by purposely sailing them in front of torpedoes or under bombs, but the fitters seemed to take the whole business personally anyway, or at least some of the ones who drank at Roscoe's did. Probably the worst of the crowd, Bunk Grantley, was staring intently at Wendell from across the bar. Bunk hated sailors the way preachers hated other people's sins. His father had been a sailor, and his mother had once been a sailor's friend for a night, so Bunk had learned to despise seafarers at his mother's knee.

"He'll find out," Birmah Mae said. She was a massive, muscular woman, who had a large red scar on her forehead, courtesy of a slag drop off of the USS *Howarth*. She had a dog named Tojo that she liked to make roll over and play dead, and a husband named Henry who was touring Italy the hard way, and there weren't many things she liked more than watching a fight.

It had started to become quiet in Roscoe's. The bartender leaned over the bar and whispered excitedly in Wendell's ear while pointing in the general direction of the street. As Reva watched, she saw the sailor break a slight smile, a smile that conveyed rueful amusement. It had grown still enough in the bar for her to be able to hear him speak.

"I really would like that beer now," Wendell said. The bartender shrugged his shoulders. He had tried to warn the boy. He pulled the pump handle, drew a draft, and placed it on the bar. Bunk Grantley began to sidle across the room. Several of his coworkers watched in anticipation. Money changed hands at various tables and along the bar, as bets were made and funded. Bunk slid onto the empty stool next to Wendell just as Wendell tipped his mug. He had not had a cold beer in six months, and he was not one of those people who could fully appreciate a hot one in a pinch, even if the Navy meant well by the offer. He was going to enjoy his beer.

"Sailor boy," said Bunk, "this bar is for folks that fix ships." Not wishing to be rude, Wendell held up his finger and acknowledged Bunk's presence as he continued to drain his glass of beer. When he finished, he placed the empty mug in front of him and sighed with contentment. He smiled at the bartender and pushed the drained vessel his way. As the barkeep hustled him another draft, Wendell turned his attention to Bunk.

"Let me buy you a beer," he offered. "You'll be fixing my ship for several days. She's a mess. You may even have to cut her up for scrap." Wendell had sailed to Navy Yard Puget Sound aboard the USS *O'Bannion*, a Porter-class destroyer that a variety of Japanese boys had been trying to sink. In their defense, it wasn't for lack of effort on their part that she was still afloat. She had been strafed by thousands of rounds by a selection of Japanese fighter planes. Her superstructure had taken a blow from a Zero after the fatally wounded pilot had nosed his crippled plane due south. A six-inch shore battery had inflicted serious damage to several parts of the ship, including a devastating hit on the number one gun turret. She had been hit by a torpedo that hadn't exploded, although the dent it had left was impressive, and she had struck a mine that *had* exploded. The *O'Bannion* had nine battle stars. A third of her original 1942 crew were dead, wounded, or missing, including the original captain, the replacement executive officer, and everyone who had been in the number one gun turret, except Wendell, when the six-inch shells had hit. The general consensus among the crew was that the old girl was crippled beyond repair and that she had done exceedingly well just getting them home.

"I don't want a damn beer," Bunk said loudly. "I told you, this

bar is for ship fitters." Wendell sighed, but this time it was not with
contentment. He turned and looked at Bunk. Why did there have to
be at least one loudmouth in every bar everywhere? It was as unavoid-
able as death, although Wendell was not sure if the alcohol attracted
them or created them. It was a chicken-or-the-egg deal, he supposed.
Why couldn't people just sit, have a drink or two, and enjoy being
alive? Why was there always one in every crowd who wanted to fight?
Wendell hated to fight. Like many war veterans, he only engaged in
the practice when it could not be avoided. But some fools loved it. He
just knew that at war's end, when he walked into a mostly bombed-out
bar in Tokyo for a cold beer, or whatever it was they drank in Japan
after a long day, there would be a drunken Japanese loudmouth sitting
there, looking for trouble.

"When you get around to repairing the *O'Bannion*," Wendell said
slowly, with restraint, "you will have to burn off a patch on the port
side, down close to the water line. It's not very pretty, but it keeps the
sea out. Or most of it, anyway. I put it there under fire. The guys who
were working on either side of me got killed doing the job. One of
them drowned. He was the best welder we had, but he couldn't swim.
He went over the side anyway, even though he was afraid, and it cost
him his life. The other man with me had a piece of shrapnel take his
head off. I took the letter he always carried with him and mailed it to
his wife. Actually, I rewrote it before I sent it to her, because the one
in his pocket was covered in blood. I made my writing look like his,
so his wife would think it was him, talking to her one more time." He
was quiet for a moment, and it was silent in Roscoe's. Then he looked
at Bunk and spoke again. "They were both my friends, and I guess if
all of that doesn't make me at least an *honorary* ship fitter, then you are
going to have to toss my young Navy ass out of here." Wendell had

slowly stood and stepped away from the bar while he was talking. "It's your choice. But what I would rather do is sit here and drink my beer. My offer to buy you one still stands. But let's do whatever it is we are going to do. I have to be back at what's left of my ship by midnight, and right now, you are sort of wasting my beer-drinking time."

Bunk did not quite know what to do. He sensed that he was not in control of the situation. Usually when he picked fights with sailors, they hopped right up and started swinging, and then he beat the living shit out of them. And normally he had the support of his peers, but from around the room he was hearing comments of "Jesus, Bunk, leave the man alone" and "Let him drink his beer, Bunk." He did not like being cast in the role of the bad guy, even though that is what he was, and he considered just letting this grievance dissipate. But Bunk Grantley was a man of principle, plus he was stupid, and in his worldview, he had no real options other than whipping the sailor standing before him. Besides, he was much bigger than his potential opponent, so he figured it would be an easy fight, even though the boy did seem wiry, and he had a look that indicated he had been around the block a time or two. Bunk eased off of his stool and stood as well.

"I said I don't want your damn beer." He clenched his fists in preparation for mayhem.

"That's good, because I want it," Reva Nichols said as she walked up to the two men. She lightly bumped Bunk out of the way with her hip before sitting on his stool and looked at him with her coal-black eyes. "Bunk, go away and leave my man alone." She had no idea what she was doing, but she was doing it anyway.

"What do you mean, *your man?*" Bunk asked. Confusion was etched on his face. He was supposed to be hip-deep in a bar fight with a sailor right now, not talking to Reva Nichols.

"Well, he's a man, and he's mine," Reva replied. "That makes him my man. And I don't want you fighting with him. So go back over there and leave us be." Bunk was adrift. He looked at the bartender for advice, but that worthy was studiously polishing his bar with a towel, so no guidance was forthcoming. He then looked at his potential opponent as if *he* might offer counsel, but Wendell just shrugged and smiled. He didn't quite know what was going on either. "Go on, now," Reva urged. Bunk turned slowly and shambled back to his seat. He couldn't say for sure what had just happened, but it sort of felt like he had lost a fight that had not even occurred. He did not know how to feel about that. Maybe a drink would help.

While Bunk was puzzling, Wendell sat at the bar next to Reva. He smiled at her in delight. He had never seen anything even resembling what had just happened or met anyone capable of pulling it off. He was enchanted.

"I guess I need to get you that beer," he said, by way of introduction. He couldn't take his eyes off of her. Her curly, short hair and piercing eyes were as black as the western horizon in the quiet hour before the dawn. She wore heavy cotton pants and a quilted flannel shirt, the standard uniform of welders the world over. Her hair was tied in a bright blue scarf. Her hands were small, but they appeared to be no strangers to hard work.

"You ought to buy me two," Reva replied. Her voice was soft, and Wendell could not quite place the subtle accent. She almost sounded like a local girl, but not quite. "Bunk would have broken you in half and then killed both of the pieces." She spoke with an ease that belied their short acquaintance. She had no idea why she had interceded on this man's behalf, but it had seemed the right thing to do.

"I wasn't worried about Bunk," Wendell said with quiet confidence, and it was true. He had spent the last two years learning that what was to be, would be. He had seen people die who had ducked and should have lived, and he had seen people live who had stood flat-footed out in the open and should have died. He had encountered the randomness of the cosmos firsthand and had emerged unscathed, so far. But he was harboring no illusions. He knew that he was a pawn on the board of the ages, and he awoke each day realizing that he was not guaranteed to see the sunset. So a fight with a drunken ship fitter was nothing to sweat. If he won the fight, it would prove only that he was either a luckier man or a better or dirtier fighter. If he lost the fight, then he was whipped, and the sun would still rise in the morning, whether he was there to see the sight or not.

"I could see that," Reva said. "But Bunk is trouble. Big trouble."

"I've been in trouble my whole life," Wendell replied in a friendly manner. "Why should tonight be any different? My name is Wendell Blackmon. I sailed in on what's left of the *O'Bannion*. I would shake your hand, but then Bunk would know we just met."

"We can shake," she said, extending her hand. "Bunk's not that bright. He won't catch on. Besides, he has been staring at a welding arc for the last thirty years, so he's mostly blind at distances over five feet." They shook. Wendell was slow to release the grasp. He liked the way her hand felt in his. It felt like it fit, like he had just donned a glove he had worn many times. "I'm Reva Nichols," she continued. "I am a welder out at the Navy Yard. I'm between ships right now, so who knows? Maybe I'll be assigned to yours. If I am, I will take care of your patch."

"It's not much of a patch, but I was kind of in a hurry," Wendell commented. "The sea will always try to kill you," he continued, mostly to himself. It was something that one of his shipmates had said, and in that man's case, it had been prophecy. Wendell seemed to drift away for a brief moment. Then he smiled and looked back at Reva. "I am curious about something. Why did you come over here? I know I am an amazingly handsome man. Was that it, or do you just break up all of Bunk's fights?" Not a large number of folks had ever tried to save him from harm, and of the ones who had, none previous to Reva Nichols had been absolutely gorgeous.

"To be honest, I can't really say why I came over here," she replied. "It wasn't because you looked all that good though."

Wendell winced.

"I was just sitting over there watching," she continued, "and then the next thing I knew, I was standing here, telling Bunk a whopper about you being my man. I don't even remember walking across the room." She thought about it for a moment. "I guess I came over here because even big, brave sailors ought to know when they should hush up and go to another bar." She realized then that the reason she had placed herself in harm's way was because she had not wanted to see him hurt. No, that was part of the reason, but not all of it. Reva wasn't like Birmah Mae. She didn't like to watch fights, and she didn't like to see *anyone* get hurt. But that feeling was intensified with this sailor. It was almost as if she felt protective of him, as if he were some-how under her care.

"Do you come here a lot?" Wendell asked.

"I have only been here one other time in the last year and a half, and I couldn't tell you for sure why I came tonight. I don't socialize that much. Usually I go straight home to my son, Charlie. He's two years old."

Two years in the Pacific theater had taught Wendell not to flinch too much when the shells hit close by, so he didn't grab his heart and fall out when he heard this bit of news. He should have realized that someone as fine as Reva Nichols would be married. She wasn't wearing a ring, but that didn't mean much. Times were tight, especially for young draftees and recruits, and many marriages were entered into with the promise of a ring after the war, if the need still existed.

"Charlie is a good name," he said. "I like it. Is your husband off in service?" Wendell was not sure why he asked this. Morbid curiosity, he supposed. Or maybe he wanted to send the guy an anonymous note of congratulations.

"He was. Is. Oh, I don't know how to say it. He was killed in North Africa. I am a widow." It was actually the first time she had ever said it out loud, and it was a strange experience for her. Truth be told, she didn't feel like a widow. She really didn't know what she felt like. She had known Ted so briefly that the void in her life had not been a large one when he'd passed, and she felt bad about that. She had liked him and was learning to love him, but he was gone so, so quickly. She was sometimes afraid that if she didn't have Charlie to remember him by, she might forget Ted altogether, and that would be an unforgivable thing to do.

"I am sorry to hear about that," Wendell said, and it wasn't just a rote line coming from someone whose mama had taught him the correct things to say. He could see the sadness in her, and he knew what a tragedy it was when a young man's time was cut short. He had seen it firsthand many times, and had seen the aftermath as well, and it was ugly every time. And he had no doubts that it was just as nasty in Japan and in Germany, when those foreign boys didn't come home. So Wendell was sincere in his condolences, and to his credit, he tried to push away the small spark of hope that had ignited when he'd heard Reva was a war widow.

"It happened a while back," she told him. "We had not been married very long when he was killed. I think the part I feel the worst about is that he never got to see Charlie. He would have liked that." She became quiet. In the background, the Andrews Sisters' "Shoo, Shoo Baby" came on the radio.

"Would you like to dance?" Wendell asked, nodding toward the dance floor, where a few couples were cutting the rug. He had become a fair dancer while in the Navy, as had many of his shipmates. It was something to do in the long, boring stretches between the short bursts of terror that came with battle.

"No, I'm not much of a dancer," she replied.

"What's the matter? Got a bone in your leg?"

"Well, no, actually, I have a tree in my leg," she replied, pulling up her pant leg. She had grown into Ronald Applewhite's old leg over time and no longer had to strap it on so tightly, but there it was in all of its bygone Seminole glory. Charlie had developed a fascination with his mother's appendage and had begun to color on it with his crayons whenever he found it unattached. Wendell looked at the multicolored prosthesis and just shook his head. He couldn't have known, but that was no excuse, and he felt about six inches tall.

"Sorry," he said. "While I'm pulling my foot out of my mouth, why don't you call Bunk back over here? He can go ahead and pound me for an hour or so. Maybe the pain will help me remember to keep my big mouth shut next time."

Reva smiled. His discomfiture was charming.

"Don't let it bother you," she said. "It didn't bother me."

"Is that why you don't dance?"

"No, I don't dance because I never learned how. My leg doesn't get in the way of welding up ships, so I don't think it would be too big of a problem on the dance floor. I'll get around to it one day. Mostly I just need a teacher and some time."

"Well, it just so happens that you are looking at the Fred Astaire of the mighty Pacific Fleet," Wendell bragged. "And I have the time, too. I don't have to be back to my ship until midnight. And if I'm late, what are they going to do? Send me someplace where burning planes will try to crash into me?" He held out his hand. He in no way favored Fred Astaire, but she was tempted to dance with him, nonetheless. She wanted to, but still she hesitated.

"No, I had better get home," she said finally. "Charlie will be missing me." She started to rise.

"One dance," Wendell repeated. His hand was still out. "Please." There was a quiet urgency in his voice. The beginning notes of "Besame Mucho" by Jimmie Dorsey came from the old Motorola behind the bar.

She took his hand, and together they strolled to the dance floor. Roscoe's was a small establishment and there wasn't much room, but that was okay by Wendell. It just meant that they had to dance closer together. One dance turned into two, and two turned into four. Wendell taught Reva to dance, and then they learned to dance together. Time passed, and songs passed, and before they knew it, it was closing time. Somewhere along the way, Wendell had fallen in love. It was as yet unspoken, but it was there. When he realized how he felt, he was content. He had been looking his entire life for someone he could love without reservation or fear. Reva, too, was aware that something was happening, but she was trying to resist loving this sailor. Not because she didn't want to, but because she was afraid to. In years to come, Wendell would say that it was love at first sight, but Reva was always the wiser of the two, and she knew better. The love had always been there. It was the dancing that had awakened it from its slumber.

"I have got to get home," she told Wendell. "I'm hours late." She had sent word to her housemates via Birmah Mae that she was on a date and not dead or kidnapped, but she did not like to be away from Charlie too long. She was always afraid that something might happen to him if she wasn't there to protect him.

"I have to get back to the ship," Wendell replied. "I am AWOL." He was quiet a long moment. "I want to see you again. I know you said that you don't get out much, but will you see me tonight, if they don't shoot me?" There wasn't much of a chance he would be shot, but you just never knew about some of those MPs. They weren't much on tangling with the enemy, but they sure liked to give the good guys a hard time.

"Yes." Her mouth spoke before her brain had the chance to intercede. Her thoughts were a whirlwind, and she needed to sit someplace quiet for a while and mull over the events of this evening. "I will meet you here at seven o'clock." They held hands as they left Roscoe's.

"You don't think Bunk will try to kill me again, do you?" Wendell inquired. He had a shipmate named Big John who might come in handy if Bunk was planning on becoming a long-term problem. Big John was an unskilled poker player who owed Wendell thirty-seven dollars, so perhaps an arrangement could be made.

"Bunk will leave you be, now that he knows you're my man." Reva smiled in spite of herself.

"*Am* I your man?" Wendell asked. He had liked the sound of that and wanted to know her feelings on the subject.

"Bunk thinks so," was her noncommittal reply, although she, too, had sort of liked the way it had sounded.

"Do you like fixing ships?" Wendell asked as he walked her to her stop. There was only one more bus scheduled to run before morning, and it was due momentarily.

"I like feeding Charlie and having a roof over my head," she replied. "I like being in control of my life. I like doing good work and people knowing it. What about you? Do you like being a sailor?" About the only part of being in the Navy that Wendell did not enjoy was when the hot steel flew, but he did not generally talk about his likes and dislikes. He had become superstitious over the last two years while standing watch opposite Emperor Hirohito and Admiral Yamamoto. He believed that if you talked about what you were fond of, it might be taken from you. And if you talked about what you didn't care for, it might gain power over you. It wasn't a rational mindset, but warfare was not rational either.

"It beats digging wells," he said absently. The bus pulled up and opened the door. He led her to the step and turned her to him. "I would like to kiss you," he said. He thought it polite to ask.

Reva intended to say no to this bold request, because she wasn't sure that it was a good idea to encourage him. But before she could speak, he placed his hands lightly on her shoulders and kissed her gently. They met each other's gaze and kissed again. The bus driver tooted the horn, waited a moment, and tooted again. Reluctantly, Wendell released her. Then she turned and was gone.

The Tuscan sun was warm on her back as she tended the Sangiovese vines. The sky was as blue as her love's eyes when they gazed into hers, the breeze as soft as his touch when he caressed her cheek or breast. The gently rolling hills of her small vineyard slowly marched to the Mare Tirreno. Although

he had always helped her at harvest and with the wine-making, her husband, Abramo, was not a farmer. He was a willing laborer who was more than happy to carry out his wife's directives, and for nearly sixty years he had done so, but he had no feel for the land and no skill with its care. He was a shoemaker, and a good one, but it had always been Bibiana who had tilled the soil, who had pruned and trained the vines, who had worked the rich, sandy earth. It had always been she who had loved the land, had respected it and cherished it like a child, had coaxed from it each year the Sangiovese and the Lambrusco di Sorbara grapes. The land had always spoken to her and made its needs known. And in return for her love and her dedication, it had always revealed its secrets to her.

Now the harvest was done, and the wine was corked. It had been a late gathering, because she had wanted this year's vintage to have a trace of sweetness. It was time for the vines to rest, and time for the vintners to lay down their burdens. Bibiana walked slowly up the winding trail to the small stone villa that had been her family's home since the time of the Medici. Even in the full warmth of afternoon, the thick walls kept the house cool.

Abramo was there. He had not arisen that morning. She sat next to him on the bed and brushed his few wisps of hair from the lifeless brow. The pain that had drawn and pinched his face for the past month was gone, and in his features she could recognize the boy she had once married. A single tear dropped from her cheek and splashed onto the bridge of his oft-broken nose.

"Abramo, my love, you have been my good husband. You have been my life. I do not wish to be without you." She bent and kissed him. Then she arose and fetched the steaming kettle from the hook over the fire on the hearth. She crushed the dried green leaves and purple flowers of the belladonna plant, the deadly nightshade, into her cup. She took the smooth

stone she had collected for the purpose and ground the mixture to a fine powder. With a steady hand she poured the steaming water and made a tea. She spooned in some honey and allowed the mixture to cool a moment. Then she drained the cup to the dregs.

Chapter Six: 1985

Sorrow Wood was the name of the mountain cave and adjoining acreage of what was once the largest farm in the county. It had originally been named Sourwood Farm, in honor of the predominance of sourwoods that grew on the knees of James Mountain. In its heyday during the latter half of the nineteenth century, it had produced cotton, corn, sourwood honey, and a variety of fruits and truck crops. The local dialect had subsequently evolved the name of the tract to *Sar*wood. For some reason, the ownership of the property had proven calamitous to a variety of people over the years, and many who occupied the farmstead had known great sorrow. Thus, finally, the short trip from Sarwood to Sorrow Wood was made.

The current owner's name was Christine Hendricksen, and she had acquired the property after her fourth husband died of heart failure. Unfortunately, his heart failed while he was falling from the patio of their sixteenth-floor apartment in Atlanta, so the debate surrounding his untimely demise churned for years. This controversy was most likely due to the fact that he had apparently fallen horizontally about ten feet before beginning the vertical portion of the trip, and a plausi-

ble explanation for this temporary suspension of the laws of gravity had
never been offered. But this mystery did not keep the grieving widow
from inheriting a respectable sum of money, as well as the mountain
and adjoining valley on which Sorrow Wood was situated.

The cavern on the property was once the only tourist attraction
that Sand Valley had ever had. It had been named Sequoyah's Cave in
honor of a man who had never been there by another man who did not
let that fact bother him. According to Wendell's mother, Eunice—
who was not present for any of the events and, therefore, could not
have possibly known any of the facts she subsequently related—the
hole that had been in the side of James Mountain since that peak was
thrust up from the sea became Sequoyah's Cave as the direct result
of the efforts of an individual with a vision. His name was Reynolds Cooper, and his quest had been to find the final resting place of
Noah's ark, which he believed with most of his heart to be somewhere
in the vicinity of Sand Valley, Alabama.

As Eunice told the tale, Reynolds Cooper had been an unenthusiastic member of General Black Jack Pershing's American Expeditionary
Force during World War One. One bleak day, he found himself in a
mud-filled hole in the middle of France with two dead French boys of
his fleeting acquaintance and three dead horses of unknown origin.
The French boys and the horses had died trying to breathe mustard
gas, and Reynolds figured to join them all in a minute or two because
he had run out of air in his gas mask. In what he thought was his final
act, Reynolds took a look at the sky. He saw some clouds and a German Fokker off in the distance, but what really caught his attention
was the angel floating directly above him, complete with standard-
issue golden aura, halo, and wings. This celestial being reached down
and touched his gas mask, and he heard a voice in his head say, *You*

will live, for the Lord thy God has a quest for you. This was good news for Reynolds because he had seen the French boys die, and it had not been a pretty sight. Then the angel proceeded to tell him that Noah's ark was at Sorrow Wood—which was still named Sourwood Farm at the time, even though a couple of its landlords had already met sad and unusual ends—and that he was to find it, so that faith and hope in the world could be renewed. The last thing she told him was to take off his mask, because the air had cleared, and it was all right to breathe again.

The first time that Reva heard this story, she was fascinated. She and Wendell had not been married long, and she had not yet met Eunice.

"Your mother said that Noah's ark was in north Alabama?" Reva asked, when Wendell told her the tale. He had been nine when he first heard the story, and he knew every syllable by heart. His wife was wearing a smile as wide as the Puget Sound.

"No, the *angel* said it was," Wendell corrected. "Mama is merely the messenger. Think of her as a living newspaper with really bad taste in men. Now, pay attention."

"Sorry," Reva replied.

According to Eunice, what happened next was not necessarily that angel's fault. It was her contention that angels were ancient creatures that had been around since the beginnings of eternity, whereas mustard gas was a new development. Thus, in Eunice's view, it was not reasonable to expect that Reynolds's angel would know that poison gas tended to settle into low places and linger. Places such as mud holes in France. So when Reynolds did as he was told and ripped his mask off, he got a whiff of the gas, and that one breath nearly killed him.

"You would have thought that the angel would have known about the gas," Reva noted.

"Maybe she was testing him."

"By trying to kill him?"

"Do you want me to tell this or not?" Wendell asked.

"Sorry again," Reva whispered sheepishly. She had yet to learn that Eunice's stories flowed better without interruption, even when a proxy storyteller was doing the telling.

In Eunice's version of world history, Reynolds Cooper spent the following year in a sanatorium in Arizona because the medical wisdom of the day dictated that the dry climate was supposed to be good for gas victims. Eventually, the doctors determined that he was going to live, so they mustered him out of the Army, and he hopped an eastbound freight train and began his slow journey to Sand Valley. When he arrived, he contacted Stewart James, who was the owner of James Mountain and Sourwood Farm, and secured permission to search for the ark. Stewart figured that the boy was crazy, and he felt sorry for him, so he granted permission. But there was another reason, as well. Stewart's son, Jackson, had also been to the war to end all wars. Unfortunately, he had not been lucky enough to find a guardian angel, and he did not return. So out of respect for his fallen heir, Stewart granted unlimited access to the mountain and farm for as long as Reynolds wanted it.

Reynolds spent the next few years combing every rock and rill of Stewart's property looking for the sacred ship. Sadly for him and Christianity in general, he never found Noah's ark. But he did find a cave that had strange writings on the walls, and Reynolds Cooper was convinced that the words were ancient Hebrew written by Noah. Stewart James was not so sure, but as a favor to Reynolds, he got a language professor from Shorter College over in Rome, Georgia, to try to read the words. It turned out that the symbols were Cherokee, and not Hebrew at all. This news broke Reynold's heart, but it gave Stewart James an idea.

Sequoyah was an important man in the Cherokee Nation before it voluntarily relocated at gunpoint to Oklahoma, and he was the one who had invented the alphabet that was represented on the cave wall. According to the professor from Rome, the author of the cave writing was an old Cherokee chief who had hidden in the cavern due to his wish to remain east of the Mississippi during a time when most of the rest of the tribe were seeing that wide river from a boat on the way across. Stewart James had never really taken to working for a living, and he was always searching for ways to make easy money. It was his thought that he could turn the cave into a tourist attraction, sort of like Georgia Animal Park down in Trenton, which used to be a big draw until the dog with five legs choked to death trying to eat the two-headed chicken. He figured to bill the cave as the birthplace of Sequoyah, even though it wasn't, and to have a museum and a zoo, with a cafe and gift shop next door.

"Did you say that the five-legged dog choked to death on the two-headed chicken?" Reva asked, incredulous. She herself had just almost choked, but it was on the bite of beef stew she was trying to eat rather than on mutated poultry.

"If you tried to eat a two-headed chicken, you would probably choke, too," Wendell replied.

Poor Reynolds was sick at heart about not finding the ark, until his angel visited him again and told him that he must have misheard her, because what she had said to him in that foxhole was that the ark was in Tibet. Stewart truly liked Reynolds, so instead of pointing out to him that *Tibet* and *Sand Valley* did not sound in any way similar to one another—even while wearing a gas mask under battle conditions—he gave him some money and told him to go find his ark. Reynolds died of cholera about a year later in Hong Kong without ever fulfilling his quest. His last words were heard by a missionary from Ireland and by two Chinese servants who couldn't understand a word that he said. "Get away from me," Reynolds said as he looked at a spot on the wall over that Irish missionary's shoulder. "Go find it yourself, if you want it so bad."

"If no one was there but the missionary and the two Chinese men, how did your mother know what Reynolds said?" Reva asked. She was still unused to Eunice's omniscient style.

"Maybe the angel told her," Wendell replied.

After Reynolds Cooper left Sand Valley for parts unknown to all but Eunice, Stewart James proceeded to inadvertently lose most of the family fortune by shoveling it into the cave, in a manner of speaking. The James family had been accustomed to wealth since the patriarch of the clan, Clayton, returned from the war for states' rights with only one eye and with a strongbox full of Yankee gold. He got both of these when his company of infantry stumbled into a column of Union soldiers guarding a payroll for Ulysses S. Grant's Army of the Shenandoah. Clayton had shown exceptional wisdom by playing dead as soon as the ball and shot began to fly, but he wasn't quite quick enough to escape totally unscathed, and a ricochet took his eye. When the smoke cleared, he discovered that he was the only man left alive on either side of the argument, so he took the gold as payment for his eye and headed back to Sand Valley before someone shot out the other one.

So Stewart was well-heeled, but he was obsessed with making even more money in the tourist trade. First, though, he had several obstacles to overcome. To begin with, there wasn't much of a path to the cave, and the only road to the town was dirt and stayed washed out half of the time. Back then, most of the people in the area didn't have cars, so the lack of roads was not a big problem for them, but Stewart wanted blacktop for his tourists to drive on, so he had a road constructed right up to the cave's front door. Once he had pavement put down from the town to the cave, he went to Montgomery and wined

and dined everyone of importance he could find, and before long, the
chain gang was out laying asphalt on the main thoroughfare to town.
By Christmas of 1928, there was a paved road joining Sand Valley
with the rest of the world, but Stewart couldn't tell it by counting new
heads in town or tourists up at the cave.

"You know, your mother was a grown woman by 1928, so this part
could actually be firsthand knowledge," Reva noted.
    "I don't think she knew Stewart James."
    "I bet they were sweethearts."
    "They weren't sweethearts."
    "Maybe he took her to Montgomery with him."
    "I don't think so."
    "It would just be sort of romantic if he did."
    "She would have told me."

Back at the cave, Stewart was open for business, but no one from Sand
Valley seemed to care, and no one from anywhere else even knew. So
he decided to conduct an advertising campaign by going into the barn-
painting business. He sent a crew around to farms located near highways,
and they offered to paint the farmer's barns for free. Most of the folks
who heard that proposition were happy to get the paint job. Times were
hard and people couldn't afford to be too particular, and the red paint
backgrounds with the large black letters that said *See Sequoyah's Cave*
didn't seem to bother the livestock too much. The foreman of the paint

crew was a hard worker, but he wasn't a natural artist, so the first project or two had to be neatened up a bit, but Stewart would have had to touch up the first few barns anyway because it turned out that the foreman wasn't a natural speller either, and it was a blow to the enterprise when it was revealed that there were no *k*'s in Sequoyah.

While the crew was out painting the countryside, Stewart was beating the bushes for curiosities to show at his attraction. He bought a two-headed pig from a farmer near Dogtown and a five-legged cow from an old maid who lived outside of Felton. He bought an egg-laying rooster from a traveling salesman, and he somehow got his hands on a buffalo, but it died when he tried to bleach it white. He bought some Indian skeletons from B.C. Munro, a drunken grave digger from Ft. Payne who called himself an archaeologist.

By this time, Stewart should have been on easy street. He had a nice highway coming into town and a good road up to the cave, and he had over one hundred painted barns in Alabama, Georgia, and Tennessee. But he still didn't have any customers. He was just about to call the whole plan off and quit throwing good money after bad, when Major Julius P. LeCroix came to town and gave him hope. Major LeCroix rolled in on a Tuesday morning, fresh from an extended tour of the crowned heads of Europe, or at least, that is what he claimed. He called himself a purveyor of oddity and amazement, and he had plenty of both packed into his three old Ford trucks.

He had a bearded lady and a stuffed set of Siamese twins. He had a genuine dog boy and the eye of Nostradamus in a jar. He had the authentic True Cross. He had Nero's fiddle and Merlin's magic wand. He had a piece of Halley's Comet and the skull of Genghis Khan. He had Samson's hair and Delilah's silk bloomers. And he had the one thing that really impressed Stewart. Major LeCroix had customers.

At two bits a head, almost every man, woman, and child in the county managed to get oddity purveyed to them by Major LeCroix. Many had gone twice, and some had gone more than that. Pop Ledbetter went six times, but all he did was stare at Delilah's bloomers until his wife, Ethel, came down and shooed him home.

"A dog boy?" Reva asked. Then she caught herself. "Sorry."

Stewart paid his two bits and sat down to talk with Major LeCroix, and before the conversation ended, he had offered two hundred dollars, cash, for the whole collection—lock, stock, and amazement. Major LeCroix was insulted and told Stewart that his collection was priceless and not for sale at any price. They eventually settled on five hundred dollars, delivered to the cave, for everything but the Ford trucks and the living members of the show. Stewart subsequently tried to hire the bearded lady, who wasn't half bad with a close shave, but she would not leave her husband, Major LeCroix. Their son, the dog boy, also decided to remain with the family business.

Stewart installed his new collection at the cave. He had spent nearly every dime he had, but finally everything was ready for the grand opening. On Thursday, October 27, 1929, Stewart James officially opened Sequoyah's Cave and Museum of the Unusual. On Black Friday, October 28, Wall Street died, and the Great Depression began.

"What a sad story," Reva said.

"Talk to the angel," Wendell replied. "Every bit of it was her fault."

It was indeed a sad ending to an improbable narrative, but Wendell Blackmon smiled nonetheless every time he recalled his mother's rendition of the tale. It was one of his favorites, and he could just see the hurt expression on the angel's face when Reynolds spoke roughly to her on his deathbed. He could imagine her being upset for days after that exchange, because she had thought that they were friends, and he could envision her trying to bridge over their differences once Reynolds passed the pearly gates.

"So, how was the trip up?" she would inquire as she folded in her wings and sat down beside him. Perhaps she would smooth the wrinkles in her robe with her perfect, angelic hands.

"It wasn't any worse than breathing mustard gas," would be his sullen reply. In Wendell's mind's eye, Reynolds had already taken the trouble to scout out Noah and had asked the pregnant question. And Reynolds had learned that the ark was not in either of the locations suggested by the angel. There was going to be trouble.

Back at Sorrow Wood, Wendell came to the rugged road that led out across fifty acres of pasture to the base of James Mountain. Though once paved, the road had suffered from the ravages of the past half century. As he bumped along the weathered track, Wendell wondered what had gotten T.F. so upset. Admittedly, it did not take much, because T.F. was an excitable man. He was also an amorous one since parting ways with the shrew fuck, and he had been dating Christine Hendricksen for close to two years. She was an angular woman with not much meat on her bones, while T.F. had enough meat on his frame for them both, plus maybe a small dog or two. So they made an odd looking couple, the Laurel and Hardy of rural Alabama. Wendell smiled as he recalled the ribbing that T.F. had endured down at the truck stop when word of his love affair had gotten out. Most of the jocularity seemed to revolve around Christine's claims that she was a witch, and that she worshipped Satan in the cave.

"Her head doesn't turn all the way around when you're screwing her, does it?" asked Tray Cash. He was a retiree from the railroad who spent most of his waking hours at the truck stop. He apparently had a bladder of iron and a prostate of steel, because he drank coffee from sunup to sundown and never took a pee.

"I guess when she gets horny, the horns are real, eh?" This was offered by Willard Perkins and received with general mirth.

"I bet she's a *hell* of a good piece," observed Claude Larkin. Two of the other regulars spewed coffee. Tray Cash pounded the table, rendered helpless with laughter. T.F. just sat quietly and ate his breakfast. Any response at all would have just made it worse.

Wendell took the slow curve around the knee of James Mountain and pulled up into the clearing that housed the cave. He wasn't quite certain what he was looking for, but he did not like what he saw. T.F.'s car was there, door ajar, and he was sitting on the hood, staring. The object of his gaze was the burned remains of Christine's house, also known as Sorrow Wood Manor. It had once been the concession stand and souvenir shop for Sequoyah's Cave, and a barn after that.

The fire was out, but the odor of smoke hung in the clearing. Wendell got out of the cruiser and walked to T.F.

"What happened?" he asked his deputy.

"I don't know," said T.F., shaking his head. "I got a call from Reva. She told me that smoke had been spotted out this way. I came out here thinking I would find a brush fire or maybe the woods burning. Instead, I found this." He gestured in the general direction of the cave and the manor.

"Where is Christine?" Wendell asked. He had a bad feeling. Her car was there, and she normally met visitors at the road.

"There's a body in the house," T.F. said. "I didn't go in, but I think it's her." He hadn't gone in because he wasn't allowed to. The rule had become necessary after he had thrown up all over the deceased Nadine Alexander a few years back, when he had been sent to check on her. She had missed her hair appointment, and he had been the first one on the scene. Foul play had not been involved—she was ninety and had peacefully gone to her reward—but the incident had been viewed as disrespectful by some of the ladies down at Whitehead Baptist Church.

Wendell looked at T.F. closely to see how he was holding up. The big man was sweating and had a case of the shakes. Dead people really upset him, especially those he had been sleeping with prior to their departure. Wendell decided that his deputy should just stay put. "Wait here and man the radio. I'll go check it out." T.F. nodded.

Wendell opened the trunk of the cruiser and removed the toolbox that he called *the kit*. It contained all of the tools he would need for his first look at the body: plastic and paper bags, tags, a laundry marker and some pens, a fresh notebook, a Polaroid camera and several packs of film, a flashlight, masking tape, some empty pill bottles, a measuring tape, rubber gloves, a magnifying glass, a pair of scissors, some tweezers, eye droppers, a blood sample kit, and a rape kit.

He walked up the gravel path that led to the rubble of Sorrow Wood Manor. On each side of the walkway was a selection of statuary depicting mythological and legendary figures and symbols. There were gargoyles and griffins, medusas and mermen. There were the Egyptian deities Seth, Sekhmet, and Osiris. The Romans were represented by Pluto, Bacchus, and Morta. The Greeks had contributed Hades, Persephone, and Thanatos. There were several renditions of Lucifer, each more menacing than the last. There was an inverted cross, an ankh, and several other symbols that Wendell did not even recognize. The common theme seemed to be a tribute to man's darker urges. Wendell had always called the pathway the Walk of Bullshit. It was his opinion that Christine's purpose in establishing it was to declare her outrageousness to the world. She said she was a witch, and she was reputed to worship Satan, but it was Wendell's belief that all of that business was just so much chaff. In his opinion, she liked the reputation of being a bad girl, and she no more believed the philosophies she was promoting than she believed that pigs could fly. But Reva had a different theory.

"I think that she might truly be evil," Reva said when she and Wendell had first discussed the subject of Christine Hendricksen. "By that, I mean that there is no goodness in her at all, and she likes to surround herself with evil. I think she is afflicted with an old malevolence that will take many lifetimes to wash away." There was an inflection in her voice when she spoke that gave Wendell a chill. Reva rarely spoke of good or evil as absolutes, and she was not prone to speak ill of others. But rare observation or not, he had to disagree.

"You are smarter than I am," he said, "and you are probably right.

But I think she is just stupid and likes to surround herself with crap."
From a philosophical standpoint, his wife's conclusion was certainly more profound than his, but he believed what he believed. "Her
crap doesn't even match. She has Christian and pagan crap. She has
Egyptian, Greek, and Roman crap. She has a swastika, for Christ's
sake. And she advertises, so people will be sure to get the point. You
wouldn't even know who or what most of that stuff was, if she didn't
have nameplates mounted on the pieces. That means she really wants
us all to *get* it. What she really needs is a statue of a little black kid
fishing in hell. Then she could offend everybody. She likes to be outrageous so that everyone will say how outrageous she is." Wendell had
known some bad people in his time, the kind of people who would kill
someone for no particular reason, and the common trait among them
was that they did not care what people thought. Christine cared. It
was important to her that people thought she was wicked.

"No," Reva had countered, "I sense darkness in her, a badness that
comes from her core." She was serious, and she was rarely wrong in
her intuitions. But Wendell just didn't buy it. He still believed that
Christine was just another rich girl playing at being a rogue. And she
was getting old enough to know better.

"Well, you may be right. All I sense is that she likes to smoke pot,
take off her clothes, and draw big stars on the floor before she gives
T.F. a little tumble." Wendell knew that the big stars were penta-
grams, but he refused to dignify the practice or the symbol by calling
it what is was. "As long as she stays inside of her cave while she does
it, I don't really care." He truly didn't. Wendell had believed for a
long time that way too many people were much too concerned with
what other folks were doing with their time. He believed that many
of the problems in the world would evaporate if most of its occupants

would simply develop the sensible habit of minding their own business. These were admittedly odd points of view for a policeman to hold, because it was sort of intuitive that cops liked to nose around a bit, but there it was. He knew that Christine and her coven—her word, not Wendell's—liked to gather in the cave, alter reality by various means, strip, and cavort. He knew this because T.F. had told him. But as far as Wendell was concerned, as long as everyone was over eighteen and no one had been dragged up to the cave against their will, then it was their business.

"But if I ever see you naked," he had said to T.F., "I swear to God I will fire you, shoot you, and then send your body to prison for life." Wendell was of the opinion that the moment he found himself viewing T.F.'s hindquarters *sans* pants was when cavorting ceased to be a victimless crime. He felt pretty much the same way about the remaining members of Christine's coven: Gilla Newman, Dixie Lanier, Otter Price, Noble Harrison, his wife Ellen, and Rita Hearst. With the possible exception of Dixie Lanier, the more clothing the group was wearing, the better.

Wendell arrived at the burned-out building. It had been a long, single-story structure, built along the lines of barracks. Its faded paint job included representations of cacti, burros, and a variety of Native Americans wearing feathers and loincloths while dancing, swinging tomahawks, and attacking a wagon train that was located on the southeast corner of the structure. These figures did not resemble any Cherokees anyone had ever seen, and it was rare to find a burro, a cactus, or a wagon train in Alabama, so Stewart James had apparently hired someone from out of town to paint the building. In its previous incarnation as a souvenir stand and snack bar, the manor had sported a large wooden teepee and a garish totem pole next to the front door. While those historically inaccurate embellishments were long gone, the log walls of the original building remained, even though the roof had collapsed in several places during the fire. The great weeping willow tree that stood in a clearing to the side of the manor had also survived the blaze. To Wendell, the tree rather than the Walk of Bullshit was the true symbol of Sorrow Wood. It stood fifty feet tall, with branches and leaves that drooped and sagged all the way to the ground. It was a tree that evoked a feeling of sadness in the beholder, as if it had absorbed all of the grief the farm had to offer and was trying to imprison it so that it could not strike again.

Wendell shined his flashlight in the front door but could not see much due to the lingering smoke. He walked around the exterior of the building and looked into each window as he came to it, jotting down his impressions of what he saw. He was a careful gatherer of evidence, and he took his time while he worked his way down the side of the building, snapping photos through each opening as he progressed. It had apparently been an intense fire. The heat still radiated from the structure's remains, and since it was already a hot day, Wendell was sweating profusely. As he worked his way up the rear of the edifice, he looked into one window and spotted what he assumed was the body of the current owner of Sorrow Wood.

The remains were situated in a portion of the building that had not collapsed, so nothing had fallen on the body, and Wendell's view was unobstructed. He looked at the scene for a moment, taking in the details and writing them down carefully. He examined the ground around the base of the window for signs of pedestrian traffic or other clues. Then he leaned over the windowsill and looked at the floor beneath the opening for the same type of telltale signs on the inside. Continuing, he took a series of photos through the window of every detail of the room that could be seen from his position. Finally, just as he was about to climb in the window for a closer inspection, he stopped short and peered hard at one particular feature of the deceased. He shined his flashlight and leaned his head to one side as he looked. Then he walked about ten feet down the wall to another window so he could get a different view, and it confirmed his suspicions about what he had just seen. Then he hitched up his trouser leg and swung first one leg and then the other over the windowsill.

He walked carefully across the floor to minimize any impact on potential evidence. He loaded a fresh film cartridge into the Polaroid and took a complete series of photos of the body at close proximity. Then he pulled his rubber gloves out of his shirt pocket and put them on. He squatted down and looked at the remains. The body was lying face down with both of its arms stretched out in front, like it had been frozen in a dive. The deceased appeared to be female. Her head was in pretty poor condition, but even so, it was obvious that the skull was caved in from behind. He looked around for any object that could explain the crevasse in the unfortunate's skull and could find nothing that might have accidentally fallen on her.

Wendell sighed and carefully raised the head to see if he could recognize the face. The heat of the fire had scorched her skin severely, but from what he could tell, the eye color and the hair color were a match for Christine Hendricksen. He gently returned her head to its former position and viewed the rest of the body. Most of the clothing was gone, but he recognized a tattoo on the victim's left buttock that was similar to one he had heard that Christine had. He noticed a bulge under her right leg, and upon investigating, he found the remains of her billfold, which had apparently been in her front pocket. The wallet was scorched but otherwise intact. Her body had protected it from the worst of the fire. He examined its contents, and then he knew. This was Christine Hendricksen, and she appeared to be the victim of foul play. Sorrow Wood had struck again. He retraced his steps to the window. He climbed out, turned for one more look at the deceased, and headed back to the cars and T.F. The deputy met Wendell's eyes as he walked up.

"Is it her?" he asked.

"It's her," Wendell confirmed. He had no doubts. "I'm sorry." Wendell hated to be the bearer of bad news. Of all of the parts of his job that he did not like, he liked that part the least. T.F. nodded, as if Wendell had just confirmed what he had already known in his heart of hearts.

"What do you think happened?" T.F. asked.

"I think she probably did not die in the fire. The back of the skull was caved in. Someone hit her with a blunt object. The fire might have been set after the fact to hide the evidence. Or maybe not. But either way, I think this is a homicide. I'm going to have Reva call the state police. Since it looks like it wasn't an accident, it's not our case anymore." The services of the state police and the mobile crime lab were required in cases of suspected foul play.

"Maybe the skull got crushed when the roof collapsed," T.F. said. He sounded almost hopeful, as if an accidental death would be somehow less final than an intentional one.

"The roof held in that room," Wendell said gently. "Somebody hit her." He walked to his patrol car, sat in the driver's seat, and picked up the microphone from his two-way radio.

"How about it, Reva?" he said. "Come in Reva. This is Wendell." The base station was in the living room of the rock castle. If Reva was home, she should hear him.

"Go ahead, Wendell," came the reply after a moment.

"We've got trouble up here, Reva. Can you get the coroner on the horn and send him this way? We also need the state police and the guys from the state crime lab." There was a long silence before her reply.

"What is it, Wendell?" she asked. "What's going on out there?"

"T.F. was right," Wendell replied. "We have a genuine sorrow fuck on our hands."

She hated the prairie. She was from a mountainous, wooded country, and she could not get used to the flatness that surrounded her. She stood on top of the dugout and looked to the east at an unbroken sea of tall grass. That was the direction from which she had come, many years ago. Then she turned and looked to the west. The views were the same, as were those to the north and to the south. It was a land with no features, and one place was as good as another. She wished that she could go back to the home she had once known, but it was too late for that. It was long ago and far away, and that path was no longer hers. She had left that land and that life behind, and she and her husband had come to this place of opportunity to build new lives with their own hands.

She climbed down the hill that provided three sides of her home and walked around it to the back side. There, in the lee of the hill, were seven graves. They had been dug at various times during the last twenty years, with the final two being excavated just yesterday. Six of the graves contained the remains of her husband and her five children. Smallpox had claimed two of her offspring. A broken neck had taken one, snakebite another. Her fifth child had died of starvation during the hard winter of the previous year. And her husband had been killed only yesterday while trying to bring down a rogue steer.

She and her family had come to the prairie to farm, but their harvest had been disaster. They were mountain people, and the flat ground had slowly and surely stolen them away. All but one. There were seven graves behind the hill. Six of them were occupied. The seventh was for her. As she lay next to her husband, she hoped that someone would cover her before the wolves came roaming in the fall.

Chapter Seven: 1944

It took three weeks to repair the *O'Bannion* and to perform a major overhaul and refit. The destroyer had spent most of the previous eighteen months continuously at sea, and during that time, she had ranged the Pacific from the freezing waters of the Aleutian Islands to the sharp coral reefs off of New Guinea. She had drawn picket duty for Admiral Halsey and Admiral Spruance, had run submarine screens for uncounted tankers and support ships, had participated in eight shore bombardments, and had weathered three typhoons. She had crossed the equator seven times, scored one direct hit on the bridge of a Japanese destroyer, shot down four Japanese planes, and picked up seventeen downed pilots, three of whom had been enemy fliers. And most of this travel and excitement had occurred at speeds in excess of thirty knots, which was all she was rated to do. She was a tired old ship that needed to retire, but there was a war on, and the only ships being retired were those retiring to the depths due to various forms of mayhem.

During those twenty-one days in the yard, Wendell was able to see Reva on five different occasions. The first of these was the night they met, and by the end of that evening, he had determined that he was going to marry Reva if she would have him. After their meeting, he

had been lucky enough to slip back aboard the *O'Bannion* undetected
and had not been shot or incarcerated for being AWOL.

"Tonight I met the woman I'm going to marry," he said to his best
friend, D.C. Becker. D.C. was a seaman aboard the *O'Bannion*. He
and Wendell were sitting on the fantail of the ship in the grey, pre-
dawn Seattle haze, smoking Chesterfields and drinking the last of the
raisin jack they had made the previous month. It was a good batch,
even though it had aged a little too long.

"Movin' kind of quick, ain't ya?" D.C. inquired. D.C. hailed from
Lake Charles, Louisiana, where he had acquired his love of the sea and
his hatred of crustaceans at a young age aboard his daddy's shrimp
boat, the *Betty Sue.*

His initials didn't stand for anything at all. He was the youngest
of the sixteen living Becker children, and by the time he managed to
get himself born, his poor, sainted mama, Betty Sue, had already lost
interest in anything even remotely associated with children, including
the naming of them. She had begun the practice of christening babies with the letters of the alphabet when D.C.'s older brother, A.B.,
was born, and it had been her intent to just go straight through the
alphabet before launching into the number line. Unfortunately, her
schooling had been rudimentary, and she was slightly dyslexic as well,
so she actually misspelled her next child's name, D.C. She died not
long after her following baby, E.F., succumbed to rheumatic fever.
Early one morning, as she was tending nets aboard the vessel named
in her honor, she stood, sighed, and stepped over the side and into
the dark, warm embrace of the Gulf of Mexico. It was the consensus
among the relatives that she had become depressed over the loss of her
child, but in actual fact, it was the upcoming arrival of young H.G.
that had led to her midnight swim.

"Well, I haven't asked her yet," Wendell replied. "But I am going to as soon as the time is right."

"What's she look like? D.C. questioned.

"She has dark hair, and dark eyes, and she is kind of curvy," Wendell said. "She's about this tall, and she has these little, delicate fingers. She has a soft voice that sometimes sounds like she's from the South and sometimes doesn't." He took another drink of the raisin jack. "Oh yeah, she just has one leg."

"No shit?" D.C. asked, his interest piqued. "One leg? Does she have a sister?"

Reva and Wendell had their second meeting the following night at Roscoe's. This time, however, Reva had not come straight from ten hours of ship repair and had been afforded the opportunity to fix up a bit. Wendell was in a borrowed set of dress whites—his own were slowly drifting in the currents of the Philippine Sea—impatiently looking for her arrival, when she came up from behind and tapped him lightly on the shoulder.

"If I had been Bunk," she said, "you would be wearing a bar stool for a hat right now, and half the boys inside would be paying off the other half." She had startled him, but he turned around and smiled at her arrival, and she gave him a quick peck on the cheek. Wendell had thought that she was beautiful in her coveralls the night before, but he was astounded at how fine she looked in the green, ankle-length skirt and white blouse she wore that Saturday night. She had applied just a bit of powder and some rose-colored lipstick, and she wore a hint of lilac. He was only eighteen, but it had been a busy eighteen years, with the two war years in there counting at least double, and she was the prettiest sight he had seen.

The entire time she had been preparing herself for her date with

Wendell, she had been telling herself that she was not going to go at all, that it was a bad idea to become involved with another man engulfed in the war. Then she had kissed the baby, handed him to Birmah Mae, and caught the bus for the waterfront.

"Bunk and I have made up," Wendell said. "We're as tight as two ticks on a hound's ear. I bought him a beer and gave him a genuine Japanese battle flag. He would take a bullet for me now. He and Mrs. Bunk are going to name one of the kids after me." Actually, they weren't quite that close yet, but at least Bunk no longer wanted to kill Wendell before dismembering him and sowing salt on his grave. It was progress of a sort.

"Where did you get a genuine Japanese battle flag?" Reva asked. She could see Bunk through the window of Roscoe's, showing the souvenir to his pals. They were all pointing at a blank space on the wall that seemed to be the likely final resting place for the war relic.

"A guy on the ship makes them," Wendell replied with a smile. "Gets five bucks. I think everyone on the crew has bought one. For two more dollars, he'll make up a great story about how many guys you had to kill while winning the flag in hand-to-hand combat. He does a good job, and he sends all the money to his sick mama. I got one for Bunk because five bucks is not much to pay for peace in the family. He can make up his own story." Wendell figured that bringing Bunk a gift was a better idea than turning Big John loose on him or braining him from behind with a stout stick of wood, but he still had those courses of action available, if the flag didn't work.

"He'll be mad if he finds out it's not real."

"He was already mad, so what am I losing? Anyway, *I'm* not going to tell him. So I guess my fate is in your hands. That makes you kind of like the Navy, only you're prettier and not painted grey. Are you hungry, or thirsty?" Wendell was both, but she was the girl and got to choose.

"No one has ever told me that I am prettier than the Navy," Reva said. "You are a sweet-talking man. I don't want anything to drink, but I am starved." He took her arm, and they walked the short distance down to Pier 54. "Do you like seafood?" she asked. There were several places down by the water that specialized in local delicacies.

"I've had seafood a few times in my life, and I thought it was great every time, except for the time I tried raw oysters." He shuddered. "I'll never make that mistake again. That was some nasty business. My favorite is fried clams." They stopped in front of a small place named Ivar's. "We don't get much seafood in north Alabama. It's more of a beans and cornbread kind of place. Deer, squirrel, and possum. Maybe a little fried pork from time to time." Very little, if you belonged to Happy Blackmon's family.

"You don't eat a lot of fish when you are out at sea?" Reva asked. "I would have thought you did." She was looking at the handwritten menu posted on the wall, next to the door. There were strike-throughs and add-ons that reflected the day's catch. In the distance, they could hear the horn of the ferry from Bremerton. It had a mournful sound as it echoed back and forth across the harbor. Closer in, they heard the *scree, scree* of the gulls as they floated effortlessly over the waves.

"We mostly eat canned and dry food," Wendell said. "Sometimes we get fresh vegetables and meat if we're near a carrier or a battle wagon. There are plenty of fish out there, but every time we stop and try to catch one, the rest of the fleet just keeps steaming along and outruns us, and then somebody shoots a torpedo at us, or runs into us with a plane." It was a real problem.

"Well, we'll be safe here," Reva assured him. "Come on. I've heard

that the food is really good at this place. Look, they even have clams."
They took a booth and shared the first of a lifetime of meals together.
Wendell had fried clams, Reva had salmon, and they both had fresh
seafood chowder. While they ate, they talked. Wendell was not much
of a conversationalist when he was the subject, but being with Reva
put him at an ease he had seldom felt, and the words spilled out. Reva
learned of Wendell's short, mean childhood, and of some of his adven-
tures in the Navy, but not the ones fraught with danger. He shared
most of the details leading up to his premature enlistment—leaving
out only those parts dealing directly with Glennice Olive Cole—and
she laughed out loud when she heard the story of Happy Blackmon
floundering in the well. Here again, Wendell edited somewhat, because he did not quite know how to present his parting gift to Happy
in a manner conducive to pleasant dinner conversation.

"I can't believe you left him at the bottom of a well," Reva marveled.
She had loved her own father a great deal and couldn't imagine an ani-
mosity such as the one that existed between Wendell and his sire.

"I can't believe I didn't shovel it in," came Wendell's reply. He probably would have, but the shovel had been down in the well with Happy.

Reva, too, told her history, and as was the case with Wendell, she
felt comfortable sharing the details of her life. Wendell learned the
facts surrounding the Martin family diaspora from its only survivor.
He heard about her unfortunate encounter with the Southern Pacific
Railroad. She told him of her short, sad marriage to a sweet but unlucky boy, and she described the absolute joy she felt every time she
held her baby. She detailed her decision to become a ship fitter and
told him of her welding lessons with Peacock. She spoke of her relocation to Seattle and her job interview at Roscoe's. As she talked, he
sensed in her both sadness at all that she had lost and a quiet gratitude

for all she still had, and these two opposites combined to produce in him a desire to protect her. He also sensed in her an enthusiasm about all that was yet to come and the courage to face whatever the future might bring. He admired this woman, both for her refusal to succumb to the daunting series of events in her past, and for her anticipation of her tomorrows.

Maybe it was the clams and cold beer, but Wendell decided during the course of the evening that he was going to ask Reva to marry him that very night. If there was one thing he had learned from his time in the war, it was that the future was not guaranteed, and *now* was all anyone really possessed. In his view, one happy today was worth more than a thousand tomorrows that might not arrive. It was his strongly held belief that he would survive the war, but he had stood at attention by the railing at way too many burials at sea during the past two years, funerals of sailors who knew that they were going to make it, too. They had all been going to start living the good life just as soon as the hostilities were concluded and they got back to their homes, wives, and sweethearts. Now they were at peace under the waves, weighted to the bottom in their canvas shrouds, waiting patiently for the last trump and a towel.

Wendell and Reva finished their meal and walked arm in arm along the waterfront. Wendell would have to be returning to the shipyard soon. The crew had been moved from the ship to a large barracks nearby, an old and drafty Quonset structure with only one door in and one door out, which would make an undetected late return from liberty difficult to manage. And Reva needed to be getting back to Charlie. If she left him in the care of Birmah Mae too long, he might end up getting a tattoo or learning to spit between his front two teeth, now that he had them. Birmah Mae was a good-hearted woman, but she and Reva differed on their theories concerning child rearing. As they walked up to the bus stop, Wendell was imbued with a sense of destiny, like MacArthur returning to the Philippines. It was now or never. He hadn't been this nervous since the day he had looked up and had seen a burning Zero heading his way.

"They say the war will be over soon," he began. The consensus was that the Germans and the Japanese were both beaten, but they were going to drag it all out to the bitter end. Like many of his shipmates, Wendell had no illusions about wars in general or this one, in particular. He knew that the five-inch gun he was a powderman for had killed many people, and he knew that he himself had escaped dying only because he was luckier than some. As was the case with many of his brothers-in-arms, Wendell's war had become a personal affair. The bigger questions of God and country, right and wrong, had evaporated over time. In response to a question from a desk sailor, a rear admiral out from Pearl Harbor on a fact-finding junket, Wendell had replied that his purpose in this war was "to survive it."

"Thank goodness," Reva replied. "It seems sometimes like it has been going on forever. Some days, I can't remember what it was like before. So many people have died. On both sides. And not just soldiers. Children. Women. Old people. I just can't believe some of the numbers I've heard." What she thought about next but didn't say was that the dying wasn't over, yet, and that the sailor standing next to her would be sailing back out into the middle of it, as soon as his ship was properly repaired.

"Have you given much thought to what you're going to do after the war?" he asked. He was trying to work the conversation around to a good spot for his proposal.

"No, I really haven't," she replied. "I try to not look too far ahead.

Every time I do, I have to change my plans." This attitude was not that unusual for the times. It was as if an entire generation of young people had placed their futures on hold, waiting to see if plans would even be necessary. There was a long silence. Then Wendell took a deep breath, as if he were about to dive under water.

"I think," he said, giving up on the *good spot* plan, "that we should get married." His delivery had not been as smooth as he wanted, but the words were out there, regardless. It was sort of like shooting the five-incher. You loaded, you sighted, you trimmed the fuse, and then you sighted one more time. But once you pulled the lanyard, the rest was up to physics, luck, or God, depending on which version of the universe you believed.

"What?" she asked. She had heard him just fine, but she needed a moment to process what he had said. She was quite aware that they had hit it off and that she had already developed her own feelings for him, but even so, the proposal was unexpected.

"I want you to marry me," he replied. "I have fallen in love with you and want you to be my wife. After the war ends, we can live wherever you want to live and do whatever you want to do, but we will do it to-gether." Wendell was proud of himself. It was going better than he had thought it might. He hadn't passed out, or thrown up, or anything.

"In about twenty minutes, we will have known each other for a whole day," Reva pointed out. "We can't get married. We're strang-ers." As she said it, she realized that the last man she had married had been a stranger as well, so she felt a little sheepish about using that as an excuse this time. Especially since she already felt closer to Wendell than she had felt to Ted.

"I don't feel like we're strangers," Wendell said. "I feel like I have known you all my life. I knew I loved you last night, but I didn't want to scare you off, so I waited until tonight to ask you to marry me." Restraint was the better part of both valor and romance.

"Yes, this is much better," she said with a rueful smile. "I appreciate your patience and all of the extra time." They fell silent then. Wendell had said all that was on his mind, and Reva had no earthly idea how to respond. She liked him a great deal. He was handsome, smart, and funny. He was a wonderful dancer. She felt comfortable in his presence. She closed her eyes for a moment, and a picture of Wendell playing catch with Charlie entered her mind. She watched them play and marveled at how natural they looked together. She pushed the thought from her mind and opened her eyes. Then she turned to Wendell.

"I don't know how to answer you," she said. "I am attracted to you. Very attracted to you. And I am lonely. And I need help raising Charlie. But I am not sure I want to get married again." She searched for the words to continue. "I would be afraid of losing you," she said, picking her way through her thoughts and feelings as she tried to elucidate how she felt. "But that's not all of it. Almost everyone I have ever loved has died unexpectedly. I don't know why, but for some reason, I think I am bad luck to the people I love."

"Don't be silly," Wendell said gently. "You have had a lot of rough luck, for sure, but none of it has been your fault." He figured he would go ahead and address the subject he knew was on her mind. She had already lost one husband to the war, so naturally she would be fearful of losing another. "If I get my killing before the war is over, it will be the Empire of Japan that caused it, not you." He thought of an argument to bolster his case. "Besides, wait until you have seen my ship. I've had plenty of chances to get mine, but I'm still here. Luck like that doesn't run out. And the Japanese are running low on everything now. They aren't going to expend any more ordnance on a patched-up old rust bucket like *O'Bannion,* or use up any of what little fuel they have left trying to chase her. These days, standing on her foredeck is probably the safest place in the war. We ought to put Churchill and Roosevelt on board for safekeeping." It was a lie, of course, but Wendell hoped she would accept the comfort it offered. She didn't.

"I don't want to be the *cause* of you dying," she said quietly. "People who love me die." Her bus arrived. The driver recognized the two from the previous night and knew he had time to light a smoke. Wendell took Reva in his arms and kissed her slowly. After the kiss, he spoke again.

"I will be a good husband to you and a good father to your boy. And I won't die for a long time. I promise." This vow was not just idle talk on his part. He had been afraid many times during the war and expected that he would be again. He had experienced the terror that came with battle and knew there was no shame in admitting it. But for some unexplainable reason, he was convinced he would not meet his end aboard the *O'Bannion.* He didn't know what else to put on the table. All of his cards were already displayed, and there was nothing up his sleeve but hope and a bad tattoo.

"I have to go," she said, quietly and abruptly. Wendell did not know it, but he had just made the same promise Ted Nichols had made before he left on his ill-fated foray to the wilds of North Africa. In Wendell's defense, and Ted's, it was a phrase that found much use in many languages during the war years.

"When will I see you again?" he asked. He sensed that he had just upset her, but he did not know what he had done.

"I don't know," she replied.

"I'm not sure when I can get another pass," he said. "Soon, I hope. But I need to know how to get in touch with you." She opened her pocketbook and removed an envelope, then wrote out a phone number on the back and handed it to him.

"I share that phone with about thirty people, but you can leave a message and I will get it." She snapped her pocketbook shut and made ready to leave.

"You haven't answered me," Wendell noted. Maybe he should have gotten down on one knee and taken off his hat.

"No, I haven't," she said. She kissed him once more and boarded the bus. As the coach receded into the distance, he spoke again, but this time there was no one to hear.

"Well, at least she didn't say *no*." He stuck his hands in his pockets and began to walk toward the ferry.

It was almost a week before they saw each other again, and during that interim they were both as busy as carpenter ants. Usually when a ship came into dry dock for a major refit and overhaul, the majority of the crew received liberty for the duration of the work. But Admiral Nimitz was putting together a fleet of 2500 ships for the final push on Japan, and he needed working destroyers to guard his tankers, tenders, and supply vessels. Since over thirty destroyers and destroyer escorts had been lost during the Pacific campaign, those that remained afloat were desperately needed in action. So while a few of the older, married hands were able to wrangle seven- or ten-day passes to go home and see their wives and children, the majority of the crew spent their time in port scraping and painting every square inch of the *O'Bannion,* while the yard crew tackled the more technical aspects of the overhaul.

World War Two-era destroyers were unique ships in several respects. They were called tin cans by those who sailed them, due to the thin three-eighths-inch steel plate that formed their hulls. They were built light so they would be fast, and most were capable of thirty knots or better. Some could do thirty-five. Although a very seaworthy ship, the World War Two destroyer tended to be top heavy due to the extras that were added as technology improved during the war. These additions included radar masts and anti-aircraft guns, as well as new and heavier gun turrets, and while these improvements enhanced the survivability of the ships in a fight and increased their abilities to search and destroy, they had the unintended consequence of causing the occasional destroyer to roll over during a typhoon.

They were expendable ships built for speed, maneuverability, and long-range operations. The ships were built quickly and cheaply because demand was constantly exceeding supply. By the end of the war, the elapsed time between laying the keel and final sea trials of a finished destroyer was less than four months. They were equipped with torpedoes, depth charges, and a variety of small- and medium-sized guns, and protection of other ships was their main role. Their job was to place themselves in harm's way and to take the bullet, shell, or torpedo that was intended for the ship they were guarding, be it a capital ship, a troop transport, or an oil tanker. Manning for the destroyer varied, but most of the Porter class of destroyers like the *O'Bannion* carried crews of around two hundred sailors. The destroyer had the dubious honor of being the warship most often sunk during the war. It wasn't the most shot at, and it wasn't the most hit. But with a hull plate only as thick as a good quality frying pan, it was the vessel that most often disappeared beneath the waves.

These were not state secrets, and even if they had been, Reva was a ship fitter and knew the limitations of the ship class quite well. The destroyer was not known for its survivability, although, to give credit where it was due, the *O'Bannion* had brought most of her crew home. As the repairs began in earnest and the full extent of the damage was revealed, Reva and her colleagues marveled that the old girl had come in at all. In addition to the patch over the hole that the mine had caused, most of the remaining bow plates were buckled and needed reinforcing. Also, there was a noticeable sag amidships. Additionally, the number one turret was out of commission, the sonar was inoperative, the port engine had seized, and the superstructure was more repair than original steel. A shortage of lead had caused the paint supply west of Pearl Harbor to dry up, so rust was in evidence throughout the ship.

Reva was assigned to the repair team working on the *O'Bannion*, and she spent most of the week preceding her third meeting with Wendell working on reinforcing the bow plates. Hydraulic jacks were used to force the bows out of the hull plates, and ribs were welded in place on the interior of the plates to help them hold their reacquired shapes. When the jacks were removed, the plates that held their shapes were left in place. Those that buckled again were replaced. It was tedious work, but routine, so Reva had plenty of time to think while she was working. As she burned rod after rod in an attempt to make the ship seaworthy again, several realizations came to her. First and foremost, she realized that she loved Wendell. It was insane to love a man she had spent less than eight hours with, but feelings aren't always logical or neat, and she knew in her heart that she had fallen for him. Being with him just felt right.

This feeling of rightness was a problem because her second realization was that she was truly afraid of loving him. Due to past history, Reva was filled with a sense of foreboding when it came to people she loved. Call it bad luck, or divine retribution, or rotten karma, or whatever. There was no denying that people she loved tended toward untimely ends. The only exception to that rule so far had been her son, Charlie, and she lived in constant terror for him. She had actually once considered putting him up for adoption so that he might escape harm. But she had been unable to go forward with the plan because it had not felt like the right thing to do. And Wendell was not Charlie. Reva's bad luck with loved ones combined with Wendell's occupation almost guaranteed that if they became man and wife, he would not die an old man someday beside her in their bed. Perhaps it would be best to just shoot him right after the wedding, to save time.

Every time she moved to a different section of the hull and struck another arc, she was confronted with the fact that the *O'Bannion* should have sunk somewhere out in the vast Pacific, perhaps taking all hands with her to the bottom. She had lost count of the number of split and cracked welds she had discovered while working her way down the hull. Even Bunk Grantley had been impressed.

"Your sailor boy is one lucky son of a bitch," Bunk had observed upon the occasion of a hull plate popping loose at a joint upon the application of hydraulic pressure. Apparently, only rust and habit had been keeping it in place.

"So far," had been her reply.

By the end of the week, Reva had mostly succeeded in talking herself out of a relationship with Wendell. In fact, she had decided it would probably be the best thing for both of them if she never saw him again, because she realized that the more she was with him, the less likely it would be she would be able to send him away. Wartime romances were a dime a dozen, and they could both just get over this one. There was no good that could come of it. Wendell was unaware of this new wrinkle and had called her and left messages on two occasions, but she had not responded to them.

Immediately prior to her third meeting with her future husband,

Reva was standing on a scaffold adjacent to the *O'Bannion*, welding out the replacement of the patch Wendell and his shipmates had installed at sea. She leaned back from her work and stopped to change rods. She raised her welding hood and wiped her sweaty forehead with the back of the welding glove on her hand. As she dropped her rod stub into the can, she heard a noise and turned to her left. There, hanging beside her scaffold in a bosun's chair, was Wendell Blackmon.

"That was a perfectly good patch you took off," he said, smiling. He was covered in grey paint, rust particles, and sweat. He was genuinely happy to see her. "I was just about to paint it."

"That patch leaked even in dry dock," she countered. "Somebody upstairs must like you." She, too, was happy to see him. Her resolve to cut him out of her life buckled like one of the bow plates of the *O'Bannion*.

"I don't think anybody upstairs even knows me," he replied. "And with the luck I've had trying to get ahold of you this week, I'm starting to think that no one in Seattle knows me, either." He handed her a sandwich wrapped in brown paper. "I brought you some lunch, if you have time to stop and eat."

"I can take a break," she said. She cupped her hands to her mouth and hollered down to her boss. "Mickey, I'm taking lunch!" Mickey looked up and waved absently before going about his business. Wendell slipped out of the bosun's chair and sat next to Reva on the scaffold. He had brought a thermos of water and a sandwich for himself as well. He unscrewed the lid of the thermos and poured a cup of water for them to share. Then he unwrapped his own sandwich and took a bite.

"Spam and onion," he said. Several of Wendell's shipmates did not like Spam and complained about the can-shaped substance, but Wendell considered it haute cuisine.

"I've never had one," she said and nibbled at a corner of hers to be polite. She didn't like Spam, and she didn't like onions, so she had no reason to suspect that she would like both on rye with mustard.

"If you are going to marry a sailor," Wendell said, "you have to learn to eat sailor's food." His unanswered proposal had been heavy on his mind all week, so he figured that this observation was a good way to broach the subject.

"I thought you sailor boys ate beans and hard tack." Reva was off balance and looking to buy a little time. It was going to be difficult enough to let Wendell down from afar, which had been her plan. Now here he was bearing gifts, which would make her task all the more difficult, even though the present was only a canned meat sandwich.

"You have us confused with British sailors. They eat bad food to keep their minds off of that junk they sail around in." Wendell had no idea what British sailors ate, and the only British ship he had ever seen looked like it was in much better condition than the *O'Bannion*. He was just trying to be clever.

"And I didn't say I was going to marry a sailor," she pointed out. She was trolling for the most humane way to let him down. Unfortunately, her rational decision to set him free did not seem as logical up on that scaffold in the full light of day. The problem was that she wanted him. And she wanted to be able to have him without worrying about whether or not acknowledging her desires constituted a death sentence.

"That's true. You didn't say it." He had thought of nothing else for nearly a week.

"To be honest, I was thinking that I wouldn't marry a sailor." Wendell could not believe it. She was saying no, although it had sounded to him like her heart wasn't in it. He didn't quite know what he should do.

"Do you love me?" he asked. Maybe it was time to get back to basics.

"There's more to it than that."

"There's nothing else *but* that. I love you more than anything. I want you to be my wife. I want to help you raise your son. I want us to have children of our own. You say you're afraid that I'll die if we get married? I don't know much, Reva, but I know in my heart you're wrong about that. You won't be bad luck for me. I know it like I know the sun rises in the east." This was a long speech for him, but it was an important subject. He placed his sandwich onto the planks of the catwalk and took her shoulders into his hands.

"I think it will be bad luck for me if you *don't* marry me. I think it's fate that we get married. Just look at all of the things that fell into place for us. I was the only guy to survive the hit on the number one turret. Everyone else got killed, and I didn't even get scratched. Then I came to Seattle on a ship that should have sunk but didn't. Somewhere along the way, you flipped a coin and decided to come to Seattle and become a ship fitter. Then, even though you never go to bars, for some reason you decided to go to one on the night we met. Then, even though you didn't even know who I was, you saved me from Bunk. I'm telling you, this is what is supposed to happen. We are meant to be married. I know it. I just know it."

Reva had been looking into his eyes the entire time he spoke. What he'd said had made sense. Their meeting and relationship thus far had been extremely fortuitous. The number one turret was destroyed, and it was a miracle Wendell had survived. The *O'Bannion* by rights should have sunk. Of all the trades and towns in the world, why had she chosen welding and Seattle? Why had she gone to Roscoe's for a drink with the girls? What had led her to intercede on Wendell's

behalf? Even today, it seemed as if there were larger forces in play.
There were fifteen ships in for repair, and there were thirty thousand
employees at the Navy Yard. What were the odds that she would be
assigned to repair the ship of the man who had proposed to her, and
that she would be entertaining him for lunch on her scaffold? Maybe
he was right. Maybe it was meant to be. It felt like it was.

"All right, Wendell," she said, finally listening to what her heart
had been trying to tell her for a week. "I believe you because I want to
believe you, and I will marry you. But I have some conditions."

"Can I have a kiss before we get to the conditions?" he asked. He
was happier at that moment than he had ever been before.

"A kiss is actually the first condition," she replied. They kissed
then—a long, slow kiss that sealed the pact they had just made. When
they finished, she laughed.

"What's funny?" he asked.

"I just kissed a man with Spam and onion on his breath. It must really be love." She smiled at him. "Are you ready for your conditions?"

"I'm ready." He had no idea what she was going to specify, but it
didn't matter. He was willing to pledge the moon, the clouds, and all
the starfish in the endless oceans of the world.

"First, you have to promise me again that you won't die. You have
to make me believe it." She wanted to hear it just one more time.

"I promise you that I will survive this war. I swear it."

"We have to get married right away, before your ship goes back
out." It was hard to explain, but now that she had made the leap of
faith, she was anxious to get on with the marriage, before she changed
her mind.

"I'll talk to the captain. I have to get his permission anyway."
This was a naval regulation for all unrated enlisted men, but Wendell

knew he would have no difficulty. Captain Mitchell was an old married man who believed that all sailors should have a good woman waiting for them back at home.

"You have to adopt Charlie and raise him like he's your own son."

"Absolutely."

"You have to be happy."

"I will be as happy as a clam."

"We have to grow old together."

"We will."

"You have to never, ever bring me another Spam and onion sandwich."

"You've gone too far now," he said.

"Kiss me again," she said. Wendell did as he was told. "Now, get out of here before you get me fired," she continued. "Mickey is glaring at us. That means he wants me to get back to work." Wendell grabbed one of the ropes suspending the bosun's chair and swung back on. He began pulling the guy rope hand over hand.

"I'll see you tomorrow!" he hollered at her. He arrived back at the deck, grabbed the davit, and climbed aboard.

"Tomorrow is Saturday," she shouted back. "I'll be off."

"I'll try to get a pass and meet you at Roscoe's."

"I'll be there at seven," she replied. Wendell waved and was gone. She fitted another rod into her holder just as Mickey climbed up onto the scaffold. He looked fussy at the end of a long week, so she placated him with a slightly used Spam and onion sandwich.

"Mickey, I am getting married!" she said to her boss.

"Great," he said as he took a bite. He pointed at the ship. "Weld." Mickey was a man of few words, and Reva knew their conversation was over. She donned her hood before striking an arc as Mickey began his climb down.

Wendell was late the next night, so Reva sat with Birmah Mae and sipped at a beer while she waited. It was boisterous in the bar that evening, with the usual Saturday night crowd working hard at making merry. In the corner, Bunk was showing the Japanese battle flag hanging on the wall to a couple of first-timers at Roscoe's. From his gestures and facial expressions, he appeared to be describing how he had defeated a battalion of samurai warriors before relieving them of their colors. Birmah Mae elbowed Reva in the ribs and nodded in Bunk's direction.

"Looks like he is describing the battle of Seattle again," she said. "What an asshole."

"I must have been taking a day off when the Japanese invaded Bremerton," Reva noted. She rubbed her ribs where Birmah Mae had nearly caved them in.

"I'm not complaining or anything, but if your sweetie had given Bunk a live grenade to play with instead of that flag, at least we could see him blow himself up." Birmah Mae shook her head in disgust. Of all the people she didn't really care for in the state of Washington, Bunk was way up the list.

"Well, there's always Christmas," Reva said. "I'll mention it to Wendell."

"I can't wait until Christmas. Tell him Bunk's birthday is in October."

"I hope Wendell could get a pass," Reva said, changing the subject. "We have plans to make."

"You're really going to marry him?"

"Yes."

"Are you sure you know what you're doing? Men get kind of funny when you marry them. Not funny ha-ha. Funny strange. Take my

Henry. When I met him, we were both working out at the yard. We would weld there all day, then come here and drink all night. Every so often, we would go to his place or mine and dance the hornpipe. We had a ball. Then I married him. Right away, he changed. He wanted me to quit working at the shipyard. Said there were too many rough customers out there. I told him he was right about that, and he had married one of them. Hell, he wanted me to stay home, keep house, and rub his poor shoulders for him when he came home from a hard day. Then he wanted me to quit coming to Roscoe's for a drink. Apparently, he didn't want any wife of his drinking beer on a regular basis, and he was afraid that my virgin ears would hear someone say a bad word."

"What did you do?"

"I told him to go fuck himself."

"I bet that really helped."

"Not as much as you might think. But then he got drafted, so the problem sort of took care of itself, at least for a while. Maybe getting shot at by Italian and German boys for two or three years will make him see that having a wife who can out-drink and out-weld him is not the worst thing in the world."

"I'm not sure about much of anything," Reva said. "But I am sure that I love Wendell. The rest of it will just have to work itself out."

"The Cadillac Hotel is right up the street on Pioneer Square. They'll rent you a room for a few hours. My advice is to get that love business out of your system, and then see how you feel about the marriage part after." Birmah Mae was not being intentionally crude. She just did not want her young friend to be making a mistake.

"Birmah Mae!" In her twenty years on the planet, Reva had never actually discussed sex or her sexual experience with anyone. Her mother had not once brought up the subject before she went to live with Aunt Velma, and the few times that Flora Hutton had alluded to sex were during derogatory monologues concerning Luke that did not seem to invite participation. So Reva was used to not talking about it. It was a private matter. After they had worked out a few details, she had enjoyed the experience with her first husband. And she was looking forward to it with her second as well, but that didn't mean she wanted to talk about it.

"Honey, you're a grown woman with a two-year-old at home. It's not like you never did it."

"I was married before, and I will be married this time. Now hush. Here he comes."

Wendell had pushed open Roscoe's swinging doors and was crossing the room. He smiled when he saw Reva. She stood, and they kissed. Then they sat back down, side by side.

"I was starting to worry that you couldn't get a pass," Reva said.

"I had to see a man about this," Wendell replied as he placed a petite parcel in front of her. It was wrapped in brown paper. There was a heart drawn on it in pencil.

"If this is a small Spam and onion sandwich, I don't want it." She thought she had been clear on that subject.

"Open it and see what it is," Wendell said. He seemed to be excited. Reva removed the paper and opened the box. It contained a woman's wedding band, a man's wedding band, and an engagement ring. No ring matched any other, and none seemed to be in any danger of being the correct size for anyone at the table, including Birmah Mae. "I got them from the guy who makes the flags. He runs a little pawn business on the side." The entrepreneurial sailor's name was Lester Harris, and from a financial standpoint, he hoped the war would last forever.

"You bought us used, pawned wedding rings," Reva said. Birmah Mae kicked Reva under the table, as if some point had just been proven. Luckily, she came in contact with the wooden leg rather than the real one, so Reva was spared a broken shin.

"These are just temporary," Wendell said. "I rented them for us to get married with. As soon as we find some you like, we'll buy those and give these back." He slipped the rental engagement ring onto Reva's ring finger. She held up her hand to admire it, and it promptly flopped over to one side. Apparently, some poor sailor on the *O'Bannion* had recently been *Dear John*'ed by a big, strapping girl. Reva removed the ring and placed it on her thumb, where it fit much better. The stone was so large that it impeded hand function. It was either made of glass, or the Hope Diamond had been sold to a deckhand, pawned to a fledgling financial baron, and then rented to a sailor in love. "Well, what do you think?" Wendell asked.

"I think they'll do for now," she said, returning Birmah Mae's kick before giving Wendell another kiss. Actually, she kind of liked the ring and the unmatched yellow gold wedding band that went with it. Wendell had gone to a good bit of trouble in a short period of time to try to do things right. Reva thought it was sweet.

"I'm glad you don't mind," Wendell said. "The captain says we can get married as soon as I get a license. I can have a three-day pass for our honeymoon. If we go get the license Monday, we can get married next Thursday if you can get off of work. What do you think?"

"I think your ship is about halfway repaired, and we had better get on with it. I'll talk to Mickey about some time off after he has a couple more beers." She let him drink until about ten before popping the question. Mickey agreed to the request, but grudgingly. Reva was a fine welder, and he knew that this was the beginning of the end of her welding career.

The following Thursday, Wendell and Reva became husband and wife. They stood in the presence of Captain Mitchell, attended by D.C. Becker, Birmah Mae Peppers, and Mickey Porch. With their backs to the slate blue of the Puget Sound, they exchanged their vows and their rented rings. Reva Anne Martin Nichols became Reva Blackmon, Wendell Blackmon became complete, and together they became as one.

The men had been gone for three days, and the woman was anxious. If the snows had been on the ground, it would not have been unusual for a hunt to go this long or longer. It was never easy finding food in the winter, and as the winters grew worse, the hunts grew longer and less productive. But during the short summer months, when the days were long and the warm winds blew, game was plentiful, and it was the rare hunt that did not bring the men trudging home by nightfall under their burdens of fresh meat and hides. Something must have gone wrong. A hunter was hurt or lost, or they had encountered a hostile band.

The men came in at midday, when the sun's orb was high in the blue sky. In addition to meat, they bore two injured members of the hunting party. The younger of the two might survive. He had been trampled by an elk, but he had shown the presence of mind to roll to the side, so the hooves had not pierced his flesh. He moaned when he moved, but he was awake and able to drink. He was the woman's oldest son. If he did not have a broken rib or a pierced lung, he would hunt again.

The older man was the leader of the clan, and he was the woman's

mate. When the elk had attacked, he had attempted to distract its attention from his son, and the large beast had made an impossibly quick turn
and had gored him. The antler tip had pierced his body straight through.
Then the elk had attempted to dislodge the antler, and it had snapped off
clean. Before he fell, the wounded hunter had buried his spear in the elk's
eye. He had thrown in anger, but it was anger at himself. He had hunted
for many summers, and he knew better than to get too close to a panicked
elk. He had seen many injuries in his time, and he knew that his wound
was mortal. Soon, he would die. Man and elk had killed each other. But
he had the satisfaction of knowing that the clan would have meat and that
perhaps his son would live.

The woman sat on the cave floor with her mate's head in her lap. He
had been a good provider. She had been his mate for many summers and
had borne him many children. Some of them had survived. Her oldest
son would assume the leadership of the clan if he was able to overcome his
wounds. If he did not, then the task would pass to another. She felt her
mate's head. It was hot, and he was restless with the fever. His breath had
grown shallow. He would soon grow still.

Chapter Eight: 1985

It was a day that had started early, and it showed no signs of ending anytime soon. Wendell was tired. The forensic investigators from the state police crime lab had come and gone, and along with them had gone the victim, Christine Hendricksen, for her autopsy and official cause of death. The body and the case were handed off to the state law enforcement officials as soon as it became apparent that the death was not accidental. And even though the deceased had not yet received a definitive identification, Wendell was satisfied it was Christine, and so was T.F. Wendell found her billfold in what was left of her jeans pocket when he examined the body. It contained her driver's license and her credit cards. Also, the body was the correct size, and it had the correct hair color. So it was either her, or it was someone who had picked a really bad day to practice her Christine Hendricksen impersonation.

As for the cause of death, the canyon-shaped crease in the back of her skull led Wendell to believe someone had hit her with a hard and weighty object, and the charred condition of the body and the premises indicated that she had then been burned. One of those two acts was the cause of death, and most likely it had been the blow. So by the time the state police had arrived with all their forensic acumen in tow, Wendell was already quite certain of who was dead and pretty much satisfied as to how she had gotten that way. He was also fairly clear on when the foul deed had occurred.

Wendell was not the biggest fan the state police had, and the feeling was, unfortunately, mutual. The reason for his low opinion wasn't that he thought they did bad work. They were competent and sincere professionals who worked very hard to solve crimes, and he would never fault their good intentions. But it was Wendell's view that they tended to see only the tree when they should occasionally look at the larger general context of the forest. As for the crime lab personnel, they all thought that Wendell relied too much on common sense, educated guesswork, and homespun luck. He never denied any of this and preferred to stick with what worked best for him.

Additionally, the turf issue arose from time to time. There was some ambiguity in the lines of responsibility when it came to a homicide. Technically speaking, the crime scene was in Wendell's jurisdiction, but the victim was under the authority of the state police. It was fortunate there were not too many cases of foul play to investigate in Sand Valley, because the two competing organs of the law did not always work well together.

As an example of their fundamental differences in approach, members of the state police were once called by an excited tourist who had discovered a deceased person in the ditch beside Crenshaw Road. When the word finally filtered to Wendell that there was one less person to protect in his jurisdiction, he climbed into the police cruiser and headed out that way. By the time he arrived, the crime technicians from the state lab had been on the scene for nearly two hours. Wendell sought out the leader of the crew, Bobby Littlefield, and asked for an update. Wendell had known him since he was a boy, and he had always thought that Bobby would someday grow up into a fine and upstanding citizen who would have an important contribution to make to society. He still believed that, although not as strongly as he once had.

"The unidentified deceased appears to be in his late forties or early fifties. Cause of death is unknown at this time. We found a pair of needle-nosed pliers, some copper wire, a roll of electrical tape, and two sharp spikes. We are not certain about the function of the spikes. This could have been some type of abduction, or perhaps a torture scenario." Wendell just looked at Bobby Littlefield. He considered going for coffee, but he couldn't do it to a fellow law enforcement official, even one as dense as Bobby.

"The deceased is Floyd Crenshaw," Wendell said. "He electrocuted himself while trying to splice a wire from his house to that high-voltage power transmission line. There's the wire he was going to run, there are the pliers, there's the tape, and those are his climbing spikes. I told him he was going to fry himself if he kept doing this, and he finally did." Wendell looked at Bobby and shrugged. It was all right there for anyone to see.

"How can you be certain who it is?" The remains were sort of charred. "We didn't find any identification on the body."

"No one lives on Crenshaw Road but Crenshaws, and Crenshaws don't believe in identification. They don't believe in taxes, vehicle registrations, or Social Security either. What they do believe in is being left alone to do exactly what they want. They all think that the less the government knows about them, the better off they are. And they may be right on that one. Floyd lived in a house he just built on the other side of those trees."

Floyd had been forced to build a new house after his old one had disappeared in a ball of flame when he had attempted to tap into the natural gas pipeline that ran across his property. He was not a destitute individual and could afford electricity and gas. But giving good money to utility companies who already had plenty of it had always stuck in his craw. It was kind of like paying the government, but worse.

Wendell continued. "His name is on that mailbox, his initials are carved into the handle of those pliers, and I've known him since he was a boy. You'll find he was drunk when he killed himself. I know that because he hasn't been sober in years."

Wendell turned out to be right on every point, but he did not even receive a thank-you note from Bobby Littlefield for the resolution of the mystery of the demise of Floyd Crenshaw. As a matter of fact, Bobby had been a bit terse with Wendell on the few occasions they had crossed paths since.

As had been the case with Floyd Crenshaw, most of the few unusual deaths Wendell had investigated in the past were of an accidental nature, such as the time Dixie Lanier sprayed her husband, Jeff, in the face with Aqua Net hairspray before sticking him in the windpipe with the pronged end of a long barbecue fork. For years, Dixie had slept with a can of Aqua Net in one hand and the barbecue fork in the other in case of burglars, and Jeff was fully aware of this habit and had always allowed for it. But unfortunately, on his final night, he had consumed one too many beers at the bowling alley, and as was always the case when Jeff got into his cups, he became amorous. So he tiptoed into the bedroom, stripped quietly, and then cut loose with a rebel yell before diving right onto his sleeping wife.

As Dixie told it later, Jeff was sprayed and stabbed more or less by reflex before she realized it was her husband and not some unknown assailant who was pawing away at her nether regions. When Wendell arrived at the scene, Dixie was sitting cross-legged on the bedroom floor in her nightgown, chain smoking Virginia Slims and reading *The National Enquirer* while trying to calm her nerves, and Jeff was already gone to that big bowling alley in the sky. But his hair looked nice. Poor Dixie was not charged in the incident, both because the death was unintended and because there did not seem to be any law on the books that fit the facts of the case. But after that night, she was never able to enjoy cookouts, trips to the beauty shop, or Sunday afternoon visits from her cousin, Aquinetta.

Unfortunately for Wendell, the current corpse did not have a barbecue fork sticking out of it, so there would have to be an investigation. And even though it was not technically his responsibility to conduct it, he felt it was his place to question the people he knew. They were his, not Bobby Littlefield's. And one of the people he would need to talk to was Dixie Lanier. In the absence of grilling utensils and the aroma of hairspray, it was not likely that she was culpable in the current fatality, but she was on the list of people who needed to be interviewed because she had belonged to Christine Hendricksen's coven. Wendell hated that word. However, it had fewer syllables than *group-of-rednecks-who-liked-to-gather-in-Christine's-cave-and-screw*, so he supposed he would continue to use it for now.

Wendell knew that Bobby Littlefield and the boys from the state police would be conducting their own inquiries into Christine's departure, and since there was nothing he could do about it, he had no objections. But he, too, would look into the matter, just in case they missed something. He was in the enviable position of being able to participate in the investigation without being responsible for the outcome. It was kind of like having a day off with pay. And if he solved the crime just by talking to a few folks around town, so much the better.

T.F. had managed to be of some use during the day, although Wendell told him early on that he ought to go home. The deputy had declined, saying he wanted to help, and he had stayed by Wendell's side. Now it was drawing near to sunset, and they found themselves to be the last two people on the scene. After the long day of hectic activity, it was calm. The sky on the western horizon was a blend of oranges and reds, as if the fire from Sorrow Wood had leapt to the atmosphere and kept burning. It was still quite warm, but a slight breeze now stirred the evening air. Shreds and tatters of yellow crowd-control tape littered the scene, as did empty coffee cups, drink cans, snack wrappers, and cigarette butts. The state police was not populated with neat people, and there had been an abundance of them scattering garbage all over Sorrow Wood during the evidence gathering.

The tree frogs and crickets began their nightly songs, and as always it amazed Wendell that creatures so small could produce such authoritative sounds. With this background of *chirps* and *skreeks*, he figured there was no better time to talk to his deputy about his late girlfriend. T.F., too, had been a member of the coven, and he might have some light to shed on the life and final times of Christine Hendricksen.

"Do you want a cigarette?" he asked T.F. Wendell had been off the tobacco wagon for a couple of years but had found a half pack in the cruiser earlier that day. The discovery had almost led him to backslide, but his willpower had revealed itself at the last minute, and he had defeated the urge. He wasn't sure if it was the stress of an apparent murder or the daylong proximity to Bobby Littlefield that had reawakened his desire for nicotine, but he knew that if he smoked a cigarette and Reva found out, there would be two murders to explore and one less person around to look into them.

"Yeah, I guess so." T.F. took one and lit up. He inhaled deeply and held it, as if he were smoking something a little stronger than tobacco.

"I need to know as much as you can tell me about Christine's last few days," Wendell said. "Who she saw, what she said, who she was mad at, who was mad at her. You know the deal. Most likely, whoever did this was someone she knew. We have to figure out who that was."

"I guess you can consider me a suspect. We had dinner last night, and we broke up. She said she didn't want to see me anymore. She said she had found someone else to scratch her itch."

"I'm assuming she didn't have poison oak."

"No, you know what itch she was talking about. She said I wasn't satisfying her needs. Then she told me I had to leave, because her new man was coming over at nine o'clock. What a chicken fuck." T.F. slumped against his car and stuck his hands deep into his pockets. His cigarette hung on his lips. He was the picture of dejection.

"I need some context on that one."

"I brought a bucket of chicken and some cold beer for dinner. Mashed potatoes, gravy, slaw, the whole deal. I even remembered plates and napkins. Then, after she ate her fill, she gave me the old heave-ho." T.F. shook his head and flipped his cigarette butt in a parabolic arc. "I can't believe she did that after I let her have both of the breasts." Wendell could tell his deputy was distraught, although he wasn't quite sure whether it was due to the loss of the white meat or the loss of the girlfriend.

"T.F., I think you're better off without a woman who would eat both of your chicken breasts knowing all the time that she was about to cut you loose." Some people simply had no shame.

"Tell me about it."

"So, after she grabbed all of the good pieces of chicken and gave you the thighs and the bad news, you didn't happen to get mad, whack her in the head with a lead pipe, and then burn the place down, did you? Because if you did, that would be great. Case closed, and we could ride on down to the rock castle and get a bite of something to eat before I arrest you." Wendell in no way entertained the idea that T.F. had anything to do with the current unpleasantness, but the chicken talk had whetted his appetite. It was the generally held opinion around town that if T.F. had not strangled his ex-wife in her sleep when he had the chance, then he was physically incapable of harming any woman ever. Still, Wendell was thorough, and somebody had to ask the question.

"No, I didn't do any of that. I just left. We didn't even fight about it. To tell you the truth, on one hand I was mad because I guess nobody likes to get dumped. But on the other hand, I was kind of relieved. When we first started fooling around, it was a lot of fun after a long dry spell. But Christine liked to get into that weird sex, and some of it was a little too strange for an old country boy like me. And it was getting wilder all the time. Like the night that she—"

"No, that's okay," Wendell said, holding up his hands to ward off the confessions of sexual deviancy. Images of T.F. dressed like Little Bo Peep entered unbidden into his psyche. "I am not your priest. I don't want to know this. I'll get back to you if I need the details. Who's her new beau?"

"I hate to tell you. It's pretty embarrassing."

"Tell me anyway. Right now you're the only suspect. If I have to put my own deputy in prison, *that* will be embarrassing. Bobby Littlefield would love it. He wouldn't be able to identify you or anything, but someone would be bound to tell him who you were, and that would be that. But as soon as you give me the name of someone else, I can rule you out and move on to some of the real prospects."

"Gilla Newman."

"Gilla Newman? You are kidding me, right? Gilla Newman? *Our* Gilla Newman?"

"I swear to you that she said her new lover was Gilla Newman."

"T.F., I have to tell you. This has not helped you. I would kill any woman who told me she had thrown me over for Gilla Newman. Whether I still wanted her or not. It would be the principle of the thing." He patted T.F. on the shoulder. "Are you sure you don't have something to tell me?"

"Wendell, I swear I didn't do it."

"You don't have your fingers crossed or anything?"

"I swear I didn't do it," T.F. said again, while showing both hands.

"What time did you leave Sorrow Wood?"

"I got home about 8:30, so I guess I left about 8:00."

"Anyone there with you?"

"No."

"You didn't happen to meet Gilla on your way out of here, did you?"

"I didn't see him on Christine's road, but I saw his Cadillac out on the highway. It was headed this way."

"Good enough for now. Let's go home." Wendell began to ease toward the cruiser. His deputy spoke again. He seemed to have the need to chat.

"You know, when the shrew fuck cut me loose, she said it was because I didn't satisfy her."

"Well, you always said she was crazy."

"And now Christine said I didn't satisfy her."

"You just can't make some folks happy." His hand was on the door handle. Five more seconds, and he was out of there.

"I don't know. It just seems funny that they both said the same thing." He was quiet a moment. "Wendell, do you suppose that I'm not a good lover?"

Wendell laid his forehead on the roof of his car. At first he couldn't believe the question, but then he thought, *Why not?* He had begun the day talking with the two biggest liars in the southeastern United States about a dead dog and how it had gotten that way. Then he had gone on to chat about naked men and high firm bosoms with his mother, which was more of a treat every time he did it. Then, at Bobby Littlefield's insistence, for somewhere around four hours he had discussed whether the burned up woman in Christine Hendricksen's house who was carrying Christine Hendricksen's identification in the remains of Christine Hendricksen's pants while sporting on her nether regions Christine Hendricksen's tattoo of a little red devil giving the finger to the world was, in fact, actually Christine Hendricksen, or merely an imposter. Now T.F. wanted to have a heart-to-heart talk about whether he was in touch enough with his feminine side. When viewed in the proper context, the current conversation actually made sense. When considered with the correct mindset, the question was somewhat overdue. Wendell should have been expecting it.

"T.F., I don't have any idea what kind of a lover you are." Actually, that was not quite true, at least as far as his past performances with his ex-wife were concerned. She was a vocal woman on many subjects, particularly as they related to T.F.'s shortcomings, and the result of this verbal largesse was the impression around the county that T.F. had not always completed his homework on time or with a passing grade. But he wasn't going to hear it from Wendell. That was between T.F., his ex-wife, and everyone else in Sand Valley. Wendell wanted no part of it.

"Back when I was in high school," T.F. recalled, "I was with a girl one time, and she didn't seem to be satisfied, either. That makes three."

"You were just a kid back then. Nobody is any good their first time or two. How did you even know she wasn't satisfied?"

"She said, 'I'm not satisfied.'" Wendell had to concede that there wasn't much ambiguity in the statement.

"She was just a kid, too. Right? And the shrew fuck was, well, the shrew fuck. But look how long you were with Christine. She always struck me as a woman who wanted her share of the cookies. Do you honestly think she would have slept with you all this time if you weren't taking care of your business?" Wendell hoped he was making a convincing argument, because he really wanted to go home. He was hungry, tired, and wanting out of the conversation in a big way.

"I don't know. She liked to use vibrators and dildos and things like that, so maybe I wasn't doing a good job with her either." An errant and unpleasant thought apparently occurred to him. He looked at Wendell with genuine pain etched on his features. "What if my dick is too short to make women happy?"

"I can't stand this," Wendell said quietly. "T.F., I swear to you that I will shoot it off if you try to show it to me. We have to get into our cars right now and go home. We'll talk about this tomorrow. Come on. Let's go."

"I think I'll stay a while."

"Uh uh. I am not going to have you mooning around up here in the dark. Get in your car. Drive to town. I'll follow you."

T.F. didn't move right away.

"Don't make me shoot you," Wendell warned.

The deputy acquiesced and entered his vehicle. He started it, backed out, and headed down the road. Wendell followed, but he drove with his two-way radio turned all the way down, in case his employee was in the mood to broadcast his penile insecurities to the populace of Sand Valley at large, and to all the ships at sea. When they got to town, Wendell pulled up in front of the rock castle. T.F. cruised the traffic circle around the statue of Black Saint Francis and parked beside Wendell, but facing the opposite direction. They rolled down their windows so they could talk.

"Go home," Wendell said. "Go to bed. Go to sleep. Don't worry about your romantic equipment. Don't even think about it. If it falls off during the night, don't reach down to pick it up. If it starts to act up, pour cold water on it. If seven naked women come over because they saw your name written on a stall at the truck stop, don't let them in. Do you understand?"

"But it just seems like—"

"Do. You. Understand?"

"Yeah, I understand." He sounded depressed.

"Great. I am sorry about Christine. If you need to talk about anything besides sexual satisfaction tonight, give me a call. Otherwise, I will see you in the morning."

T.F. motored toward his home, and Wendell exited the cruiser and headed into the rock castle.

When he got to the living quarters upstairs, he noted that Reva had already gone to bed. There was warm supper in the oven and a place set for him at the table. He added a bottle of beer to the equation and sat. Supper was pot roast, carrots, and potatoes—one of his favorite meals. Reva had a habit of trying to make something he liked when she knew he'd had a bad day, and she'd hit the nail on the head this time. The stress of the day manifested itself in an overwhelming hunger, and Wendell cleaned his plate. After he finished, he rinsed his dishes at the sink. Another urge for a cigarette came over him as he walked to the bedroom with his beer. He would have to keep an eye on that. Reva was reading a book and waiting for him.

"Big doings, huh?" she asked.

"Well, it looks like there's an actual killing to solve. Somebody whacked Christine Hendricksen on the head and then burned the place down. I think the whack is probably what killed her, but we'll find out for sure when the autopsy results get back. Unless Bobby Littlefield loses the body or forgets to call us."

"Are there any suspects?"

"T.F. could have done it, but I think his pecker is too short."

"What?" She looked at him over the top of her reading glasses.

"Inside joke," Wendell said. Then he explained the issue to his wife. Once she heard the explanation, she shook her head.

"And he's serious about that?"

"He seems to be."

"I will never understand men's preoccupation with the subject."

"That's too bad because I was hoping you would talk to him tomorrow. Maybe reassure him. Give him the old *size doesn't matter* talk."

"You want me to talk to your deputy about his . . . area?"

"He has a lot of respect for you. He'll listen to what you say. You could tell him that his ex-wife told you that she left him because he was just too large. That she just couldn't handle him. Be sure to mention she was always totally, 100 percent satisfied though, right up until the day she left."

"I have a better idea."

"What's that?"

"No." She kissed him on the cheek and switched off the light. "Good night."

"Boy, ask for one little favor around here," Wendell said to the darkened room. He finished his beer, undressed, and climbed in the bed beside the love of his life. Then he closed his eyes and drifted slowly to sleep, like a rowboat that had slipped its line and was gently bumping its way down an easy, emerald river.

The following morning, Wendell was awakened by the crackling and popping of bacon frying and the aroma of biscuits browning in the oven. Wendell and Reva were early risers, and over the years breakfast had evolved into the main meal of the day. Reva generally awoke first and prepared the meal, and the late riser dealt with the clean up. It was a fair system that worked for the best because Reva was the better cook, and Wendell did not mind doing dishes. On this morning, he arose and prepared himself for the day. His ablutions were timed to perfection, and he walked into the kitchen just as the biscuits came from the oven. He stepped behind his wife, encircled her waist with his arms, and kissed the nape of her neck.

"Good morning."

"There you are," she said. She turned in his arms and kissed him. "I thought I was going to have to come wake you up this morning."

"Investigating foul play and talking to deputies about their dobbers always wears me out. I'm halfway tempted to just go back to bed right now."

"A little breakfast will improve your mood." She took the biscuit pan to the table and placed it on a pot holder. Wendell noticed she was limping a little this morning. Even after all these years, some days her leg gave her trouble.

"Sit down," he said. "I'll put the rest of it on the table." She sat, and he poured each of them a cup of coffee. Then he plated the bacon onto one side of the old ironstone platter Reva had used for years and shoveled the scrambled eggs out of the pan onto the other side. He put the platter on the table and sat beside his wife.

The mantle clock in the living room chimed six times, signifying it was almost certainly not six o'clock. The old timepiece was the only heirloom Reva possessed from her childhood, and it was dear to her. She didn't count the leg as a memento, since she still used it every day. The clock had a mind of its own, however, and periodically— sometimes on the hour, and sometimes not—it would strike six times. Wendell liked to say the clock had one chance in fourteen hundred and forty of being right, and if it ever was, he was going to either buy a lottery ticket or duck because something either really good or really bad was about to happen.

"Sounds like breakfast time," Reva said absently. She took a spoonful of eggs and a slice of bacon. Then she buttered a biscuit for herself and one for Wendell.

"Lucky we have all this breakfast food then," he replied. They both ate quietly while reading separate sections of the paper. Then Wendell spoke.

"We made the Birmingham newspaper," he said. "Our mamas can be proud of us now. Get a load of this headline. 'Local Witch Burned in Sand Valley.' It sounds like something out of the seventeenth century. I don't like to speak ill of the dead, but I think I hate her more now than I did when she was alive." He read on for a moment. "Listen to this. 'Constable T.F. Morgan reports that mystical sexual rites were performed by the deceased in a cave known as Sorrow Wood.' Mystical sexual rites? What is so mystical about a cave full of people getting drunk and stripping down? I am going to be performing a mystical ass-kicking rite with T.F. just as soon as I see him." Wendell slumped in his chair. He already felt the beginnings of the headache he had joked about earlier, and the sun was not yet fully above the horizon. There was real potential for this day to become as bad as yesterday had been.

"Well, look on the bright side," Reva said. She was trying without much success to hide a smile. "At least T.F. didn't mention that he learned everything he knows from you."

"The story is continued on page seven. That part is probably over there. I bet they got a copy of my driver's license picture to run next to the article." Wendell had what he considered the worst driver's license photo ever taken. In his opinion, his facial expression in the likeness was similar to that of Charles Manson if he had sat on a tack.

"Have some more bacon," Reva offered. She pushed the platter his way.

"No, I'm too upset to eat bacon." Wendell loved bacon. It was a sacred food for him, and he didn't want to sully the experience by partaking of it while in a dark mood. "I didn't even see any reporters yesterday. How did I miss T.F. talking to a reporter? Every time I turned around, he was standing right there with me. He must have run up on one when he went to the john. We're lucky the headline didn't read 'Cave Fuck Reported by Local Policeman with Short Dick.' We'll be the laughingstock of the whole state. *Sixty Minutes* will be down here wanting to probe us. I would just shoot myself now, but I don't want to deny myself the pleasure of killing T.F. first."

"You're sure you don't want some more bacon?" Reva asked, trying to lighten his mood.

"Maybe just a piece," Wendell relented. He crunched on a strip. Then another. The salty pork had a calming effect, like warm, chewy opium with streaks of fat and a rind. He took another sip of coffee before he spoke again.

"Well, I knew he was kind of slow when I hired him, but he's loyal, he works cheap, and he supplies his own car." Wendell had entered the phase of aggravation where he attempted to put the best face on a bad situation. It was one of his strengths.

"That's true. He launders his own uniforms, too."

"I don't have to kill him all the way dead," Wendell concluded, reaching for one more slice of bacon. "Maybe just most of the way dead. We could leave the actual final outcome in the Lord's hands. If he dies, it will be by divine providence. My conscience will be clean."

"You could just wing him, to teach him a lesson," Reva suggested.

"But if I catch him around any reporters today, you may be arraigning me."

"I'll keep your bail low," she promised. "Now that we have that settled, what about the investigation? You didn't talk about it very much last night. How's that going to go? You know you don't get along very well with Bobby Littlefield."

"That part hasn't changed. He's such a pain, especially when he is 'in charge.' Bobby made it clear yesterday that he wants me to stay out of his way. So I thought I would stay out of his way today while talking to all the members of Christine's mystical sexual rites association. I doubt if it will occur to Bobby to do that right away, and it's a good place to begin. I started with T.F. yesterday. About the only useful information I got out of him was that Christine had thrown him over for Gilla Newman. If there's one thing you can say for sure about her, it's that she had unusual taste in men."

"I wonder if Gilla's wife knows about the affair?"

"She was probably paying Christine to amuse Gilla so she wouldn't have to do it herself. That's what I would have done." Gender issues aside, the very thought of anyone sharing intimacy with Gilla made

Wendell's skin crawl. He shuddered.

"No, really. Do you think she knows?"

"I don't know. Anna Newman is one peculiar woman. I mean, she married a guy who looks like a cartoon gorilla but isn't quite as smart as one. Gilla has screwed around on her before, and she either doesn't notice or doesn't care. She likes living up in the big house, and I guess that whatever comes with that is okay by her. Still, if she did know, that makes her a suspect. With my luck, I'll end up talking to Newmans all day. I wonder what the kid was doing the night before last." Wendell was referring to Gilla's offspring, Stanley Newman Jr. He was an eight-year-old boy who did not look or act anything like a blue primate wearing a derby, so perhaps Anna was finding useful ways to spend at least some of her long afternoons while her husband was out dallying with girls from the village.

"Well, if you wind up talking to Mr. Frank, remember to hold your temper. Every time you arrest him or write him a ticket, I end up with Charnell Jackson in my office bending my ear for half the day." Charnell was the Newman family attorney. He lived across the Georgia line in Sequoyah, but the legal pickings were relatively slim over that way, so he was admitted to the bar in both states. Or at least, Wendell assumed he was. He supposed he needed to look into that subject one day.

"Me and Mr. Frank are just like this," Wendell said, holding up two fingers stuck together. "And Charnell and I are even closer than that." He bent and kissed her cheek before heading for the rigors of the day.

"Yes, your relationship is truly amazing," she replied. "I'll give your best to Mr. Frank and Charnell when they come in to complain about you."

T.F. was leaned against his car sipping on a cup of coffee when Wendell came out of the rock castle. It was early yet, and the air was still cool. That respite would dissipate as soon as the sun climbed a little higher in the sky. Wendell leaned up next to T.F., and the deputy handed his boss a cardboard cup.

"How do you like your coffee?" T.F. droned. It was the setup line of their daily coffee joke.

"I like it with real cream, two sugars, and a Marlboro 100. But I'll take it black." This was Wendell's standard reply. He had suffered a little angina a few years back, and as a punishment for this offense, the doctor had made him give up almost everything he loved, including cigarettes and dairy products. He only got to keep Reva because he had lied about bacon and sex, but it had been worth it.

"What's the plan today? T.F. asked.

"Well, provided we don't have to spend too much time talking about your love life or running our mouths to reporters, I thought I would try to get in a few interviews with potential suspects while you ran patrol." He took a sip of his coffee and winced. It needed something.

"Reporters?" T.F. asked. Wendell removed the folded newspaper from his back pocket and slapped him in the chest with it. The offending article was highlighted with bacon grease. The big deputy read in silence for a moment. Then he looked at Wendell. "Boss, I swear I never talked to any reporters." He crossed his heart.

"They don't always have buttons that say 'Press.' That's only in *Three Stooges* episodes. Did you talk to any strangers yesterday?"

"Well, there was this one guy, but he never said he was a newspaper reporter."

"If you see that one guy today—or any other day—send him to me. Don't even talk to him. Just point in my direction while making encouraging sounds. As a matter of fact, until the investigation is over, don't talk to anyone you haven't known for at least twenty years. That ought to keep us safe."

"Okay Wendell. I'm sorry." He became quiet and hung his head. Disgrace was heavy upon him.

"Don't worry about it. Now, before we go to work, do we need to talk about the other matter? The one that had you so torn up last night?" Wendell hoped not, but T.F. was the sort of person who could not always put an issue out of his mind. If the notion of shortness was still troubling him, then it would have to be dealt with.

"No, I thought it over, and you were right yesterday. Nobody is much good when they're in high school, and I don't really care what the shrew fuck says. But like you said, I kept Christine happy for a long time."

"So you don't think that you have any . . . issues . . . down south?" Wendell had been fully prepared to take up Reva's slack and tell his coworker that his former spouse had dumped him because of his enormous penis, but now it appeared he would not have to perjure himself after all.

"Nope, I looked it up, and I am exactly average."

"You looked it up?" Wendell asked. "This information is actually in a book?"

"It's in the encyclopedia."

"The regular encyclopedia, or something you got through the mail?"

"The regular one."

"The one that's in the school that the kids can get to?"

"I guess."

"I keep hearing that test scores are down. I know why now. All the young boys are down at the library, trying to find out if they are manly enough. Excuse me—all the young boys and my deputy. Okay. You start off by heading out to Sorrow Wood. Make sure the barricades are still up, and remove any rubberneckers that are hanging around. I'm going over to the truck stop to see if I can catch Gilla Newman having his coffee. I'll call you on the radio after I am through with Gilla."

"Ten four, Wendell. Gilla was at the truck stop when I got our coffee."

"All right, then. Let's go to work." They entered their vehicles, and T.F. headed for Sorrow Wood while Wendell made his way to the truck stop.

The truck stop had been a thriving establishment for many years but was now in its decline. It was situated on Highway 11 and had once catered to the large numbers of truckers who fought their rigs down that curved and hill-bound north-south artery. It was literally an island on their highway of life, and it sustained them by providing diesel fuel, ham and eggs, coffee, cigarettes, magazines, showers, companionship, and a place to sleep. But then the interstate had been built, and due to budget restraints, the exit that had been slated for Sand Valley remained on the drawing board. Now, only locals visited the premises, and the bustle of the establishment's past was replaced by the slow trickle of farmers and retirees as they came by for coffee and pie.

The bell at the door tinkled when Wendell entered. He looked around the café and noted that there were several patrons in attendance that morning, including his intended interviewee, Gilla. Heads nodded and hands waved as he crossed the floor to the counter and

ordered coffee from Dixie Lanier's daughter, Savannah. She was a
pretty girl of eighteen, a living portrait of Dixie as she had appeared
two decades ago. She had been the apple of her daddy's eye, and the
domestic strain brought about by the accidental barbecue fork in Jeff's
windpipe had led Savannah to move out on her own the previous year.
She was named after the city she was conceived in, and Wendell always thought it was a mercy that Jeff and Dixie had not gone to Walla
Walla on their honeymoon. Wendell picked up his third coffee cup of
the morning while silently vowing to make it his last. He had a long
day ahead and did not want to commit any caffeine-induced gaffes,
such as grabbing Gilla or Mr. Frank by the lapels, slamming them up
against a convenient wall, and inquiring as to their whereabouts on the
night in question. He walked to the booth occupied by Gilla and sat
down opposite. Gilla looked up from his paper at his new companion
and frowned.

"What the hell do you want?" he asked. Wendell and Gilla did
not have a long history of warm moments together, but even allowing for that, the greeting was a bit terse. Wendell supposed that Gilla
was battling grief due to his new girlfriend being dead and his sex cave
being closed until further notice, so he tempered his reply.

"A forty-foot cabin cruiser made out of mahogany, not fiberglass,
and a wide, calm ocean to sail her on. I would name her the Reva
Ann, and I would never willingly set foot on land again." Wendell
took a sip of his coffee. "Instead, I get to talk to you. If you ever get
the feeling that the big man upstairs doesn't have a sense of humor,
think again. I see you're reading about our witch burning. What are
your thoughts about that?"

"Terrible. Just terrible. This is the kind of thing that can set a town
back ten years." Gilla shook his round head. He was bald except for

an anemic fringe around the sides that gave him the look of a Roman senator. He was a tall, potbellied, pear-shaped man, prone to wearing shirts one size too small and pants one size too big. Wendell noted that he had some additional distinguishing features this morning, as well. Both of his forearms were scratched and bruised, and his right eye was puffy and blue, like a plum that had been in the sun too long.

"It can set the burnee back even further than that," Wendell noted.

"Terrible. Absolutely terrible." Gilla's concern for the economic impact of Christine's demise was touching, but Wendell figured they had covered the *terrible* aspect of the crime sufficiently, so he attempted a change in course.

"It looks like it probably happened late Tuesday night or early Wednesday morning. I am in the process of talking to all of the people who knew her socially. When was the last time you saw her?"

"I don't remember for sure when I last saw her. I really didn't know her that well." Wendell sighed quietly. He had been hoping that Gilla would just hand him a signed and notarized confession. Then he could go back home and have some more bacon, and maybe watch some daytime television.

"Gilla, everyone in town knows that you were one of the charter members of her coven. The one that has gotten together every Monday night for the last couple of years. The one that meets in the cave at Sorrow Wood. Christine's cave. With Dixie, Otter, Noble, Ellen, T.F., and Rita."

"Oh, you meant *including* coven meetings. Well, yeah, in that case, I saw her Monday."

"But for sure you didn't partake of her favors some time after nine o'clock on the night she died? That was Tuesday night."

"What do you mean, *partake of her favors?*"

"Well, let's see. Make love. Screw like a wild rabbit. Have sex. Achieve nirvana. Climb the stairway to heaven. Shag. Copulate. Do any of those work for you? I'm an old Navy man, so I can give you a few more, but some of them are really graphic."

"You know damn well I am a married man."

"I know a lot of things. I know that Ellen Harrison has been your full-time girlfriend since high school. I know of at least six other women you have cheated with besides her. I know you were Christine's current boyfriend. I know you did the love dance with her. I know you were out at Sorrow Wood the night she died. I know you think you're slick. And I know that every lie you tell me is another nail in your coffin. Now, do you want to try it again?" *You always had to do it the hard way with Gilla,* Wendell thought.

"I don't have to talk to you, you know."

"That's true. You can just sit there and shut up, or lie, which is worse, and before you know it, I'll have this whole mess tied up neatly and dropped right in your lap. I *like* all of my other suspects, so I have no trouble at all with you being the last guy standing when the music stops. By the way, what happened to your arms? Did you fall down while you were picking blackberries, or have you been in a fight?" Gilla mulled Wendell's words while considering the hard look in his eyes. Then he spoke.

"Okay. I slept with Christine a few times, but I went out there Tuesday night to break it off."

"Why were you going to do that? You had only been her official boyfriend for a day. Was it not working out between you two?"

"Anna is pregnant, and I realize that I have been a bad husband. We're going to try to make our marriage better." Gilla sounded about as sincere as an alligator assuring a chicken that everything was going to be all right.

"No, really. Why did you want to dump Christine? And if you lie to me again, I will arrest you for something." Gilla cleared his throat.

"Daddy has been trying to buy Sorrow Wood from Christine. He wants to build a luxury subdivision out there. When he found out that I was sleeping with her, he went nuts. He asked me how in the hell was he supposed to be able to do business when I was sleeping with the enemy. He was the one who wanted me to break up with Christine."

"How did she take the news?"

"She didn't take it all that well. I have never seen her that way before. She came at me, slapping and scratching. She even threw some chicken legs at me. She knocked the hell out of my eye. Told me she would kill me before she let me go. Told me she wouldn't think twice about putting a little shit bird like me right into the ground." Wendell had never cared much for the deceased, but he had to admit he was warming right up to her. He would jot the *shit bird* comment down later. It had a nice ring.

"So she came at you, and you killed her in self-defense? Good deal. Charnell can probably get you off with involuntary manslaughter, if you can give me a good explanation for why you decided to burn the place."

"Hell, no, I didn't kill her. You are not pinning this on me. She was too upset to talk, so I just left. But she was alive and well when I got out of there. That was about ten o'clock."

"Did anyone see you with her or see you leave?"

"No."

"So you're telling me that she loved you too much to abide losing you?" Wendell was having trouble with the concept. It was just too foreign.

"Lord, no. Christine didn't love anybody but Christine. She was just pissed. You didn't dump her. She dumped you. She always had to be the boss."

"How did you feel about her?"

"Pussy. *Good* pussy, but just pussy." Wendell made a mental note to be sure that Gilla was not put in charge of arranging for the epitaph on Christine's headstone. He didn't think one of his tributes would fit in with the somber sentiments chiseled into the other stones at the town cemetery. He stood and patted Gilla on the shoulder.

"There. Don't you feel better, now that all of this is off your chest? Tell Anna I said congratulations on her maternal condition. How about doing me a favor? Would you tell Mr. Frank that I would like for him to drop by the rock castle this afternoon about three o'clock? Tell him I said to bring Charnell Jackson with him if he wants to. I need to talk to him about this real estate deal."

"I'll tell him. Now you do me a favor. Tell me who you think did it."

"I don't know yet. It's too soon to tell. The forensic evidence isn't even back yet. So for now, all I know is that I didn't do it. Everyone else in the county is a suspect." Wendell paused a moment. "Of course, you are the *best* suspect at this point."

Wendell left the truck stop and climbed into the cruiser. He sat a moment and recapped his thoughts about what he had learned thus far. He supposed that T.F. was a suspect of sorts due to his relationship with the departed, but Wendell had to admit that he wasn't much of one, even if he took into account the chicken breast hoarding incident. The deputy was an honorary suspect, at best, and Wendell wasn't really even considering him too much as one of those. T.F. was, respectively, too nice to kill someone and too stupid to try to cover it up. If he had done it, he would have driven straight to the rock castle, locked himself into the cell, written his confession, and waited for justice to find him out and bring him lunch.

Gilla was a stronger candidate, but not by a large margin. He could have killed her accidentally while trying to fend her off, Wendell supposed, but it didn't seem likely. During the interview, it had been apparent that there was no love lost between the two, their physical relationship notwithstanding, so Gilla would have been more likely to simply turn and leave. It was just sex, after all, and in Gilla's worldview, there were around three billion other potential vessels for his love offerings, not counting farm animals and inflatable dolls. The two big surprises of the morning were Anna and Mr. Frank. Anna Newman's pregnancy made her a person of interest in Wendell's opinion. Whether or not she normally liked her husband or cared what he did, he felt that her enhanced maternal instincts might lead her to a different view of her husband's infidelities. Mr. Frank, on the other hand, would do anything for money, purely and simply. He would cave in a skull and burn down a house for a lot less reason than the deed to Sorrow Wood.

Wendell keyed the microphone on his radio and called for T.F. to come in. He made two more attempts before finally getting his response.

"This is T.F., Wendell. Go ahead. Over."

"I can tell it's you, T.F. Do you have any company out there?"

"That person you told me not to talk to was out here when I got here, but I told him that you said I was not allowed to talk to him, and I sent him to find you. Over."

"Thanks. T.F., I know when you're finished. You don't have to say *over*."

"Roger. There have been a couple of sightseers, but I ran them off. Also, Dixie Lanier, Otter Price, and Rita Hearst are up at the cave. They wanted to know if they could have a little service for Christine. I told them that would be fine. I figured you would want to talk to them anyway, and it would be handy to have them all in the same place."

Actually, it was usual investigative procedure to keep witnesses and suspects apart until their statements were gathered, but what was done was done. Wendell liked to encourage initiative in T.F. whenever it presented itself.

"That was good thinking. Keep them there praying or whatever it is that covens do. You can join in, if you want to express your respects. But everyone needs to have their pants on when I get there."

"Roger that. Out." Wendell started the cruiser and began the drive to Sorrow Wood. On the way, he again keyed the radio and called for Reva. After a moment, she came on the air.

"Go ahead, Wendell."

"Do we have any visitors?"

"There's a reporter here to see you. He's waiting out in his car. He says he wants to talk to you about your censorship of the story of the decade."

"I have never been anything but cooperative with the press. Send him out to talk to my mama. She can tell him the entire history of Sorrow Wood. Names, dates, when unidentified trees fell in the woods, the whole bit."

"You're joking, right?"

"They call it deep background. If he doesn't slit his own throat by this afternoon, then I might have time to talk to him. In the meantime, I'll be out at Sorrow Wood. Some of the members of the coven are having a wake for their absent leader. I don't want to miss it."

"Okay. Anything else?"

"You will be seeing Mr. Frank and Charnell Jackson about three o'clock. I'll probably be there, but if I'm late, entertain them."

"Have you already had a fight with Mr. Frank?" Reva asked with reproach.

"I haven't even seen him yet. But according to his boy, Frank was trying to buy the scene of the crime from the victim. I suppose that makes him worth a conversation. I sent word for him to bring Charnell, because you just know he would have showed up with him anyway. Mr. Frank doesn't go to the bathroom without Charnell. This way, it's my idea, not his."

"Pretty impressive. Just like the boys downtown do it."

"I haven't watched Magnum all this time for nothing. Speaking of the boys downtown, call me if Bobby Littlefield comes up with anything today."

"Okay. I'll get ahold of you. Let me go. I need to send that reporter to see your mama. If he hurries, he can get there in time for breakfast."

Reva signed off, and Wendell made the remainder of his drive in silence. When he arrived at the crime scene, he parked beside T.F.'s car and exited the cruiser. He noted that Dixie Lanier's Jeep and Otter's old GMC truck were also in the yard. He raised the crime scene tape and stepped underneath. Then he walked up the Path of Bullshit, past Sorrow Wood Manor and the weeping willow tree, and on up to the cave.

Wendell entered the cavern, and as usual he was impressed. The entrance portal was about twenty feet wide and ten feet high, and a smooth, flat pathway had been cut through a forest of stalagmites and stalactites. About fifty feet in, the roof and walls receded and the portal opened into what was once called the Grand Hall. This room was as wide as two football fields and as long as four. The roof soared one hundred feet overhead. At the back of the room, a waterfall shot out of the wall eighty feet up and fell to a pool in the cave floor. This was the Diamond Pool that was once the focal point of the cave during its abbreviated tourism days.

A river of bitterly cold, crystal clear water left the pool and the hall down a passageway in the eastern wall. Local legend had it that this subterranean river ran the length of the mountain and made its exit from the mouth of Johnson's cave near Sulphur Springs, fifty miles down the valley. Wendell had heard all of his life that it was possible to make this journey on foot, step by dark step through the passage the river had carved over the millennia through the soft stone. His mother had told him that Reynolds Cooper had made the trip numerous times. Indeed, it was said that the mountain was completely honey-combed with such avenues, and that the Cherokees had once used the secret ways as hidden highways, far from the covetous eyes of the long knives. Later, it was rumored that the legendary underground railway utilized some of the mountain caverns during the movement of its human cargo. Wendell himself had once lived in the cave for a week while hiding from Happy. During that time he had, out of boredom, followed the river down the passage for a day, but first his lantern, and then his nerve, had failed, and he had retreated to the world of light.

Christine had spent a substantial sum of money renovating the lighting that had once been installed in the cavern by Stewart James, and in Wendell's opinion, it was one of her few positive accomplish-ments. As he stepped into the Grand Hall, he was greeted with a bluish light in the upper reaches of the cavern that seemed to fade to gold as it neared the floor. All of the geological features of the cave were backlit with a hazy ruby. Periodically, each of the hues would morph into one of the others, and this continuous color pulsation had a mesmerizing effect on Wendell. He thought it was beautiful.

In the middle of the glory of the colorful Grand Hall sat some of the remnants of the Sorrow Wood coven: T.F., Dixie, Otter, and Rita. They sat shirtless in a circle on the smooth stone floor in the middle of the cavern, eyes closed, murmuring an incantation as they paid homage to their fallen leader. All except Otter, that is, who was taking this opportunity to pay visual homage to Dixie Lanier's bosoms. Wendell caught his eye and motioned him to the cave entrance. Otter looked slightly guilty as he eased himself out of the group and made his way to Wendell.

"You seem to have gotten over your grief," Wendell noted.

"Dixie's boobs can help a man do that."

"Bless her heart for that. Do you know anything about what happened up here?"

"No."

"Did anybody threaten Christine lately? Did she have any enemies that you knew about?"

"Uh uh."

"Was she ever your girlfriend?" Wendell had always figured that Otter's interests up at Sorrow Wood had leaned more toward the physical than the spiritual.

"I wish."

"Where were you Tuesday night?"

"I was with Deadhand the whole night. He can vouch for me."

"Having Deadhand provide your alibi can get you hung in some states. It's almost like an admission of guilt."

"We were at the beer joint. Several of the boys were there all night with us. Termite Nichols, Shorty White, a couple of the others." It sounded to Wendell like it had been a fine old night over at the bootlegger's. It reminded him it was probably about time for a drop-by.

"Okay. You can go." Otter started back into the cave, but Wendell stopped him. "You can look at Dixie's breasts later. Right now, I need for you to clear on out of here."

"You know, I have some rights." Otter said sullenly.

"You absolutely do. But I have actually read the entire Constitution, and it doesn't say a word about Dixie Lanier, with or without her shirt on. So go on. I will consider it a personal favor. It will buy you some slack the next time you screw up. You and I both know it's only a matter of time."

Otter slowly began moving toward his vehicle. A get-out-of-jail-free card from Wendell was no small boon. Wendell walked back to the Grand Hall. The prayer meeting seemed to have broken up. Dixie and Rita were decent again, and T.F. was buttoning up. Wendell walked up to his deputy.

"Good to see you back in uniform," he noted quietly. T.F. started to protest, but Wendell held up his hands. "Yeah, I know. I said to keep your pants on. Don't worry about it. Do the girls know I need to talk to them?"

"They're ready to help. Do you want me to move them outside?"

"I kind of like it in here," Wendell said. "It's a lot cooler than outside, and I like the lights. If you don't mind, I'd rather we just sat back down and talked." Everyone agreed that this was a good idea, and they all sat.

"Did anything unusual happen at Monday's meeting?" Wendell asked.

"No, it was pretty much business as usual," Rita Hearst began. Wendell had always liked Rita. She was actually one of Glennice Olive Cole's children—although not the one that had caused Wendell's enlistment—and like Glennice, Rita was somewhat luckless with men. She married Stanford Hearst six days before he shipped out for Vietnam and twelve days before he died. Since that time, she had searched in vain for some meaning to life in general, and to hers in particular. She was the sometime companion of Otter Price, but she was angling for the position full-time, and Wendell figured she had only joined the coven in an attempt to keep an eye on him. She continued with the description of the evening's events.

"We drank some wine, and then we prayed awhile. Then we ate some mushrooms Christine had."

"Snacks?" Wendell asked. "That was a nice touch."

"No, it was a different kind of mushroom."

"When you pray, who or what are you praying to?"

"We pray to our inner god or goddess. Christine always taught us that the divine was in all of us."

"Got it."

"Anyway, the spirit came on Christine, and she and T.F. went to the back of the cave." T.F. looked embarrassed. "Then we prayed some more, and Gilla and Ellen Harrison went over by the entrance. Then we prayed some more, and the spirit came on Noble, so him and Dixie headed off yonder-way toward the pool. That left me and Otter."

"Did the spirit come on Otter then?" Wendell asked. He could not resist.

"The spirit is always on Otter," was Rita's laconic observation. Wendell had suspected that Otter was the spirited type.

"Does the spirit ever tell him to go off into the cave with someone else?"

"Not if he wants to keep his spirit-catcher attached, it doesn't," she replied firmly.

Wendell was both confused and disappointed. Whenever he had considered on it, which admittedly wasn't that often, he had always assumed that the scene in the cave was a bit wilder than the tame version of Sand Valley public sex he had just heard about. He had thought there was a little more cavorting going on in the Grand Hall. Perhaps some variety in partnership. But Gilla had been fooling around with Ellen Harrison off and on since high school. T.F. and Christine had been a pair for some time. Otter and Rita were a couple, and if Otter wanted to keep all his parts attached it had apparently better stay that way. The only real surprise was Noble Harrison and Dixie Lanier, and the surprise there was Dixie. As for Noble, he was as misnamed as Happy Blackmon had once been. There was no nobility in him. He would have slept with a goat, if he could have found one that would let him—but goats are notoriously particular. So it was no mystery that he would ease on off to the back of the cave with Dixie Lanier. Dixie was the odd part of the equation because she was at least as particular as a goat and much more attractive, and she had never shown the least interest in walking on the wild side until about two years after she had skewered her husband. She had joined the coven at that time, and it just wasn't like her. She wasn't the kind of woman who would take off her shirt in front of people who weren't her husband or her doctor, and she was not the type to eat mushrooms unless they were sautéed in butter. As for sleeping with Noble, well, it was just too strange.

"Okay. Thanks, Rita. T.F., will you walk Rita out? I need to talk to Dixie for a moment." The deputy gathered his charge and made for the entrance. Wendell sat in silence for a moment with Dixie.

"Dixie, this has nothing to do with the investigation, and you can tell me to go take a hike anytime you want—but why do you fool with this crap? It's just not you." It really wasn't any of his business, but he felt like he needed to say it anyway.

"What *is* me?" she asked. He looked at her closely, and in the pastel hues of the cave, it was as if he were truly seeing her for the first time. She was an attractive woman, with shoulder-length brown hair accented by a few streaks of gray. The gray was a recent addition. She had acquired it in the aftermath of sending her husband to the big cookout in the sky. She had brown eyes, high cheekbones, and a compact mouth. She wore no makeup.

"A nice girl who finds a good man and settles down. Raises a family. Helps cook supper at the church on Wednesday nights and teaches Sunday school." Wendell did not believe this prescription was right for every woman, but Dixie was an old-fashioned girl, and he thought it was what she needed to make her happy.

"Well, I did all that, and I had all that. Then I killed my husband. Now no one wants to be around me. All of the friends we had were married, and you know how that goes when a single woman or a widow starts hanging around. They have all been right funny about me down at the church, too. I guess they think I'm bad because of what happened. They quit asking me to cook on Wednesdays, and the last two times I had Sunday school, no one was in there but me. My own daughter moved out, and she won't even talk to me. She blames me for her daddy's death." There were tears in Dixie's eyes.

"Dixie, it was an accident. It was just one of those stupid, crazy things that sometimes happen. Everyone knows it. Jeff knows it, too. If he could find a way, he would tell you that. You have to let it go."

"I would be happy to let it go. It's everyone else that's the problem." She began to cry in earnest. Wendell did not quite know what to do, so he hugged her clumsily. She held onto him tightly, desperately, as if she were holding to a life ring from a swamped and sinking ship. She sobbed, and he patted her back and said, "There, there," as the cave changed from blue to gold to ruby. She finally cried herself out. Wendell held her for another moment before helping her to her feet.

"If it makes you feel any better," he said, "Otter thinks you have great breasts." They began to walk toward the sunlight.

"Great. What I really need is Rita shooting at me from the ridge top."

"But seriously, Dixie. You won't find what you're looking for in this cave. It probably doesn't matter anyway, now that Christine is gone. I suppose the coven business will just sort of peter out. Look. Why don't you come to the Methodist church with us? Meet some new folks. Reva keeps them so torn up they'll never even think twice about you."

"I always thought you didn't believe in religion."

"I don't believe in religion, but I do believe in God. There's a big difference between the two. And I absolutely believe in keeping Reva happy, and she likes for me to go to church. She says it's good for me. Kind of like skim milk, only not quite as watery."

"Is it good for you?"

"That's kind of a hard question to answer. I can't really see that it hurts me to go. But we're Methodists, after all. God is our pal. We would go ride around and drink beers with Him if the Bible would tell us what brand He likes. But anyway. Reva likes for me to go, and I like Reva, so there it is." Dixie gave Wendell another hug. They had reached the entrance.

"You're a good man," she said. "Unfortunately, you're taken." Then she turned and walked to the Path of Bullshit.

"That's true," he replied, but there was no one there to hear. "I've been taken for a long, long time."

Cateline knew that something was terribly wrong. She had labored for a night and a day, and still the baby wouldn't come. She was horribly tired and did not know where she would find the strength to continue with the birth. This was her first child. She was nineteen years of age, and she was afraid. Her husband, Gustave, had been with her the whole time, and he had assisted to the limits of his knowledge and ability, but he was a forester, not a deliverer of children. He had bathed her face and given her sips of water, and mostly he had prayed that his wife and child would be all right.

Finally, the midwife arrived. She was an ancient woman named Olympe, and in her time she had delivered everyone that Cateline knew. She told Gustave to go hold his wife's hand, and with him out of the way, she stripped her sleeve and examined Cateline. She muttered to herself as she tried to reposition the baby. Then she came close to Cateline's ear.

"The baby is too large, and he is feet-first and will not move. I must take him out of your womb or you will both die." Cateline nodded. She knew that she could not go on as she was, and she trusted Olympe.

The old woman gave Cateline a piece of soft birch wood to bite upon and told Gustave to hold his wife's hands tightly. She had performed this procedure four times in her long career. Once the mother and the infant had both died, twice she had saved the babes but had lost the mothers, and once the mother and the child had both lived. So the chances for a happy outcome were poor, but they were better than no chance at all. She whetted her knife, positioned the point below Cateline's sternum, and made her cut. Cateline seemed to unfold, to open like a flower, exposing her son to the light and air of the medieval world. Olympe worked quickly to remove the child. Cateline had lost consciousness, which was a mercy. Olympe handed the baby to Gustave. Then she stitched the young mother back up.

"Will she live?" Gustave asked. His voice was shaky.

"That is in God's hands now. Come. Let us clean your son."

Cateline lived for three days before the trauma of the birth ended her young life. She was unconscious for most of this time. Gustave sat by her bed and held her hand. His son, Jehan, was being tended and nursed by a woman in the village who had recently lost her own child. On her final day, Cateline awoke and looked at her husband.

"How is our baby?" she asked weakly.

"He is fine," Gustave replied.

"A boy?"

"A fine boy."

She smiled. Then she slept.

Chapter Nine: 1945

After their wedding, Reva and Wendell had the remainder of Wendell's three-day pass in which to conduct their honeymoon. This left approximately two and a half days to get stocked up on wedded bliss and to discuss and arrange the practicalities of marriage, because it had been decided by the Navy that the *O'Bannion* was sailing with the tide on Sunday next. The ship's basic structural and mechanical issues had been dealt with, meaning she would float and could propel herself through water, and whatever else had not been refurbished by early Sunday morning would have to be repaired at sea by the crew, or perhaps at anchorage when she was back on station. The war would not wait, and it was time for Wendell's ship—and Wendell's hide—to both get back into the fray.

"I am afraid for you," Reva said. They were lying beside each other on silk sheets and pastry crumbs in the bridal suite of the Claremont Hotel. Her head rested on the right side of his chest, and her right arm lay across him. She had already instinctively found the position she would occupy for a good portion of the rest of her days. Sunday morning had arrived, and Wendell had to be back on board the *O'Bannion* by noon. He had awakened early, and while his bride still slept, he had slipped down to Pike Place for flowers, coffee, and a selection of pastries: Greek baklavas, Russian piroshkies, and almond kuliches. He had been advised by the vendors at the market that these weren't exactly breakfast fare and that the three delicacies weren't normally found together on the same plate, but Wendell didn't care. They were fancy and special, which was what he was after. He wanted to have a memorable breakfast in bed with his new wife, before he had to go back to the war. It just did not seem like an oatmeal kind of morning.

"Don't be afraid. This war is running out of steam. It will probably be over by the time I get back out to it. I made a promise to you that nothing would happen to me, and I never break a promise." He held her closer and fed her a nibble of baklava. Crumbs fell to his chest. She had already eaten two of the pastries and was addicted for life.

"You talk a good game, but I am still going to worry. I really don't think I can help it. I remember this part from my last marriage. It's hard to be the wife of a man gone to war," Reva said, giving voice to the wisdom of the ages. The curtains at the window danced, and the morning breeze caressed them, as if all her departed sisters throughout the long millennia were sighing in agreement. She shivered.

"It's too late for an annulment," he pointed out as he pulled the sheet up around her shoulders. He brushed a lock of her hair with his fingertips and kissed her.

"I'll say," she confirmed. They were quiet for a while, each with their own thoughts. Reva was woolgathering, and her mind jumped from Wendell to Charlie, to a pretty house in the country, to maybe a little girl in the years to come, and other children after that. Wendell's musings were more specific. He finally had somebody worth living for, and he hoped he could do just that. In the meantime, Reva had turned to the business of married life.

"We haven't really talked about it, but I want to keep working at the shipyard. It's important work, and it's good money. I hope that's okay with you." She didn't think that her new husband would be like Birmah Mae's Henry, but she supposed now was the time to find out. If Wendell didn't like the idea, it was still too late for an annulment, but it was never too early for an attitude adjustment. She wondered how marriages preceded by long engagements unfolded. Her two forays into the realm of wedlock had been spur-of-the-moment, to be sure, but she enjoyed the discovery phase that followed. It seemed to her that if a woman knew everything there was to know about a man before marrying him, then too much of the decision was made by the head and not by the heart.

"Are you kidding? You make twice as much money as I do, and they don't shoot at you nearly as often. What we ought to do is get the Secretary of the Navy to let me quit. I'll raise Charlie, and he and I will both be clean shaven and standing at attention at the door when you come home in the evenings. The house will be neat, and the supper will be on the stove. He'll hand you your newspaper and say, 'Hello, Mother,' and I'll hand you your pipe and slippers and say, 'Hello, darling.' It'll be great."

"You really don't mind?" She toyed with the hair on his chest with the fingers of her right hand.

"I really don't mind."

"I was just asking because Birmah Mae said that her husband got kind of funny about her working after they got married."

"The man had to be a little odd to start with, to marry Birmah Mae. He's just mad because she has better tattoos than he does and can beat him arm wrestling. If Uncle Sam had sent Birmah Mae to the European Theater in place of Henry, the war would be over by now." He could just see Birmah Mae attacking a pillbox, Thompson submachine gun in one hand and grenade in the other, the pin from the grenade and a Lucky Strike clenched in her teeth. The Germans would be shooting each other as the lesser of two bad outcomes.

"Also, until the war is over and we decide what we are going to do next, I would like to stay at the boarding house. Until I met you, those girls and their kids were the only family Charlie and I really had."

"I think that's a great idea. I won't worry about you two nearly as much if you're staying there. Just don't let Birmah Mae take Charlie out drinking."

"I wonder how Charlie is doing this morning," Reva mused. While on their abbreviated honeymoon, Wendell and Reva had spent the days with Charlie, taking the first steps toward becoming a family. Charlie was not accustomed to a male presence in his world, but he and Wendell had developed an almost instant rapport, and Reva was satisfied that the father and son dynamic she had hoped for was developing nicely. They had gone to the zoo, visited several parks, and enjoyed ice cream and soda pop. They had walked the waterfront of Seattle, waving at ships. Sometimes they strolled a little ahead of Reva, and the sweet sight of the small boy holding the big sailor's finger as they meandered brought tears to her eyes and a lump to her throat. At those times, the two were father and son. But at night, Birmah Mae kept the boy so that Wendell and Reva could take their first steps toward becoming lifelong lovers.

"I am sure he's fine," Wendell said. "You've done a good job with that boy, and I'm going to enjoy being his daddy." Wendell took seriously the fact that he had assumed the great responsibility of raising a child. He had been on the receiving end of a poor effort at that sacred task, so he knew the long list of what not to do, and he had made a solemn vow to himself and to his new wife that he would be a good father. Also, he owed it to a man he had never met, a fallen brother in arms, to do his level best to properly raise the boy. Wendell felt like he was in a partnership of sorts with Reva's first husband, and he was committed to finishing what the other man had started.

"I had a lot of help. Ivey. Peacock. The girls at the boarding house. Mickey. Birmah Mae."

"I wish Charlie could come to the dock today. He loves ships. I bet he would like to see mine sail."

"Don't worry about that. At his age, I can point to any ship in the harbor and tell him, 'There goes Daddy,' and he'll be fine."

"Do you want him to call me Daddy?" They had not discussed this, either, but Wendell liked the way it sounded.

"Well, having him call you Mr. Blackmon is a little formal, don't you think?"

"You know what I am saying. I would love for him to call me Daddy, but I don't want to disrespect your first husband."

"When the time comes, when he's older, we will both tell him about Ted. But that will be a long time from now. In the meantime, you're his daddy."

"Thank you. I won't mess that up." Wendell meant it.

"I know you won't. Now I am ready for another treat."

"We are out of baklava and kulich."

"I wasn't talking about baklava and kulich," she responded, lying back.

Later that day, the *O'Bannion* sailed. She was an aging destroyer that had seen better days, a grey warrior easing out of the dry dock, another in a seemingly endless succession of fast ships heading back out into harm's way. It was a somber embarkation in a cold drizzle. The mist clung to the water like a white beard. There were no brass bands or flapping pennants, no hoopla or fanfare, just the mournful horn from the ship and the answering whistles from the tugs as they nudged her away from the pier and back into service. Very few family members were present at the sailing, because it was not the *O'Bannion's* home port, but Reva was there, her breath steaming in the morning mist, and she waved at Wendell until his ship was out of sight.

She waited until her new husband was nothing more than a speck on the horizon before she let the tears come, because she did not want him to see her cry. But once they began, they came in torrents she could not control. Her sadness was like an anchor on her chest, so heavy that she had difficulty finding her breath, the weight of it crushing her spirit. She sat on a spool of cable beside the dry dock and cried bitterly in the chilly rain, inconsolable at the thoughts of all she had already lost, as well as what she now risked. Mickey Porch found her a little later, still sobbing.

"Reva, you'll catch your death out here," he said. He had been at the office shack working on his rosters for the coming week. There weren't ever enough hours to get all of his duties performed, and it was the rare day that he did not come down to the docks for some reason or another. But he would have come even if he had no job at all. The sea had taken more than his leg. It had taken his soul, and he needed it like an opium addict needs his pipe and a place to recline. But with his old injury, Mickey could no longer stand before the mast, so for him the next best thing was to remain on the quay and watch the vessels come and go. It was his connection to a life he could no longer live.

"It's not my death I'm worried about," Reva replied. She pointed at the empty dry dock. Out in the sound, the tugs were maneuvering around a damaged destroyer escort that was to take the *O'Bannion's* place. Lines were shot and secured, signals exchanged. From the looks of the escort's decks, some Japanese guns had been brought to bear upon her.

"Reva, I've been around ships and sailors my whole life, and I've learned to spot a survivor. I'm one, and so is our old buddy Peacock. He and I both should have died when the *Jacob Jones* went down. Most everyone else on board did. But we weren't ready to die. Your man is like that. He has already walked away from a double armload of shit that would have killed most other folks. But he's still here. And if you'll pardon my French, he's also the luckiest son of a bitch I have ever seen, and there ain't a damn thing wrong with that either. I would rather be lucky than good anytime. You need to believe me when I tell you that if he has to swim all the way home from Japan to get back to you, he will do it. You'll see him again. I know it. I can feel it. Now, go home and get out of this rain. You're back on the schedule for next week, and I don't need you sick." Reva stood and hugged Mickey gratefully. He was not an eloquent man, but he had presented the right combination of words this time. She released her boss.

"Thanks, Mickey." She wanted to say more, but with Mickey, a simple *thanks* was enough.

"Out," he said, pointing to the gate. "You are officially still on your honeymoon until seven in the morning. Go write your husband a letter. Do *not* tell him about sitting on the docks, crying in the rain. That is not the kind of thing he needs to hear from you. Then spend the rest of the day playing with your kid." Reva gave him one more quick hug, then did as she was told.

Out on the ship, Wendell, too, was melancholy at their parting. He had sailed many times from many ports, but this was the first time he wished he was still on the pier. He loved the sea and being at sea, loved to stand on the weather deck at dawn and taste the spray on his lips, loved to step onto an unknown shore and feel the newness wash over him like a wave, loved to stand at the stern at midnight on a night with a new moon and stare at the phosphorescent trail left by the ship. But he knew already that he loved Reva more than all of those things and that to choose between his love of the sea and the love of his life was no choice at all. It was like choosing between eating and starving, water and thirst, living and dying. Once the war was behind him, his days at sea were numbered. They would fall by the way like grains of wheat from a sheave, until they were no more.

The *O'Bannion* sailed to Pearl Harbor, where she took on supplies, ammunition, bunker fuel, and crew. Some of the veterans aboard the ship were not impressed by the quality of the replacements coming up the gangplank. At least two of Wendell's shipmates were downright disgusted.

"Damn," said D.C. Becker. "I've needed to take a shit longer than some of these boys have been alive. They keep getting younger and younger." D.C. was a constipated twenty. He could not believe what the Navy was doing to him. He shook his head.

"I guess they're weaned, or they wouldn't have let them join," said Lester Harris. He was twenty-one, the official old man of the peanut gallery. He pointed at one timid-looking young man in the middle of the line. "They need to throw that one back."

"They'll do," said Wendell. He tended to not hold excessive youth against someone who really wanted to be a sailor. He was eighteen, married, with a child, and he was a two-year war veteran on top of all that. He wondered what some of the comments had been when *he* had first walked the deck.

Despite Wendell's contrary assurances to Reva, the war in the Pacific continued to grind men and machines at a horrific rate. The *O'Bannion* sailed from Pearl early in October and arrived back on station with the Pacific Fleet at the month's midpoint, just in time to stand in support of the Sixth Army's invasion of Leyte in the Philippines. She was one of fifty-seven destroyers assigned to Admiral Halsey's battle group off of Cape Engaño in the Philippine Sea, and she was in the group that crossed Admiral Ozawa's tee, when Japanese naval power was once more tested and was, at long last, found to have lost its razor edge. Over a four-day period of continuous naval battles, the Imperial Navy lost five destroyers, three battleships, six cruisers, four carriers, and most of their carrier-capable aircraft, while inflicting much less damage in exchange. It wasn't all good news for the U.S. Navy, however, since it was during these engagements that the Emperor first initiated the use of the divine wind, the kamikaze. Three of these suicide attacks came the *O'Bannion's* way during the Battle of Leyte Gulf alone, but luckily all three were shot down before striking the ship. When the first of these attacks occurred, some of Wendell's crewmates had difficulty assimilating the fact that the whole purpose of the flight was to crash it.

"I think that dumb bastard is trying to fly his plane into the ship!" D.C. Becker yelled from his seat on the dual 40mm Bofors cannon. He had never before seen such foolishness.

"Maybe he has oil on his goggles," Lester Harris surmised. He was D.C.'s aimer, and he couldn't believe it either.

"Why don't you boys shoot his ass down before he kills all of us?"

Wendell hollered as he ran by on his way to his battle station. D.C. took Wendell's recommendation, but he just couldn't get over the effrontery.

As the days turned into weeks and the weeks into months, the Japanese strongholds fell one by one, but ever so slowly, like dominoes on the moon. Leyte, Mindoro, Luzon, Corregidor. Manila, Bataan, Iwo Jima, Mindanao. The battle for Okinawa—the Typhoon of Steel—lasted four months at a cost of 100,000 combatants' and 150,000 civilian's lives. To the east, the British worked their way through Burma, reopening the Burma Road and retaking Mandalay. By April of 1945, when Franklin Roosevelt left Warm Springs, Georgia, to go join his ancestors, the landings were all made except for the last one on the Japanese mainland, the strategies were all agreed upon, and all that was left to do to conclude the war was to add tens of thousands of additional casualties to the butcher's bill, while the Japanese came to the slow understanding that the gamble was lost, that they had indeed awakened a sleeping giant, and that the rising sun was destined to set.

By the time the Germans reached their own conclusion to that effect on May 8, 1945, ground, air, and naval superiority had been established by the Allies in the Pacific, but still the Japanese would not admit that the end was preordained. In May, Japan announced its formal plan to fight to the last man, woman, and child, when their homeland was invaded. In June, Japanese resistance ended on the Philippines and on Okinawa. Daylight B-29 raids over Japan flew from all the surrounding islands. General MacArthur and Admiral Nimitz began to lay their plans for Operation Olympic, the invasion of the islands of Japan, which was to commence on November 1. It was estimated that the offensive would cost upward of one million lives.

In light of the contemplated slaughter that would surely be the outcome of the assault on Japan, Plan B did not look as horrible as it otherwise would have. On August 6, 1945, hell reigned at Hiroshima when Harry S. Truman allowed a bomb named Little Boy to be dropped from a B-29 named the *Enola Gay*. The bomb killed 70,000 people outright and another 60,000 over the coming year from radiation poisoning and lingering injuries. The atomic age had begun with a bang. When no general surrender followed this action, the atomic age continued three days later as Little Boy's brother, Fat Man, was dropped at Nagasaki, with much the same toll. After this second bombing, the enemy finally realized that the struggle had become as futile as trying to walk on water. On September 2, 1945, the Emperor of Japan signed an unconditional surrender on board the *USS Missouri*, which was at anchor in Tokyo harbor. Of the estimated seventy-two million deaths attributed to World War Two, well over half were in the Pacific Theater of operations.

As he had promised Reva, Wendell survived the war, although it had been a close scrape on three occasions, two occurring on the same day. As the four-month-long Battle of Okinawa progressed, the *O'Bannion* was struck five times by kamikaze attacks. During the first of these divine winds, D.C. Becker, his quad-mount Bofors guns, and fifteen other sailors all went to that much recommended better place. Wendell had been talking with D.C. until moments before the attack, when he had stepped to the stern for a smoke. Later that same day, after the second of these suicide attacks, Wendell had been engaged in fighting the ensuing fire when a shell cooked off and exploded in his vicinity. Of the six sailors on the fire hose with Wendell, only one other survived, and he was burned so badly that he was on his way to the Philippines before nightfall, and on the way to his maker before the following dawn. Wendell caught two pieces of shrapnel—one in the leg and one in the back—but his injuries were not life threatening, so he was patched up on the ship. As was his habit, the following day he wrote his weekly letter to Reva. And as also was his custom, he lied like an old hound about the gravity of his situation.

> Dear Reva,
>
> I hope you and Charlie are well and happy. We are back on tanker escort and nowhere near any fighting. Tanker escort is boring but not dangerous. It is like I told you before I left. The war is pretty much over out here. Nothing is going on and no one is getting hurt. I am playing a lot of poker (which is where the enclosed $50.00 came from) and getting a sun tan. It is like being on an ocean cruise except I bet they don't have canned turkey as much as we do, and I bet everything doesn't smell like bunker fuel because of the tankers. I love you and Charlie and will see you soon. I miss you both very much. I've got to go for now.
>
> Love,
> Wendell

Wendell didn't mention that the reason he had to go was that he had burial detail and there were twenty-one sailors waiting with infinite patience to be committed to the deep.

Wendell's third brush with permanent mishap occurred during night shore-bombardment duty. The *O'Bannion* was placing fire on a hill to soften it up for an infantry assault the following morning. It was a moonless night, as dark as the bottom of a deep, dry well. Sometime during the bombardment, Japanese swimmers attached magnetic limpet mines to the hull of the ship. This had become a common tactic during the Okinawa campaign, so much so that Allied sailors who were decent shots with rifles were posted at the rails to shoot any swimmers that came near. But they did not spot the boys who had attached these mines. Their bodies were blackened with grease, and they were trained to swim slowly and quietly, to not make so much as a ripple on the surface as they delivered their deadly cargoes. They were human torpedoes, suicide swimmers, and, as such, they were not concerned about the trip back.

When the mines were set off, several sailors found themselves blown into the water, and Wendell was one of these. For the rest of his days, he remembered the sequence of events surrounding the explosion as if they had occurred in slow motion. The deck seemed to lift him gently but insistently, and then to flick him away from the ship like a cigarette butt. There was no air around him, as if it had all been sucked away. After he and the steel deck separated, he rotated as he continued his upward trajectory. He recalled being upside down at this point, and as he looked back at his ship, he noticed the glow of the fire on the deck and spreading over the water. He also saw that there was a large hole amidships where one should not be. He was happy for a brief moment then because he believed he was looking at his ticket back to Reva. Surely the *O'Bannion* would be headed to Bremerton for repair. Then he was looking at the surface of the water as it approached on a collision course. The force of the impact with the sea knocked him unconscious, but he had been wearing his Mae West life jacket when the mines detonated, because the ship had been at general quarters, so he did not drown while he slept.

When he regained consciousness the next morning, he found himself floating alone in the grey-green waters off the island of Kurawa. He had a headache, and his back hurt. He had swallowed some salt water, and the taste lingered. He also noticed that he was missing a shoe and his rented wedding ring. It had always been a trifle loose, and he supposed it had been blown off his hand. Wendell wondered if the ring's landlord, Lester Harris, would consider an act of war sufficient cause for breaking their agreement. Knowing Lester, he had to conclude that this was not likely. His next thought was that he could sure use a smoke and a cup of coffee, although a handful of aspirin and a glass of water might be a better choice. His headache was worsening, and he was thirstier than he could ever remember being. He wished it would rain so he might catch a drop or two of rainwater on his lips.

As soon as he saw the first shark fin break the water's surface, however, he mentally offered to swap the nonexistent cigarette, the imaginary aspirin, and all the rain in the world for something a little more lethal to the aquatic population, like maybe a depth charge and a destroyer to fire it from. Wendell was not a nonbeliever, but neither was he among the group of the faithful who gathered on Sunday mornings in the mess hall for prayer meeting. But there are no half-way believers in foxholes, hell, or in the shark-infested waters off of Kurawa, so Wendell dashed off a quick prayer in the direction of the sky. While he was doing that, he removed his clasp knife from his pants pocket and opened the longest blade because it was not like him to go down without a fight. The Navy actually recommended hitting an attacking shark on the nose as a means of discouragement, but Wendell had never held with that theory, and neither had many of his crewmates. It seemed like a good way to lose a fist.

"I'd like to meet the stupid son of a bitch who wrote that," D.C. Becker commented when he had first encountered the information. "I'd smack *him* in the nose and then feed him to a shark." D.C. had not been overladen with respect for the writers of Navy manuals.

Wendell did not ask for deliverance in his prayer, because it looked to him like his number had finally been called and it was time to catch the big boat. He was a bit surprised because he had truly believed that he was destined to survive the war, but facts were facts and fins were fins. Rather, he requested that whoever would tell Reva the bad news would do it kindly. He asked for a fatherly chaplain to be sent, but he knew there was a war on and he could not be too particular. Knowing the Navy, he figured they'd probably send the guy who'd written the shark manual. Then he asked that Reva and Charlie find happiness in his absence. Finally, he prayed that his end be a quick one. He hoped it wasn't a tiger shark that got him. The scuttlebutt in the destroyer fleet was that, of all the man eaters, the tigers were the absolute worst. They attacked even when they weren't hungry, just to be killing, and they would tear a man to pieces before leaving what was left for the scavengers. Tigers had also been known to get their meals to go, and he did not want to be dragged halfway across the Pacific before being consumed by a fourteen-foot-long fish with sharp teeth and a really bad attitude. It was Wendell's intention to make the shark a one-eyed shark if he was lucky and a blind shark if he was lucky and fast. He knew that his own final outcome would not change, but it was his intention that the shark have a bad day to go along with his snack.

However, it was apparently not Wendell's time after all, or else the Almighty had admired the courage and style that is implicit in a man-shark knife fight. Either way, salvation arrived in the form of a mosquito boat, a PT boat that roared in from Wendell's left and scattered the mingling sharks with rapid fire from her two Lewis machine guns. The boat circled back, lowered a line, and retrieved Wendell from his watery predicament. She was the *PT-633*, and in Wendell's opinion, she was the finest craft that had ever dared to sail the wide seas.

"You guys have good timing," Wendell said, as he accepted a smoke from one of the gunners on the PT boat. "I was about to be fish food. I'm from the *O'Bannion*. We must have hit a mine, or maybe a torpedo got us. I got blown into the water sometime last night. Anyway, have you heard what became of her?" The sailor was quiet for a moment. Then the captain came up. The sailor whispered to him. The captain turned to Wendell.

"Son, I am Captain Mullins. I hate to have to be the one to tell you, but your ship went down. It was probably a mine that got her. But whatever it was, it broke her back. We were out looking for survivors when we found you. What's your name?"

"Seaman Wendell Blackmon, sir," Wendell said, saluting. "Have you found anyone else?" He had lived on that ship for over two years, and he knew almost everyone on board. He hated to think who might no longer be around.

"You're the first one we've picked up, Blackmon, but there are a lot of mosquito boats out looking. I know that most of the crew got off before she went down. I don't know how many are dead. C'mon. Let's get Doc to look at you." While the corpsman gave Wendell the once-over, Wendell sat, smoked, and considered. The *O'Bannion* was gone. He knew men who had lost their ships before, and some of them said it was like losing a family member: a wife, a brother, or a child. Wendell didn't know about all that, but he did feel the sadness that comes from losing a good and trusted friend. The ship had been his home. On her rolling decks, he had known great fear and staggering boredom and had tasted some sorrows that time would never erase. He had grown from boy to man on the grey confines of a small, expendable warship, a floating, self-contained world, forty feet wide and three hundred seventy feet long, a vessel that up till now had always nurtured him and brought him home safely.

"You're all right," the corpsman said. "You took a pretty good hit on the head, but I don't think anything is cracked. You'll just have a big goose egg up there for a few days. I'm sorry about your ship. I was on the *Wasp* when she was sunk. I know how you feel." He offered his hand. "They call me Doc."

"This is my lucky day, I guess. Thanks for patching me up. My name is Wendell Blackmon. It's good to meet you." They shook hands. "Hell, it's good to meet *anyone*." They felt the rumble as the three Packard twelve-cylinder engines got them underway. The captain came below.

"He's fine, sir," Doc said. He saluted and went aft.

"Blackmon, what were your duties on the *O'Bannion*?"

"Sir, I was a seaman. My battle station was powderman in one of the gun turrets."

"Well, you're short a ship, and I'm short a seaman and a machine gunner. Have you ever thought about serving on mosquito boats?" Wendell had not thought about it, but now that the idea was planted, he found it had some appeal. He did not want to serve on another destroyer. It would be kind of like remarrying after your first wife was sunk by a limpet mine. And the rule of thumb in the Navy was, the bigger the ship, the heavier the load of shit that had to be borne by the crew. So he did not want to transfer to a cruiser or a battleship. Wendell understood discipline and the need for order, and there had been both aboard the *O'Bannion*. But the captain had not been obsessive about it. As long as a man did his job, he was allowed a little breathing room. But that was not always the case on the capital ships.

"I guess I'd be willing to give it a try, Captain." From what he had seen of *PT-633*, she was both shipshape and casual. Captain Mullins needed a shave and sported an open collar. Both of these were good signs to Wendell.

"Excellent. I'll send Smitty back to get you squared away and get you checked out on the Lewis guns." Wendell was between Smittys, so it was indeed his lucky day.

In the Navy, possession was nine-tenths of the law, and Captain Mullins went to work formalizing the transfer of his new seaman and gunner, Wendell Blackmon, whose predecessor had gone to meet his maker during a night torpedo run on a Japanese destroyer in the South China Sea. That had been six weeks ago, and no replacement had yet graced the *633's* deck. So when the captain hauled the mostly uninjured and obviously lucky sailor aboard, it was his opinion that the good Lord helps those who help themselves. The transfer put his ship's complement back at fourteen, and that was where Captain Mullins liked it. Wendell's weekly letter home to Reva reflected his new status as mosquito-boat sailor, although he neglected to put in all the details of the transfer.

> Dear Reva,
>
> Well, I have been transferred to a mosquito boat. They call them that because they buzz around the bigger ships and drive them crazy. My new station is aboard the *PT-633*. I will be a seaman and gunner, just like I was aboard the *O'Bannion*. My luck is still holding out fine. The day after I was transferred, the *O'Bannion* was sunk by a mine. So I guess that was pretty good timing. I will miss the old girl though. She took me through a lot. Then you fixed her, and she took me through a lot more. The *633* is a fast little seventy footer that will do forty-five knots in a pinch, which works out to about

sixty miles per hour. She is made out of mahogany, though, not steel. That will take some getting used to. You don't need to worry about me having PT duty, either. It used to be tough service on a PT boat, but now there are not many Japanese warships steaming around to attack. And usually the kamikazes won't fool with something this small. We go out mostly at night, but so far all we've done is ride around burning up gas. I feel like the commodore out on his yacht. I have to go now. I love you and Charlie.

Take care,

Wendell

He mentioned neither being the intended entrée on the shark's menu nor the twelve-hour swim he had taken, and the timeline surrounding the details of his transfer was a little hazy in a couple of spots. He did not like being dishonest with his wife, but she had been so nervous about his redeployment that he felt he needed to shelter her from the worst of what he was experiencing. He planned to tell her all the gorier details once he was home. In the meantime, he did not want her falling off a scaffold because she was worrying about him rather than about repairing ships.

On the other end of the pipeline, in the city beside the Puget Sound, Reva, too, was withholding information. By the time she received the letter from Wendell informing her of his new status as a PT boat sailor, she was six months pregnant. It was early March of 1945. She had wanted to tell him the good news since the moment she had found out, but she had hesitated because she wanted him keeping his mind on the business of staying alive and not on his future brood. But once she received the news that he had transferred, she decided she had waited long enough. Wendell's contention that he was safe on a mosquito boat sounded reassuring. Of course, he had also assured her he was safe on a destroyer, and now that ship was the backbone of a coral reef. Reva finally came to the realization that she was going to have to rely on her husband's promise that he would come home. It was really all she could do. So she sent Wendell a letter detailing all of the current events from home, including the fact that he was going to be a father. He received the letter on a rainy day in early April, the same day that marked the demise of President Roosevelt.

Dear Wendell,

I am happy to hear that you are on a PT boat. It sounds safer than a destroyer, and I want you to come back to me in one piece. I have some wonderful news. You are going to be a father. We are having a baby. I don't know if it was the kulich or the baklava, but it had to be one of them. I am about six months along, so it will be sometime in June. We never really talked about children, but there has been so much we haven't talked about. I hope we have a little girl, but I bet that you want a boy. As soon as you get this letter, send me your picks for names, because I am likely to see the baby before I see you. I am not showing too much, and Mickey says I can work one more month if I feel well enough. He is mad at me for being pregnant. You know how he is. He said, "I knew it, I just knew it. One of my best damn welders, too." He talks tough, but he is a nice man, and he has always been good to me. Don't worry about our money. I have been able to save most of your pay plus all of your extra money from playing poker. So we will be fine when I quit. I asked Mrs. Bellamy about staying on at the boarding house after the baby is born, and she told me that I had better. So that's settled. I will work another month or so, then I will quit working at the shipyard and have your baby. Then I will wait for you to come home and hold him or her. I love you. Be safe.

Reva

Wendell couldn't believe the news at first. He reread the letter and then read it again. It was wonderful news. First he had found the woman of his dreams, and now they were going to have a baby together. The only way it could get any better would be if people would quit trying to kill him, and with the way the war was going, Wendell knew he only had to make it a few more months. The shark incident had strengthened his conviction that he was going to make it, that he was destined to survive. His new friend and shipmate Smitty had hit the nail on the head with his observation on that encounter: "Boy, you should be shark shit on the bottom of the sea right now." He was a plain speaker, a career sailor who had been busted back to seaman so many times he wasn't sure what his actual rank should be. Wendell had to agree with Smitty's assessment. He immediately wrote Reva a return letter.

Dear Reva,

I am very happy for us. I kind of hope we have a little girl, too. Then we'll have one of each. But really, it doesn't matter. As long as you and the baby are okay, I will be happy with whatever you have. Why don't you pick out the names? If it is a boy, please do not name him Wendell, Junior. For that matter, don't name him Happy, either. Other than that, it is up to you. I am enclosing some more poker money be-

cause the boys on the *633* don't play cards any better than the
boys on the *O'Bannion* did. Speaking of the *O'Bannion*, Lester Harris went down with the ship. He was the guy I rented
the rings from. I don't know anything about his family, so I
guess they are ours now. Or at least, yours are. Mine slipped
off my finger somewhere, and I can't find it. I guess you have
quit work by now, and I hope you are doing all right. My
mother never seemed to have much trouble having children,
so maybe you will just breeze right on through, too. Take care
of yourself and Charlie. Take care of the baby, too. I hope I
will see you soon.

Love
Wendell

By the time Reva received this letter, the war in Europe was over,
and she was optimistic that the war in the Pacific would not be far
behind. She worked at the Navy Yard until April. Then she resigned
to have her baby. On June 22, the same day the Japanese surrendered
at Okinawa, she delivered an eight-pound baby girl. Reva named her
daughter Abby Louise, and she was perfect. She had her father's blue
eyes and her mother's black hair. Wendell received word of his new
baby in July.

Dear Wendell,
We have a little girl. She was born on June 22, and I
named her Abby Louise. She was born with a head full of hair,
and she was as mad as a wet hen when she got here. I didn't
have any trouble to speak of. Charlie is very good with her
and wants to help me with her. I let him rock her some, and

he sings to her when he does. Now you have three good reasons to get yourself back here. You can't see it in the pictures I have sent, but she has blue eyes just like you do. Mickey came to see her, and he said that she had welder's hands. I think he must be looking for my replacement. Birmah Mae says to tell you hello. She has heard from Henry, and they are about to ship him home. She says that seeing Abby has made her want to have a little girl, and if Henry wants to be involved in making her, he had better get on back. I hope your turn comes soon. To get on back, I mean, not to make a little girl with Birmah Mae. Please, please be careful. As we get closer to the end of the war, I get more and more afraid that something will happen right at the very last. You have to keep your eyes open a little while longer and not let that happen. It would be too cruel. I have already had one husband who never got to see his child. I could not stand for that to happen again. I love you. Be careful.

Reva

During this letter's circuitous journey to Wendell, first Hiroshima and then Nagasaki were sacrificed to the gods of war. On August 14, the Japanese accepted the terms of an unconditional surrender. And on September 2, 1945, Harry Truman declared VJ Day. It was done. All Wendell had to do now was not drown or slip on a bar of soap as he made his way back to his family. His intuition had been correct. He had survived the war.

Amisi began to cook the evening meal as the sun dipped toward the horizon. She intended to prepare a honey omelet and seed cakes to serve to her husband, Ibana, along with bread beer. They did not eat this well every night, but tonight they would celebrate. She was with child again, and Ibana would be pleased. He was a worker at the tomb and was paid his daily wages in bread, so they had plenty of that staff of life to eat and for the preparation of beer. He had worked at the tomb since he was a boy and had been there for five years when the two had married. Amisi had been twelve, and Ibana had been fifteen. In another year her oldest son would begin his career there. Soon after, her second son would join them. There were 20,000 workers at the tomb—men, boys, and women—and it was said that the labor would last for more than a lifetime.

Amisi had been disconcerted since awakening early that morning, when she had discovered her husband's cat staring with unblinking eyes at Ibana as he slept on his mat. She did not like the cat, but her husband doted on him, and Amisi had to admit that the animal kept the snakes and rats under control in their dwelling. Her mother had believed that cats could move between this world and the afterlife and that they were portents of disaster. Amisi did not know if that was true, but she knew she did not like the cat, and she did not like it staring at her husband while he slept. She shooed the feline away before waking her husband and sons. She fed Ibana gruel and cold bread for his breakfast. Then she sent him out to meet the morning.

They brought Ibana home as the last of the light melted into the waters of the Nile. He had been helping to unload a block of stone from a barge, when the cradle had broken and he had been crushed. He was not dead,

but it would have been better if he had died immediately. He lingered through the night, attended by his wife, his two sons, and his cat, which sat and quietly stared at him. At the first hint of the rising of the sun, Ibana's final breath rasped as it flowed over his pale lips. His cat hissed, arched his back, and ran out the door of their dwelling. He ran across the dooryard, through the small irrigated patches of garden that belonged to the work-men, and out onto the rich delta that bordered the river. He ran hard to catch his master, who had already gone before him to meet Ra.

CHAPTER TEN: 1985

Wendell arrived back in town at two thirty. As he came in sight of the rock castle, he noted with no great surprise that Mr. Frank's Cadillac was already there. Frank Newman liked to start early, stay late, and be a pain in the neck during the interim. It was the method by which he had made his fortune. Wendell thought it was a little unusual that Charnell Jackson's Lincoln wasn't also in town, but maybe they had ridden together, or maybe Charnell had hung himself in disgust for being Mr. Frank's lawyer. He drove around the traffic circle and pulled up behind the vehicle. He decided to sit for a few moments to gather his thoughts, both about what he had already learned, which wasn't much, and about what he wished to discuss with the patriarch of the Newman clan.

He had to admit that he was a little shy of viable suspects so far. T.F. was the jilted lover, which was always a good bet for a heat-of-the-moment killer, but the big deputy had been a little too relieved at being the cuckold to be a serious candidate. Wendell was no longer surprised by much, but he would be taken aback if T.F. turned out to be his man. Gilla Newman did double duty as the new boyfriend and as the person who had dumped the deceased, and he had even confessed to a tussle with Christine before she died. As much as Wendell would like to pin the whole mess on Gilla and send him on over to Limestone for thirty years or so, the fact was that the younger Newman just didn't feel like a good fit for the deed. He would not want to have to defend his theory formally, but he believed Gilla just wasn't mean enough, smart enough, or ambitious enough to be a killer. Still, he might have committed the crime accidentally, so he couldn't be ruled out completely. The rest of the members of the coven seemed to lack some combination of motive, means, or opportunity. Most of them lacked all three. He still had to talk to Ellen and Noble Harrison and Anna Newman, and, of course, he had the upcoming interview with Mr. Frank. But so far, he had no really outstanding suspects or leads. He wondered if the official investigator, Bobby Littlefield, was doing any better.

Wendell got out of the cruiser in the shadow of Black St. Francis, the statue that occupied the position of honor in the center of the traffic circle opposite the rock castle. The concrete patriarch had resided in the middle of town for a decade, donated by that most holy and devout of Catholics, Frank Newman. Actually, Frank wasn't all that pious, but he had converted to Catholicism, nonetheless, after experiencing an epiphany of sorts on the nature of forgiveness. As he had gotten older, he had begun to worry about going to hell when he died. He had not always been a nice man, and in his time he had done some very bad things in the name of profit. And the thought of eternal damnation made his feet get hot every time he considered on it. Then he discovered what he liked to call The Big Loophole. It came to his attention that in the Catholic faith, it was possible to have his sins washed away merely by owning up to them and asking for forgiveness. While researching the matter, Frank had apparently skipped over all the parts that dealt with true contrition, living a good life, and honest faithfulness. But regardless of those details, he liked a religion that would let you do whatever you wanted to do, provided you stepped into the confessional once a week and promised you were sorry as could be and you wouldn't let it happen again. It was like having a personalized get-out-of-hell-free card.

So Frank converted, and he made Gilla follow suit. It had been the talk of Sand Valley because at that time the Catholic presence in the area had been small. There wasn't even a church for them to attend, and Frank and Gilla had to drive to Fort Payne or Rome every Sunday so Frank could receive his weekly dose of absolution.

"Frank thinks God is stupid, I guess," Wendell said, when Mr. Frank made his leap of faith. "He wants to have his cake and eat it, too. If I can figure out his angle, I am fairly certain the big man upstairs will have no trouble sorting out the fact that Frank is playing both ends against the middle."

"Frank has a young soul," Reva had once observed. "Once it cures out for forty or fifty more lifetimes, he might be all right."

"If you say so," Wendell had replied.

The Newman conversion was the precipitating factor in the arrival of Black Saint Francis on the town square. One of Frank's conceptions about his newfound faith was that he should donate lavishly on behalf of the church, so he commissioned a statue to be made for the town. Unfortunately, granite and bronze sculptures were very expensive, and Frank didn't want to spend too much money while securing his place in heaven. So he selected concrete as his medium of worship, and he chose Saint Francis as his subject because the artisan he had hired, Burton Cale, already owned a large mold of that particular pillar of the church. In reality, Burton's expertise lay more in the direction of septic tanks and cemetery vaults, but he had acquired a few statue forms over the years to help make ends meet when business was slow. The finished product had been a very good likeness of Saint Francis, but it had been awfully white, so Frank had instructed Gilla to have the statue painted black with a top coat of dark green. He wanted it to look like an old iron statue that had weathered over time, and according to *Southern Living*, this was the way to accomplish that look. The paint job had gone awry, however, which is how paint jobs will sometimes go if Otter Price is performing them for drinking money, and the resulting statue had been as black as a tar pit at midnight. This unusual color had been noticed right away at the unveiling. Frank had let Gilla take care of all of the details involved with the dedication ceremony and had not actually seen Saint Francis after he had been painted. Thus, he was a bit surprised when he snatched the sheet away and, along with most of the rest of Sand Valley's residents, gazed upon the inspirational features of Black Saint Francis, patron saint of animals, lace makers, and cut-rate paint jobs.

"I thought Saint Francis was a white guy," T.F. had observed.

"Mr. Frank is going to hell now, for sure," Wendell had whispered to Reva. It was kind of exciting, in a damned-for-eternity sort of way.

Now, ten years down the road, Black Saint Francis had weathered to an extent, but he was still pretty black as he stood up there on his pedestal, as were the birds on his shoulder and the little rabbits nibbling concrete lettuce at his sandaled feet. Wendell wasn't sure what the half-life of cement was, and he didn't know if the stature would survive long enough to ever look like aged cast iron. But that was okay. He had grown to like Black Saint Francis just as he was. In Wendell's mind, he had become the patron saint of Sand Valley. A flawed town needed a flawed benefactor, one who could understand the less-than-perfect nature of those under his care and protection.

As Wendell stepped onto the sidewalk, he noticed Frank New-man's Cadillac was parked right next to the fire hydrant in front of the rock castle, and he stopped for a moment to write out a parking ticket and slip it under the wiper. He could have let the transgression go, he supposed, but with Black Saint Francis looking on, it just hadn't felt right to turn a blind eye. He walked up the steps and entered the rock castle. Mr. Frank occupied one of the leather chairs in the lobby area. The other was filled by Charnell Jackson. Wendell nodded at both men as he joined them.

"Mr. Frank," he said, shaking hands with the old man for the sake of civility. Frank's grip was weak and clammy. "Charnell," he continued, clasping the attorney's hand as well. "Come on into my office." As they all settled around the desk, Wendell took in Frank Newman's appearance. Much like Black Saint Francis, the old man had weathered some since Wendell had last seen him. He was decked out in a coat and tie, as always, and he wore a dapper straw fedora, which covered a freckled, balding pate. The arthritis in his left knee was getting worse, and he had taken to walking with a cane. He still had one long eyebrow rather than the customary two short ones, and it was still as white as unpainted concrete, but it had seemed to thicken as the hair farther north had thinned. His lifelong habit of scowling had resulted in a deeply lined face, with creases at his forehead, below his green eyes, and triangulating from the outer edges of his nostrils toward the corners of his mouth. His chin was decorated with a neat, white beard, and the petite wedge of whiteness in the sea of his scarlet complexion was striking, like a white cloud floating across a red dawn. His skin hung in loose folds at his neck. All in all, Mr. Frank cast the impression that he was an unpleasant and crotchety old man, which was convenient because he was.

Charnell, on the other hand, did not appear at all like the extremely intelligent and competent lawyer that he was. He looked like he was fresh off of the farm, just in town to pick up some seed corn and the mail. He was fiftyish with long ears and a big nose. He was constantly in need of a shave, and his stubble was as gray as a winter day. He wore dark glasses indoors and out, and he was never seen without a pipe clamped in his jaw, although it was rarely lit. He wore a baseball cap with *Case* emblazoned on it, a blue-striped golf shirt, and a pair of beige khaki pants. He was as skinny as a starved cat everywhere but his belly, which poked out like a little watermelon. The impression he cast was that of a bumpkin, but nothing could have been further from the truth, as many an opposing counsel had discovered over the years when Charnell rolled right over them in the quest for truth, justice, and lucrative legal fees. Sitting together, Charnell and Frank made an odd-looking pair. Wendell had known Charnell a long time, and he considered him a friend. He had once asked him why he was Frank Newman's attorney.

"Well, I could tell you that it is every American's right to have adequate legal representation and that Mr. Frank is entitled to the same Constitutional guarantees as all of the regular, decent people," Charnell had said. "But the truth is, someone has to walk around behind the old bastard with a shovel, and it might as well be me getting paid for it." That was one of the reasons Wendell liked Charnell: he told it like it was.

"I appreciate you both coming in," Wendell said, beginning the meeting. Charnell nodded cordially, while Mr. Frank just sat there with a sour look on his face. "I am in the process of talking to everyone who had any recent dealings with Christine Hendricksen."

"What the hell does this have to do with me?" Frank Newman spat. "I am a busy man, Blackmon. I don't have time to jawbone with you about dead people all afternoon." Charnell held up his hand to silence his client.

"How can we help you, Wendell?" he asked. Wendell directed his reply to Frank.

"Gilla told me this morning that you were trying to do some business with the deceased." Frank did not like the Gilla nomenclature, and as a courtesy, Wendell did not usually use it in his presence. But the old man had dispensed with the courtesies right at the starting gate today, thus setting the tone of the interview, so all bets were off. "What can you tell me about that?"

"I was trying to get her to sell me Sorrow Wood. I made her a hell of an offer, too. I offered her close to a million dollars for the farm and the mountain, but the damn woman wouldn't sell." Frank Newman sounded disgusted.

"Thinking about going into the tourist business, Frank?" Wendell asked. He, personally, couldn't see it, but you just never knew what a Newman might do.

"Hell, no. There ain't nothing to tour out there except that damn cave, and I told her that she could keep it. I just wanted the farm and the mountain. I'm going to build a luxury subdivision out there. You probably don't know this, but Sorrow Wood is the exact midpoint between Birmingham and Chattanooga. Look on a map if you don't believe it. Ninety miles each way to town, right up and down the interstate. Just right for a nice commute for the rich folks. And I am going to put two hundred high-dollar homes on that property and sell one to every doctor and lawyer in both of those cities who has enough money to buy in."

"I'm missing something," Wendell said. "To hear you talk, it sounds like the deal is already made. I thought you said she wouldn't sell the property to you."

Mr. Frank sighed. "You don't understand business. She was negotiating. She was sweetening the pot. Sooner or later, we would have found a price we both could live with, and then we would have dropped the hammer."

"When did you last see her?"

"It was last Wednesday. That was the day she told me she wouldn't sell the property. Charnell was there." Charnell nodded. "This past Monday, I sent word to her by Stanley that I wanted to meet with her again. She called me and told me she would see me today. But I guess that's out now." He sounded peeved that Christine would not be making her afternoon meeting.

"What will you do now about your subdivision?" Wendell asked. "Give up on the idea?"

"Give up? This is a setback—that's all. Now I'll have to deal with whoever inherits Sorrow Wood. I have Charnell tracking that down right now. I know that woman had a grown son. Maybe he will like the sound of a million dollars. Anyway, to answer your question, I am still going to put in my subdivision. Did I tell you what the name is going to be?"

"You didn't say, Frank." Gilla's Grotto? Mr. Frank's Revenge?

"Newman's Retreat," Frank said with a flourish. He was like a child with a Snickers bar.

"That's nice, Frank. Real fancy. Gilla said you told him to find another girlfriend."

"Damn right I told him. I told that boy to put his dick back into

his pants before he ended up costing me some big money. I told him
he had a perfectly good wife at home, and if he needed some love, that's
where he was supposed to get it. I told him I had better not hear anymore talk about him rolling around in a cave with some floozy. Here
I was, trying to work the woman, and behind my back, my own boy
was working her, too, if you catch my drift. Sleeping with the enemy.
Guess how I found out? When she called me this past Monday to tell
me we would meet today, she told me herself. I am not shitting you!
She said "Oh, by the way. I am screwing your boy, and that's going to
cost you a few grand extra." I have only been speechless four times in
my life, and that was one of them." Wendell was afraid to ask about
the other three.

"How did Gilla take it when you told him he had to break off
the romance?"

"*Stanley* does what I tell him to do."

"Did his wife know about the affair?"

"I don't know if she did or not, but she's no dummy. She might
have an idea that something was up. But in case she didn't, I don't
want you talking to her and letting the cat out of the bag."

"Well, Frank, I am going to need to talk to her. But I will try to
be discreet."

"Why the hell do you have to bother the poor woman?" Frank
asked. "She has enough on her mind, what with being pregnant and
all." Wendell was inclined to agree that anyone who had made the unfortunate choice of becoming pregnant twice by the homeliest member
of the Newman family was probably dealing with about all they could
handle, but he still intended to have a chat with her.

"To be honest, I need to talk to her because she had a motive. She
is the betrayed wife. Sometimes betrayed wives just let it go, kind of

like they appreciate the extra help. Sometimes they decide to kill their husbands. And sometimes they choose to take out the competition. Just like sometimes disgruntled businessmen have to remove obstacles when those obstacles won't be reasonable." Wendell threw that one in just to see if Charnell was awake. He was.

"Whoa, whoa, whoa. Time out," Charnell said, making the "T" sign with his hands. "We came down here voluntarily to try to help you with your investigation. There is no call to be talking about removing obstacles."

"You're right," Wendell agreed. "For the record, I don't think Frank did it. The reason I don't think he did it is because the victim's demise is likely to cost him time, money, and trouble. He would be better off with her alive—although that cane he's carrying would have made a nice crease in the back of her head, if he had been so inclined." Frank looked at the cane in his hand, then dropped it like a hot poker. "And I really don't think Anna had anything to do with it either. But I have to talk to her.

"Frank, I have also talked to a lot of folks who aren't related to you, so it's not like I'm singling you out. Charnell, you're welcome to be there when I talk to Anna, if it will make Frank any happier." Since he billed by the hour, Charnell nodded at the idea. Frank grunted his assent, so Wendell and Charnell made the plan to sit down with Anna the following day, Friday. They agreed to meet at the truck stop at eight o'clock for breakfast and a chat, provided it was a good time for Anna.

"I notice you didn't say you didn't think Stanley did it," Charnell said.

"No, I didn't," Wendell agreed. He couldn't rule *everyone* out. If he did, that would leave only suicide, and it would be tough to explain how Christine had killed herself by hitting the back of her skull with a blunt object before lighting her own remains on fire. The scenario had some logistical problems that would be difficult to put to rest.

"Are we through now?" Frank asked. He was feeling beside his chair for the dropped cane.

"I have one more question," Wendell said.

"I was playing poker with him and some of the boys at the club until the early hours of Wednesday morning," Frank said, pointing at Charnell. "My own lawyer won a thousand bucks off of me. Does *that* finish us up?"

"We are through," Wendell said. The three men stood, and he again shook Charnell's hand. Frank decided to forgo the niceties and just stomped on out to his car. The attorney started to leave, but Wendell held him up a moment. "Wait a minute," he advised.

"Damn it!" Mr. Frank hollered from his vantage point next to the ticket under his wiper blade. "Charnell!"

"As a favor to me, I wish you would quit messing with him," Charnell said, turning to go. "I will have to listen to him raise hell all the way back to his place now."

"To enforce the law without fear or favor," Wendell replied, quoting the motto written on the door of the cruiser. "But seriously, I will tear up the ticket if you get me hooked up with one of those nice homes at Newman's Retreat. Maybe something with a swimming pool. No tennis court though. Reva can't run, and I don't want to."

"No can do," Charnell replied. "It's going to be a restricted community."

"No minorities?" Wendell asked.

"No Blackmons," Charnell replied. He left the building, and Wendell could hear him out front, settling his client. If Mr. Frank didn't calm down, he was going to have to spend extra time in the confessional the next time he went down to the church for a tune-up. Wendell put his visitors out of his mind and went upstairs to check on Reva. She was usually in her office at this time of the day, right down the hall from Wendell. But today, the door had been shut and the light was off.

He found her asleep in her easy chair. Her left leg was propped on her ottoman, and she had removed her right. He sat quietly in his own chair directly opposite her, and for the next little while, he watched her as she slept. He had always loved to watch her in slumber. She was one of those people who did not take the cares of the waking world with her when she went to sleep. When she drifted off, the years seemed to melt from her face like wax from a candle. Wrinkles and worry lines fell like leaves from a tree in autumn, and what was left was the young woman he had married highlighted with traces of the little girl she had once been. It was a magical transformation, one that Wendell never tired of seeing.

The phone rang, startling him from his quiet observation. He hopped up and snatched the receiver from its cradle before the second ring.

"This is Wendell," he said.

"Wendell, this is Bobby Littlefield. As a courtesy, I have some information on the victim."

"Shoot." Wendell pulled out a legal pad, clicked his ballpoint pen, and prepared to take some notes.

"Dental records, tattoos, plus the ID you found on the body all confirm it was the Hendricksen woman. We got eight out of ten of her fingerprints as well. We don't have the results back from Atlanta yet on those, but I'm sure it's her. There was no smoke in the lungs. The pathologist ventures a guess of about midnight Tuesday night as the time of death. She had traces of marijuana and cocaine in her system, but no poisons that we could identify. She had Kentucky Fried Chicken and beer for her final meal. She was apparently a white meat girl. We think the fire may have been accidental in nature. It looks like it started when some candles got out of control. Plus, no one could screw up arson this bad. My dog could burn a building better than this. Almost no forensic evidence was destroyed. We even got fingerprints. Lots and lots of fingerprints. I think everyone in town has been in her house lately. Anyway, it looks like it was a single blow to the head from behind that killed her. The weapon was a smooth, tubular-shaped wooden object, like maybe a ball bat. From the one small splinter we got, we think it was hickory. There were the barest traces of some type of color particles embedded in the wound that suggest the weapon may have been painted. Red and green. As you know, she wasn't robbed. And the rape kit came back clean." Bobby paused to breathe. Wendell was impressed with the report. Bobby might be coming along after all.

"Anything else?"

"She had some skin under her fingernails, and we found five different tire imprints. It rained Monday night, so assumably they belonged to her Tuesday visitors."

"Okay, Bobby. Thanks."

"Anything for me?"

"No, I've been staying out of your business like you asked me to." Mostly, anyway. Wendell hung up the phone.

"Was that the forensic report from the crime lab?" Reva asked from her chair. The phone call had awakened her.

"That was it, and I wish Bobby hadn't disturbed your nap. Speaking of your nap, are you all right?" It was very unusual for Reva to sleep during the day. She looked tired, with the barest hint of darkness under her eyes.

"Yeah, I'm okay. I'm a little worn out, and my leg has been killing me the last few days. I think I'll wear my new one for a while." Reva now had two artificial right legs, the original wooden one Ronald Applewhite had unknowingly bequeathed her all those years ago, and a newer, aluminum model she had owned for about ten years. She preferred her old prosthesis, but from time to time, it made her leg sore. When that happened, she wore her new one when she had to go out and just did without when she was at home. "What did Bobby have to tell you? Did he do a good job?"

"He absolutely did a good job. He found a little bit of everything. According to the forensic evidence, somebody with fingers who had access to a sporting goods store and the paint department down at Poteet Hardware drove five cars to Sorrow Wood and killed Christine Hendricksen before accidentally burning the place down."

"Well, that ought to be fairly easy to pin down," Reva replied. She sat up and began to massage her leg. Wendell stepped over, sat on the footstool, and took over for her. "How did it go with Frank and Charnell? They got here at two. I gave them a chair and a cup of coffee. Then I came up here for a nap. Charnell was nice, as usual. But Frank seemed like he was loaded for trouble. And just a little while ago, I could have sworn I heard him cussing out in the street."

They had probably heard him over in Sequoyah.

"You did. I gave him a ticket for parking in front of the fire hydrant out front." He continued his massage. Then a thought occurred to him. "Do we have a law on the books about cussing in public?"

"You do love to stir him up," she observed.

"I do for a fact, but he was already stirred up this time. He didn't like being questioned, and for some reason he didn't like that I'm going to talk to his daughter-in-law tomorrow. And it really made him mad when he found out I wouldn't rule out Gilla as a suspect."

"Gilla is a suspect?"

"Sort of. He was her boyfriend for about a day, and he got into a slap fight with her the night she died. Actually, I think she was doing the slapping and he was doing the ducking. And he doesn't have a good alibi. He's the last person to have seen her alive, he admits to having an altercation with her, and I bet you a dollar to a doughnut it is *his* skin under her fingernails. So given all that, I can't just say 'nah.'"

"No, I guess not." She began to put on her faux appendage.

"To be honest, though, I don't have a really good suspect. T.F. *could* have done it. Gilla *might* have done it. Mr. Frank is *capable* of having done it. The rest of the coven *may* have done it, as a sacrifice to some of the uglier members of the Walk of Bullshit. But none of them feels like the culprit. Anyway, I'm going to talk to Anna tomorrow. After that, we'll see." He stepped behind her chair and rubbed her shoulders. "I don't like this tired business. You're never tired, and you never take naps. Why don't we get Dr. Mize to take a look at you?"

She sighed. "Wendell, I am sixty-two years old this year. I am getting to be an old woman. Old women sometimes take naps."

"That's what I get for marrying an older girl, I guess," he said wistfully. "All the other women warned me this would happen, but I wouldn't listen."

"What other women were those?"

"You know, the legion of other women who wanted to marry me. But I chose you instead."

"Lucky me. Funny, I don't remember the line to get to you being all that long."

"Well, it was a long time ago, and you may be having a little touch of the old timer's disease," he commiserated. "Don't worry though. I'll stick by you."

"Thanks. You know, when the official 'spring chicken' of the relationship is pushing sixty with both hands, there could be more than one touch of the old timer's disease floating around," she observed. "By the way, that's you," she clarified.

"I got it. I got it."

"Besides, I had to deal with Otter today. That always takes it out of me."

"Did he pay his fine?"

"He paid his fine and brought me a message from his partner in crime."

"What was the word from Deadhand?"

"Deadhand said he wasn't going to pay. He sent word that he had thought it over, and it wasn't right he had to pay a fine when it was his dog that was dead. He told Otter to tell me to just have him arrested." Wendell grimaced and shook his head. From time to time, the enormity of the unfairness of the world would wash over Deadhand, like a tidal wave over a Pacific atoll.

"I don't want to arrest Deadhand," he said. "If I arrest him, I'll have to bring him *here,* and I don't want him here." It was a problem. The last time Wendell had been forced to arrest Deadhand had been five years previously, on the occasion of the maimed veteran's thirty-fifth birthday. At that time, Deadhand had decided to commemorate the happy day by treating himself to a celebratory blow job. To assist in this endeavor, he hired the services of Blossom Hogan, and for close to an hour, poor Blossom attempted to provide value for the twenty dollars she had been paid. Unfortunately, Deadhand was unresponsive, as if the lack of feeling in his hand had been secretly infiltrating other areas. Blossom consulted her friend and mentor, Edwina Blansit, and together the two women spent another hard hour at the task, with no tangible results. Finally, macular fatigue had forced them both to abandon the quest, which is when the trouble began. Although a total of three woman-hours had been devoted to the project, Deadhand requested his twenty dollars back because he had not been able to achieve his desired goal. The girls pointed out that they had never encountered this particular problem before, so perhaps the problem was Deadhand's, not theirs. As the difference of opinion escalated, Wendell was called, and when he arrived on the scene, he found the opposing points of view holding each other at gunpoint in the yard outside of Blossom's house.

"What's going on?" Wendell had asked quietly as he eased slowly out of the cruiser. He held up his empty hands so all three of the armed individuals could see that he, at least, was not a threat. If they were determined to shoot, he wanted them shooting at each other, not at him. He was not being foolhardy by arriving unarmed. If he needed it, the shotgun was within easy reach on the driver's seat.

"I gave them twenty dollars for a blow job, and they didn't finish it," Deadhand said, succinctly stating what he believed to be the facts of the case. "I want my twenty dollars back."

"We gave him his blow job, and a damn good one, at that," Blossom replied. "It's not my fault if his dick doesn't know a good blow job when it gets one." Edwina nodded and cocked her pistol. She didn't like disparaging remarks concerning her work ethic or expertise. She was proud of both.

"I want my money," Deadhand repeated.

"How about if I just shoot your dick off instead?" Edwina proposed. "It don't work, anyway." She shifted her aim from his head to an area south of there. Blossom kept her bead on the spot between Deadhand's eyes. Deadhand pulled his other pistol from his jacket pocket and leveled it. Wendell sensed that the situation was about to degrade.

"All right," he said. "Everyone lower the guns." No one complied for a moment. Then, slowly, Deadhand's left pistol wavered a bit, and Blossom dropped her sights from Deadhand's head to his chest. It felt like progress to Wendell. "I mean it," he continued. "If you shoot each other in front of a policeman, the people who live will be going to jail for a long time. And if you shoot me by mistake, you'll be in even worse shape. Put the guns down." Slowly, the firearms eased toward less lethal positions as tempers seemed to cool.

It had been Wendell's intention to confiscate the pistols and to ignore the twenty or so misdemeanors and felonies that had been committed by the three members of the birthday brigade during the course of the afternoon, but Deadhand had it in his head that he had been duped, and he would not give up on his twenty dollars. The more he insisted that Blossom provide a refund, however, the less inclined she was to do so. Wendell even offered to provide the refund himself as a method of defusing the situation, but Deadhand was deep into the realm of principle by that time and would have none of it.

"I want *her* to give it to me," Deadhand said petulantly, pointing at Blossom.

"Okay, I will give her the twenty, and she can hand it to you," Wendell proposed.

"If you give me twenty dollars, I am splitting it with Edwina," Blossom clarified. "Floppy, here, didn't pay us near enough for our trouble, anyway. I still can't close my mouth all the way."

Hell hath no fury like a woman scorned.

"Don't call me that," Deadhand warned.

"Floppy," she said. "Floppy, Floppy, Floppy."

"I give up," Wendell said. "Everyone get in the car." He felt like
the captain of the Titanic as he ran the whole crew in. The ensuing ten
days had been long ones, and Wendell had not recovered fully over the
following five years, so he was in no mood for a repeat engagement.

"I'll stop by Deadhand's place tomorrow and see if I can't talk
some sense into him," Wendell said. "If not, he likes pinto beans for
his supper."

"Try really hard to talk him into paying his fine," Reva replied. "I
will make it worth your while. Country fried steak. Sex. Whatever
you want, it's yours. But if you do have to bring him in, leave Blossom
and Edwina at home. I hereby acquit them for whatever they have
done in their entire lives." Reva, too, remembered the birthday party
and its aftermath.

Later, after the sun had set and the supper dishes were dried and
stacked, Wendell and Reva made their way up the circular iron stair-
case to the roof of the rock castle. They sat side by side, holding hands
while sharing the quiet of two people who were not compelled to make
conversation just to fill the silence. They rocked in their oak rockers
and listened to the sounds of the night: the creak of the weathered oak
runners and joints, the murmur of an unknown conversation drifting
up from the vicinity of Black Saint Francis, a lone dog's bark out in the
darkness, a screen door's slam, and a car horn from a few streets away.
Overhead, the evening star shone brightly, twinkling like a sparkler
on the Fourth of July. Cumulus clouds had piled on the horizon, visible only when the heat lightning flashed within them and silhouetted
their forms against the backdrop of the black velvet sky. The occasional rumble reached their ears, but the sound was an empty boast.

From the shadows he heard a sigh.

"What is it, babe?" he asked.

"The bear is loose," she said. *The bear* was Reva's term for one of her precognitions of change. She had a nose for future happenings, and when she sensed a portent, it was no parlor trick of mirrors and lighting. Once, when they were a young married couple, they looked at an old farmhouse to buy. It was a beautiful dwelling surrounded by fir trees, the kind of home that could provide the foundations for the building of a family. It had double-hung windows that would let in the light and air, and window boxes filled with red geraniums and purple phlox. The rooms had tall ceilings that would be cool in the summer, heart of pine floors, and plastered and papered walls. It was everything that the young Blackmons had been seeking, and more. But halfway through the tour of the house, Reva stopped cold. When she turned to Wendell, her face was as white and stiff as a starched Sunday shirt.

"We need to go," she said, quietly but urgently.

"Let's look at the kitchen," Wendell suggested.

"We need to go *now*," she said. She was holding Charlie's hand, and she pulled the boy close to her. Wendell was carrying the baby in his arms, and his wife's strange behavior unsettled him. He held Abby Louise tighter, in an attempt to protect her from a danger he could not see.

"Is something wrong, dear?" asked the lady who had been showing them the place. She and her husband had lived there for thirty-eight years prior to his passing. Now she lived with her daughter, and the house was for sale.

"Something bad is going to happen in this house," Reva said. "I don't know what, and I don't know when. But it will be soon. Please don't stay here."

Wendell apologized to the woman as he hustled his family out the door, and he and Reva had not spoken of the incident again, because she hadn't seem inclined, and he hadn't known what to say. One week later, the house burned in the night. The fire chief listed the cause of the blaze as a short in the wiring in the kitchen. But Reva knew better. The bear had lit that fire.

Over the years, Wendell had learned to trust his wife's premonitions implicitly. He could not even begin to comprehend how it was possible for someone to know when change was about to arrive, but his lack of understanding of the mechanics of the gift did not alter the fact that he knew good advice when he heard it. From a cosmic standpoint, when Reva said "duck," it was time to hit the deck. The problem was that she seldom knew what was going to happen, or when, exactly. She just knew that the bear was in the neighborhood, and he would drop by presently. She called it her curse, because she could only dread the future. The bear never gave her enough information to alter outcomes.

"I hate the bear," Wendell said, back on the roof of the rock castle.

"I haven't felt him this strongly since Charlie died." She had cried for a full week prior to their oldest son's unexpected death in 1969, sobbing so desperately and miserably that when the bad news finally arrived, it had almost been a relief to learn that the bear had not been hungrier, that he had only wanted one child and not the entire family.

"What do you need for me to do?"

"I need you to hold me."

Wendell could not do much, but he was the best there was at doing that. He sat and held Reva, rocking her gently in the oversized rocker, until she and the bear drifted into slumber.

The following day dawned bright and clear, but the heat that enveloped the town had not dissipated overnight. It was August, and the dog days had come to Sand Valley. If the day ahead was true to form, the temperature would top one hundred degrees by noon and would still be hovering in the nineties as the lights of the town began to flicker off at bedtime. Wendell had a quiet cup of coffee with Reva, and then was out of the rock castle by seven o'clock. Due to Reva's bear alert, he was not looking forward to the day. But perhaps he would solve the mystery of the demise of Christine Hendricksen today. At the very least, he hoped to avoid arresting Deadhand Riley.

Before he commenced his duties, he walked behind the rock castle and then down the narrow trail that led to the river. The Echota River meandered like a drunken snake through Sand Valley, northeast Alabama, and northwest Georgia. It began on Lookout Mountain and emptied itself into the Tennessee River, but between those two fixed points, it crossed back and forth from Alabama to Georgia five times, as if it could not make up its mind where it was headed. It was a deep, lazy, green river, full of striped bass and crappie, bream and catfish, shell crackers and carp. The far bank was the border of a two hundred-acre tract of heavy woods and thickets, and from Wendell's vantage point on his bench, he had seen otters, muskrats, river turtles, and the ubiquitous opossums. He had spied raccoons, moles, chipmunks, and squirrels. His vigilance had once been rewarded by the sight of a red fox, but that had been years ago, and he believed the species to be gone from the area now. He had witnessed cottonmouths, rattlers, and green snakes from his vantage point. He had seen an alligator once, and the fact that no one believed him only served to make the sighting more special, as if the reptile had surfaced and made its way slowly upstream for Wendell's sole benefit.

Wendell sat on his bench. He began many of his days, and concluded more than a few, on the bench he had placed on its bank years ago. He kept some fishing tackle in a plastic bag under the bench, and sometimes he fished as he sat. But most times he just watched the river flow from right to left as it made its easy way to the Gulf of Mexico. His intention was to watch the water while he cleared his mind of the turmoil of the past few days. He also needed to compartmentalize Reva's bear warning, or he would end up spending the day hunting the beast rather than doing his job.

The river was fifty yards wide at this point. The bank was steep on Wendell's side, but the opposite bank was shallow and grassy. As he watched, a doe carefully poked her head from the trees and inspected the area carefully. Then she slowly stepped out and walked to the water, followed by two fawns. The two miniature deer walked unsteadily on spindly legs. From the spots on their backs, he judged them to be about a month old. They tentatively touched their noses to the water and drank as their mother watched for danger. Then she took a quick sip before herding her brood back into the safety of the woods. The sight of the three deer had been a gift, and a good way to start the day. Wendell stretched and stood. It was time to ride to the truck stop.

Charnell Jackson was already in a booth drinking coffee when Wendell arrived, so he stopped at the counter and got his own cup from Savannah before joining the attorney.

"I saw your mama yesterday," he said to Dixie Lanier's daughter. "She seemed kind of sad to me. I think she might like to see you." It was not his business, but he didn't care. Savannah glared at him and did not answer. "She's the only mama you will ever have," Wendell continued. "If you woke up tomorrow and she was gone, you would spend the rest of your life wishing you had been to see her today, after you got off of work." He picked up his coffee, walked to the booth, and sat down opposite Charnell.

"Can I buy you some breakfast?" the lawyer asked.

"No, I am just going to have coffee. Is Anna on the way?"

"Yeah, she had to drop the kid off at Bible school. She'll be here in a minute." Charnell took a sip from his cup. "How are you going to handle the subject of Gilla's extramarital excesses with Anna?"

"Well, provided she doesn't walk in here spattered in blood, with a crazy look in her eyes and a baseball bat tucked into her pocketbook, it's likely to be a short interview, and I will try not to bring the subject up. Gilla has been screwing around on her forever, and I guess she would have wiped out Ellen Harrison or one of his other girlfriends years ago, if that sort of thing bothered her. But you know the drill. She has a motive, so I need to talk to her."

Charnell nodded as the subject of their conversation entered the truck stop and walked to the booth. Anna Newman was a few years younger than Gilla's forty. She had thick, curly, brunette hair, cut shoulder length. Her nose was a trifle big for her face, which made it interesting, in Wendell's opinion. Her mouth smiled easily, showing straight, white teeth, but her hazel eyes rarely shared the sentiment. They were cold, as if they had been chiseled from a block of green ice. She wore a white blouse, a denim skirt, and leather moccasins. There were diamonds on five of her fingers, both of her ears, and hanging from a golden chain around her neck. She had once been a beauty and was still considered attractive by most, but it seemed to Wendell that her years with Gilla had left her looking pinched and somewhat drawn. She sat next to Charnell, opposite Wendell, and smiled absently at both men.

"Good morning, Anna," Wendell said. "I appreciate you taking a minute to talk to me."

"I am glad to help if I can, although I don't know how much I can tell you," she said. "I really barely knew the woman. She was more Stanley's friend."

It seemed to Wendell that he heard a slight inflection when she said *friend.* "Were they close friends?"

"Well, he has been going to church out there for the past two years. At least, that's what he called it. I call it something else. He has always been a restless man, always trying to find whatever it is he thinks he's missing. I've told him that he can find himself right out at the Baptist church with me and Stanley Junior, but for him, the grass is always greener on the other side." Anna had never joined the Newman family conversion.

Savannah came to the table with her order pad, and Mrs. Newman asked for a cup of coffee and a lightly buttered biscuit. Then she continued. "This killing is a terrible business. You expect this sort of thing to happen in the city. But not out here." She shuddered.

"Stanley tells me that you two are expecting."

"Yes," she said, and again, her mouth smiled, but her eyes were as hard as a shelf of mountain slate.

So much for the bundle-of-joy angle, Wendell thought. "Well, there's nothing like a new baby," he said. "Congratulations." Anna nodded in acknowledgement. Observing the look in her eyes, Wendell hoped she didn't eat the new arrival at birth. He thought it might be time to change the subject.

"Anna, I'm trying to construct a chronology of events leading up to the murder of Christine Hendricksen. Have you seen her at all during the past two weeks?"

"I don't think I've seen her for several months," Anna replied. "Stanley has tried to get me to come with him to her services, but I have to be honest and tell you I don't believe in all of this voodoo mumbo-jumbo."

"What do you mean?" Wendell asked.

Anna looked at him with arched eyebrows. "Wendell, I am not a stupid woman. I know what has been going on up there in that cave. And I know what my husband has been doing, and with whom. They have a little sex club up there, although why anyone would want to roll around on a cave floor is beyond me. He was out there Monday night, I guess with Ellen Harrison, who's his usual girlfriend. He went back out there Tuesday night. I don't know who he saw or what they did, but if there was any praying going on, I'll be really surprised. I went to bed at ten o'clock that night, and he wasn't home yet. I don't know when he came in."

Her biscuit arrived, and she took a nibble.

"So," Wendell said, "you know that sometimes Stanley . . . strays?" Charnell lightly kicked him in the ankle.

"The first time Stanley 'strayed,' we had been married eleven days," Anna said in a matter-of-fact manner. "It used to bother me a great deal. I would cry myself to sleep some nights, wondering why I couldn't satisfy my own husband. Then I finally came to realize that it wasn't me. He's insatiable. He would have sex ten times a day if he could find enough partners. Back before I stopped counting them, I knew of seventeen different women he had slept with since he married me. That was before he joined the coven, so there are more now. But I quit worrying about all that a long time ago. Now I don't care. He can have all the girlfriends he wants, as long as he keeps his hands off me."

She took another bite and had a sip of coffee. It was quiet at the table. Wendell did not know what to say, and Charnell seemed to be studying a fertilizer truck parked out by the pumps.

"I, uh . . ." Wendell began. Then he just stopped.

"I'm thinking you would like to know how I got pregnant," Anna said.

"Well, I was going to ask about that because I *am* curious. But it has nothing to do with what happened at the cave, so it is really none of my business."

"I'll tell you anyway," she said. "You'll love it." Charnell cleared his throat and shook his head. "The hell with you, Charnell," she said to her solicitor. "Drink your coffee." Then she turned her attention to Wendell. "I haven't slept with my husband in about five years, and that arrangement has suited me just fine. I didn't care who or what he was sticking it into, as long as he was leaving me alone. But I'm a heavy sleeper, unfortunately, and I take a sedative, as well, so imagine my surprise about four months ago when I awoke to the sight of that smiling grimace on the bastard's face as he was just finishing up his business. The son of a bitch raped me in my sleep, and now I'm pregnant again." Her voice shook with barely suppressed fury. "You are right, by the way. He looks just like a gorilla."

"Why haven't you filed charges?" Wendell asked.

She laughed bitterly. "I'm a mere woman, married to a rich boy with a powerful father. There was no point in filing charges. You know it, I know it, everyone knows it."

"Why do you stay?"

"I stay because I have no place to go. I stay because my father-in-law pays me to stay. Two million dollars to raise Stanley Jr. until he is eighteen. Another three million for whatever is in the oven right now. Mr. Frank didn't like the price increase, but I explained to him that it was simply inflation, a sign of the times. So, five million dollars plus a deadbolt on my door and a pump shotgun to prop beside my bed is the price he's paying me for heirs to the kingdom." Anna looked at Wendell. "You don't have to worry about whether I killed that woman. If she kept my husband happy and off of me just once, then she was my friend for life. What you need to worry about is what's going to happen to him if he ever touches me again."

"I think that'll be enough, Anna," Charnell said quietly.

"I think you may be right, Charnell." She took a final sip of coffee before gathering her pocketbook and standing. "I am sorry to put a pall on this breakfast gathering," she said. "I have to go now." She smiled her best smile before heading for the door. Wendell and Charnell were quiet for a long while. Then Wendell spoke up.

"Most of that was news to me. How much of it was news to you?"

"I drafted the monetary agreements. I was not aware that Gilla had forced himself on her."

"How is her alibi?"

"Rock solid. Watching a sick kid all night with two of the hired help right by her side."

"What did she mean about raising heirs for the kingdom?" Wendell asked. "Isn't Gilla going to inherit the Newman fortune?"

"Frank intends to take care of him financially, but he would like someone a bit sharper running things," Charnell replied.

"Do you think she'll shoot Gilla someday?" Wendell asked.

"I think *I* would shoot him."

"Rough talk from the family attorney."

"You never heard any of it from me," Charnell said simply. "Anyway, Stanley is not my client. He fired me a few years back, and I have never let him change his mind. As you have no doubt noticed, it's bad enough having to deal with the rest of them. Legally speaking, they are one messed up group of folks."

"Well, since we're not talking anyway, here's a hypothetical question for you. I have just been informed of a crime of rape. Knowing the accused, I believe Anna's story. What kind of case can be made?"

"Even if she would testify—and she won't—she was right on the mark in her analysis of the situation. Rape victims always have to prove themselves innocent before they go on to prove the rapist guilty. Married rape victims have it even worse. She's sort of stuck." He was reflective a moment. "Of course, if you have to be stuck, being stuck with five million dollars is the way to go."

"I would need to have more than that to sleep with Gilla," Wendell said simply.

"I have to be in court over in Sequoyah at ten," Charnell said. "Are you through talking to Newmans today?"

"I guess I am," Wendell replied. The only one left was eight years old and was at Bible school anyway. He was not a good candidate. Wendell paid the check, and Charnell left the tip. Then they walked together to the parking lot and headed their separate ways.

Wendell tried to mentally review his small trove of facts as he drove to Deadhand's place, but his heart wasn't in it. The interview with Anna had upset and depressed him. He could not for the life of him imagine why any two people would want to continue along in a relationship like theirs. But he tried not to judge. He had not walked in Anna's shoes, so he did not know what factors had led her to stay. His own daughters' paths to happiness had not always been straight and true, but they had eventually found their way. Wendell just could not envision either of them having to sleep with a shotgun propped by the bed.

Wendell pulled into Deadhand's yard and exited the cruiser. He had to step around a freshly mounded grave that was in the center of the driveway. Rusty had found his eternal home, as indicated by the inscription in black Magic Marker that had been freehanded onto the pressure-treated two-by-six that formed the crosspiece of the tomb marker. The tribute was exquisite in its simplicity: *Rusty. He was a dam good dog.* Wendell was touched. In the world of dog eulogies, it said about all that really needed to be said. He walked up to the steps at the door of the trailer and knocked loudly. A minute passed with no response. He banged again, louder this time. When he still got no answer, he tried the door. It was unlocked, and he slowly opened it and trod the steps carefully as he went up. Just inside the door on the right was Deadhand's table. There was a note taped on the blond Formica top.

> Hello Wendell,
> You have just broke into my trailer, but that's ok because I would of let you in any way. Ha ha. I guess Otter told you I am not going to pay my fine. Nothing personal, but I don't have the money, and it ain't right anyhow. I don't want Judge Reva to throw me into a cell, so I guess I will head up north for a while to visit some kinfolks I have up there. I will see you sometime. Keep an eye on Otter. He will take it hard.
> Deadhand

Wendell finished reading the note and placed it back on the dinette. If Deadhand was truly gone, it was the end of an era. His first thought was that maybe this was the bear Reva had sensed, but then he realized he couldn't be that lucky. Still, he didn't have to arrest the reprobate, and that was good news. He went back to the cruiser and raised Reva on the radio. She signed on, and he took a moment to present the facts of Deadhand's flight from justice. When he finished, Reva was silent for a minute.

"Do you think he's really gone?" she asked finally.

"All I have is the note to go by, but it takes something exceptional for Deadhand to put pen to paper, so maybe he really has headed for bluer skies." Wendell figured Deadhand had probably headed to Detroit to see his brother and would be back in two or three months, once that living arrangement wore thin. But in the meantime, a respite was a respite, even if it turned out that Deadhand was just hiding behind some trees on the other side of the yard.

"I guess you're pretty upset, huh?" Reva asked.

"Actually, I was just wondering if he still wanted his trailer. We could drag it to the lake, and it could be our own little romantic getaway spot."

"That would be great," she said absently. "You let me know when you get it down there, and I'll start chilling a bottle of champagne. In the meantime, there's a delivery here for you from Bobby Littlefield. I guess it's the forensic report. He is certainly being nice."

"He needs for me to solve his case for him. I'm about to go see the final coven members, the Harrisons. Then I will come read the report and tell you who did it."

"Impressive. How did your interview with Anna go?"

"Those Newmans are some strange folks. I'll tell you about it when I get back. Have you heard from T.F. this morning?"

"Your deputy has been silent."

"Have you heard the bear growl again?"

"No, but he's around. Drive safely, and wear your seat belt."

"I will, and I'll see you in a bit." Wendell signed off and began his drive to the log cabin that was Noble and Ellen Harrison's home. Noble was an antique dealer who operated a monthly auction in a large barn on the Harrison property. Although he claimed to be a purveyor of historic commodities, he had a merchant's heart and thus did not limit himself strictly to the buying and selling of aged merchandise. Wendell enjoyed attending the sales, both because he was a connoisseur of old junk and because he loved to see what Noble had acquired to sell. During the first hour of his most recent sale, Noble had offered an eclectic collection of merchandise that had included a Staffordshire flow-blue jardinière that he called a coffee cup, a Persian rug stamped "Korea" on the back, a pottery jug signed "Sand Mountain," a cardboard box of Harlequin Romances, three Carson City silver dollars, a sackful of estate costume jewelry, a hand-carved dough tray that had split in half over time and been glued together poorly by Noble Harrison, a set of cane-bottomed bentwood chairs, a chocolate cake from the Baptist Ladies Association, a Gary Lewis & The Playboys album, and a rusty axe head. There was no rhyme or reason.

Wendell entered the drive and pulled up to the house. Ellen was sitting on her front porch in denim jeans and a halter top. It was a cool outfit for a hot day. Her thick, honey-blond hair was pulled back into a ponytail. According to T.F., who had apparently been peeking, it was her natural color. She waved at Wendell and motioned him up to sit with her.

"Good morning, Wendell," she said. "Or, rather, good evening." It was just past noon. "I'm about to have a sandwich. Would you like one?" She had been painting her fingernails and was allowing the ceiling fan overhead to dry her enamel.

"You know, I *am* a little hungry." She invited him in and seated him at the kitchen table while she prepared tomato and mayonnaise sandwiches for them both. She poured two large glasses of sweet iced tea. Then she sat. Wendell took a bite and was rewarded with the fresh taste of the garden tomato, lightly salted and peppered, nestled in the rich flavor of the mayonnaise. Tomato sandwiches were one of his summer favorites.

"I bet you're here to talk about Christine," Ellen said. "I have been dreading it since Wednesday."

"It's no big deal, Ellen. I just need to know whatever you can tell me. Is Noble here? I would like to talk to him as well."

"No, he left Tuesday morning on a buying trip up North." Once a month, Noble would take ten thousand dollars and head out in his twenty-foot-long truck. He would stay gone until the truck was full of untapped profit. By leaving on the Tuesday morning before Christine died, he had removed himself from the suspect list.

"There he goes, emptying the North of all of its valuables again," Wendell said between a bite of sandwich and a sip of tea. Ellen made good tea: very sweet, no lemon, a touch of mint.

"He always claims he's just bringing it back to where it was before the Yankees stole it all."

"I like a man with a good grasp of history and economics," Wendell noted. "The sandwich was great. Thank you." Ellen nodded in acknowledgement of the compliment. "So, can you help me out with Christine? Do you have any idea why someone might want to do her in?"

Ellen sighed. Then she looked at Wendell.

"I have given that a lot of thought since I heard about it. She was more popular among the men of our group than the women, but I can't imagine anyone doing this to her."

"How did you feel about her?"

"I didn't have anything against her until she tried to take Stanley away from me. She started in on him a couple weeks ago, and I knew what she was trying to pull. But I wouldn't kill her over it. Lord, if I was to kill every woman Stanley slept with, I would always be killing someone." She took a sip of her tea. "There's no need anyway. He always comes back to me, sooner or later." She spoke wistfully, as if she wished her reality contained kinder facts.

"Ellen, I am not trying to hurt your feelings or get up into your personal business, but I have just got to ask. You have been Gilla's girlfriend for twenty years, since long before he was married. You obviously love him. Why didn't you marry him when you had the chance?"

"He never asked me. Mr. Frank didn't want him to marry a girl raised in the mill village, and he didn't have the guts to stand up to Mr. Frank. My daddy was a truck driver, and my mama was a weaver on the second shift at the cotton mill, and we just weren't fine enough for the Newmans. I couldn't put my life on hold forever. I was lonely more times than not, and I wanted to have children, too. So when Noble asked me, I went ahead and married him. And Stanley eventually married Anna because his daddy made him do it."

A love story from hell.

"Tell me something, Ellen. He screws around on his wife with you. He screws around on you with other women. He screws around on the other women with more other women. First off, I don't understand the attraction. Secondly, and this one is the real puzzler, I don't get why any of you put up with it."

"I can't speak for anyone else," she said. "But as for me, I love him. It's that simple. He is a weak man when it comes to matters of the flesh, and he is a coward when it comes to Mr. Frank, and he has done me dirty so many times I have lost count. But I love him and always have. I think he loves me, too, and someday he will realize it and want to be with only me." Her voice trailed off.

Wendell believed everyone had one dream that made the days more bearable and the long nights shorter. He had just heard Ellen Harrison's. He feared that in her case, the dream would be unfulfilled, and he felt sorry for her in that regard. A leopard could not change its spots, an elephant could not fly, and Gilla Newman was not capable of being a good man to any woman.

"Well, I hope it works out for you, if that's what you want. For the record, did you kill Christine Hendricksen?"

"Lord, no."

"Where were you Tuesday night?"

"I was at my mother's house. I spent the night with her and Daddy."

"That's good enough for me," Wendell said. He stood and made his way to the porch. She followed and watched as he drove out of sight. He could see her in the rearview mirror, her right hand to her brow, forming a visor against the bright sun.

Wendell arrived back at the rock castle around two. Reva was out, so he sat and read the forensics report from Bobby Littlefield. But he was unenthusiastic about what it contained. Bobby had already covered most of it over the telephone, and there was nothing new in the text and photos worth any additional excitement. He sat in the semi-dark coolness of the rock castle and thought about the case. So far, he had talked to everyone who had been in contact with the deceased during her last days as the Queen of Sorrow Wood. It seemed to Wendell that there was a mostly ambivalent attitude toward her among the people who had known her. They could all sort of take her or leave her. And everyone had an alibi, anyway. Except for Gilla.

The phone rang and snapped Wendell from his reverie. He crossed the room and picked up the receiver.

"Wendell," he answered.

"Wendell, this is Padgett Mize," came the voice of the town doctor.

"Hey, Doc," Wendell said. He heard an inhalation from the earpiece, as if the doctor were about to dive into water.

"Wendell, Reva has had a heart attack. She is in an ambulance on the way to the hospital in Rome right now. You need to get over there."

Wendell quietly replaced the receiver in the cradle. Then he straightened his shoulders and headed for the cruiser. The bear had arrived.

No one in the village was quite sure how long the fires had burned. The old woman, Biyu, said they had begun with a lightning strike when she had been a little girl, a bolt from the heavens that had caused the very ground beneath them to smolder and hiss. But Chuntao did not know if that was the truth, or just the meanderings of a grandmother who made up stories to pass the time. Whenever and however they had started, though, they had been burning for as long as Chuntao could remember, and she would be thirty-eight that winter. Today was her final day in the only home she had ever known. Tomorrow they would leave on their three-day journey to the far end of the valley.

It was not the ground that burned, but the coal. The fire had eaten its way along the coal seams like a slow and deadly cancer, and over the years the land beneath and around the village had become riddled. Once the coal burned away and the fire moved on, glowing sinkholes and smoking crevasses would appear at random along the paths of destruction. It was because of these deadly traps and the heavy smoke that clung to the floor of the valley that the governor had ordered the villagers to move. The earth throughout the entire village was warm to the touch, and when the snow fell, the flakes would melt as they touched the soil. When the rains fell in the spring, the village steamed and sizzled.

Chuntao's husband, Dingxiang, was a coal miner, as were all the men of the village. Each morning he would leave with his basket and digging tools and go to the coal field. There he would excavate from his bell-shaped hole until the light in the west began to fail. Then he would trudge home with a black, shiny harvest for her to sell at the market. They had been husband and wife for twenty-seven years, and in that time he had dug thirteen holes. When they arrived at their new home, he would begin to dig his fourteenth, but it would be at the far side of the vast coal deposit in the valley, the end that was not consuming itself.

Dingxiang was late, and Chuntao was worried about him. He was a predictable man, and he always arrived home just as the final light of day faded behind the rim of the mountains. Now it was fully dark, except for the eerie red and white glows from the fissures and cracks in the ground, and still he was not home. She wet a scarf and tied it over her nose and mouth. Then she walked toward the coal field. At the outskirts of the village, she discovered a new sinkhole in the earth. It was irregularly shaped, fifty feet across at its widest point, and it was flaming brightly, like a brazier dug straight into the valley floor. Often when the ground opened and fell in upon itself, the fires within would burn brighter for days as the fresh supply of oxygen invigorated the blaze. Next to this new hole, she saw Dingxiang's basket. The coal it contained had spilled onto the warm soil. His bronze-tipped digging stick lay nearby. Chuntao sank slowly to the ground next to her husband's pyre. She began to quietly cry. She would be making her way to her new home alone.

Chapter Eleven: 1945-1953

Wendell was mustered out of the Navy in late 1945 after spending most of his final four months in the service decommissioning PT boats. Decommissioning was the Navy's official term for running the boats up on shore, removing the engines and armaments, and burning the rest because they felt that it would be more cost effective to burn them than to maintain them. In Wendell's opinion, it was a waste of good craft that deserved better treatment. But as was their habit, the admiralty had not asked him what he thought before they decided upon a course of action, so although he performed his duty, his heart wasn't in it. He found it strange that he and his mates on the demolition crew were responsible for more destroyed PT boats than the Japanese Navy had been, but he supposed that was just one of the ironies of war. He spent his days dismantling fast wooden ships of war, and he spent his nights dreaming of Reva and home. When the war was in full force, the days had always seemed short to Wendell, even the ones that weren't etched onto a backdrop of terror. The hours shot by like a runaway freight train. But now that he was just marking time waiting for his enlistment to expire, each moment slowed to a lame turtle's pace. Although some of his comrades on the wrecking crew liked to discuss the physics of this phenomenon, Wendell did not encourage the conversations. He only wanted to go home.

"Do you think time really slows down when you're doing something you don't like to do?" asked Smitty Smith for what seemed like the tenth time. They were stripping a pair of Bofors guns from the deck of a boat.

"No."

"Well, do you think time speeds up when you're afraid?"

"No."

"Do you think that red-headed nurse we saw yesterday over at the airfield will go out with me?"

"No."

Finally, after what seemed a short eternity, he was assigned to the USS *Millicoma*, a fleet oiler making its way to San Francisco for a decommissioning of its own. He served as a deckhand and rode the tanker first to Pearl Harbor, and then on to San Francisco. He arrived back on the mainland on the nineteenth of November 1945, and by the following Monday, he was an unemployed sailor riding a bus toward home.

Wendell was reunited with Reva at the bus station in Seattle. He climbed off of the coach after a sixteen-hour journey that had included a stop at every wide place in the road between San Francisco and the Puget Sound. He was worn out from the trip but excited to finally be at this destination. He had been to the ends of the earth and had walked through the fires of hell—or near enough to it—to get back to Reva. He placed his duffel on the floor of the terminal and began searching the milling crowd. While Wendell looked east, Reva slipped in from the west and encircled his waist with her arms.

"If I were Bunk Grantley, you would be wearing a bus hubcap

for a hat right now," she said quietly. He turned in her arms and held her gaze for a moment. Then he kissed her for a long time. A couple of bystanders applauded, and one old man who looked as if he might make his living at sea patted Wendell gently on the shoulder and advised him to let the girl get a little air. The vicarious participation in the reunion was all good-natured. People were happy that the interminable war was finally over, and they merely wanted to share in the joy of the moment of return. The kiss ended, but still they stood and held each other. Reva was crying, and Wendell had to blink a tear as well. It was good to be alive, and home, and in the arms of the woman he loved. Finally, Reva spoke again.

"You told me you'd come back," she whispered. "I told myself and everyone else I believed that, and I really tried to. But I was afraid the whole time." She took a shaky breath and held him tighter. "I thought I would never see you again. But here you are." She felt his cheek with her fingertips, as if she were sightless and trying to memorize his features by touch.

"Here I am," Wendell confirmed. "Still have all my fingers and toes, too." He did not mention the scars he had acquired in other areas. She would find out soon enough. "Where are the kids?" He wanted to see how much Charlie had grown during the time he was gone, and he wanted to see his daughter.

"Birmah Mae has them at the new apartment. I didn't want to bring them to the bus station, so she took the day off and kept them. Charlie has turned into a runner, and he's too hard to catch in a crowd. And Abby is a little chunk of lead. We'll meet them in a little while. First, though, I have something to show you."

She led him by the hand from the bustle of the bus terminal out to the street, where she had a taxi waiting. The driver already had the address. They sat in the back, holding hands and chatting about nothing much at all, until he pulled up in front of the Claremont Hotel, where Reva had once again reserved the bridal suite. Wendell looked at her in surprise, until she explained that in her opinion, their honeymoon had been rudely interrupted by a war, but now that the war was over, they should get back on schedule. They crossed the lobby and rode the elevator in silence, shy in the presence of each other, the elevator operator, and the other occupants of the car. They reached their floor, and Reva led him down the hall and into their rooms. There was a can of beer chilling for him in a bucket of ice.

"You Seattle girls sure know how to show a sailor a good time," he said as he closed the door behind them.

"We do," she said. "Have your beer. Then go freshen up. You had a long bus ride."

Later, as he stepped from the bathroom, he asked what it was she had wanted to show him.

"It's in here," she called from the bedroom. "Come see."

The ensuing weeks strolled past, and Wendell settled into the routine of civilian life. He was offered employment out at the shipyard, and he was considering taking Mickey Porch up on the offer, when he found a job with the Black Ball ferry lines as a deckhand and line handler. Once he got back onto the deck of a vessel, he considered himself to be one of those rare individuals in life afforded the opportunity to both own and eat their cake. During the days he was on the water, where he loved to be, and even though the Puget Sound wasn't the open sea, it wasn't Kansas, either. And at night, he got to hold his family in his arms in their apartment on King Street, just off Pioneer Square. It wasn't the best neighborhood in town, but it was fine enough to suit a young couple who had seen many of life's harder moments and had not quailed. Plus, the apartment was close to the waterfront, and they both liked the smells and the sounds that drifted up from the chilly waters of the Sound. It was Wendell and Reva's first real home together, and they were happy there.

Wendell's wife and children were a source of unending delight for him. The idea of a family being a haven from the harsh realities of existence, a respite from the bumps and scrapes of the world, was a new concept to him. In his experience prior to marrying Reva, families were combat zones in which only the strongest, the luckiest, and the meanest survived. Wendell had gotten out only by the sheer audacity of marooning his father in a dry well, and he knew that if he ever wanted to go back for a visit with his mother and sisters, he had better go armed because Happy was not the sort of man who would forgive or forget. Now, though, Wendell would come home from his days as a deckhand on the Bremerton ferry and bask in the warm glow of the life he and Reva had cobbled together from the shards of other, less perfect existences. He would hold Charlie's hand and walk with him through the cool streets of Seattle, or down by the waterfront if the breeze was not too stiff for the boy, and he would point out to his son all of the magic wonders of the world.

When Wendell was a boy, flights of fancy had not been allowed, as if the act of childhood itself had been forbidden. It was his intention that this shortfall in his own upbringing not be repeated during Charlie's journey to adulthood. Thus, an old man in a porkpie hat shuffling down the thoroughfare became the traveling King of the Gypsies, searching the Pacific Northwest for his lost queen, his old

mule and wagon, and his bag of spells. A rust-streaked coastal freighter limping out on the Sound was transformed into a pirate ship bound
for plunder, glory, and all of the ports and riches of the Orient. A long,
black, chauffeured automobile motoring down Alaskan Way morphed
into a limousine belonging to a notorious gangster looking for a fat
bank to rob. A multiengine airplane buzzing miles overhead was a silver dragon flying to its home behind the sun. As Wendell spun these
yarns, Charlie listened with eyes wide and mouth open.

In addition to the happiness that Charlie brought him, Wendell
was constantly amazed by the perfection that was his little daughter,
Abby. He loved to sit with her in the rocking chair he and Reva had
bought at the secondhand furniture stall over by Pike Place. He would
cross his right leg over his left, lay her on her back in the cradle formed
by his limbs, and rock her for hours on end while humming melo-
dies to songs that did not exist, keeping time with the creaking of the
runners as he rocked. He would tell her stories, as well, tales he had
heard from his mother about the people and places of Wendell's childhood world. Abby could not understand the words, but the cadence
and tone of her father's voice would calm her when she was fussy and
would make her smile more times than not. She was the prettiest baby
Wendell had ever seen, with her thick, short curls as black as midnight
and her eyes as blue as the atolls off of Kwajalein. He loved her chubby
little legs and the way her hair smelled and how her miniature hands
would grasp his fingers and hold them while she slept.

"I think Abby may be the prettiest baby in the world," he said to
Reva one bright morning. "We should enter her into a contest."

"All fathers say that about their daughters," Reva replied.

"Yeah, but the rest of those guys are wrong. They're just saying
it to make their wives happy." Wendell wasn't saying the other babies

weren't pretty, but there could only be one prettiest.

At night, after the babies were fed and washed, down and quiet, Reva and Wendell would take time for one another. Although they had been married going on two years, they were still on their honeymoon in many respects, as Reva had pointed out at their reunion. So on many evenings, they made love until they fell into exhausted sleep in each other's arms. Both had experienced sex prior to their current relationship, and both had found it to be an activity worth engaging in. But with each other, the act was exponentially better. It was as if each had needed the other their entire lives, and now that they had finally found each other, they were complete. So they played, and they learned, and they loved each other with their hearts, minds, and bodies.

Other nights, they lay in the bed, her head on his chest as they talked the quiet conversations of two people at ease.

"Are you happy?" Reva asked one night. Wendell had been home for six months.

"I am happier than I ever thought I could possibly be," he replied. "How about you?"

"I think our life together is perfect," she said. Then she reached up and knocked on the headboard three times with her fist. "Knock on wood," she whispered to herself.

"What was that?" Wendell asked. He had been almost asleep.

"Nothing," Reva replied, patting him gently. "Nothing at all."

The weeks grew and became months, and the months formed the bridge first to 1947 and then to 1948. Wendell and Reva were deep in the business of life together. They felt the bad times were behind them, and they were optimistic about the future. Wendell continued to work the ferries and rose to the second mate position. He hoped to someday acquire his master's license so he could begin to pilot the big boats. Occasionally, on nights and weekends, he picked up the odd shift out at the shipyard. Mickey Porch would call him when he was short a welder, and Wendell was happy to get the extra work. He wanted the best that he could provide for his family, and the best took money. Charlie had started school by that time, and his parents were finding out that education was expensive. Also, they were saving up a down payment for a house. They liked their apartment on King Street, but they both believed the children needed a yard to play in.

Sometime late in March of 1948, Reva became pregnant again.

"You know, I like Wendell as much as anybody does, and I like him more than Bunk Grantley does," Birmah Mae observed, when Reva shared the news that she was with child. "But you could tell him 'no' from time to time, just to keep him honest." She was a firm believer in telling Henry "no," just to keep him honest. Henry Peppers was arguably the most honest man in Seattle, and perhaps in the entire state of Washington.

"I occasionally say 'no,'" Reva replied. But she preferred saying yes, most times. She loved Wendell, and she enjoyed the more physical aspects of that love a great deal. And she and Wendell wanted to have a houseful of children anyway. So it was a win-win situation, in her opinion.

"Not much, you don't." When Henry had come home from the war in Europe, he and Birmah Mae had taken the apartment down the hall from the Wendell and Reva's lodgings, and the walls were thin. "You're making me look bad."

On December 25, 1948, Reva gave birth to another little girl. The baby made the decision to arrive a couple weeks early, and Reva was sort of famous for short and dramatic labor, anyway, so Wendell was caught unawares out on the Puget Sound when the birth occurred.

He had volunteered for the Christmas Day run to Bremerton for the extra pay it brought. By the time the ferry docked that afternoon, the delivery of his third child was all over, including the naming. Birmah Mae met him at the pier and gave him the good news. Henry was home babysitting Charlie and Abby, while their mama was out getting them a new sister.

"You're a daddy again, Ace," she said sullenly, although the tone was wasted on Wendell. He was too happy to pick up on nuances of voice at that moment. "You have a little girl," she mumbled, gesturing at the old 1939 Chevrolet sedan she and Henry owned. "Of course, Reva did all the work." She drove Wendell to the hospital.

"I wanted to name the baby something Christmasy," Reva told him as he stood beside her bed in the maternity ward.

"Santa?" he asked. "Comet?"

"Natalie," she replied. "It means *Christmas joy*." She had bought a book titled *10,000 Baby Names and Their Meanings* early in the pregnancy and had read it from cover to cover. Of all the names in the volume, she had liked *Natalie* the best. "Do you like it?" she asked Wendell.

"Well, it's not Santa or Comet, but it's a pretty name," he said, smiling. Then he kissed the mother of his children.

They brought Natalie Michelle Blackmon home on New Year's Day, 1949. She was smaller than Abby had been when she was born, but she was a carbon copy of her in every other respect, with a head full of curly black hair and piercing blue eyes. She cried more than Abby had, but not much more, and she was still a good baby. There were no photographs of Reva when she had been a baby, but Wendell was certain that both of his girls were living portraits of what their mother must have looked like.

With the addition of Natalie, the apartment on King Street was officially crowded. Charlie and Abby slept in one bedroom, and the baby's bassinet was in the other bedroom with Reva and Wendell. Although they loved their apartment, it was time to move forward with their plan to buy a house.

"How much money do we have saved up?" Wendell asked Reva. He was not good with money, but Reva could squeeze a nickel until it screamed for mercy, so by mutual consent, she had become keeper of the accounts.

"We have $742.71 in savings," she said.

"How much more do we need to buy a house?" he asked. He had no idea about house costs, mortgage rates, or the price of tea in China. He turned everything he made over to Reva and promptly forgot about it. Historically, money had not been that important to him, except as a means of keeping score in poker games, or as a medium of exchange when purchasing Japanese battle flags. He had never had much of it and did not think it likely he ever would. Even now, it only mattered to him in that a certain amount of it was necessary to support his family comfortably.

"I think that if we have one thousand dollars to go toward a nice house, the bank will loan us the rest. There will be some other expenses, as well, when we set up housekeeping. We will need a little more furniture, and I bet we will have to put up deposits for utilities. So we should try to have twelve hundred dollars in the bank when we get ready to make our move."

"If I work every Saturday and Sunday for Mickey, could we have the rest in a year?"

"I think so." So that became the plan. Wendell worked seven days out of every week, and Reva made every dollar do the work of two, and over the course of the year they made their slow march toward twelve hundred dollars and a little house in west Seattle or out at Bremerton that the sum had come to symbolize.

Out in the wide and uncaring world, 1949 stumbled along and eventually became 1950. American military personnel quietly eased into a backwater known as Vietnam to advise the French how to defeat their tenacious opponent, Ho Chi Minh. Harry S. Truman authorized the development of a hydrogen bomb in response to Joseph Stalin's insistence upon conducting atomic tests in response to Harry S. Truman dropping two atomic bombs onto the Empire of Japan. Joseph McCarthy, a second-rate senator from Wisconsin, began his search for communists in Hollywood and the District of Columbia, two likely hotbeds of Marxism. Birmah Mae and Henry Peppers became parents to a bundle of joy they named Henrietta, much to Henry's delight. And on June 25, 1950, Kim Il-Sung decided North Korea should invade its neighbor to the south.

On June 30, Reva had her first official encounter with the bear. She had experienced small inklings and premonitions throughout her life, but this was her first full-blown certainty that an unknown event of mythic proportion was rolling down the highway of fate toward the Blackmon family. It was a Friday, and Wendell came home late after taking an extra run to Bremerton. He was happy because the captain had let him take the wheel, and he was whistling as he let himself into the apartment.

It was dark in the domicile except for the reading lamp behind the rocker. Reva sat there, slowly rocking. It was long past the children's bedtimes, and they were sleeping peacefully. She turned as he entered.

"Supper is on the table," she said. Wendell stopped in his tracks. There was a catch in her voice he did not like.

"What's wrong?" he asked. She stood and took a ragged breath before answering.

"I don't know," she responded. "But something is."

"I don't understand," he said, coming close.

"I don't either," she replied. "Hold me." Wendell sat in the chair and took her in his lap. She buried her face in the crook of his neck and held on to him tightly. He stroked her hair as he rocked her. The chair creaked like an old screen door as he went back and forth. Finally, after nearly an hour, she spoke.

"I was doing the books today, and I was so happy that we have over eleven hundred and fifty dollars in savings, that we almost have enough for our house. And then, out of nowhere, it hit me that something big and unexpected is about to happen."

"Something bad?" he asked. He did not doubt that she knew what she knew.

"Bad, good, I don't know. All I know is that it is about to happen." She looked at her husband. A tear rolled down her cheek. "I hate this," she said. "What must you think of me?"

"I think we should let it go for tonight. Whatever it is, we will deal with it tomorrow."

But they did not have to deal with it the following day, or for several weeks thereafter, because the bear was hanging back, waiting for his moment in the sun. Reva was on the tips of pins and needles the whole time, because she knew that change was in the wind. Wendell was more concerned with his wife's well-being than he was with whatever was lumbering their way. He believed her, and he believed in her, but he knew there wasn't anything he could do but wait. Whatever was going to happen would happen. And then, at the end of August, the wait was over. Wendell received a letter from the Navy Department, advising him that his services were once again required on the open seas, and that he was to report for duty on September 13.

"Well, *that's* a damn bear," he said, after he read the news to Reva. The bear had been named. Wendell was in a daze. He had been in the ready reserve since leaving the service, but he had certainly not seen this coming.

"This is what I've been worrying about all summer," Reva said. "Now I know what it was. Do you really have to go?" She had hoped and prayed she would never again have to be a war wife, and she didn't even want to think about the renewed possibility of becoming a war widow.

"I don't see much way out of it," he said. "You know, this is really a washtub full of shit. They're calling it a police action, but a police action is what two cops do on a Saturday night when a drunk gets up in their face. This is a war. When two large groups of people who don't want to be there start shooting at each other, that's a war." Wendell was pacing while he talked. "Hell, I don't even know where Korea is, and I don't know anyone who lives there, either. I wouldn't know a Korean if one fell on me. Besides that, I fought my war. It is somebody else's turn. There are plenty of young boys out there they could send." Wendell was only twenty-four, but he was too old for this. And unlike the last time he had sailed into the sights of the enemy, this time he had too much to lose. He had a wife with an amazing nose for trouble, three beautiful children, a future in the ferry boat business, and a house to buy. He hated that the South Koreans were having a tough time, and he hoped everything worked out okay for them, but this was none of his affair.

There were indeed plenty of young boys scattered over the countryside, and some of them were eager for their own chance at glory, or at least for the opportunity to get out of town. But the Navy needed

boys who recalled how to sail destroyers and fire deck guns, and the
Air Force needed boys who could already fly fighter planes and bomb-
ers, and the Army needed boys who remembered how to shoot straight
under pressure and could keep their tanks from running off cliffs.
At the end of World War Two, there had been a general exodus of
men and women from all branches of the service. And vast numbers
of fighting machines—ships, tanks, and airplanes—had been stored,
mothballed, or simply scrapped. Unfortunately, this leaner, peacetime
version of the military was simply not sufficient to the demands of the
moment once the North Koreans decided to drop in on their relatives
to the south, and Wendell was not the only retired warrior to receive
his letter that summer.

He reported for duty in San Diego and was assigned to the *USS
Bandy*, a World War Two-era Fletcher-class destroyer that had been
in the mothball fleet since 1947. He and his crewmates spent the remainder of 1950 putting the venerable ship back into fighting trim,
and they departed for the Korean coast in May of 1951. Although
Wendell was less than happy to be back in uniform, he was pleasantly
surprised to be reacquainted with Smitty Smith, who had also been
recalled from his civilian pursuits in San Diego and been assigned to
the *Bandy* as well.

"They got you, too? I do not believe this shit," Smitty said as
they shook hands. "There I was, selling faucets and minding my own
business, and the next thing I knew, I was a sailor again. Sheila was
pissed." The two men had not seen each other since Wendell sailed
into the sunrise aboard the USS *Millicoma*. Smitty's enlistment had
expired in 1947. He had returned to his home in San Diego, married
a cocktail waitress named Sheila, and fathered a little girl. He was
a hardware salesman, and he was about as happy to be back on a

destroyer as Wendell was.

"They got me, too," Wendell confirmed. There really wasn't much else to say. Misery supposedly loved company, but Wendell drew very little comfort from the fact that Smitty's future, too, had been placed on hold. The knowledge actually made him feel twice as bad.

The *Bandy* arrived on station off the Korean coast late in May. Her duties included blockading the North Korean coast, shore bombardment, and aircraft carrier escort, but mostly what she did was fish downed pilots out of the Sea of Japan. It was a different type of war than Wendell, Smitty, and the other World War Two veterans were used to, a secondhand war that was happening somewhere off in the distance, a war they were in support of, but not a part of. No one was shooting at them on the *Bandy*. They weren't being strafed, shelled, or torpedoed. Young North Korean boys weren't swimming out to greet them with limpet mines, although submerged mines were a problem close to shore; all five of the Navy ships lost during the entire war were lost to mines. But for the most part, the *Bandy* was one step removed from harm's way.

Dear Reva,

Well, I never thought I would ever be writing to you from a destroyer in the middle of a war zone again, but I guess that's what I get for thinking. I suppose we had better leave the thinking to you in the future. I don't seem to have the knack. I know you have heard it from me before, but I swear to you that I am as safe as a baby in his mama's arms out here. I am not lying to you this time. This whole business seems to be a land and air war—whoops, I mean police action—and from what I hear, I would hate to be one of those poor guys

on the ground. They are having a tough time. I know for a
fact that I would hate to be one of these pilots. Especially one
of the jet pilots. We fish one or two Banshees or Panthers a
week out of the drink. Some have been shot up, and some of
them just miss their landing wire and run right off the end of
the ship. If they miss their wire, they are supposed to power
back up and try to take off again. Sometimes they make it,
and sometimes they don't. I never was a big believer in trying to land an airplane on a ship, anyway, and that was back
when they were all propeller driven. Now that the Navy is
switching over to jets, I don't know where they are finding
guys crazy enough to fly them. I miss you and the kids, and
I wish I was back home. I am afraid my heart is not in this
war. I feel bad for the guys who are up in the thick of it, guys
who are fighting and dying right now. They are getting the
worst of it. And for what? I really don't care if North Korea
takes over South Korea, or vice versa, or if China takes over
the whole place. The Chinese were our friends during the
last war, but now they don't seem to love us anymore. Anyway, it is the Korean's country, not mine, and they can work
it out. To me it is kind of like back during the Civil War in
our country. I swear I don't remember my mama telling any
stories about Korean boys coming to help, and I don't believe
she would have forgotten something like that. Give the kids
a kiss for me, and show them my picture so they don't forget
what I look like. Don't you forget what I look like either. I
was hoping I would be coming home soon, but the news I am
hearing is not happy. I don't think we will lose, I just think
it may take a while to win. We sort of started out in the hole.

Kind of like last time, come to think of it. So maybe I will
be home in time to watch Charlie graduate. But I am not
going to worry about that unless you have one of your feelings. Then I'll worry.

Love,

Wendell

Back on the home front, Reva had her hands full, but she was
managing to work out her domestic difficulties with the help of Birmah Mae. Henry had gone back into the Army, but he had not been
called up, as Wendell had been. Rather, he had joined, and he had requested combat. This action had been a mystery to Reva, but Wendell
understood Henry's point of view perfectly. If he were married to Birmah Mae, he would have just stayed in Europe at the conclusion of the
last war, to begin with. And if he had made the mistake of coming
home, he wouldn't have passed up the opportunity of another war as a
means of escaping the sweet snares of Birmah Mae's love.

Both Wendell and Henry took substantial cuts in pay when they
reentered the services, so the girls put their heads together and came
up with a workable plan for economic survival. Birmah Mae moved
into the apartment with Reva so they could share expenses. They
flipped a coin, and the loser—Reva—went back to work full-time at
the Navy Yard Puget Sound, while Birmah Mae kept house and raised
the babies. It was a good plan, and it worked so well, financially, that
Reva was even able to contribute a bit of change from time to time to
the house fund. This was a huge relief to her. When Wendell had
been called up, she'd been certain that before he got home, she would
have to use their entire nest egg to supplement the household income.
And while she was grateful that it was there if she needed it, she would

prefer to buy a house with it, if she was able.

Life went on at its own pace with little regard for the plans Reva and Wendell had laid. First 1951 became 1952, and then 1952 evolved into 1953. The front line moved dramatically back and forth across the Korean landscape before finally settling around the thirty-eighth parallel, which was more or less where it had started. Harry S. Truman fired Douglas MacArthur for insubordination, much to the amusement of most of the crew of the *Bandy* when they heard the news.

"I wish the son of a bitch would fire *me*," said Smitty Smith as he swabbed at the deck with a stiff brush and some elbow grease.

"I'd settle for going down on short time," Wendell responded. The *Bandy* stayed on station in the waters surrounding the Korean Peninsula, and sadly, neither Wendell nor Smitty were let go, so they stayed on station aboard the *Bandy*. It was at this time that Happy Blackmon set sail for the Promised Land, where the faithful could expect farms full of sons, wells full of water, and lives full of peace and contentment. Birmah Mae's husband, Henry Peppers, was killed by a MiG-15 fighter that was flown by a Soviet pilot who was officially not there at the time, but he was dead just the same, leaving a widow who could out-weld him and a daughter who would know her father only through pictures and reminiscences.

Late in 1952, Reva found a house. It had everything she had been looking for. It had four bedrooms and a big kitchen, with Dutch doors that led out to a back porch with a view of the Sound. There was a breakfast nook and a pantry, and a window complete with a window box over the kitchen sink. The bathroom was huge, and the cast-iron tub it contained would hold all three of Reva's children plus Henrietta. It was not a new house, and it needed a little work, but it was what she wanted. It was owned by a woman whose husband had died at Bataan in the previous war, and whose son had just been shot down over the Yalu River in the current unpleasantness and was now a prisoner of war. She was a motivated seller who only wanted to go home to what was left of her people in Missouri, and there was more than one potential buyer looking at the property. So Reva made the decision to buy the house.

Dear Wendell,

I always took you at your word when you told me I could have whatever house I wanted. I found us the perfect house out in Bremerton, and I bought it. I have enclosed a picture. It's a great house on a big lot with a yard and a fence, and we bought it for $3400.00. The lady took $1000.00 down and she will let us pay her the rest by the month, so we didn't even have to go to the bank. I hope you are not mad, but she couldn't wait and I couldn't pass it up. The kids love it. Charlie is already asking for a dog. Birmah Mae has been pitiful since Henry was killed, and I can't just leave her on her own. So I told her she could live with me and the kids in the new house until you get back. I promise that she won't be any trouble, but right now she needs a friend and some support, and I still need a baby-sitter while I am at work. Please don't be mad. She didn't ask. I volunteered. I know what it is like to have a baby and no husband, and there were many times I wished that someone would take me in. It is the right thing to do. I miss you so much. I have been hearing they are making progress at the peace talks, but they have been saying that for a year, so I don't know what to believe. Maybe you'll be home soon. I hope so. I am ready to have another baby, and I will

need your help with that. Take care of yourself, and don't let
Smitty get you into trouble.

Love,

Reva

When Wendell found out that he was a homeowner, he bought
himself and Smitty a cigar at the ship's store, and they sat on the fantail to smoke them. It was close to sunset, and a hot breeze tugged at
their shirts and caps. In the distance they could hear the roar of Panthers taking off from the carrier they were escorting.

"If I just stay out here and keep sending my pay home, Reva will
make me a rich man," Wendell bragged. He had never been a man of
property before, and he liked the way it felt.

"You're lucky," Smitty said. "I send money home to Sheila, and
she buys more shoes with it. The girl is not good with money. We
will never even have our own pot to piss in, never mind a nice house."
He was morose.

"But you'll have nice shoes," Wendell pointed out, trying to cheer
his friend. It was the least he could do.

"Yeah, well," Smitty said dubiously. A Claxton horn sounded, and
the *Bandy* turned hard to port. It was time to fish another pilot from
the warm waters of the Sea of Japan.

On July 27, 1953, a ceasefire-in-place was declared by the peace
negotiators at the ancient Korean city of Kaesong. After three years
of fighting, two million military personnel killed, wounded, or taken
prisoner, civilian casualties on both sides greatly in excess of that number, and billions of dollars spent, the border between North and South
Korea was basically back where it had been the day before the war
began. To quote Dock Farris, they had taken the long way around

the barn to get back to the door. Wendell and a large number of his comrades-in-arms considered the entire episode a waste of lives, time, and money. But as was generally the case, no one much cared what the consensus was among the troops, down where the bullets met the meat. And regardless of the overall insanity of the outing, the fact was that Wendell was willing to take good news any way he could get it. The war was over, he was alive, and he was going home.

The execution was scheduled for sunset, but the crowds began to gather long before the appointed time. Inmaculada herself had not intended to witness the event. She had been selling vegetables at the marketplace all afternoon and was preparing to make her way home when she noticed the gathered crowds. She had lived in Portucale her entire life. Home for her was a small stone hut perched atop a gentle slope overlooking the sea. She had lived there alone for the past two years, since her parents had succumbed to the Great Death. She was seventeen.

There was a carnival atmosphere in the market. Vendors were selling meat pies and sweets. A juggler was entertaining the mob until the main event began. When they brought the boy out just before sunset, the crowd cheered. Inmaculada gathered her belongings and began to leave. She had no interest in watching someone die. But she ventured one glance at the condemned young man. He appeared to be about her age. He was tall and broad-shouldered, with brown, curly hair and defiant blue eyes. It was his gaze that snared her. She could not look away. His eyes held hers as he was marched to the platform. His piercing stare would not release her as he was presented with his opportunity to kiss the crucifix and make his peace with God, and she flinched when he smiled a contemptuous smile and spit on that symbol of the Savior's sacrifice. She wished to look away, but could not, as his neck was settled onto the block. His blue eyes bored into hers until the axe made its arc.

Inmaculada was an attractive, propertied woman, but she had never married, although it was not for a lack of suitors. Many young men came to call over the years, and some of them would have made fine husbands. But the blue eyes still held her, and they would not let her go.

Chapter Twelve: 1985

Wendell sat by Reva's hospital bed and held her hand. She had not roused since his arrival at her side several hours earlier. She looked small and helpless, more like a sick child than the woman he had lived with for over forty years. Her leg leaned in the corner, forlorn and alone, like an orphan on a street corner. The emergency room doctor he had spoken with had said that she was sleeping due to the morphine, which had been administered for chest pain. She was stable, and according to the medical staff, she was out of danger for the present, but it had been a very serious heart attack.

Wendell was grim. He patted the back of his wife's hand carefully, so he would not disturb the IV needle that was threaded into the vein there. Reva had small blood vessels that tended to run away from needles, so medical personnel had to take insertions where they could find them. It was twilight out in the world of the hale, and except for the small amount of ambient light that filtered in through the open curtains and from the crack under the door, it was dark in the room. Wendell smelled Lysol, a slight odor of bleach, and the barest hint of urine. He hated hospital rooms, and he hated this one most of all, because it contained Reva. From the hall, he heard a clatter that might have been a food tray hitting the floor, followed by a muffled male voice saying, "Dammit."

The door opened behind him, and Dr. Mize came in. He was sixty or so, with wispy white hair, a hideous tie, and a permanent scowl. Wendell had once seen a photo of Padgett Mize from when the doctor was about thirty, and the only feature that had changed during the ensuing years was the hair color. He was a good physician who cared about the welfare of his patients. He squeezed Wendell on the shoulder before switching on the wall light. He picked up the chart that was hanging at the end of the bed and read the top page, then flipped it up and read the sheet below. Then he looked at his watch, scribbled a quick note, and replaced the record.

"How are you holding up, Wendell?" he asked quietly.

"How is *she* holding up?" The folks at the hospital were kind and seemed to be extremely competent, but Wendell wanted to hear the news from the Blackmon family physician.

"She appears to be out of danger at the moment and is resting comfortably. It was a bad infarction. We will need to run some tests to determine how much damage her heart has sustained and to evaluate the condition of her coronary arteries. After that, we'll see. Right now, she is on blood thinners and has a steady heartbeat. The morphine is keeping her blood pressure low and keeping her out of pain."

"What happened? What caused this?" He felt responsible somehow for not spotting the trouble before it had arrived. He was a policeman. He was supposed to notice and act. It felt like he had been asleep on his watch, like he had let the enemy sneak in under the wire.

"It is hard to say right now. She didn't smoke, which means she won't have to quit. She's carrying an extra pound or two, but she seems to be in pretty good shape overall. I know her mother died young with heart trouble. A lot of what happens to us is determined by our genetics. Stress can sometimes be a factor as well. She was actually in my waiting room when she had the attack. I don't know why she wanted to see me. She didn't tell Dixie when she made the appointment, but Dixie told me she sounded odd when she called, and that she looked upset when she came in." Dixie Lanier was Doc Padgett's receptionist, helper, and unofficial nurse on Mondays, Wednesdays, and Fridays. "It was a good thing she was in the office when this happened though. I was able to get right to her. I think we might have lost her, otherwise. Someone upstairs is keeping an eye on Reva."

Wendell supposed it was true, but the thought came unbidden that a more effective method of divine intervention might have been to have made those coronary arteries a little wider in the first place. Still, Doc meant well, and he had a point. If you had to have a heart attack, the doctor's office was one of the best places to do it.

Doc switched off the light. "She will sleep through the night," he told Wendell. "Why don't you go home and get some sleep yourself, and I'll meet you back here in the morning?"

"Thanks, Doc, but I can't leave. I need to stay with her. She might wake up, and I don't want her to be in a strange place alone. Especially not in a hospital. She hates hospitals."

"I figured you would say that. I'll see if they can scratch you up a pillow and a blanket at the nurse's station, and I'll stop by first thing in the morning. Do you think you might need a little something to help you sleep?"

"No, I guess I'll drop off after a while." If not, he had a pint of medicinal Jack Daniels in the trunk of the cruiser, and a swallow or two of that would make him drowsy.

After Doc left, Wendell sat in the dark with his wife of many years and wondered what he was going to do if she slipped away. The subject was not dear to him, but that was where his mind kept going. He had always considered her and the children to be the main event, in a manner of speaking, while he was merely the side show. It was as if he were a supporting actor in her days and times, rather than the star of his own production. Reva and his family were the Great Wallendas performing under the lights in the big top, and he was just the dog boy, in a shabby tent down at the end of the midway, next to the sword swallower and the girlie show. He had married her when he was just a youth, and she was a part of nearly every adult memory he possessed. She was woven into the fabric of his life as surely as fibers intertwined to become cloth. They were so inseparable he could not conceive of existence without her.

Wendell supposed he should call the children and let them know what had happened to their mother, but inertia had settled over him, a deep tiredness that would not allow him to stir from the chair he occupied. Abby lived with her husband and two children in Bremerton in the house where she had grown up. Reva and Wendell had kept the dwelling when they'd moved back to Sand Valley and had rented it out to a succession of tenants. When Abby Louise met and married John Brazelton in 1964, she expressed a desire to move back to the Northwest because she had not taken to Sand Valley when the Blackmon family had moved there in 1960. Wendell could certainly understand that point of view, because he had not really cottoned to the area as a youngster either, so he and Reva had given the house to Abby and her new husband as a wedding gift.

Abby's younger sister, Natalie Michelle, lived in Yarmouth, Nova Scotia. She had relocated to that cool and misty locale in 1968 because it was where the love of her life resided. She had always loved being near big bodies of water anyway, and because she did not love what she thought her birth country was becoming during the late sixties, she moved to the Bay of Fundy with her sweetie. Wendell and Reva had discussed the move the day after Reva had learned of the new living arrangements.

"Who is this guy she's going to shack up with?" Wendell asked. "Have we met him?" He supposed with modern times being what they were, a wedding ring was out of the question.

"It's not a guy at all," Reva replied. "And don't say 'shack up.' I don't like that phrase. Her name is Amanda Peace. Our daughter does not like guys." Reva had been aware of her daughter's preferences for some time but had been waiting for the right set of circumstances to present themselves before she told her husband. That moment had apparently arrived, and she was not completely sure how he would take the news. Mostly what he was thinking was that the wedding ring issue was now moot and that you could call shacking up baking a cake if you wanted to, but it was still shacking up.

Wendell was quiet for a couple of minutes before he spoke. "Well," he said finally, "I don't like most guys either, so I guess she came by that part honest. But why in hell do they have to live in Nova Scotia?" Wendell realized he didn't care who his baby girl slept with as long as he or she was good to her, but it would be a long drive when they wanted to visit, if she insisted on living in Canada. He already had to drive four days each way to visit Abby and her family.

"Natalie thinks our country is conducting an illegal and immoral war in Vietnam and does not want to live here anymore," Reva replied. She had been aware of Natalie's political point of view for a good while, as well, and was again waiting for the opportune time to break the news to her husband, who was, after all, a veteran of two wars, although he wasn't obsessive about it.

Wendell was again quiet for a couple minutes before he spoke. "She's probably right." He thought the current war was a good place to get killed, like all wars tended to be, including the two he had visited. "But why does she have to move to Nova Scotia?" That drive was going to be a long one, and there was no way he was going to fly. He had seen too many pilots die in his time. It was his studied opinion that flying was way too dangerous a pursuit, even if no one was shooting at the plane.

The third of the Blackmon children, Charlie, would be much harder to reach. He had died in 1969 after first surviving a tour of duty in Vietnam, during which he had been decorated for bravery in action. When he had arrived home, he'd been pestered into conducting a radio interview to discuss the particulars surrounding his exploits in the jungle, but it had not gone as well as the journalist had hoped it would. Charlie had developed a taste for liquor while defending the world from the communist hordes and had knocked back most of a pint of Southern Comfort before putting on the headphones and sliding the microphone into place. His resulting candor was more than his audience was expecting.

"Can you tell our listeners about the events that led up to you being awarded the Silver Star?" asked Parnick Stevens, the five hundred-watt voice of Sand Valley on WSVA.

"I was decorated for not leaving my post and for showing conspicuous bravery in the face of the enemy. But in reality, I was surrounded by about half of the North Vietnamese Army at the time and didn't have a hell of a lot of choices. I would have hauled ass in a country minute, but there was no place to go. So I shot at everything I saw until the Air Cav came and got me out of there. My post, by the way, was a little bump of high ground on the side of a rice paddy. It smelled like shit and blood and cordite. Real strategic spot. I was there because our lieutenant wanted to be a hero, so he led us on a wild goose chase straight into a trap. Most of the guys in my squad were killed right away when Captain America marched us into a minefield full of Bouncing Betties. That's a mean little spring-loaded mine that jumps up about waist high before it explodes and blows your dick off. Whoever invented it is going straight to hell. Anyway, there were mines popping up and going off all over the place, and everyone in the squad but me got wounded or killed right off. There was a lot of screaming going on.

"One guy we called Doobie cussed the lieutenant's ass for five minutes straight before he died. Cussed the L-T's mama and his wife, too, for having him and for marrying him. But a couple of the guys lived, including the lieutenant, which is why I got the medal. You have to have witnesses to get medals, and they like for the witnesses to be officers. I'll tell you this though. If I had known at the time that he was still alive, I think I would have shot him myself because he sure got a lot of guys killed, and some of them were my buddies. He's a captain now, and they'll probably make him a general before it's all over with. They love guys like him. But if I had seen him move or heard him groan, they might have been digging Yankee steel out of him before they loaded him onto the plane.

"Anyway, I had the .50 cal and six or eight M-16s, because everyone else was dead or wounded. I dragged the two guys who I knew were alive over to my hump in the rice paddy. We called one of them Zombie because he always looked like he had been dead for a few days. He looked even worse than usual after the Betty blew a hole in his leg, but he could still shoot, so I tied off his leg and put him on the

Thumper—the grenade launcher—and while he was blowing up shit, I cooked off a big pile of ordnance with everything else. If it moved, we shot at it. We got a water buffalo and two pigs, among other things. I know Zombie blew down a whole lot of trees."

There was a long silence on WSVA as the interviewer attempted to regroup. He cleared his throat and swallowed. Charlie offered him a taste of the Southern Comfort, but he declined. The call-in line was blinking frantically.

"I understand that you were credited with shooting over twenty NVA regulars as well as several Viet Cong guerillas," Parnick finally said, trying to steer his interview back to God and country while he still had a job.

"That's what they tell me, but I never saw any of the bodies. I saw one old dead guy with no shirt on. What people back here in the world don't get is that most of the body counts they hear are total bullshit. It's like with me and Zombie. We unloaded for a solid hour, and I'm telling you I saw one dead guy. And I didn't see a gun next to him. Hell, he may have been dead before I even got there. But back at Division, no one is going to say, 'we lost half a platoon, but we got one old farmer.' So they make the shit up. If the Army had really killed as many NVAs and VCs as we claim we've snuffed, there wouldn't be anyone left to shoot at. The war would be over.

"So I may have killed twenty or thirty of the enemy, or I may not have. I really don't know. Or Zombie may have gotten them all. He got a medal, too, but he lost his leg. I thought it was a bad trade. The wound got infected in that rice paddy, and they couldn't save it. It happens all the time. That paddy water is the nastiest liquid you'll ever see. Take the worst swamp you can imagine, and then mine it and pour it full of water buffalo shit. The VC like to put sharpened stakes under the water so that guys walking patrol step on them and end up losing their feet. Anyway, I don't know who killed what. I wasn't being too particular about what I shot at, and I wasn't taking notes about which ones went down and didn't get back up. I saw a lot of little people coming at me with rifles, and there was no doubt in my mind that those guys were there to finish off what was left of my outfit. So if I saw a branch move or heard a twig snap, I cut down on it.

"There is kind of a funny story to go along with the medal. The .50 cal has an interchangeable barrel. You're supposed to change it out before it gets too hot and warps. The same day I got my star, I was informed by my new second lieutenant, who was an even bigger shithead than my old one had been, that the Army would be deducting the cost of a replacement barrel out of my pay because I had warped one during the fight. I told that prick I would have changed it out, but I was kind of busy at the time, and who the hell knew where the asbestos gloves were anyway? So the damn Army gave me a medal *and* tried to send me a bill for holding off an enemy attack, and I spent the rest of the day cleaning out the shitters because I had run my mouth to the L-T. I guess I am lucky they didn't charge me for the bullets I used."

There was silence out in radio land after this soliloquy.

"Well, I thought it was kind of funny anyway," Charlie finally said.

At that point, Parnick Stevens faded into a commercial for Bell's Hardware and Appliance, and when that tape had run its course, Betty Rupp, the Happy Homemaker of Sand Valley, started her regular morning broadcast a little ahead of schedule.

"That's our boy," Wendell said. He and Reva had listened to the interview on the radio in the kitchen at the rock castle.

"I'm just glad he got out of that place," Reva replied.

"He hasn't quite gotten all the way out yet," Wendell told her.

"But he's working on it." Wendell knew it usually took longer to leave the war zone than people realized. He still had nightmares twenty-something years later about many of the scenes he had witnessed during his time on the *O'Bannion*. Some of them he knew he would never be able to put fully away. They were engraved onto his memory like garish tattoos.

Before this, Charlie had graduated from high school in 1961 and spent the following four years pursuing a college degree in political science down at the University of Alabama. Wendell wasn't exactly sure what political science was, but he knew what a draft deferment was, and with the war in Southeast Asia beginning to pick up more speed as each week went by, he was as happy as he could be for Charlie to become a political scientist.

"Is it like being a Christian Scientist?" he had asked Reva. He wanted to bone up on the subject so he could have intelligent conversations with his son when he came in on the weekends.

"No, I think it's different. Maybe one of the girls will know."

Charlie had graduated in 1965 with his bachelor of science degree, but he'd wanted to gain some real-world experience before moving on to his graduate studies. It was his intention to become a professor of political science and to perhaps someday run for office. But he believed he needed some practical knowledge to go along with his head full of theory, so he made the decision to join the Army for one tour of duty. Wendell was not pleased with his son's resolution.

"I know you have noticed there's a war going on, and it seems to be getting worse," he pointed out to his fledgling political scientist. Wendell had made many a misstep along his own path and was a believer in allowing the children to commit their own mistakes, up to a point, but Charlie had crossed the line of non-interference with this

decision. Wendell felt the young man was now careening down a bad
road toward a hairpin curve in a car with faulty brakes. He could see
no positive outcomes to his son's intended course of action, and there
would be hell to pay when Reva heard of Charlie's plan.

"You went off to war when you were a lot younger than I am,"
Charlie pointed out.

"That's true. But you don't have woman trouble, and we have
plenty of water. So there is no need for you to go. Plus, I had no idea
what I was getting into, and that was a whole different kind of war
anyway. I think you should just stay in college, work on another diploma, and let all of that business over there work itself out."

"I don't know what you mean when you say that World War Two
was a whole different kind of war. Wars are wars. Good guys are good
guys, and bad guys are bad guys. You don't think I should fight for my
country?" Charlie asked. Wendell sighed. Was this what they were
teaching down at political science school?

"It is not as simple as that. In World War Two, we were attacked
first. Our country was threatened. If North Vietnamese boys were
marching down that road out there, threatening Mama and your sisters and maybe Grandma Eunice, then you and I would go and do
everything in our power to stop them. We would be fighting to protect our own loved ones and our home. Good, bad, right, and wrong
would all be pretty clear, at least to us. Whatever the outcome of that
battle, it would have been our duty to fight the good fight. And if we
died, we would go out knowing that protecting our family was one of
the very few things worth dying for, and we wouldn't feel like we had
given our lives for nothing. And Mama and your sisters would not
feel like we had wasted our lives either. That part is important because they would be the ones living on without us. They would miss

us and grieve for us, but they would understand the necessity of the sacrifice. When you weed out all the crap, that is what World War Two was about."

"But . . ."

"Let me finish. If those same North Vietnamese boys were coming down the road over in the next town, in Sequoyah, threatening somebody else's mama and sisters, you and I *might* look within ourselves and decide that as neighbors and friends, we *ought* to go try to help defend those people's loved ones and homes from a threat by strangers. Or we might not. But we probably would because good and bad would still be fairly obvious to us. We would be fighting to protect our neighbors and their people because we had decided it was the right thing to do, and maybe because we knew we might need similar help someday. Whatever the outcome of that battle, we would have freely made the decision that the welfare of another man's family was something we would give our lives for. And if we died, we would go out knowing that protecting that guy's family was another one of the very few things worth dying for, and maybe we wouldn't feel like we had given our lives for nothing. That's also what World War Two was about. Don't ever forget the dying part though. If you choose to fight, your life is at stake every time. Everything you are or will ever be is at risk. You are betting every dollar you have. You are all in."

"What about . . ."

"You asked me what I thought, so let me tell you what I think. Now, let's talk about Vietnam. Those North Vietnamese boys are coming down the road somewhere in South Vietnam, threatening someone's mama and sisters over there. You don't know any of the people. If you are like me, you don't even know where Vietnam is. You have no idea why the North Vietnamese are really coming down

that road, or why the South Vietnamese don't want them to. You don't
have enough facts, and you can't trust the few pieces of information
you do have, because everybody is saying something different, which
means some of them are lying. So what is right, and what is wrong?
Who is the good guy, and who is the bad guy? What is your motiva-
tion to risk your life? What makes you sure you are any better than
the guy walking down the road? That's Vietnam, and that was Korea,
too. I feel sorry for most of the people in both of those countries, the
women and the children and the farmers who are just trying to mind
their business and live their lives, but they are not my people and I am
not willing to sacrifice my only son to save them. And, by the way, I
didn't see any Korean or Vietnamese boys trying to pull me out of the
water after the *O'Bannion* went down." Wendell held up his hands, as
if to ward off Charlie's next point. "Yeah, I know I have a really simple
view of things. But there it is. That's what I think."

"Just because I don't know the people over there doesn't mean I
shouldn't try to help them," Charlie said.

"I can name you five other places in the world right now where
innocent people are being screwed over by people with guns. What
makes Vietnamese people special? I hope you are not buying into
that line about making the world safe for democracy. That's not what
this war is about. And there are a thousand ways you can help people
without getting your ass shot off doing it. You can be a doctor. You
can work with poor kids. You can join the Peace Corps. You can be
a college professor like you're planning to be and teach young people
how to make the world a better place. But you have to listen to me
on this: I have been to two wars, and they are bad business. The first
one probably had to be fought, but that didn't make it any prettier or
quieter, and every single person who was killed in that war is abso-

lutely and positively dead. No do-overs. They didn't get to see their families again. They didn't get to see their children grow up. Maybe their deaths were necessary, maybe not. I don't claim to know all the answers. But I do know they are gone, and they left behind crying mamas and wives who had to explain to crying children why their daddies weren't coming home."

Wendell paused for a moment. Then he continued. "The second war I went to was total bullshit. All the bad things I just talked about happened then, too, but there was another part to it. Guys were going out wondering if the sacrifice was worth it. There wasn't any certainty you were right. At least, that's the way I saw it. This war is bullshit, too. It has nothing to do with fighting for your country. Vietnamese boys are not trying to invade us. You don't have any relatives over in Vietnam who need to be protected. You don't own any land over there. So for you, for us, there is nothing in Southeast Asia worth betting your life against."

"There are bigger things in this world than just our families—things worth fighting for," Charlie argued. "Great truths like liberty, justice, and compassion."

"If you want to fight against oppression and injustice, you can find both of them a lot closer to home. As for the great truths, let me tell you the one and only great truth I brought back with me from seven years of being in wars. When a guy is dying, you can look into his eyes and tell he doesn't want to die. You can boil it all down to that. Sometimes he's crying. Sometimes he's screaming in pain. Sometimes he's asking for his mama. Sometimes he just looks sad because he knows it's all over." Wendell was quiet for a moment. Then he played his last, best card. "I never had the honor of knowing your father, but I do know he never got to hold you in his arms." Reva and

Wendell had told Charlie about his biological father on his sixteenth birthday. "He never got to take you camping or teach you how to ride a bike. He didn't have the privilege of seeing you grow up into a fine young man. He missed all of it. That is what a war will do for you."

"I don't want you to go. I don't want to lose you. Don't go." Wendell had spoken passionately, and he was out of breath. He hoped Charlie had been listening.

"What about all the guys who are getting drafted and have to go?" Charlie asked. "It isn't right that I have a choice and they don't." Wendell was proud of his son's sense of fairness and honor, even as he was trying to talk him out of the dangers of a military sabbatical.

"Life is not fair. I wish those boys had the choice, but if they don't, they don't. You do. Take the gift."

That had concluded Wendell's anti-war diatribe, and while he'd hoped it would have some influence on Charlie's final decision, he hadn't been confident it would. Charlie had said he would consider Wendell's words, but Wendell could tell by the set of his shoulders and by the look in his eyes that his son had already determined to test his mettle against the Asian Menace. He was stubborn, and he believed he must pay his dues. In the summer of 1965, Charlie joined the Army and requested to be assigned to the infantry. He was offered Officer Candidate School because he was a college graduate and showed potential, but he chose to serve in the ranks. By the fall of that year, he was at Ft. Benning, Georgia, learning how to cause a casualty rather than be one. And by September of 1966, he was on station in Vietnam, one of the 385,000 American troops who would swelter there by year's end.

The year that followed was hard on the home folks. As Wendell had predicted, Reva was not happy with her son's choice of employment. She was in a constant state of anxiety, and no amount of reassurance from her husband could calm her fears. She had sensed the bear, and she knew for a fact that he was lurking in the deltas and jungles of Vietnam. This was not an exceptional example of precognition, admittedly. He was in a war zone, after all. And most of the mothers of the soldiers serving in Southeast Asia probably felt the same way. But Reva's track record with bear divining made Wendell nervous, nonetheless.

"Something is going to happen to him over there," she said to Wendell, when they found out that Charlie had received his orders to ship out to Saigon and points north. Wendell wanted to tell her that she might be wrong, but the fact was that she was almost never wrong. "Why did they have to send him to that place? Not everyone has to go there, you know. Some of them go to Germany, some go to Korea, some stay here in the states."

"He volunteered. He wants to go. I don't know why it's so important to him. But it is. I tried to talk him out of it, but I think he believes he has something to prove." Wendell had no words to comfort his wife, so he sat and held her. It was enough, but only just.

Charlie was a voracious letter writer, and it was the rare week that Wendell and Reva did not get two or three letters from him. Additionally, Wendell got the occasional note written only for him. These correspondences were addressed to Wendell via T.F.'s home address, so Reva would not have the opportunity to read them. The first of these, in particular, affected Wendell deeply, and he kept it in the back of his bottom desk drawer and read it frequently. It disturbed him a great deal when he read the words his son had penned, but he was unable to leave the letter in its envelope. Charlie had been in-country about four months when he posted it to his father.

Pops,

Well, we just got back in off a night ambush, and I thought I would write you a letter. This one's not for Mama. She'll get her usual three this week, and I will complain about the food like I always do and tell her I work at the motor pool and the only way I could get hurt over here is if someone ran over me with a Jeep. I try to be very upbeat in my letters to her because I don't want her worrying too much. I know she does anyway, but maybe it will help some. I know you would never say I told you so, but you did tell me so. I don't know what I am doing here or what I thought I would accomplish. For a small-town policeman who didn't finish high school, you are a pretty smart guy. You remember that talk we had about North Vietnamese boys walking down the road, and when a fight was worth fighting, and when it wasn't? You were right about this war. This is not our war, and these people's problems are not our business. If I manage to get out of here with my ass still attached to the rest of me, I promise I will never do anything this stupid again.

We are real big about going out on night ambushes. We leave camp late in the day and walk eight or ten klicks out. Then we set up our ambush, hunker down, and wait. If we're lucky, we sit there all night in the rain and nothing happens. Then we go home and get drunk or high. If we are unlucky, an enemy patrol will file past. When that happens, it is show time. Everyone cuts loose on both sides, and you are as likely to be killed by friendly fire as not. Trip flares are going up, claymores are shredding the jungle and everything else, and guys on both sides are chunking grenades just like they can see or something. Sometimes an air strike or an arty mission will be called in if we have a fresh lieutenant who just can't resist, and when that happens, it is time to get real small. It's dark, and no one can see shit, and then the bombs start hitting all around. If we are really unlucky, then it is us who gets ambushed while we are on the way to ambush them. When that happens, it is best to be on point. They will let the point man go by so that more of the squad will come up into the kill zone. Whichever way it goes, we never find many VC when it is all over, but we always seem to find a GI or two either dead or dying. Seems like it is mostly FNGs, too. That's fucking new guys. I guess I was just as raw when I got here, but I swear that some of these new boys have a death wish. I have seen some bad shit since I have been here, shit I want to forget but know I never can. You were also right about what you can see in the eyes of the guys who are dying. It is there every time. Don't worry about me being a hero. I intend to commune with the ground every chance I have and to get the hell out of here the first opportunity I get.

Your son,

Charlie

That opportunity presented itself in August of 1967. Charlie had been in Vietnam for eleven months and some change, and he had started to allow himself to believe he might survive. His platoon was trudging its way back from an unfruitful night patrol. Charlie was on point and was stepping carefully down the same trail they had used some eight hours previously. He was a good point man, just a whisper in the pre-dawn darkness as he slipped toward the safety of the base camp, invisible as a forgotten dream. As he stepped over a root, though, he felt rather than heard the click when his foot armed the mine. Either the trail had been mined during the night, or else all thirty of the feet in the platoon had missed it on the way to the ambush spot. Pure reflex caused Charlie to leap to his right as the mine bounced up to a height of about three feet. When it exploded, most of Charlie was behind the big tree that bordered the trail. The Betty must have been old or defective, because the blast was much smaller than normal. Even so, a jagged piece of shrapnel entered Charlie's right leg and shattered his hip. The platoon hit the deck in place and conducted a firefight with the surrounding jungle for a minute or two, until the sergeant got everyone's attention.

"Cease fire, God damn it! Cease fire! What the hell are you shooting at? Jesus Christ! It was a mine! Prettiest, get your ass up there and see about Blackmon."

"Am I going to die, Prettiest?" Charlie asked as the medic made his examination. The medic's name was actually Woodrow Anderson, but everyone called him Prettiest Medic in the Army because that was what he was. Charlie didn't feel any pain yet, but he knew that situation would change.

"Naw, man," Prettiest replied as he spit tobacco juice on the tree, the ground, and some of the bandages. He wrapped the hip tightly. "You're going to the house with this one. You are one lucky mother. You stepped on a bouncer, and you still have your dick. Not everyone can say that. Now lay back, and let old Prettiest make the colors come." Charlie felt the prick of the needle. Then a warmth spread throughout his body, centering on his chest. He felt a bit nauseated as he slipped into the hot embrace of the morphine, and he heard Prettiest fussing and muttering as he tended to his patient. "Luckiest mother I ever saw . . ." Then he felt nothing at all.

A week later, Charlie and his new hip were in Germany at Ramstein Air Force Base. Once the wound healed, he would have an angry red scar on his right leg that began two inches above his right knee and ended at his hip. The Army kept him at Ramstein for two weeks so they could monitor his recovery, and because they needed to treat him for an infection that had set up at the entry wound. They also wanted to slowly ease him off the large doses of morphine he had been receiving regularly since that night on the trail. Finally, the medical staff was satisfied that he could travel, and he was shipped to Fitzsimmons Army Hospital in Denver, where he would learn how to walk again. He made good progress in the mile-high city, and eight weeks later, he found himself being picked up by his parents at the airport in Birmingham. Reva and Wendell watched as he limped across the tarmac toward the terminal. He still walked with a cane, but in his letters to his mother, he had assured her that this was a temporary condition. Reva had tears streaming down her cheeks as she spoke to her husband.

"He looks terrible," she whispered. Charlie was gaunt, and his color was bad, his skin as pasty as biscuit dough. His uniform hung off him like it was several sizes too large. He stopped once to catch his breath as he crossed the parking ramp. He looked like a sick, tottery old man, not like the muscular and healthy young warrior they had fare-thee-welled a little over a year ago.

"He looks alive," Wendell responded as he took her hand. "That's what matters. We can fix everything else." He didn't know all the specifics of Charlie's war, but drawing from his own experiences, he knew that where there was life, there was hope. Charlie had come home. "We'll see a big change once we get some of your home cooking into him." He was a big believer in the healing properties of Reva's food preparation.

"I still feel the bear," Reva said. She was crying openly but quietly now.

"I thought it was the bear that bit him on the hip," Wendell replied.

"I thought it was, too. But that wasn't it. Or not all of it, anyway. He is still out there somewhere." She removed some tissue from her pocketbook and dabbed at her eyes.

"Well, whatever it is, we'll deal with it." Wendell wanted to reassure his wife, but he didn't know what else to say. "Come on. Wipe your tears and we'll go welcome Charlie home. Let's don't let him see you crying."

They retrieved their son and took him to the rock castle. They had kept his room for him, just as they had for the girls. The living space at the rock castle was large and roomy, and each of the children's rooms remained as they had been when occupied, like shrines, but with posters on the walls. Both Wendell and Reva had been without homes at one time or another during their lives, and it was important to them that their children never knew the empty feeling that comes with not having a place to be. During the months that followed, Charlie continued his physical recovery. He began to walk without his cane, although he still had a pronounced limp. He gained a few pounds, and the afternoons he spent weightlifting paid off as his body slowly built its way back to that of a younger man. Spring of 1968 came, and he moved his weights and bench out behind the rock castle. The exercise sessions in the Alabama sun gave him back some of his color, but the dark circles under his eyes and the haunted look in them were slow to fade.

Mentally and emotionally, Charlie was not doing well. He had once been a talkative person, but now he rarely spoke, although it was during this period that he conducted his infamous radio interview. Loud sounds caused him to flinch, and a couple times he had actually dropped to the ground upon hearing noises he could not identify. Sometimes Wendell would find him down by the river, staring at the emerald currents as they eddied and swirled. At these times, it was hard to rouse him. It was as if he were in a trance, as if his body was on the bench on the riverbank, but his spirit was floating down the river toward the southern delta. Charlie had also developed a craving for alcohol. He started each day with a few beers, but he was always into the hard liquor by early afternoon. Then he would drink steadily until the early hours, until he had finally drowned his demons and quieted their rasping voices. Then he would pass out and sleep fitfully, but never more than four or five hours at a time. He would twist and struggle through the dark of night, and sometimes he would awaken still under the gun.

"No! No! No!" he would yell from the battle site in his dream. "Get down, damn it! Get down!" Then he would moan and stir. "Aw, shit. Why didn't you hit the dirt? Hold on, man. Medic! Prettiest! Over here! Shit." He would awaken, drenched in sweat and shaking with fear, searching for a cigarette. After weeks of this, Wendell sat with him early one morning at the kitchen table to talk about the dream. He had waited as long as he had and longer than he should have because he hadn't been asked for help, and some problems are personal. And he knew from his own experience that some issues have to be worked out alone. But finally, Wendell interceded on Reva's behalf. Her son's duress was nearly as hard on her as it was on Charlie. She still sensed the bear's presence in the vicinity of the rock castle, and her sense of foreboding was heightened.

"Charlie, your mama and I have noticed that you aren't sleeping too well," Wendell said. "You're hitting the juice pretty steady, too. If there is anything you need to talk about, I'm a pretty good listener." He was proceeding slowly and delicately.

"There isn't much to talk about," Charlie said. "It's just something bad that happened I can't get out of my mind." He was drinking a can of beer and smoking a Camel. It was four in the morning.

"Talking about this kind of stuff sometimes helps." Wendell had been lucky back in his day to have Reva's willing ear when he needed to talk.

"You know, not to change the subject, but I never saw you going through this kind of shit when I was a kid. You fought in two wars, and you didn't fall all to pieces and become a drunk."

"You're not a drunk, and I don't think you are falling to pieces. Those were different wars, and you and I are different people. You can't compare the wars, and you can't compare us. I had a friend back during World War Two who just couldn't wait to get into a submarine. He always said it was all he ever wanted to do. It killed him, but that's beside the point. You would have had to shoot me to get me into one of the damn things, but he volunteered for the duty. It just goes to show you that all people are not the same. Different things bother different guys. About the only thing I can think of worse than going down in a submarine would be to have to walk through a jungle knowing that there might be boys drawing a bead on me at any time. It makes my skin crawl just thinking about it. I don't know how you did it." He stood and refilled his coffee cup.

"Getting shot at is getting shot at, regardless of where the bullet comes from," Charlie said. He lit his next Camel off his last one and retrieved another Schlitz Tall Boy from the refrigerator. "It's how you handle it that separates the men from the boys, and I am definitely not

handling it well at present. That is kind of what is so crazy about the
whole thing. When I was over there in the middle of the shit, I didn't
have bad dreams. I would drink myself to sleep after a patrol, or get
high, but I would be out like a dead guy and wake up ready to go. I
thought about dying, but I didn't think about it too much. I figured
it was way out of my hands. But now that I'm back and safe, it's like
I am punishing myself for getting out of there. Does that make sense
to you?"

"It makes good sense," Wendell answered. "When I was in my
first war, I started out being sure that I wasn't going to get killed. As
time went on and more and more guys around me bought the farm, I
became less convinced I was going to make it. Don't tell your mama
that, by the way. I lied to her a pretty good bit during that time because I didn't want her to worry. Kind of like you did when you sent
her the nice letters and sent me the real letters. But mostly, I tried not
to think about dying too much. Like you said, there wasn't anything
I could do about it anyway. But after I got back, I would sometimes
think about some of the boys who weren't coming home, including
your father. And I would feel guilty because I made it and they didn't.
I think that it must be a natural reaction to surviving a bad situation.
Or at least it was for me, and it sounds like it is for you, too. So don't
beat yourself up over it." They were quiet for a while. Then Charlie
began to speak. His voice was atonal, as if he were reciting a poem
from memory for a class at school.

"We were on a night ambush, and we had a new kid named Glass
with us. I don't know what his first name was. Never did. We tried
not to get too close to the FNGs—the fucking new guys—because
about half of them didn't make it. Once they got back from a few
patrols, then you knew they might have what it took to stay alive.

That they were either lucky or had some skill. You had to have luck or ability, and it was better to have both. But on those first few patrols, they were kind of on their own. It was just too hard to start liking a guy, and then to end up having to find his pieces and put them in a bag. And poor old Glass didn't have the look of a survivor to me. He just seemed confused most of the time. You could almost pick out the ones who weren't going to make it." He paused for a drink of beer. Then he continued.

"It was about one in the morning, hot as hell and raining like pouring piss out of a bucket. I had the watch, and I was sitting there in my poncho, hoping like hell that it was too wet for our little friends to come out and play. All of a sudden a trip flare went off out in front of me, and there they were. Fifteen or twenty NVA regulars, about fifty yards out. When they moved into our kill zone, I started setting off the claymores and toe-poppers, and the other guys were coming awake and firing by reflex. Another flare went off, and there were ten more of the bastards off to my right, trying to flank us. Everyone was grabbing ground and returning fire. The L-T shot up a couple flares to keep the enemy illuminated. Then he got on the radio. He loved that damn radio. We always used to say that he couldn't take a dump without calling it in. There were tracers zipping by, and grenades going off, and guys hollering in two languages. We had gone from zero movement to a firefight from hell in about three minutes."

He was standing now, pacing as he talked. Wendell could tell Charlie was looking at the battle in his mind's eye, like he was watching a movie.

"Right in the middle of all this shit, Glass just stood up. I don't know what he was thinking. I hollered at him, but he just stood there. He wasn't even pointing his rifle at anything. It was like he forgot where he was. Or like he couldn't deal with the reality he was in and just decided to get it over with. Anyway, what seemed like about half of the North Vietnamese Army shot him. He got hit from all over. The shots knocked him into a tree, and then he just sort of fell in on himself. I was the first one to get to him, and he was still alive, but I don't know how. He was cut to pieces. It was the worst I ever saw. There were guts hanging out, and chunks of him were missing. I have never seen that much blood come out of one man. It was everywhere. He just looked at me, and that look you told me about was in his eyes. He couldn't talk, but he was moving his mouth like he wanted to tell me something. I hollered for Prettiest, but about all he could do was hit Glass with the morphine. Sometimes, when you could see that a guy wasn't going to make it, Prettiest would be real liberal with the morphine. He would say there wasn't any use in flying coach to the Promised Land when you could travel first class. He wants to be a doctor if he lives through his tour. I hope he makes it, because I think he'll be a damn good one. But Glass died on his first patrol without ever firing a shot. He is not going to be anything but dead. I don't know if he had a wife or a kid. I don't know where he was from. I don't even know what his first name was. I know that I didn't help him, though, and I wish I had. He was just a wasted guy. They should have just shot him right after they drafted him, and saved all the trouble." Charlie sat back down.

It was quiet in the rock castle except for the *tick tock* of Reva's mantle clock. Finally, Wendell broke the silence.

"Several people had a hand in killing Glass, and each of them is a little responsible for his death," he said. "But you weren't one of them. The people who started the war killed him. The people who inducted him killed him. The people who trained him killed him. And all of those North Vietnamese boys who shot him killed him. We won't count your medic. He did him a favor. Glass was already dead by then."

"If I had taken him under my wing and given him some pointers, maybe he would have made it," Charlie said.

"Maybe. Maybe not. No one will ever know. What did I always used to tell you when you were a boy about *if*?" Wendell asked.

Charlie smiled a ghost of a smile. "You used say, 'If a frog had wings, he wouldn't bump his tail when he jumped.'"

"I read that in a book, so it has to be true."

Charlie's mood seemed to improve in the days after his talk with Wendell. His drinking slackened, although it did not cease. He seemed to be sleeping better, as well, and Wendell and Reva began to hear him talk about going back to school in the fall. Then one morning at the breakfast table, Charlie announced he was taking a trip to see some of his Army comrades in Los Angeles, including Prettiest, who had survived the war and was back home. Charlie's plan was to drive rather than fly so he could see some country on his way to and from California. His westward route would carry him through Mississippi, Louisiana, Texas, New Mexico, and Arizona. His homeward journey would take him through Oregon to Washington, where he planned to visit the old home in Bremerton. He wanted to see his sister and her husband. When he left Washington, he planned to travel to Idaho, Montana, North Dakota, Minnesota, Wisconsin, Illinois, Indiana, Kentucky, and Tennessee. He was going to be gone for eight weeks, which would put him back in Sand Valley by midsummer. This July return would still leave him time to make the final arrangements for his schooling. Charlie had purchased a 1964 Ford Galaxie Country Squire station wagon for transportation. It was a barge of a car, with plenty of room in the back for camping. He was looking forward to the trip, and Wendell thought it was a good idea that he go, although Reva was not so sure. She was still on bear alert, and in her opinion, a two-month road trip had numerous opportunities for encounters with *Ursus americanus.*

Charlie left early on a fine May morning. From Wendell he had inherited the need to get on the road before the sun rose, so he could make some time, and they said their goodbyes in the predawn darkness in the street in front of the rock castle. Wendell shook his hand and reminded him to check his oil and his maps often. Reva hugged him and told him to not pick up hitchhikers. Then the elder Blackmons stood arm in arm and waved as Charlie left on his adventure.

"Do you think he'll be all right?" Reva asked.

"He's more all right than he has been in a while. The trip will be good for him. And when he gets back, he'll be starting school. The war was hard on him, harder than we know, but he may be starting to get over it."

The trip to Los Angeles took a week and passed without incident. From the postcards Reva and Wendell began receiving a few days after he left, it was apparent Charlie was taking the scenic route and enjoying himself. He was in no particular hurry and on no set schedule. If a particular sight piqued his interest, he stopped and investigated. He spent a full day in New Orleans, walking the French Quarter while sipping on a series of cold rum drinks. He took another detour at Carlsbad Caverns in New Mexico, where he spent the day in the Big Room, enjoying being cool, dry, and alive.

While in the City of Angels, he had a good visit with Prettiest and with some of his other war buddies, but after a week or so of carousing in the hot California sun, he was ready to move on. He and his comrades had rehashed the old, good times, but they ran through those fairly quickly, and none of them wanted to relive the other, darker memories. So Charlie loaded the station wagon and headed north. He was taking Wendell's advice and checking his oil daily, but it was during his drive to Washington that he disobeyed his mama and picked up a young woman he referred to as *Teeny* in his postcards. He acquired her just south of Eugene, Oregon, and she accompanied him to Bremerton, where she, as Abby Louise put it, "horned in on what should have been a nice family reunion."

"I don't like her, and I don't think you will like her, either," Abby said to Reva over the telephone, when Reva called to check on her son. Charlie and Teeny were riding the ferry to Victoria, British Columbia, at the moment, so his sister felt she could speak freely. Not that she would have tiptoed much, even if Charlie had been there and on the extension. "Sugar wouldn't melt in her mouth, and she is hanging all over him, but when I look into her eyes, it's like they're empty."

"I wonder why Charlie doesn't see that," Reva wondered. She had done her best to raise perceptive children.

"He's not looking at her eyes," Abby replied sardonically.

Regardless of how his mama and sister felt, however, Charlie was enthralled with Teeny. In fact, he decided to bring her home with him to meet his parents. Wendell and Reva first heard this good news via a postcard from Moscow, Idaho, which was Charlie's first stop after leaving Bremerton. He had only stayed at his sister's house for a week, although he had originally intended to stay longer. Teeny and Abby Louise had engaged in a loud argument the morning the latter had discovered the former going through the mail, and the atmosphere around the house had been a touch frosty since.

"I don't like it that he's bringing home a girl that he picked up on the side of the road," Reva said.

"Well, I picked you up in a bar, and that worked out all right,"
Wendell pointed out. In his opinion, Charlie's love life was one of
those things he couldn't do much about.

"That was totally different," she replied. "Anyway, I picked you up."

Charlie's daily postcards continued to filter in, marking his east-
ward progress. Mail greetings flitted in from Missoula, Billings, Rapid
City, and Minneapolis. Then, oddly, they stopped. On the first and
second days without correspondence, Wendell and Reva didn't worry
too much. There had been gaps in the deliveries before. But by the
third day, Reva was convinced something was wrong.

"He said he would send us a postcard every day," she reminded
Wendell.

"Maybe he's just in a place that doesn't sell postcards," he replied,
trying to soothe her fears. "Or he might be out of stamps." But he was
starting to worry as well. On the fourth day, Wendell was in his office
at the rock castle working on some paperwork when the phone rang.
He picked up the receiver on the third ring.

"This is Wendell," he said as he continued to write.

"Is this the Sand Valley police?" came a voice from the receiver.
Wendell did not recognize the caller.

"It is."

"Hello. My name is Steve Wilson. I'm a police officer in Fond du
Lac, Wisconsin." Wendell stopped writing. The realization hit him
that he had been expecting the bear all morning. But he had never
heard of a bear using a phone. The officer continued. "I could sure
use your help in locating the next of kin for a drug overdose I have
up here. Right now we're treating it as a suicide. Kid's got no track
marks anywhere; then he loads up on enough smack to kill a cow. The
name on his driver's license is Charles Blackmon. The address is Sand

Valley. Do you know his people?" There was a long silence broken only by the sound of Wendell trying to swallow the sob that was trying to claw its way to freedom. He finally gained enough control to allow himself to speak.

"It's not a suicide," he managed to croak.

"I'm sorry?" Officer Wilson replied.

"Charles Blackmon is my son," Wendell said so quietly it was almost a whisper. "It wasn't suicide." This time the long silence was from Wisconsin.

"Oh, man," said Steve Wilson. "Mr. Blackmon, I am so sorry. I had no idea . . ."

"Don't worry about it. You didn't know. What happened?"

"We found him in a motel room. He had been in there for a while. He overdosed on heroin."

"Was there a girl with him?" Wendell asked. He was scrambling to try to fit the pieces of this tragedy together.

"No. No girl. Just him."

"Did you find his car? It was a white Ford station wagon." Wendell could not believe that he was asking standard cop questions at a time like this. It was like he was floating behind himself, watching another Wendell talk to the officer from Fond du Lac.

"No car either."

"Did you find any money in his right shoe? He always carried an emergency stash under the liner of his right shoe. Usually it was a couple hundred dollars."

"We didn't even find his shoes. Tell me more about this girl and the car."

"I'll call you back. Right now I have to go tell the bad news to my wife." Actually, that was not the case. When Wendell got to the kitchen of the rock castle, Reva was sitting on the floor beside the table, sobbing. She already knew.

Wendell broke from his reverie and found himself back in the present, still sitting beside Reva while she slept in her hospital room. It was dark except for the light he had left on in the bathroom, and it was quiet except for the hum of the ventilator in the wall. He didn't know the time, but he felt the calm he normally associated with the very early hours of the morning. The room was cold. He took his wife's hand once again to warm it. It felt small and fragile in his grasp, and he noticed that some blood had backed up into the IV tube. If someone didn't come in presently to flush the line, he would call the nurse.

A tear made the short trip from his eye to dampen the tangle that was his beard. Thinking about Charlie always made him blue, even though he had been dead sixteen years. They had never found Teeny, or the car, or the shoes, and Wendell and Reva had never found solace for their loss. There was a crevasse in their world that could not be spanned, a fissure large enough to admit a bear and remove a life. Steve Wilson changed the official cause of death to *accidental*, and he had felt so bad about the manner in which he had notified Wendell of his loss that he would have listed Charlie as *still living* if he had been asked. But it wouldn't have helped. Charlie was gone to that other realm, where perhaps Private Glass was waiting to take him under his wing. He had survived a terrible war, only to succumb to bad heroin in a cheap motel in Wisconsin. Wendell sighed deeply and shifted in his chair. He was an old man in the dark. The best part of him, by far, lay in the adjacent bed, and it was a long, long time until the dawn.

Kirima was alone on the white expanse of the frozen polar sea. Her soli-
tude was absolute, but this bleak world she called home had no tolerance
for inattention, so her senses were fully engaged, nonetheless. She heard
the frigid ocean slosh as it lapped the shore along the edge of the ice shelf,
whittling and sculpting it into an endless series of peaks and whorls. In the
background, she could hear the ice pop and grind as it sought to organize
itself. The wind moaned and whistled as it sprinted across the seascape.
The sun was a large, red orb balanced carefully on the horizon. It pro-
vided little light and no warmth. She sniffed the breeze. She could smell
the salt of the water, and her own sweat, and the cold itself. She breathed
in with her mouth open and tasted more than scented the slightly musky
odor of her pursuer. It was faint, but it was there. The white bear that
had killed her husband earlier that day was still on her trail. The lone
male bear would not give up the chase and would eventually catch and kill
her too, Kirima knew.

She did not blame the bear for its persistence. He was merely trying to
find food, which was what Kirima and her husband, Anuniaq, had been
doing at the seal's blow hole when they ran afoul of the bear. Kirima had
not yet properly mourned her husband's death. She had been occupied
with avoiding the same fate for herself and her unborn child. Once she
had escaped the danger that stalked her, she would remember the fine man
and husband that Anuniaq had been.

She walked along the ice shore until she found what she was looking
for, a small piece of ice jutting out from the shelf. She stepped onto this
miniature icy peninsula and began to gouge with her knife where the for-
mation joined the shore. Her knife was made of chipped stone, and it took

a long while to separate her ice raft from its mooring. Eventually, however, her persistence paid off, and she broke free. She knew that she could never outrun the bear. But if she could stay downwind of him, she could out-float her hungry opponent. As she settled in for a long voyage to she knew not where, Kirima allowed her mind to travel to Anuniaq. Now she could bid him goodbye.

CHAPTER THIRTEEN: 1985

Wendell was awakened when the lab technician came in to draw Reva's blood. He had apparently drifted off in his chair, and he was disoriented for a moment, not remembering where he was or why he was there. Then it all came back to him. He was in the hospital room with Reva, and she had suffered a heart attack. He was as stiff as a rusty crowbar when he stood and stretched. He watched as the young medical assistant attempted without success to find a vein. He didn't think Reva could feel the multiple sticks, but he felt each one on her behalf, and it made him queasy to watch.

"I'm going to go find a cup of coffee," he said to the woman. She reminded him of his own daughter, Natalie. "I am not getting into your business, but the back of her other hand might be your best bet."

He followed the aroma of slightly old coffee down the corridor to the nurses' station, where he found an unattended pot of thick brew and half a box of stale doughnuts. He helped himself to a cup of the coffee and two of the doughnuts and walked around the corner to the waiting room to take a break. There, asleep on the couch with his service revolver in hand, was T.F. Morgan. Wendell sipped his coffee, which was foul, and ate both of the purloined pastries. The he placed his hand gently on top of the gun—he didn't want to get accidentally shot if T.F. was having a bad dream—and awakened his deputy.

"Expecting trouble?" Wendell asked.

"I didn't want anyone to steal it," T.F. replied sleepily. He yawned and scratched his temple with the barrel of his revolver.

"You could have left it in the trunk. We are sort of out of our jurisdiction over here, and in a hospital on top of that, so it would have been all right." T.F. took his duties seriously and was a deputy twenty-four hours a day, seven days a week. According to the shrew fuck, he even took his trusty Smith and Wesson—wrapped in a baggie—into the shower.

"I didn't think of that." He yawned again. Then he bolted upright as he remembered why he had come. "How's Reva?" he asked as he holstered his pistol.

"She had a heart attack. Everyone tells me that she's doing okay, but she's been asleep since I got here yesterday, so I haven't gotten to talk to her. When she wakes up, she'll tell me how she's doing. Then I'll know how she's doing." It wasn't that Wendell didn't trust Dr. Mize or the folks at the hospital. He had complete confidence in them. But he wanted to hear from Reva that she was on the ups. Then he would believe it.

"Man, that's a real heart fuck," T.F. commiserated. "I'm sorry. But if I know Reva, she'll be up and home in no time."

"Thanks."

"Where did you find that coffee?" T.F. asked. He had experienced a short and restless night on the waiting room sofa and was having difficulty getting fully awake.

"It's around the corner. It tastes like burnt motor oil, but it will get you going." T.F. moved down the hall while Wendell looked through the stack of magazines on the table in front of the sofa. He was without reading material, and he selected a couple out-of-date periodicals to take with him back to the room. His deputy came back with two steaming Styrofoam cups in his hands and the remainder of the box of doughnuts under his arm. The coffee smelled much fresher than it had when Wendell had poured his first dose.

"Someone made a pot," T.F. said as he handed a cup over.

"Bless them."

"How do you like your coffee?" T.F. asked.

"Not this morning, T.F.," Wendell said, not unkindly. He was not in the mood for the coffee game. "How did you find us? I couldn't get you on the radio all day yesterday, and I didn't have time to leave a note."

"I ran into Doc Mize in town last night, and he told me what happened and where you were. I came on over, but you were asleep in the chair when I got here. So I came out here for a little nap, myself."

"Where were you yesterday?" Wendell asked.

"I was sitting in the cave most of the day, thinking things over. I didn't love Christine, but we were together for a long time. I got to feeling kind of bad that nobody else was feeling bad that she was gone." He looked at Wendell. "Everyone ought to have someone miss them when they're gone. So I spent yesterday missing her. I feel better about things now, and wherever she is, I bet she feels better, too."

"You are a good man, T.," Wendell said. "Your wife must have been crazy to let you slip through her fingers."

T.F. looked abashed. This was high praise.

Wendell moved on to current events. "I'll be here for a day or two, so you're going to have to keep an eye on things in town for us."

T.F. looked surprised. Then he swelled visibly with pride.

"You can count on me, Wendell," he said with emotion.

"I know I can."

"Do you want me to continue the investigation?"

"No, I think it will keep for a day or two. Bobby Littlefield is running the show. We'll let him run with it for a while longer. Who knows? He might even solve the case, if whoever did it gets to feeling guilty and turns themselves in. No, I want you to take patrol and keep the peace. Tell anyone who asks—and who has some reason to know—what happened to Reva, and where we are. Except reporters. Remember that you are not talking to any reporters. Or strangers. Remember we are not talking to them either. And if anyone says they're coming for a visit, send me along a change of clothes and a toothbrush. And don't shoot anybody. And don't fall asleep driving home." Wendell felt like a mother sending her little boy out into the wide world for the first time.

"Got it, boss." T.F. saluted before shaking Wendell's hand. Then he left. Wendell drained his coffee cup and walked back to the room. The clock at the nurse's station informed him that it was six o'clock. It was almost sunrise, and he had left his wife alone long enough. When he entered the room, he was surprised to see Reva was awake. He had kept the vigil by her side for part of a day and all of a night in anticipation of her awakening, and she had managed to return from sleep during the fifteen minutes he had been gone. It figured. He felt a small pang of remorse about the coffee break, because he had thought it important that she see him first when she awoke. He hoped she hadn't been anxious.

"Hey, babe," he said with tenderness. "I didn't think you would be awake yet." He sat back in his chair, placing one hand on her forehead and the other on her midriff.

"I wouldn't be, but some little girl was in here trying to kill me with a needle. She stabbed me several times."

"Was she kind of short with curly black hair?"

"That was her. She sort of looked like Natalie."

"She was from the lab. She was here getting blood."

"Thank God. I thought Deadhand had hired a hit person to take me out. I'm thirsty. Can you get me a drink?" Wendell poured a drink from the pitcher beside the bed and helped Reva sit up to drink it. After several long sips through the straw, she lay back. The act of drinking had tired her out. "Did I have a heart attack? I remember being in Dr. Mize's waiting room, waiting and wishing he would hurry along. Then I felt a terrible, hard pain right in the middle of my chest. There were other pains shooting up into my left jaw, and I felt like I was going to throw up. Then I guess I passed out, because the next thing I knew, that little curly-headed girl was trying to kill me." Her voice was gravelly, and Wendell had to lean forward to hear her. "I'm still having some twinges, but nothing like I was having. It was awful."

"Well, they say you did have a heart attack, but it was a mild one."

"You lie," Reva said with a tired smile.

"I have never lied to you in my life," Wendell protested.

"There's another one," she said. "You lie all the time when you think you're sparing my feelings or keeping me from worrying. But you are such a bad liar that I know when you are doing it, every time." She was still smiling, and there was fondness in her eyes. "You can't even lie in a letter."

"Name one time I have lied to you," he challenged.

"How about when the *O'Bannion* got blown out from under you and you got tossed into the water and almost eaten by a shark?"

"But how—"

"How about the money you've been sending to Abby every month for the last fifteen years?"

"I can explain that."

"How about when you say you like my beef Wellington, and then you throw it away when I leave the room and pretend that you ate it?"

"Enough," he said, raising his hands in surrender. He was caught, and he was beaten.

"I can give you several dozen more off the top of my head," she offered.

"No, you win. I am a liar."

"Yes, but you're a sweet one," she said. The weariness in her voice was increasing. "Now tell me about my heart attack."

"Dr. Mize says it was a serious one, but he thinks you're out of danger. He said it was a good thing you had it while you were in his office. I have the impression we might not be talking if you hadn't been." A tear welled up in his eye. Even alluding to losing Reva made him emotional. "They'll run some tests today, I think, and then they'll decide what to do after that."

"It *felt* serious," she confirmed with closed eyes. She was quiet then for a long while, and Wendell thought she had fallen asleep until she spoke again. "Thank you for telling the truth. It suits you much better." He patted her hand. Minutes later, almost imperceptibly, she made one last comment. "Just like my mother," she mumbled as she drifted into the healing embrace of sleep, leaving Wendell with his thoughts and fears.

Wendell was totally unprepared for Reva's illness. He had always assumed she would outlive him by many years, and he had simply never considered the possibility that she might go first and he might someday be left alone. Now he had been forced to acquaint himself with the idea, and he was afraid. She had been by his side for so long he could not envision any scenario in which she did not play a role. If she died, he would not know what to do or how to be. He was a life-long member of a pair, and he had no experience with being solitary. He was sitting in his chair, with his thoughts as bleak as an ice storm at midnight, when Dr. Mize walked in.

"Morning, Wendell," he said as he snapped on the light. He moved to the foot of her bed and began to read the new entries on her chart.

"Hey, Doc."

"Did she have an easy night?" Dr. Mize replaced the chart and stepped to the side of the bed. He felt her head and checked her pulse.

"She slept the whole time. She woke about six o'clock for a little while. Talking tired her out, and she drifted back off." The doctor placed his stethoscope over her heart and listened. Then he moved to the foot of the bed and made a couple more notations on her chart. "How is she doing this morning?" Wendell asked.

"There is really not much change since yesterday. Her vitals are pretty good. Some of the blood work we did yesterday is back. She has suffered some heart damage. A cardiologist will come by this morning on rounds. His name is Dr. Sevier. He's a good doctor."

"You won't be her doctor anymore?" Wendell didn't like the sound of that.

"I will always be her doctor," Dr. Mize assured him. "But Dr. Sevier specializes in treating heart attack victims. We need to bring him in on this so she gets the best possible care."

"Will she recover okay?" Wendell asked. "She seems awfully weak."

"Give her some time, Wendell. She's pretty sick. Give Dr. Sevier a chance to treat her. We are going to have to deal with whatever it was that caused the heart attack. Then we'll need to determine the extent of the damage the heart attack caused and how best to treat it."

"Just tell me she's not going to die, and I will leave all the details to you and the other doctors."

"There are no guarantees. You and I could both drop dead from heart attacks right now, and Reva could go on to live forty more years. But she's stable, and in a good hospital, with good doctors seeing to her care."

"Thanks, Doc." Dr. Mize hadn't given him the guarantee he had requested, but Wendell felt a little better, nonetheless. If Padgett Mize had a special strength, it was his comforting presence. More than one of his patients had recovered over the years simply because of that intangible. The doctor shook Wendell's hand. Before leaving, he assured Wendell he would return that evening to check on his patient.

After the departure of Dr. Mize, Wendell selected one of the *Better Homes and Gardens* he had purloined and settled in for the long vigil. While he flipped pages and attempted to stay out of the way, a succession of medical personnel came and went about their business. More blood was drawn, and IV bags were changed. Reva's vitals were taken, and she received a big shot of some miracle drug straight into the muscles of her stomach. Dr. Sevier visited his new patient, did a thorough examination, and read every word on her chart before adding several more of his own. Then he did something Wendell liked a great deal. He roused Reva and asked her how she felt.

"I feel like hammered shit," she replied groggily and uncharacteristically. "And my chest hurts." The doctor smiled at the first comment and frowned at the second. He assured the Blackmons he had a regimen in mind for both of the conditions she had mentioned. Then he continued along with his rounds and left them alone.

"I can't believe I said that," she said. "I have been around you too long. I'm hungry."

"Me, too," he replied. "Let me run down to the nurse's station and see what I can do for you." He was gone only a minute before he was back with the bad news. "They said you can't eat until Dr. Sevier says okay, and he's still making his rounds. How about a Life Saver?" He placed the candy on her tongue.

"This tastes delicious," she said as she savored the cherry-flavored confection.

"If you clean your plate, I'll give you an orange one for dessert."

"I wonder why they have me on the 'no eat' list."

"I guess they're just being careful. As soon as they say you can have a bite, I will go get you whatever you want."

They were quiet a moment. Then Reva spoke.

"I dreamed about Charlie. It always makes me sad when I start remembering. He would be forty-three if he had lived. Do you know I still think about him almost every day? He would have a wife and children by now. He always said he wanted to have children." It did not surprise Wendell in the least that she had picked up on his own train of thought while she was sleeping. He had long since accepted that his wife was in touch with the world in a different manner than he was. It was as if he received his version of events via a minimum-wattage AM station situated down low on the dial, while Reva tuned in on clear-channel FM stereo.

"I know."

"We would have more grandchildren. I think he would have had two girls and a boy, just like we did." She sounded so sad that it made his own heart hurt.

"Probably."

"I believe he might have stayed close to home," Reva said. "I don't think he would have moved off to the ends of the earth like the girls did. He thought Sand Valley was a fine place to be." It was true that Charlie had liked the country life, the slow talk, and the lazy days. In one of his letters to Wendell, he had vowed that if he made it home, he would never leave again. Wendell remembered the pledge sometimes, and he wished Charlie had kept it.

"I know, babe." He lowered her bed rail and hugged her as best he could around all of her attachments. She started to cry. It began slowly, with a sniffle and a shudder, but before Wendell realized it, his wife was racked with grief, sobbing bitterly. Her jag went on for several minutes before tapering. Finally, her bout of sadness began to abate.

"I'm sorry," she said. "I don't know what's wrong with me this morning."

"You don't have anything to apologize for. You can cry if you feel like it." Wendell, too, felt a little depressed. "I may cut loose any minute myself." It was a blue morning, a morning of loss.

"Do you ever wonder what happened when Charlie died?"

Wendell was surprised at the question. Reva had never ventured into this territory before, which had led Wendell to believe she accepted that her son was the victim of an accidental overdose. Wendell had always had a few questions in his mind about the terrible incident, but he had never voiced them, out of respect for his wife's feelings.

"I think about it quite a bit," he said. "I could never quite believe it was an accidental overdose, because I don't think Charlie took drugs. Not heroin anyway. He might have smoked a little marijuana when he was in Vietnam, but mostly he liked alcohol. He liked it way too much sometimes, but we were working on that. So the drug business never really rang true to me. I have always wished we could have found that girl, Teeny. She might have been able to shed some light on the whole deal."

"What would you have done if you had found her?"

"I don't know, specifically. But I would have tried to get some answers. She might not have known anything, but I have always thought it was strange she and the car were gone. Why did she run? What did she have to hide?" There was a quiet knock, and Dixie Lanier peeked her head around the door.

"Can I come in?" she whispered.

"Absolutely," Wendell said. "Come on in here." She pushed the door open and entered the room. She handed Wendell a large brown paper bag.

"Here's a change of clothes, your deodorant, your toothbrush, and a comb," she whispered. "T.F. sent some quarters, too, so you can get some crackers or something out of the machine if you get hungry."

T.F. was turning into a detail man, and Wendell was impressed.

"Dixie, you can quit whispering. Reva is awake and right here."

"Hey, Dix," Reva said.

"Oh, my goodness," Dixie said, when she noticed her friend was awake. "You poor thing." She bit her lip and blinked a tear. Then she moved to the bed and gave Reva a long hug. "How are you feeling?"

"Be careful when you ask her that," Wendell advised Dixie. "The morphine makes her always tell the truth. Watch this. Reva, do you still love me?"

"No, but I have too much time invested in you to cut you loose now." She smiled as she spoke. Then she yawned and closed her eyes.

"See? What did I tell you? She's tough." He bent over his wife and kissed her forehead. "Dixie, can you sit here with Reva while I clean up and change?"

"I would be happy to."

Wendell stepped into the small bathroom with his paper sack. Fifteen minutes later, he emerged a new man. Dixie had turned off the wall light and opened the curtains to the morning sun. Reva had drifted off once again.

"Can you stay another minute while I run down and get something for breakfast? I'm starving, but I don't want to eat in here. She's hungry, too, but they don't want her to have any food just yet." Wendell wasn't a medical man, but he knew the prohibition probably meant surgery or some other procedure that involved anesthesia must still be a possibility.

"Take as long as you like. I don't mind sitting with her at all. I just wish I could do more for you."

Wendell left the room and went to find the cafeteria. He got there just before they finished serving breakfast for the day, so he loaded up his plate with what was left on the steam table: some very firm scrambled eggs, two soggy biscuits, one slice of bacon, two pancakes, and some chewy hash browns. He added a cup of coffee and a glass of juice, paid for the unappetizing tray, and headed toward the dining room. He was genuinely surprised when he entered the cavernous hall to see one other lone diner, Otter Price. Wendell crossed the room and sat.

"Otter, what are you doing here?" he asked. It was not like him to venture this far afield, or to cross a state line into a jurisdiction where there were several outstanding warrants bearing his name.

"Dixie wanted to come over and see about Reva, but she was afraid to drive to Rome." He sipped his coffee and shrugged. "I guess she don't get out that much. Anyway, I told her I would bring her."

Wendell was touched. He realized that Otter's silent campaign to get into Dixie's pants had played a major part in his mission of mercy, but it was still a nice gesture.

"How is Judge Reva?" Otter asked.

"She's doing some better. After I eat, I'll take you to see her if you'd like."

"No, Wendell, I don't mean no disrespect, but it wouldn't be right for me to see the judge while she's sick and in her gown and all. You tell her I'm thinking about her, and I'll see her the next time I have to go to court." This show of professional courtesy demonstrated a level of sophistication he had not been aware Otter possessed.

"Fair enough."

"That prick Bobby Littlefield came to see me last night. He questioned me about Christine. He was going around talking to everybody, just like you did. I told him you had already covered all of that ground, and asked better questions, too. I told him that if he wanted to solve the crime, he should just come talk to you." He lit a cigarette. Wendell was certain they were in a no-smoking cafeteria, but they were alone, and maybe Otter would smoke fast. "It really pissed him off when I told him that. His face turned as red as a Folgers can. He told me that when he needed your help, he'd ask for it. What a little piss ant. That boy couldn't find his own ass with both hands if he was standing between two mirrors." He put out the butt in his coffee cup. "Anyway, this morning at seven o'clock he walked into the truck stop with about half the Alabama State Police behind him and arrested Gilla Newman. They say that Gilla was flat hollering for Mr. Frank while they dragged him out of there." Otter chuckled. "I don't think Gilla killed Christine, but I like it that Bobby sort of ruined his day."

The news surprised and amused Wendell. He agreed with Otter

on his two main points, which was unusual because he generally didn't agree with Otter on anything. Bobby couldn't find his hind-quarters with both hands, and Gilla probably didn't do it. Still, he would have paid cash money to have seen Gilla dragged protesting from the truck stop.

"Sounds like Charnell Jackson is going to have a busy day," Wendell noted. He had finished his breakfast and was taking a final sip of coffee.

"Yeah, I bet Mr. Frank is screaming at him right now."

"I need to get back to the room. I'll tell Dixie where to find you. I appreciate the good word for Reva." He shook hands with Otter.

"If I knew where Deadhand was—which I don't—and if I had talked to him—which I haven't—he would have said to tell Judge Reva to get well, too," Otter said.

"Theoretically," said Wendell.

"Huh?"

"Never mind."

Wendell stopped in the lobby and made three phone calls. The first was to Natalie in Nova Scotia. No one was home, so he left a message on the answering machine that he would call back later. He did mention that Reva was admitted to the hospital for tests, but he downplayed the seriousness of her condition so their daughter wouldn't worry. Due to the time difference, he awakened Abby Louise when he called her. The news frightened her, and she immediately wanted to fly east. Wendell calmed her fears and assured his daughter that Mama was doing much better, and he would call her back that evening. The third call he made was to his mother. After a goodly amount of shouting, he was finally able to convey the necessary news to her. He was also able to discourage her plan to have Jacob drive her over for a visit. The last thing he needed was the pair in intensive care or at the funeral home because Jacob forgot to apply the brakes before taking a mountain curve. Once he completed his notification duties, Wendell made his way back to Reva's side.

Dixie had been busy while Wendell was away. She had given Reva a sponge bath and combed her hair. The bed was smoothed and the room neatened. Several vases of flowers had arrived with the morning deliveries and were strategically placed. Reva was awake and seemed comfortable. The room wasn't exactly cheerful, but it was certainly less gloomy than it had been.

"Dixie, you are amazing," Wendell told her. "It's like a fine hotel in here. I feel like I need to tuck in my shirt."

"Don't make such a fuss. All I did was a little straightening. Now that you're back, I guess I need to be going." She seemed to be in a hurry all of a sudden.

"Otter is waiting for you in the cafeteria. Whatever you do, don't let him buy you lunch. He'll think you have an arrangement, and he might try to pull the old 'out of gas' routine on the way home."

"I know to keep an eye on Otter, but it was sweet of him to drive me. It has gotten to where I hate to drive over the mountain. All of those curves scare me." She gave both the Blackmons a hug. "You two are in my prayers," she said. "I'll see you tomorrow if Otter will bring me." She waved as she left the room.

"It was nice of her to come," Wendell said as he settled back into his chair. "Otter and Deadhand send their best."

"Deadhand is here?"

"Otter can neither confirm nor deny the existence of Deadhand, but if he did exist and was hiding somewhere in the county, he would have told Otter to tell you to get well soon."

"I appreciate the thought from both of them. But Deadhand needn't think he can sweet talk me out of his fine. He had better show up at the rock castle pretty soon with one hundred dollars. Otherwise, one of my first official acts when I get better will be to send you to find him and bring him to me. If he doesn't think I'll give him thirty days, he needs to think again." She paused for a breath. "Well, maybe just fifteen days, since he's trying to be nice." Wendell groaned, then changed the subject.

"Big news from town. Bobby Littlefield arrested Gilla Newman this morning at the truck stop and charged him in the death of Christine Hendricksen. I don't know what the charges were, but Otter said there are claw marks on the truck stop floor where they hauled him out of there."

"But you said you didn't think he did it."

"I don't think he did it. I think Bobby has done his usual fine job of investigation and has come up with the wrong answer. But who knows? Maybe he found some incriminating evidence in that pile of forensics he was sorting through. Even a blind pig finds an acorn every now and then."

"You should call Bobby and tell him you don't think Gilla did it."

"I will, I will. Just as soon as we get you home, I will give my colleague a shout and share information with him. But he won't want to listen to it." In the meantime, it wouldn't hurt Gilla to chill out a bit in the cool confines of the county lockup, at least until Charnell could get him out on bail.

"I have some news as well," she said. "The doctor came in while you were gone. They're going to run some dye through my heart to check for blockages. If they find what they expect to find, I will probably have to have bypass surgery." Wendell had been expecting and dreading this course of treatment. He had a personal fear of bypass surgery, because the procedure involved the induced stoppage of a beating human heart that already wasn't working properly. To him, it just seemed like asking for trouble.

"When are they going to do it?" he asked.

"The dye procedure will be in a little while. The surgery will be tomorrow."

"No pun intended, but what does your heart tell you about that?"

"I am more afraid of that dye business than I am of the surgery. Dr. Sevier explained the procedure to me, and apparently they run a catheter inside your arteries all the way from your groin to your heart. They shoot the dye into your heart from a wire they thread in through the catheter. Then they watch the dye as it travels through your heart. That's how they find blockages." An involuntary shudder crossed her features. "The doctor assured me it was a safe procedure, but it sounds dangerous." She looked at Wendell with a small, rueful smile. "Besides, anything that involves a catheter can't be good." She gestured at her urinary tube.

"I can't argue with you about that. But on the bright side, maybe you can have something to eat after you have the dye test."

"I wish they would just go ahead and do the bypass surgery. I'm going to need it, anyway."

"You don't know that."

"Yes, I do." She spoke with such certainty that Wendell had no rebuttal. They were quiet for a moment as they absorbed the facts of the moment. Then Reva changed the subject. "If I die, I want you to get married again."

Wendell frowned. This was a topic they had discussed before, and it always annoyed him. He did not like to talk about death in general, and he did not like to discuss Reva's death in particular.

"Can I bring my new wife to the funeral?" he asked.

"I'm serious. You will not do well alone. You will need another wife so you won't be lonely. I can just see you eating out of cans, and smoking, and wearing wrinkled clothes, and drinking by yourself late at night because it's too quiet. That won't do." There was sadness in her eyes when she spoke.

"I don't want to get married again, and I don't want to talk about you dying."

"You should marry Dixie. She's a nice person, and she's been alone since she stuck Jeff with the barbecue fork. You two would be very good for each other."

"Now you're fixing me up?" Wendell couldn't believe it. Life was too strange sometimes.

"I think she kind of likes you," Reva noted. A thought occurred to Wendell.

"Did you talk to her about this while I was eating?"

"I might have mentioned it."

"Quit doing this! You're not going to die! And I don't want to get married again if you do! And if I did want to get married again, I could find someone on my own!"

"Well, she does like you," Reva said quietly. Then she quickly moved to a new spot of ground. "There is something else we need to talk about. I am not quite sure how to begin, or where."

"I don't want to talk about anything else to do with dying."

"This is about dying, but not like you think." She took a deep breath. Then she took another and began to speak. "Bobby Little-field is wrong, and you are right. Gilla Newman didn't kill Christine Hendricksen. I killed her. It was an accident, but I did it. Once all of this heart business is over with, I intend to turn myself in. I think the stress and guilt I have been feeling since I did it are what caused the heart attack anyway. I feel better already, now that I've gotten it off of my chest."

"I don't understand what you're saying." He had heard her words, but they made no sense to him.

"About six months ago, I got a call from a lawyer in Atlanta who was trying to locate Christine Hendricksen. It was something to do with her late husband's estate and some papers that needed to be filed over here. But when he called, he said he was calling on behalf of 'Teeny Hendricksen.' Now, I know there are probably a million Teenys out there, but that was only the second time I had ever encountered the name. So I hired an investigator and had Christine's background and history checked out. And to make a long story short, a couple of weeks ago, I found out it was her. She was Charlie's Teeny. Back then her name was Christine Rivers, but it was her."

"Why didn't you tell me?" Wendell asked. It was a big piece of news.

"Looking back, I should have told you right away. But at the time, I felt like I needed to talk to her alone. I can't say why, for sure. It just seemed important, and you know I always try to go with my feel-ings. Anyway, I went out to Sorrow Wood. When I asked her about Charlie, she told me that the sixties were just one big, thick fog and she didn't remember him. I told her to try harder because that wasn't good enough. I described the trip she had taken with him, and his car, and that motel in Wisconsin, but she still said she didn't remem-ber. Then I showed her the picture of Charlie I always carry. She looked at it for a long time. Then she handed it back, smiled at me, and said 'sorry.' And I believed her. She honestly didn't remember him. I could see it in her eyes. I have thought about him every day since he died—my poor baby boy—and so have you, but to the person who may have caused or somehow contributed to his death, he was just another face in the crowd. Someone she 'screwed in the sixties,' as she put it. Something in me snapped. I think it must have been that smile. So I slapped her. I have never hit another human being, but I slapped her hard. Then I slapped her again. She didn't handle that well. I have never seen anyone turn mean as fast as she did. She called me a damn, stupid bitch and stepped over to a table that had several candles burning on it. I guess it was more like an altar. There were curtains hanging on the wall behind it. Anyway, she picked up a knife that was on it and came at me. She was going to stab me, Wendell. I could see her intentions as clear as day. I turned to run, and you know what happens when I try to run."

"Your leg fell off," Wendell said quietly. It happened every time.

"My leg fell off, and I fell down. Then she was bent over me with that knife, and she had an evil look in her eye. A deadly, animal look. The knife looked evil, too. It had a demon or something on the handle, and whatever it was had red eyes, like rubies. She raised her hand up over her head, like she was ready to plunge it into me. And then I guess my survival instincts took over, because the next thing I knew, I was on my knees with my leg in my hands, and she was flat on the floor. She wasn't moving. I checked her pulse, and she didn't have one." Reva paused briefly in her narrative to catch her breath. Then she continued. "I remember swinging the leg at her twice. Once at her knee to knock her down, and once at her head to finish her off. It's strange, when you think about it. I'm not afraid to die, but I was damned if *she* was going to kill me. She had already done enough damage to my family."

"You brained her with your leg?" He had lived with Reva for a long time, but she never ceased to amaze him.

"I did. So I was kneeling there wondering what to do next when I saw that some of the candles had caught the curtains on fire. We must have bumped the table when we were fighting. Anyway, the fire was getting out of hand quickly. By the time I got my leg put back on, the place was filling up with smoke. I barely got out of there."

"So Christine was Teeny," Wendell said. "I wish she had remembered something though. We still don't know how he died."

"No, we still don't know. But somehow that chapter feels closed to me now. I didn't go out there to kill her. But it doesn't feel wrong that she's gone. Maybe that was why I felt like I needed to go alone. Maybe I was supposed to balance the scales." She shrugged and looked at him earnestly.

"Even Charnell won't take on a 'she needed killing' defense," Wendell replied, "and he doesn't cull much. We'll need to come up with something different. I was thinking that claiming self-defense would be a better way to go."

"But I started it when I slapped her."

"No, she started it when she killed our son. And one way or another, I am convinced that she killed him. She either got him hooked on drugs or slipped him some without him knowing it. And she didn't even care about him. He was bringing her home to meet the folks, which means he was thinking about marrying her, and she didn't even remember what he looked like. So, no, you didn't start it. You just finished it." A thought occurred to him. "You know, Bobby Little-field already has his man. Why mess up his day? If we keep this to ourselves, we can kill two birds with one stone."

"We can't let Gilla take the blame for something I did."

"Sure we can. He may not have done this, but he has done *something.*" Wendell was thinking of the rape of Anna Newman. "It's a kind of cosmic justice. That ought to appeal to you."

"No," she said. Wendell sighed. It was such a good solution, too.

"All right," he said dubiously. "We'll do it your way. We'll hire a good lawyer and get you off. I'll let T.F. arrest you. He always forgets to read people their rights, and that could come in handy." He held her hand and smiled at her. Oddly, he was sort of proud of her.

"I am glad I told you," she said. "I should have told you right away, but I was at wit's end. I haven't killed anyone in several lifetimes, and it caught me off guard."

"I'm glad you told me, too."

"I love you."

"I love you, too." He sat at her side while she drifted off for a nap, and he was still at her side an hour later when the nurse came for her. He continued to hold her hand as the bed was wheeled down the labyrinth of hallways toward the cardiac area of the hospital. Dr. Sevier met them at the door to the cath lab.

"This will take about an hour," he told Wendell. "There's a waiting area right down this hall. I'll be out after the procedure to tell you what we find." Wendell nodded his thanks to the doctor. Then he leaned over his wife and kissed her. The nurse began to wheel the bed through the double doors.

"I will see you soon," she said. "Wait for me."

"I always have," he said to the closing door. "And I always will," he said, but she was not there to hear him.

EPILOGUE: 1990

Wendell leaned on the rail of the slow freighter and lit another cigarette. He didn't have the midnight watch, but he had always liked the quiet and solitude of being on deck while the ship slept, and he had found in recent years that sleep was no longer his friend. His dreams were as sad as the funeral of a child, and when he awoke from one of them, he was so full of sorrow that he had difficulty swallowing. It was as if sadness had been poured into him until he could hold no more. So most nights he slept little and arose in the small hours. He would sit on a coiled hawser on the fantail, smoking cigarettes, drinking bourbon, and watching the luminescent trail that marked the path the *Miss Jean* had followed on its lumbering journey from one port of call to another. Sometimes, toward dawn, when the bourbon had softened the edges of reality and he was able to see around the corners, he would talk to his wife, but she wouldn't answer. Wendell supposed the silence was her way of signaling disapproval for the alcohol and the tobacco.

Reva had been gone for five years, but Wendell's grief was still as acute as it had been on that terrible afternoon, when he had looked up from *The Ladies Home Journal* and seen Dr. Sevier standing there, downcast and grim-faced.

"Mr. Blackmon, she went into cardiac arrest when we released the dye, and I couldn't save her," he said. Wendell stood, and the journal fell to the floor. His knees began to buckle, so he sat back down before he collapsed. He wanted to talk to Dr. Sevier, to garner more details, to try to put some order to a world that had just flown apart. But he had no voice. He nodded as his silent tears began to flow, and he reached out to clasp the cardiologist's hand. He held it tightly for a moment. Then he released it and turned away.

Wendell remembered very little about Reva's funeral. He realized later that he had been in shock, but at the time it had been as if he were watching a stranger make the preparations for her trip to the afterlife. She had wanted to be cremated and scattered into the Puget Sound, so he proceeded with those arrangements. He had her remains committed to the flames, except for her leg, which he kept, and he placed her ashes into an urn made by Abby Louise and painted by Natalie. He held a memorial service for her in Sand Valley that was attended by almost everyone in town. Anyone who wished to speak was allowed, and the farewells were many and poignant. Then Wendell and his daughters took their wife and mother on one last, long drive to the sea. They scattered her in the Puget Sound on a chilly, choppy morning, when the mist stuck to the water's surface like ink to paper.

"Bye, Mama," Abby Louise said.

"We love you," Natalie whispered.

"I hope you made it, babe" Wendell said. "But if you didn't, I'll see you in a little while." He could never quite put her last words from his mind. "I will see you soon," she had said. "Wait for me."

Wendell returned to Sand Valley, but not to stay. He knew he could never live alone where he and Reva had lived together. The

sense of loss would be too great. But they had resided in Sand Valley
for twenty-five years, so he did have some business to conclude. He
gave Abby and Natalie all of his and Reva's things. What they didn't
want, he donated to the Methodist Church, keeping for himself only
some clothing, some pictures, and a few personal effects. He told his
mother he was going away, but Natalie was going to move home from
Nova Scotia and wanted to build a house right there on the farm so
she and her husband would not be left alone. Natalie's long-time companion, Amanda, had died unexpectedly, and Natalie, like her father,
could not live a solitary existence where she had once lived happily as
part of a pair.

Wendell contacted Bobby Littlefield to get Gilla Newman off the
hook, but it turned out that time and a lack of evidence had already
done that, and Gilla had been released. Bobby had no other suspects
and didn't know what he was going to do next. Wendell wished him
luck with his case and bid him farewell. He resigned and recommended that T.F. Morgan become his replacement. T.F. was overcome with
the enormity of the honor and appalled at the responsibility it brought.
Wendell told him that he would be fine, provided he kept his pants on
in caves. The last wrinkle that he had to iron was Dixie Lanier.

"Dixie, I am leaving Sand Valley."

"I see that. Did you know that Reva asked me to keep an eye out
for you?"

"I know she did."

"I was kind of hoping that when the time was right, when you
were ready, you would give me a chance to do it."

"Dixie, I appreciate that you are willing. If I was going to be with
anyone, it would be with you. But I can't stay here, and you can't go
where I am heading." He reached out to touch her cheek. "Take care

of yourself."

Over the years, Wendell had stayed in contact with his boyhood friend, John Frank Henson, and even though John Frank never did learn to swim, he did become highly placed in the Seafarer's International Union. With his help, Wendell obtained his union card and went back to sea.

As his time on the water expanded, the news from his old life on the land became more scarce, but the occasional letter would find its way to him. Abby Louise had adopted a baby, bringing her total to three, although the first two were grown. Natalie and Amanda had managed to find a way to give him a grandchild as well, before Amanda had died. He wasn't sure he understood all the details of that process, but he was proud of his grandchildren, nonetheless. Their pictures were all taped on the bulkhead above his bunk. Back in Sand Valley, Dixie Lanier married T.F. Morgan, and T.F. was planning on running for sheriff in the fall. Otter Price and Rita Hearst tied the knot as well, and they opened a combination coin-operated laundry and flea market. Deadhand Riley was killed by a bear that he was attempting to train to fight, but the bear escaped into the piney woods and was not seen again. Bobby Littlefield never closed his case, and his failure to solve the biggest crime in the county's history broke his spirit. He resigned from law enforcement and began to write a book about UFOs. Mr. Frank died suddenly when he choked on a communion wafer. He went straight to hell, and Gilla stepped into his empty, smoking shoes, at least until Stanley Junior, turned eighteen. He bought the Sorrow Wood estate from Christine Hendricksen's heirs for three million dollars, and he went on to build Newman's Retreat, an exclusive development for the discriminating buyer.

As for Wendell, he had lost his greatest love and so had reverted in his desolation to his first love. He sailed the Pacific routes as much as possible because he knew Reva was out there somewhere, that she had made her way up the Puget Sound to the vastness of the western sea. It was a comfort to him to know that she was always there, and that he was always just one step away from being in her warm embrace once again.

Epilogue: 1995

The two young women sat at the kitchen table and became acquainted over morning coffee. The house was new, as were all of the homes in Newman's Retreat. In the den, the women's babies slept side by side in the playpen. The baby boy was fussy; he had never been a good sleeper. He wiggled and twisted until his companion—the baby girl with the twisted right foot—reached out in her sleep with a chubby hand and touched him. He calmed, then, and slipped into a peaceful slumber.

Be in the know on the latest
Medallion Press news by becoming a
Medallion Press Insider!

<u>As an Insider you'll receive:</u>

• Our FREE expanded monthly newsletter,
giving you more insight into Medallion Press

• Advanced press releases and breaking news

• Greater access to all of your favorite
Medallion authors

Joining is easy, just visit our Web site at
<u>www.medallionpress.com</u> and click on the
Medallion Press Insider tab.

Want to know what's going on with your favorite author or what new releases are coming from Medallion Press?

Now you can receive breaking news, updates, and more from Medallion Press straight to your cell phone, e-mail, instant messenger, or Facebook!

Sign up now at www.twitter.com/MedallionPress to stay on top of all the happenings in and around Medallion Press.

For more information
about other great titles from
Medallion Press, visit

 m e d a l l i o n p r e s s . c o m